Dakota
LOVE

Dakota LOVE

Rose Ross Zediker

BARBOUR BOOKS
An Imprint of Barbour Publishing, Inc.

Dear Readers,

Welcome to the area I call home, eastern South Dakota. Although its true western South Dakota is a tourist destination, eastern South Dakota boasts the Sioux Falls, pristine farmlands, and charming small towns, all of which you'll find covered in the setting of this series of three contemporary novels. I wanted to share with my readers the distinct change of seasons in South Dakota and how the weather affects daily living. Each book takes place in a different season with a theme based on the Bible verse that corresponds with the biblical quilt block each heroine patterns in their story to show how their reliance on God brings them through a dark season in their life, strengthens their faith, and opens their hearts to love in a later stage of their lives.

I hope you enjoy visiting eastern South Dakota within the pages of this book and journeying with the characters as they discover true love isn't just for younger couples. I love connecting with my readers and look forward to hearing from you.

May God be with you always,

Rose Ross Zediker
www.roserosszediker.blogspot
www.inkspirationalmessages.com

LILY OF THE FIELD

To my favorite quilter, Marion Hummel Ross.
Mom, I love you and I miss you.

Chapter 1

Caroline slipped into the pew just as the first chords of the processional rumbled from the organ pipes. The spirited notes hushed the congregation's murmured conversation.

With a halfhearted smile, she nodded her greeting to the family sharing the pew before she feigned interest in the worship bulletin. She used to enjoy arriving early to converse with fellow congregants, but since Ted's death, she'd grown tired of answering the question, "How are you doing?" She knew they didn't want to hear about her struggle with finances. They expected a positive answer, and quite frankly, after fourteen months, she still couldn't provide one.

A tap to her knee drew Caroline's focus back to the service. The congregation was standing. The young boy in her pew offered her a hymnal. Caroline mouthed, *thank you*, as she took the book. The child responded with a toothless grin and inched back to his mother's side. A happy young family. She remembered those times.

Caroline fumbled through the pages as she rose from the pew, the hymn and worship response a distraction from her troublesome thoughts. Once she was again seated, her mind reverted back to her worries. Hanging clothes on a line to dry in the summer would save her money. But what did a retractable clothesline cost? Could she install it herself? If not, what was the cost of that? The lectionary's words turned into a drone. Since Ted's death, her savings dwindled with each passing month. Caroline mentally rearranged her monthly budget for the hundredth time. The answer always came out the same. She was short on funds.

"Caroline Baker."

My name. Caroline's heart thumped in her chest. Panicked questions replaced her mental laundry list of her financial miseries. She hadn't been a lector since Ted's death. Why was her name being called during the church service? Had she been caught not paying attention like a grade school child daydreaming in class? Did it require her to answer? Was everyone looking at her, waiting for her response?

Moisture beaded her upper lip as she scanned the service bulletin in an attempt to figure out where they were in the church service.

"She is my joy," said a familiar voice somewhere behind Caroline. A sniffle followed the statement.

Caroline's eyes fixed on the words *Joys and Concerns* in her bulletin. They were *that* far into the service. Didn't they just sing the opening hymn?

She recognized the voice and knew all eyes would be on the speaker, Mildred Welch, yet Caroline's pulse built speed, beating a drum solo in her ears. She peeked over her shoulder. Mildred stood in a center row, dabbing her eyes with a tissue. Caroline turned sideways in the pew. Mildred's face beamed with joy when their eyes met.

"She restored and finished a quilt my late daughter-in-law started. Now it's a beautiful heirloom for my grandson."

Delight bubbled inside Caroline and urged a smile to her lips. A genuine smile, not a forced one like she'd pasted on for some time now. Caroline turned back to face the front of the sanctuary. Mildred's praise reminded her of the one positive thing in her life—her newfound occupation.

That Jason doesn't approve of. Her smile drooped. She pursed her lips into a grim line. Her usually supportive son thought her purchase of a long arm quilting machine was a huge mistake that she'd come to regret. He felt she'd never recoup the investment, let alone turn a profit or provide a steady income from this business venture. She'd reasoned that although she'd given up her teaching certificate in home economics, she could still use her sewing skills to earn a living. As a last resort she explained to Jason that the life insurance money had paid the funeral expenses and the mortgage but didn't leave enough to cover monthly living expenses for an extended period of time. Still he refused to budge on his opinion.

The rustle of people standing indicated to Caroline that once again, she'd lost track of the service. Why did she even bother coming every Sunday? Hadn't God forsaken her when He called Ted home at such a young age, leaving her in this predicament? She stood as she scanned the bulletin for a page number, then opened her hymnal and joined the congregation on the second verse of the praise song.

Caroline fidgeted during the benediction. She'd forgotten to scope out her escape route. Since Ted's death she tried to avoid congregants. She'd grown tired of turning down "enough time has passed" invitations and listening to "fifty is the new thirty—you can still find love" lectures. Although her church family was well meaning, socializing and finding love were the least of her worries.

As soon as the organist hit the first notes of the recessional, Caroline scanned the sanctuary for the fastest exit route. She slipped her coat over her sweater and jeans. Uncrowded, the side door seemed her best choice. She could zigzag through the empty pews to make her escape. Focused on buttoning her coat, she maneuvered to exit the pew and almost mowed down Mildred.

Mildred reached for her hand. "My grandson was so pleased. He remembered his mother working on those quilt blocks. She used pieces of his shirts and blue jeans that he outgrew as the Fisher Boys' shirts and overalls."

"I'm so glad he liked it. A quilt is a special gift, in my opinion anyway." Caroline squeezed Mildred's hand, happy to know her hard work hadn't been in vain. All the Fisher Boy pattern pieces had been basted on the blocks but not appliquéd. By the time she'd finished the quilt top, she'd mastered the appliqué stitch.

"I hope you don't mind, but in my excitement I showed everyone the quilt, even my yardman, Rodney Harris."

"Is he related to Clara Harris?" Caroline asked. Clara's pies sold first at any bazaar the church sponsored. Sadly, she had passed away a few months after Ted.

"Yes, Rodney's her son. He has a quilt he'd like you to look at and see if you can repair. I told him you'd be happy to. I hope that was okay."

"No, that's quite all right and the best kind of advertising. Go ahead and give him my name and number. Better yet, I'll give you a business card to pass on." Caroline released her grasp and tried to pull her hand free of Mildred's.

Mildred's grip tightened. "I'm glad you feel that way. I'll introduce you." She started toward the main door, pulling Caroline behind her. For a woman pushing eighty, Mildred's strength surprised Caroline. Mildred paused long enough for them to murmur acknowledgments to their pastor but not shake hands.

"Yoo-hoo, Rodney," Mildred called.

A tall, slender gentleman, head shaved clean, turned from the group of people he'd been chatting with and waved. Caroline didn't recognize this man. How long had he attended their church?

As Mildred pulled her down the cement stairs, Caroline said a silent prayer of thanks for the January thaw that blessed this South Dakota winter. The balmy forty-degree weather was a respite from the below-zero temperatures in December. The church stairs were free of snow and ice, so it was easy for Caroline to descend two steps at a time and keep up with Mildred to prevent her arm from being dislocated. Actually, Caroline didn't remember the sidewalks, stairs, or parking lot of the church ever being this clear of any residue the South Dakota winters dealt them. She wondered who the church custodian was now that

Mr. Carter had passed away.

Mildred stopped beside the man and released Caroline's hand. "I'm so glad we caught you." Mildred, puffing from her exertion, patted Rodney's arm.

Caught him? Caroline frowned. It hadn't looked to her like he was going anyplace.

"Rodney, this is Caroline Baker, the woman who repaired and completed the quilt I showed you."

Caroline started to replace her frown of confusion with a practiced smile, but when she looked at Rodney, she just naturally smiled.

"I'm Rodney Harris. I've seen you many times in church. It's nice to finally meet you." Rodney held out his hand to Caroline.

She grasped his hand. "Finally meet me?"

His fingers tightened around hers. His warm touch and welcoming smile made her wish she'd taken care with her appearance today. How long had it been since she'd worried about being attractive? Oh, she'd combed and ponytailed her strawberry blond hair. She'd brushed powder on her face to eliminate shine. However, her height matched his, and they stood almost face-to-face. With her minimal makeup and the direct sunlight, he was sure to see the effects of her age.

"Yes, I've been attending church here for the last nine months, and I think you are the only congregant I haven't met."

Nine months and she'd never noticed him. Really, that didn't surprise her; she'd only been going through the motions since Ted's death. She arrived at church with minutes to spare and snuck out the side door whenever possible.

"Well. . ." Caroline began to stammer an excuse, then stopped. She owed no explanation, even if his caramel-colored eyes sent a warm shiver through her. She cleared her throat. "It's nice to meet you, too." She opened her purse and pulled out a business card holder.

"Mildred says you have a quilt in need of repair." She slid out a powder blue card and handed it to Rodney. "You can reach me at that number or stop by the shop during the listed hours."

Rodney read the card before unzipping his coat halfway and tucking it in the pocket of his gray-and-white-striped polo shirt. "That's a residential address. Do you work from your home?"

A slight wind chilled Caroline's hands. She pulled her gloves from her coat pocket and put them on. They were her insurance against chapped hands that might crack and snag delicate fabric or leave soil on a quilt.

"Yes, I live in a split-level with a side entry that makes easy access to my basement workshop. Although my business is new, I learned early on that I had to set regular hours or people would expect me to be open at their beck and call."

Why had she rambled? A simple *yes* would have sufficed.

Laugh lines crinkled the olive-toned skin of Rodney's face as he chuckled at her remark. "I can relate. My house, well, garage actually, is my main business base. I get calls at all hours. Thank goodness for answering machines."

Caroline grinned and nodded her head knowingly. Normally during a break in conversation, she'd focus on something else, but Rodney's face captivated her. Blond eyebrows accented his brown eyes. Full lips revealed straight teeth. Deep parentheses semi-circled his mouth when he smiled. A firm jawline not yet affected by age met at the cleft in his chin.

"We just firmed up breakfast plans. Would you care to join us?" Rodney motioned toward the group of people he'd been visiting with when Mildred interrupted.

For the first time in months, she wanted to accept this invitation, yet she hesitated. She'd stopped socializing when Ted died, uncomfortable being a third or fifth wheel. She glanced toward the group. She knew all of them, and most were single or widowed. Dining with a non-couples group might feel different. Maybe she could try it just this one time.

"I guess it'd be all right."

"Great!" Mildred said. "I'll ride with you, dear. We don't want you to change your mind."

At the restaurant, the hostess seated the large group. Caroline planned to sit by Rodney to discuss his quilt. Her business had slowed about a week before Christmas. She needed to fill her time and bank account. Good health insurance came with a hefty premium.

Thanks to Mildred's interference, her plan came together. Rodney sat in clear view across the table from her. She guessed his age close to hers from the telltale lines that settled in to stay on a person's face, a fact she knew from the mirror's reflection of her own etchings.

As he discussed the breakfast choices with the gentleman who sat to his left, Caroline studied Rodney. He wore no wedding band. Hard to imagine he wasn't taken, because he was cute. Mature men probably appreciated being called handsome or dashing or good-looking. Rodney was all of those and cute, too.

Mildred lightly touched Caroline's arm. "See anything you like, dear?"

Caroline turned her head to respond to Mildred's question concerning her breakfast choice. Mildred's raised brows and grin clarified the double entendre. A flush, which had nothing to do with menopause, warmed

Caroline's face. She'd been staring at Rodney. Thankfully, their waitress began to take orders, giving Caroline the diversion she needed to recover her composure.

Orders taken and drinks served, Caroline lifted her mug. "So, Rodney, you said you have a quilt in need of repair?" She blew across the top of the cup, then sipped the rich brew.

"Yes." Rodney dipped his herbal tea bag into his cup. "I have to be honest. It's in bad shape. Although Mildred assures me that you are a magician in this area, I just don't know." He shook his head.

Caroline laughed. "I wish I could wave a magic wand to restore a quilt. Unfortunately, it's not quite that easy, and sometimes only portions can be salvaged. Tell me a little bit about it."

Rodney shrugged. "It's yellow with white flowers on the back. Some of that material is used in the design on front, but there's also white and yellow in the front."

The waitress cut short their conversation with the delivery of their breakfast. Caroline noted Rodney had ordered oatmeal with whole wheat toast versus the large egg, meat, and potato platters Ted always used to order. Had Ted been more health conscious, he'd be alive today. Rodney's mindfulness of his health was obvious, not just because of his food choice but also in the visible fitness of his body.

After Mildred said grace, the table quieted as everyone began to enjoy their breakfast. Caroline had eaten at home, so she'd ordered light. She halved her banana nut muffin and buttered the top.

"I found the quilt in a trunk in the basement, wrapped in tissue paper, so it must have meant something to my mom. I'm certain the damage was done prior to that storage. Nothing else in the trunk showed signs of spoil." Rodney took a bite of dry toast.

Since dry toast was usually only eaten to calm an upset stomach, this seemed to push fitness a little too far. Caroline swallowed a bite of muffin and washed it down with her coffee. "Is the quilt soiled or has the fabric rotted?"

"Not stained. Some of the seams are coming apart, one area is ripped, and the fabric looks like something chewed on it."

"You don't remember seeing it or using it as a child?"

Rodney smiled and shook his head. "I don't remember it at all."

"It's not something your mother pieced together?"

"Mom was a cook, not a seamstress. She seldom mended. I don't know where she got it." Rodney shrugged.

"My curiosity's piqued. There's a story behind every quilt made, you know. I'd love to see the quilt even if you don't commission me to repair it."

"It's a deal." Rodney patted his shirt pocket. "I'll take a look at my schedule and the weather forecast. Maybe I'll be able to bring it into your shop this week."

"Weather report? Are you going somewhere?"

Rodney shot her a surprised look. "No, if it snows, my crew and I'll be working." He held up his left hand and crossed his fingers. "I know everyone else enjoys this January thaw, but it's giving us quite a bit of free time."

"But Mildred called you her yardman." Caroline wrinkled her brow in confusion. "I just assumed—"

Mildred laid her hand on Caroline's arm. "Dear, Rodney runs a lawn care and snow removal business. The church hired him last summer, at a significant discount I might add." Mildred smiled approvingly at Rodney. "It was in the monthly newsletter."

A flush of heat crawled up Caroline's neck and settled on her cheeks, giving away the fact that she didn't know. She'd stopped reading the newsletters. She scanned them for death notices, then pitched them into the trash.

Not missing a beat, Mildred added, "It just must have slipped your mind. You've had a lot going on, opening a new business and all."

"Yes," Caroline managed to croak out, avoiding eye contact with anyone. She reached for her cup and took a long drink, trying to gain composure.

This was a bad idea. What had she been thinking, accepting the breakfast invitation in the first place? Her social skills were too rusty. She wanted to make a professional impression; instead she'd managed to show her lack of interest in her church. Thank goodness Mildred stopped her before she'd made a complete fool of herself. Attending the same church and not even knowing the caretaker work Rodney did for them. She needed to pay more attention.

Or did she? She'd done all the right things, and what did she have to show for it? A lot of worries and nothing else, that's what. No husband. No future. No steady income. God forced her to let go of her security by taking Ted from her. Maybe it was time for her to let go of something else—what little faith in God she had left.

❧

Rodney caught his reflection in the bathroom mirror as he gathered dirty towels. He'd worn a grin since leaving the restaurant. His awareness of that fact widened his grin into a smile. He'd admired Caroline from afar for quite some time. He always preferred strawberry blonds with ivory skin and pert noses. When he'd inquired about her, he learned she'd recently lost her husband. As one month turned to the next, her grief seemed to deepen, not ease. He prayed she'd find solace. Her acceptance of the breakfast invitation and the few times her blue eyes sparkled briefly before the dull fog of sadness settled back over them were a good sign.

Those beautiful eyes, unencumbered by makeup, showed the love of her work. Her face lit up at the mention of the quilt. He'd wished he'd had more information on it to keep the conversation flowing and her eyes shining.

He also wished he knew what caused her to bite at the corner of her lip and withdraw from conversation half-way through breakfast.

Rodney carried the basket down the basement stairs, past his elliptical and treadmill, and set it on the edge of the washer. Caroline's questions about the origins of the quilt got him thinking. Where *had* it come from?

He stuffed the load of towels into the washer, added detergent, then selected the water temperature and wash cycle. He set the laundry basket on the floor and closed the washer's lid. His baby sister, Michelle, would be making her monthly trip to Riverside to check up on him. She might remember something about the quilt.

He headed back to the main floor to the guest room and retrieved the quilt from the trunk. With care he laid the blanket across the extra bed to avoid additional damage. Rodney ran his fingers over it. Whatever was in between the back and the front of the quilt bumped up in some spots and felt nonexistent in others.

The back door opened, and the rustle of plastic sacks announced Michelle's arrival. He walked down the short hall of the ranch-style home and into the kitchen.

Michelle stood at the counter. She pulled individual storage containers from the discount store bags.

At forty-seven, five years his junior, she still remained petite. She favored their paternal grandmother, small framed and fair skinned. With her blond hair held back in a headband, dressed in jeans and a USD Coyotes sweatshirt, she looked like she should be the college freshman, not her oldest son.

"What'd you bring me this time, sissy?"

Michelle turned and wrinkled her nose at Rodney. He laughed. That was the exact reaction he'd expected when he called her by her old nickname.

"Don't be giving me the evil eye. You are my sissy." He exaggerated the hiss of her nickname as he walked over and gave her a one-armed hug, then leaned against the counter and crossed his arms.

"Of all the big brothers in the world, I had to be blessed with you." Michelle pulled a face to emphasize the sarcasm in her voice.

Rodney put a hand to his heart and feigned hurt. Michelle smiled and turned her attention back to the bag.

"I brought lasagna and chili made with ground turkey breast. My family really liked it. They didn't even notice it wasn't red meat."

"That's because you're a good cook, just like Mom." He hoped his brother-in-law and nephews didn't hate him for the heart-healthy menus his sister now served, although most of the dishes in which Michelle substituted turkey or chicken for the red meat tasted as good as the originals.

"Do you want me to leave anything out, or should I put all the containers in the freezer?"

"Leave a container of the lasagna in the refrigerator. I'll have it for my dinner." Rodney peeked over her shoulder. "What, no desserts?"

Michelle lifted two containers. "Cherry pie and apple crisp. I had to hide it from my boys. So how are you feeling?"

"Great."

"You're staying in the pickup and plowing with the blade while your crew runs the snowblower and hand scoops?"

"Yes."

"Wearing your mask when you're out in the cold?"

Rodney drew a deep breath. "Yes." He exhaled to show his annoyance.

"No side effects from your meds?"

"Aren't you a pediatric nurse?" Michelle grilled him with the same questions on every visit.

She raised her eyebrows in a warning fashion. "Answer the question."

Since he moved back nine months ago, this was their monthly ritual. "I'm fine. I've hired a dependable crew, stuck to my diet, eliminated stress, exercise daily." He pulled at his black sweatpants. "A picture of health. My doctor is pleased."

"Don't be flippant." Michelle wagged a finger at him. "I'm still not over losing Mom. I don't want to lose you, too."

Rodney put his palms in the air. "Okay, but I'm fine, really. Speaking of Mom, I have something to show you."

Michelle followed Rodney down the hallway. "I found this in a trunk in the basement." He grasped a corner of the quilt and rubbed it between his fingers and thumb. "It was wrapped with care, so I'm guessing it was special to Mom, but I don't remember it. Do you?"

"Nope." Michelle pursed her lips and shook her head in emphasis as she ran her hands across the quilt top. "I've never seen it before. Looks like it's seen better days, though, doesn't it?"

"Yeah, it does. Did she purchase things at auctions, rummage sales, or secondhand stores?"

Michelle snorted. "I don't think so. You know how she felt about used items."

Rodney smiled. "Yeah, she had her fill of hand-me-downs, growing up in the Depression. I thought maybe she'd had a change of heart as she grew older."

Michelle's hearty laugh filled the room. "It got worse. She didn't even want me to reuse any of my baby items, and the boys are only three years apart. Had you visited more often, you'd know that. Minneapolis isn't *that* far."

Rodney chose to smile at the thought of his mother's vehement view of hand-me-downs and ignore Michelle's dig at his past. He looked at his sister.

With downcast eyes, she said, "Sorry, it slipped out. But we all missed you."

"I know." Rodney sighed. He'd loved his occupation and his life in Minneapolis. An award-winning adman with national and local accounts, deadlines and stress energized him. Meetings, networking, and award ceremonies kept him in metropolitan areas. His walls had filled with accolades, and his family life paid the price. Not just the one he'd had since birth, but the one he should have been making for himself. He rubbed the back of his neck, feeling the slight stubble of hair growth. Best to just change the subject.

"Do you think Mom could have inherited this from someone in the family, after we left home?"

"I don't know; she could have." Michelle shrugged.

"Think Aunt Katherine could help? I can snap some digital pictures and e-mail them to her."

"Worth a try, I guess. Maybe you should include everyone in the family. Why are you so interested in it?"

"I'm thinking about having it restored. Caroline, a lady at church, started a quilting business after her husband passed away. I've seen her work, and she does a good job."

"I see. So it's not so much about repairing the quilt as it is about getting to know the woman."

"What?" Rodney frowned at his sister. "No, I know how hard it is to be self-employed. And if this is a family heirloom, it should be preserved."

Michelle cocked an eyebrow at him. She wasn't buying it. He knew what little dare followed that look.

"Look me in the eyes and say what you just said without a smile."

"I'm not playing childish games." Rodney focused his gaze on the quilt.

"Because you can't do it, never could. I'm right. You're interested in. . . what was her name?" Michelle pretended she'd forgotten, then snapped her fingers. "Caroline."

Rodney's shoulders sagged. His sister knew him too well. He might as well admit the truth. He raised his eyes to meet his sister's and nodded his head in the affirmative. "Originally, I thought of this"—Rodney lifted a corner of the quilt—"as my icebreaker, but today when I approached her about it, she asked the history of the quilt. She said each one has a story. That got me wondering about this quilt."

Michelle grazed a block with her fingertips. "That story part is probably true. This quilt's pretty old. We'd best get some pictures taken, downloaded, and e-mailed off to relatives. Are you sure getting to know this woman is worth the cost of fixing this quilt?"

"First, she hasn't seen it yet, so I don't know if she can repair it. Second, I don't know what she charges. And third, I can afford it."

Michelle rolled her eyes at her brother. "Go get your camera."

Rodney snapped several photos of the quilt. He went to the den to download them while Michelle brewed two mugs of herbal tea.

"I think these are the three we should send." Rodney pointed to the pictures on his computer screen. Michelle set his mug on a stoneware coaster and peered over his shoulder.

"I don't know. I think this one where we flipped the corner over the quilt shows the back fabric better." Michelle tapped her nail on the computer screen.

After a few minutes of sibling deliberation, Rodney attached the pictures Michelle thought best represented the quilt to a brief e-mail message asking their family members if they remembered or knew anything about this quilt. He thanked them in advance for any insights and hit the SEND button. He sent up a silent prayer that he'd receive a positive reply before tomorrow, when he planned on making an appointment with Caroline.

Due to his former occupation, Rodney could converse with anyone, but today at breakfast revealed that quilting sparked Caroline's conversation and nothing else. Unless he surfed the web for general information, he knew only two things about quilts. They were pretty and warm.

For the remainder of the afternoon, Rodney and Michelle caught up on their activities from the previous month. At five o'clock Rodney watched Michelle pull out of the driveway. He knew in an hour, she'd call to say that she'd arrived home safe and sound. A habit she'd started in college for her parents. A consideration he never gave his family. He'd leave after a visit, and by the time he arrived at his destination, his thoughts would be deep into his current or next project.

The sunset cast orange-red hues in what remained of the clear blue sky, the clouds puffy and white with no threat of snow. It appeared the January thaw would continue tomorrow. The previous snow cover, melted to small patches throughout the yard, would be gone if the unseasonal temperatures held.

Rodney went into the living room. He picked up the television remote, pressed the POWER button, and then entered the station numbers for the local news. He increased the volume before heading into the kitchen, using the time before the weather forecast to heat his lasagna in the microwave and fill a glass with water. He set his drink on the coffee table and took his usual spot for dinner on the arm of the sofa. He forked a bite of lasagna as he watched the graphics while the weatherman described the change in the jet stream.

Above-average temperatures and no snow predicted for the first three days of the week. Last week he'd scowled at that forecast. This week he smiled. He picked up the powder blue business card he'd laid on the coffee table and reread the business hours. At ten o'clock sharp, he'd call Caroline and see if she'd work him into her schedule.

Chapter 2

*O*ffer *him refreshment.* The thought nagged at Caroline from the moment she hung up the phone with Rodney. Normally she didn't serve beverages to potential customers, well, any customers. She shook her head. How silly was this?

Not as silly as changing out of sweats into jeans and a sweater, applying makeup, taking her hair out of the ponytail, and trying to style it so the strands of gray weren't apparent. She'd tried to convince herself a serious businesswoman needed to look presentable, which was true but, in her case, inaccurate.

Rodney's presence triggered a strange reaction in her, an awareness of her appearance. It had happened on Sunday and then again today on the phone. Truth be told, he probably wouldn't even notice. Although Ted complimented her new outfits, he paid little attention to a change of hairstyle or makeup.

"Where are you?" She searched through her cupboard for powdered creamer left from making hot chocolate mix before Christmas. She removed boxes and pushed containers to the side. Standing on tiptoes, she took the items from the top shelf and placed them on the counter. Who designed these cupboards that ran to the ceiling? How did short women manage? Taking a few steps back, still on tiptoes, she saw a bright red cap hiding in a corner. She pulled a step stool from the broom closet, retrieved the creamer, and reshelved her pantry items.

She carried the step stool back to the closet before taking the creamer downstairs. She set it on a card table beside the coffee carafe filled with hot water, two mugs, instant coffee, several types of tea bags, spoons, and napkins. Rodney had used two liquid creamers in each cup of his tea at breakfast yesterday. She drank coffee and tea black, so she never bought that type of creamer. Would powdered creamer be acceptable?

Caroline heard knocking on the side door. She started to hurry up the steps, then slowed her pace. Although she was anxious to see his quilt and possibly commission a new project, she concentrated on one step at a time to maintain a professional decorum. She could see Rodney through the door window. He wore a blue stocking cap and jean jacket with a wool collar. His focus was toward the street.

When Caroline reached the landing, she sucked in a deep breath and released it in an effort to calm her jitters. When she reached for the doorknob, her movements caught Rodney's eye. He turned toward the door window and smiled widely. A puff of his breath turned to vapor in the January air. He lifted a shopping bag with one hand and pointed at it with the other.

A rush of excitement made Caroline's hand tremble as she turned the doorknob. So much for deep breathing. As soon as the bolt retracted, a gust of wind forced the door open, causing her to lose her grip on the knob. The glass in the door rattled when it bumped into the wall.

"Good morning," Caroline said, grabbing for the door-knob. She leaned against the door with hopes of composing herself. The cool winter air penetrated her clothes and sent a shiver through her.

"Good morning. Thanks for letting me come over on such short notice." Rodney stepped into the entryway.

Caroline pushed the door closed behind him. "Not a problem," Caroline said as she rubbed the chill and hopefully the nervous shake from her hands. "I was working on my own project anyway. My studio is at the bottom of the stairs to your left."

Rodney wiped his dry boots across the entry rug, slipped the stocking cap from his head, and stuffed the cap into his coat pocket. "After you."

Caroline held on to the safety rail and led the way down the six stairs to her work space. She walked into the room, but Rodney's footsteps stopped in the doorway.

She followed his gaze as he took in her work area. Since Jason's outburst about her major purchase, she braced herself for negative comments. Rodney looked from the corner that held the cabinet with her traditional sewing machine to the other corner where several different-sized hoops for hand quilting stood. When his eyes rested on her long arm quilting machine, he let out a low it's-a-beaut whistle. Caroline laughed, releasing her defenses. Most people never realized the size of a quilting machine.

"Wow, that is quite a contraption!" Rodney walked over to the quilting machine and looked it over as if it were a classic car on display.

"It is, isn't it?" Caroline joined him by the table, which was really a frame with rollers that held her long arm model. The sewing machine head and table ran the length of the room. "It's easier to use than you'd think."

"I'll take your word for it," Rodney said, shaking his head. He walked over to her display board and studied the small quilt pinned to it. "Is this your project?"

Caroline's heart swelled. "Yes, I'm going to be a grandma." She'd shared this news with few people, the neighbors and her good friend in Arizona.

Not because it bothered her like it did some women her age. Who did she have to tell? She was an only child, like Jason, and both of her parents had passed away. She'd stopped socializing with their couple friends after Ted's death.

"Congratulations! Judging by the pink and white colors, it's a girl."

"Well, it could be." Caroline's cheeks grew warm when Rodney's brow wrinkled in confusion. "My son and his wife, Jason and Angela, don't want to know the sex until it's born, so"—Caroline walked over to a worktable and unfolded a blue bundle—"I'm prepared for both."

Rodney's laugh echoed in the basement. "I can tell you're excited about the new addition to your family."

"Very much. Do you have children or grandchildren?"

"No." Rodney sighed the word more than said it. The smile slipped from his face. His eyes glazed with a faraway look as they rested on the blue quilt she held.

She'd managed to ask the wrong question, again.

"I'm sorry, I didn't mean to pry." Judging by his wistful expression, she'd hit a tender spot in his heart.

Rodney lifted his eyes from the quilt. His face brightened. "I have two nephews, though, fifteen and eighteen. It's hard to remember them small enough to be covered with a quilt that size." He shrugged. "But I wasn't around them much as babies either."

"I was around Jason all the time and it's still hard to remember him that small." Caroline rubbed her palms together. "I'm anxious to look at your quilt. Is it in the bag?"

Rodney held the shopping bag out to Caroline with the handles resting on two gloved fingers.

Caroline lifted the bag and carried it to a long white table in the center of the room. "You can have a seat. Help yourself to some coffee or tea. The carafe is filled with hot water." Caroline motioned toward the card table in the corner. She set the bag on the table and removed the quilt.

"Thank you." Rodney slipped off his gloves and coat. He rested them on the chair before unwrapping a tea bag and pouring hot liquid over it.

Caroline held her breath until Rodney reached for the creamer and measured out two spoonfuls. Guess she'd worried for nothing.

"I'd like to look at the quilt with you." Rodney stirred the powder into the liquid as he walked over to the table.

"Sure," Caroline said as she scrutinized the tattered block in the quilt top before turning the quilt over. She inspected the muted yellow fabric with small white daisies. "Hmm, just what I thought."

"What?" Rodney stepped closer to her.

"The quilter used flour sacks as the fabric. See where it's seamed together to make the back big enough for the quilt top?" She ran her fingers over several horizontal seams in the back.

"Is that bad?"

Caroline smiled at Rodney. "No, not bad. It just means it's older. Fabric flour or feed sacks disappeared sometime in the 1950s."

"I don't remember ever seeing flour in a fabric sack."

"Me either, but my grandmother showed me one of her aprons made from flour sack material. She said sometimes it was hard to find enough of the same patterned sacks to actually make an item." *Stop rambling. Focus on the quilt.* Caroline cleared her throat. "By the size of the pieces on back, I'd say whoever made this quilt bought their flour in ten-pound sacks and at the same time."

"Hey, that might give me a clue to go on." Rodney laughed.

Caroline furrowed her brow at him. "What do you mean?"

"Yesterday, you said every quilt had a story. I know that my mom didn't make this quilt, but now I'm wondering who did and how it got in Mom's possession. I showed it to my sister, Michelle, and she doesn't remember it either."

"Do you have any relatives who quilted?" Caroline laid the quilt with the top faceup on the table.

"I'm one jump ahead of you. Michelle and I e-mailed digital pictures to all the relatives in my address book to see if they can shed some light on it."

"Smart thinking."

"Thank you, my lady." Rodney rolled his free hand in front of his waist and bowed, holding his cup steady with the other hand.

Caroline smiled at Rodney's playfulness. *You used to be lighthearted before Ted's death.* She felt her shoulders sag at the thought, but she managed to keep her smile in place. Ted's death brought more than the loss of a loved one. Her basic necessities were covered, but. . . Aware that her mind had started to wander, Caroline pushed her financial miseries from her thoughts and focused on her profession.

" 'My lady'?"

Rodney chuckled. "Well, according to Mildred, you are the Queen of Quilting." Rodney straightened to his full height.

The title catching her off guard, she stammered, "I don't know about that. . . ."

"Your repair work was a blessing to Mildred. She gave a piece of his mother's love to her grandson, and Proverbs tells us, 'She makes coverings for her bed; she is clothed in fine linen and purple,' so I think it's okay to call you a queen."

Proverbs 31. She'd read that scripture many times in church on Mother's Day. "Okay, but I hope I live up to her and your expectations."

"I'm sure you can." Rodney affirmed his statement with a firm nod of his head, then sipped his tea.

A lump formed in Caroline's throat. No one had ever displayed that type of confidence in any work she'd done, not her parents, Ted, or Jason. Although she knew they loved her, none of them expected her to want to be more than a wife and mother. Flustered, she cleared her throat and turned her attention to the quilt.

After inspecting a few of the quilt blocks that formed the top, she looked up at Rodney.

"Well, is it worth repairing?"

Caroline laughed. "All quilts are worth repairing. Some just can't be restored, but yours is in pretty good condition." She pointed to the blocks' seams. "This quilt was hand sewn and used, maybe not by your mother, but someone. The stress of being used and laundered pulled at the seams until the thread broke. Cotton thread was used back then and didn't stretch like the nylon type made today."

"You got all that from looking at a block? What else can you tell me?"

"Well, the quilt was tied together versus quilted." Caroline pointed to knotted string in the corner of one block. "That will make it easier to repair. The cotton batting in between the top and back needs to be replaced. It's separated in spots from use. That's why the quilt is bumpy."

Caroline grabbed the quilt with both hands, held it firm, and tugged. "The fabric shows no signs of rot or it would've pulled apart. This"— Caroline ran her fingers down the ragged hem fold of the quilt—"is not rot; it's wear."

"What about that block in the corner of the top? The way the cloth looks, an animal chewed it."

"Well," Caroline said, fingering the block, "it looks more like it got caught in something with gears, maybe the wringer of a washer? See these small black marks?"

Taking reading glasses out of his flannel shirt pocket and slipping them on, Rodney took a closer look at the quilt block Caroline held up. "Grease stains?"

"That's my guess. And that block is the problem if you want the quilt restored. The block will need to be replaced. There's a quilt shop in Sioux Falls that carries replica feed sack material, so I may be able to match the fabric. If you want it repaired, I can work around it, but the quilt will be smaller because I'll have to take blocks out."

Rodney removed his glasses and returned them to his pocket. "Okay."

Caroline knitted her brows. "Okay to which option?"

"I don't know." Rodney shrugged his shoulders. "I thought you'd just tell me what needed to be done and I could say do it."

"Don't you want an estimate of the price for each?"

"No, that doesn't matter."

"Wow, I should have gone into lawn care and snow removal instead of quilt repair." The words were out before Caroline realized how it sounded. She could never be that casual about money, especially now. She lived on a tight budget, but that didn't give her the right to be rude. "I'm sorry. I didn't mean that the way it came out. It's just since Ted died, I keep a close watch on my finances."

Rodney finished his tea. "Don't worry about it. Another lifetime ago, I excelled as an ad exec and made good investments."

"Impressive and exciting. A boomer with good career planning in your youth, so you were able to retire"—Caroline made air quotes with her fingers—"at a young age."

"It wasn't quite like that."

"Nothing goes as planned, I guess. I dreamed of an exciting career in clothes design but played it safe and got a teaching degree in home economics." She shrugged.

"You traded it for another dream, a home and family?"

"You might say that a heart attack stole that dream away from me, too." Caroline sighed. What was wrong with her? She seemed to spill out personal information around Rodney.

"Health issues can do that, but maybe that's God's plan."

At one time Caroline would have agreed with that statement, but not anymore. God wasn't a topic that she wanted to discuss. She'd respected her parents and husband's wishes as instructed in His commandments, and what did it get her? A life filled with uncertainty. Not that it was any of Rodney's business. Before she blurted out any more of her personal life, she steered the conversation back to business. "Are you interested in the name of your quilt block?"

"Quilts have names?"

Caroline grinned. "The blocks do. Mildred's was the Fisher Boy. I think yours is a lily of some sort. I can try a search on the Internet. Or maybe you don't have time or aren't interested?"

"Unless a blizzard just blew in, I have the time and I am interested. Knowing the name of the block may be another clue to the quilt's story." Rodney rubbed the back of his neck with his hand. "Or at least jog someone's memory." He walked over to the table. "Can I fix you a cup?"

"I'll join you." Caroline slipped the folded quilt over her forearm before grabbing the dish with the tea bags in it and the instant coffee jar. "My computer is upstairs, so let's just take the carafe up with us."

Caroline led the way to the den. Rodney set the decanter on the bookshelf. Caroline measured some instant coffee into her cup while Rodney removed a tea bag from its packaging. He shook creamer into his cup while Caroline poured the hot water into the mugs. Rodney slipped his free hand into his front jeans pocket and watched as Caroline booted up her computer and accessed her Internet provider.

She typed *lily* and *quilt block* into the search feature and hit ENTER. She sipped her coffee as the results appeared on her screen.

"I know it's not a Carolina Lily because that is usually an appliquéd block." Caroline clicked on another web address.

"Appliquéd?"

Caroline turned and looked over her shoulder at Rodney. "Like Mildred's quilt blocks, where the pattern pieces are sewn onto the background material with decorative stitching around each piece. I did a tight zigzag stitch on Mildred's."

Rodney nodded.

"Your quilt is a pieced block, which means the pattern shapes are cut out and sewn together to create the block, pattern, and background." Caroline pointed to the small seams within the patterned block on Rodney's quilt between the plain yellow, white, and flour sack material, then turned back to the computer screen. "Well, this has been no help," Caroline said. "Not one of these blocks matches your quilt. Perhaps I'm wrong that it's a lily."

"Maybe if one of my relatives recognizes it, they'll know the name of the block."

"If you want to forward a digital picture to me, I'll try to upload it to my website. My e-mail address is on my card. I'm a member of a few online quilt groups. I can inquire there and point them to the picture on the website. I do have several books I can look through, too. I'm just certain I've seen that pattern before."

"You have a website? I didn't notice the address on your business card."

"I had the cards printed before I realized I needed a website. It's not very fancy. I just used a free service with basic templates."

"What's the web address?"

"It's cbakerquilts.com."

"Do you mind pulling it up? I'd like to see it."

"Really?" *Is he just being polite?* "Again, it's not much. . . ." Caroline bit at her lip as she turned to the keyboard and typed in the address. What would an experienced businessman like Rodney think of her amateur site?

❧

Rodney assessed the basic layout of Caroline's home page. Based on her comments about her finances, she needed her business to succeed. But this layout wouldn't do much to grow her business. She'd chosen a good readable font, but the content lacked flair. He liked the white background with black lettering; however, some color was needed to attract attention.

In addition, Caroline's lackluster website wasn't an appropriate showcase for her work. The one-page site needed links to pricing, to a contact address or phone number, and to pictures of her studio and repaired quilts. Adding a patchwork border under her name, various quilt blocks to the left for the information links, and a snazzy paragraph or two about the services she provided on the right would be a definite improvement. A more attractive web page promised double site hits, which, in turn, would bring in more customers.

"You don't like it."

Caroline's words broke into his thoughts. He turned to her, and her shoulders sagged. Disappointment filled her pretty blue eyes and pulled her lips into a grim line. Her body language said that she had tried her best with the website. Caroline's talent lay in creativity with fabrics, not website design. No shame in that.

Rodney, pulling a trick from his adman's hat, flashed a reassuring smile. He'd lead with all the appealing things her website had going for it, and then he'd talk about improvements. "Sorry, it's the adman in me. For a first attempt, your site is eye pleasing—easy-to-read font that's black on white with no loud colors or music."

"Do I hear a *but* floating around in there?" Caroline raised her eyebrows in question.

She was pretty and intuitive. No use in sidestepping around issues. "But this layout won't sell your business and bring in customers if that's what you want it to do."

Caroline sighed and placed one elbow on the computer desk, then rested her chin in her hand. "It is. I ran an ad in a couple of quilt magazines, but everyone at the quilt conference I attended insisted websites attract customers."

"It's true. We live in a computer era. After all, where did you go to look up the quilt block name?"

"The Internet." Caroline nodded. She lifted her cup and took a sip. "Since this is how I earn my living, I guess I should hire someone to design my website. Trouble is, I don't know anyone who does that. Do you?"

"I know someone who can do it."

"Do you know what they charge? Is it expensive? I can't afford too much."

Rodney fought the urge to use his thumb to rub away the worry indent that formed between Caroline's brows when she frowned. The deep crease indicated she wore that expression often. To keep his hands busy, Rodney slipped his fingers into the front pockets of his blue jeans, hooking his thumbs in the belt loops. "Well, I work pretty cheap. Maybe a home-cooked meal or two."

Caroline shook her head. "You're retired from that type of business. I can't ask you to do that."

Rodney's insides wrenched at the word *retired*. He enjoyed his life now but seldom felt the vibrancy that came with selling a product, especially one he believed in. He believed in Caroline's products and her business. It had nothing to do with his interest in her personally. She was a good quilter and deserved to succeed.

"Caroline Baker, are you a hard sell? Because I must warn you that was my favorite kind of potential client when I worked in the ad game."

"Hard sell?" Caroline's eyes began to twinkle. "You say that like it's a bad thing."

"Not a bad thing, but I'm afraid my persuasive skills are rusty and I'm tired of eating my dinners perched on the arm of the sofa while I watch the news. So what do you say? Let me punch up your website. Please." Rodney clasped his hands together in a begging fashion.

Caroline laughed out loud. "All right, but no backing out if you don't like my cooking. And don't even expect pie for dessert, because there is no way I can compete with your mom's."

Laughter relaxed the tense expression Caroline usually wore. Her curly hair, touched with gray, framed her face. She looked carefree. An expression she should wear more often. It suited her.

"I like chocolate cake, too," Rodney offered with a wink.

"Thanks for that subtle hint." Caroline continued to chuckle. "Any other requests?"

"Yes. That you work with me on the website. I'll need to study the template; then I'll update and add links. You'll need to supply the pictures of quilts you've made or repaired, your studio, a price list—" Rodney stopped when Caroline held her hand up.

"I meant food requests. I make a mean pot roast."

"Oh." Rodney smiled sheepishly. He'd kicked into autopilot on this new project, a habit he thought he'd broken. In his excitement to work on Caroline's website, he'd forgotten about his diet restrictions. Good thing she asked. "I prefer chicken, turkey, or fish."

"Really?" Caroline's tone showed her surprise. "My dad and Ted loved red meat. It's Jason's first choice, too." She shrugged. "I just assumed all men did."

Not long ago, his diet consisted of red meat and other rich, fatty foods. His mouth watered at the mention of pot roast. "Sorry, I don't mean to be finicky. It's just that I—"

"Don't be sorry. I love trout almandine but seldom made it because it wasn't well received at our table. Maybe if Ted had eaten less red meat and more fish, he'd be alive today." Wide-eyed, Caroline stopped. Embarrassment flushed her cheeks. "Sorry, I didn't mean to say that out loud."

Rodney decided there'd be a better time to explain as strain replaced the lightheartedness in Caroline's features. "Well, it sounds scrumptious to me."

"Okay, we have a deal, then." Caroline held her hand out. "I'll cook."

Rodney clasped the offered hand—dainty and smooth against his weather-worn skin. They shook on their agreement. "And I'll design your website."

"Now what do you want to do about your quilt?"

"You're the professional—you tell me." Rodney released her hand, then closed his into a loose fist in an attempt to hold on to Caroline's warmth that lingered on his skin.

"I prefer to restore quilts, if I can. The fabric may be impossible to match, but like I mentioned, some companies replicate flour sack material. It'd be worth checking into to fix the torn block. If we found material and you chose to restore, I'd snip the ties and rip the hem edge out to separate the quilt top from the quilt back. Then I'd machine sew all the seams on the front blocks and back. If the fabrics raveled too much, I'd reinforce the blocks and use a tight zigzag or appliqué stitch on top of the seams to correct the problem. That would also add contrast to the block pattern. I'd replace the batting and retie the front to the back; then, using quilt binding, I'd finish the edges."

Rodney appreciated that Caroline pointed to the areas of the quilt as she spoke, or she'd have lost him at "snip the ties."

"If the fabric can't be matched, then what?" he asked.

"You have a couple of choices. Many times, quilters make a mistake on purpose in a quilt. They'll sew a block upside down or use opposite colors than the other blocks in the quilt, just so it's not perfect. I could take the spoiled block out and replace it with a block made out of contrasting color, say, just white and yellow."

Rodney tried to picture the quilt with a mismatched block. He wrinkled his nose.

The sweet tones of Caroline's laughter bounced around the room. "That look has veto written all over it."

"Can I veto the Queen of Quilts?" Rodney raised his eyebrows.

"Of course you can. It's your quilt."

"Then, in my opinion, it'd distract from the eye appeal of the quilt. What's my other option?"

Caroline folded the quilt down to the row that held the shredded block. "I'd take the quilt apart like I described before. Instead of reinforcing these seams, I'd use a seam ripper to loosen the thread and take that row out of the quilt. Then I'd move the bottom row up. Your quilt will be shorter, almost a foot because these blocks are roughly ten by ten. I'll have to cut the back to fit the new length of the front. The rest of the process is the same. I can use the good blocks and the fabric from the back to make pillow shams or a table runner. I'd have to put other fabric with it, but at least there'd be no waste of your heirloom, except for the ripped block."

Rodney rubbed the back of his neck. His pinkie brushed the stubble at his hairline. "I'd like to try to restore it first."

"Okay, the search for retro flour sack fabric is on!"

Caroline typed *flour or feed sack fabric* into a search engine and hit the ENTER key. She sipped her coffee and browsed the links that appeared on the screen. After viewing several different sites, they found unique and pretty patterns but none matching the fabric in Rodney's quilt.

Although Caroline delighted in searching the Internet for matching fabric, Rodney's interest waned. He enjoyed Caroline's company, but he'd imposed on her time long enough. No sense wearing out his welcome. "You mentioned a fabric store earlier that might carry it."

"Yes, it's a quilt shop. They carry some replica fabric. If they don't have what we need in the store, they may be able to special order for us. I advertise there. They direct clients my way. I have some quilts to pick up sometime this week, so I'll take yours with me and maybe they can help us out."

"Would you like company?"

Caroline frowned and sucked in a corner of her mouth.

Was she afraid that this was a date? Although he intended it to be, he tried to alleviate her apprehension. "I have some errands I need to run. We might as well save gas."

After a few minutes, Caroline said, "I guess it'd be all right." Worry continued to etch her features. "What day were you thinking?"

"It depends on the weather for me. Can I call you after the six o'clock weather report?"

"Sure. Meanwhile I'll look through my quilt books and see if I can locate the name of this block."

"I might have a response to my e-mails that sheds some light on the quilt's origins. I probably should get going."

"I'll get your coat."

Rodney waited by the door and watched Caroline descend the steps with his quilt neatly folded over her arm. Who knew this morning that he'd be designing a website and accompanying Caroline on a shopping trip? Rodney peered through the door glass at the winter sky and found his answer. A cloud blocked the sun, yet its rays broke through, casting shafts of light that seemed to connect heaven to earth. No longer taking anything for granted and knowing who was in control, Rodney whispered, "Thank You, Lord, for all the plans You have for me."

Chapter 3

The unpredictable South Dakota weather postponed the trip to the quilt shop for about a week and a half. Temperatures dropped into the teens with some sort of precipitation every other day. Between plowing driveways and making sure his crew finished his clients' sidewalks by either snowblowing or hand scooping, Rodney redesigned most of Caroline's website.

Vitality surged through Rodney, a feeling he'd thought he'd never experience again and decided he missed. His creativity ebbed and flowed while working on Caroline's website, forcing him to not only challenge but frustrate himself. The text he contributed had provided the right marketing punch. Credit for the eye-pleasing and user-friendly layout of the web page went to his former intern, Allison. In the short year since his resignation, the rapid change in technology stumped him more than once, so he called in a favor and asked Allison for help.

Today, God blessed him. His morning workout had seemed effortless as he mentally planned their day in Sioux Falls. Now Caroline's flowery fragrance filled the pickup cab.

"I love the improvements you made to the website. It looks so professional."

His chest swelled with pride at Caroline's ecstatic reaction to the basic website changes. He did give his all to his current occupation, but clearing a driveway didn't quite provide the same sense of accomplishment.

Caroline's excited chatter about which quilts to photograph and upload to her website fueled his exuberance and made the hour-long drive between Riverside and Sioux Falls fly by. Nothing could do his heart more good.

"Lucky for me I photographed Mildred's quilt. Your quilt will make great before-and-after pictures."

The sun through the windshield accentuated the various tones of red in Caroline's unencumbered curls. She pulled a white notepad from an oversized tote bag. "I'll put that under 'website plans.' I'm writing down all the suggestions since my memory isn't always reliable."

"Don't forget to include those two baby quilts, unless it will spoil the surprise for your son and his wife."

Caroline sighed. "I doubt it will. I'll make a note of it."

When Caroline looked up from the pad, concern replaced the twinkle in her blue eyes. In the past week he'd noticed the look every time she spoke of her son. He assumed it was Angela's pregnancy, but when he asked, Caroline said everything was going great.

He regretted not having more family experience. Not knowing what to say to put her mind to rest, he prayed nightly that Caroline's burdens would ease so everyday decisions would no longer cause her anxiety.

"Have you given any thought to Allison's suggestion of posting a blog or newsletter on your website? She says either could increase hits to your site."

"I'm leaning toward a blog, but I just don't know yet. I want my business to succeed, so I weigh every decision carefully."

Caroline sucked in the corner of her lower lip and turned toward the window as they passed dormant winter fields speckled with snow patches and cornstalk nubs.

Rodney's people skills, honed to perfection from his previous career, included awareness of body language. The way Caroline turned from him and focused on the passing landscape indicated there was another reason she weighed every business decision. He suspected it had to do with money, but then again, he'd been wrong about her daughter-in-law's health. He wished Caroline would confide in him, but it was too soon; even *he* knew that.

He did, however, intend this day to be fun. The business side of Caroline's venture never failed to dampen her spirits. Her passion lay in the creative side of quilting.

"So you mentioned you had quilts to pick up today. For repair?"

Caroline shifted in her seat to adjust the fur-lined hood of her white parka over the shoulder belt. A royal blue turtleneck that deepened the blue in her eyes peeked out above the zipper.

"No, these quilts belong to the owner of the store. I do his quilting."

"*His* quilting?" Surprise filled Rodney's voice. "Isn't the name of the store Granny Bea's Quilts?"

"Yes, but Mark Sanders runs the quilt shop and fabric store. It's his family's business. He took over for his mom when her MS progressed, then continued to run the store in her memory. He buys quilts and quilt tops online or at auctions. I repair or finish them; then he uses them for display before he sells them at the shop."

Rodney chuckled. "I see. I thought you meant he quilted."

Caroline raised her eyebrows. "Some men do quilt. It is an art form. There's nothing wrong with that."

"I didn't mean to imply that there was. It's just that I don't know any..." Rodney laughed. "Actually, I don't know anyone but you who quilts, so I stand corrected."

"Mark's a salesman. The only time I've seen him sew is while he's demonstrating sewing or quilting machines to a customer. I purchased my regular sewing machine from him."

"He's an advertising opportunity then." *And a better son than me.* Sure, Rodney had taken care of his mom before she died, but only because his own health demanded a life change.

"What do you mean?" Caroline's sharp tone jolted Rodney back to the present. "Mark's my friend. I don't want to jeopardize our friendship."

Something inside Rodney bristled at her last statement. Was Mark the reason she insisted this trip was strictly business? Her potential interest in another man never crossed his mind. Everyone at church agreed Caroline had crawled into a shell like a hermit crab after her husband's death. He glanced at Caroline, the deep crease once again formed between her brows, a constant reminder of her worrisome nature.

Rodney gripped the steering wheel until the urge to massage the distress from Caroline's forehead dissipated. He didn't think his comment insinuated that Caroline should use Mark on the basis of their friendship.

"I meant, he believes in your work, so if a customer needs a service you provide, he'll recommend you. Plus he displays your work in his shop." Rodney hoped his explanation would ease her tension.

"Oh, word of mouth." Relief erased the worry from Caroline's features. "Just like Mildred."

"Yes, just like Mildred. Her enthusiasm about your work is great advertising. The day I told her about Mother's quilt, she almost marched me over to your house then and there."

"I wish I could share my mental picture of that." Caroline giggled. "Her sweet-heartedness compensates for all of her shortcomings. You're right; that is the best kind of advertising because it's free. I could ask Mark if he'd place a sign by the display quilts, saying 'Quilted or repaired by Caroline Baker.' And"—Caroline lifted the tablet from her lap— "I should include photos of the quilts I've worked on for Mark on my website. I'll ask Mark if he took pictures of the Nine Patch, Log Cabin, and Flying Geese." Caroline clicked her pen and began writing again.

Rodney shook his head. *Must be quilter's language.*

As the outskirts of the city came into view, Rodney glanced at the clock on the dashboard. He'd mentally formulated the itinerary of their day while doing his three-mile morning run on the treadmill. He hoped Caroline found his schedule agreeable. Although he wanted to consider this outing a date, several times during the week Caroline had stressed that this was a business trip.

Rodney slowed his pickup at the speed limit sign, followed the highway around the curve that led to Sioux Falls, and prepared to stop as the first traffic light on the highway turned yellow. "Shall we grab some lunch, run my errands, and then stop by the quilt shop? That way we can take our time there and not be rushed."

The right corner of Caroline's bottom lip disappeared under her white teeth as the line between her brows began to deepen. She seemed mesmerized by the taillights on the car stopped in front of them.

My treat popped into Rodney's head, but thankfully God was with him because he thought twice before he said it. "Have you eaten lunch already?"

Caroline's expression held as she shook her head.

"What is it then?"

She turned her gaze to him and pursed her lips. He braced for another conversation about this not being a date.

"Well, I don't know how to say this." Caroline actually began wringing her hands. "I don't want to sound forward or insult you, but. . ."

Her voice trailed off just as the light changed. Rodney focused on the traffic flow. This sounded like the start of a breakup speech. Although he hoped this would be a date, she didn't. She'd made her stance on that clear. In the few seconds it took Caroline to clear her throat, doubt chipped away at the bravado of his meticulous planning. Tension pinched his shoulders as he flexed his biceps and tightened his grip on the steering wheel.

"I guess I'll just say it." She turned farther in her seat and looked directly at him. "I don't want to offend you in any way, but since you drove, I'd like to buy your lunch." Caroline didn't wait for his response. "I haven't held up my end of the bargain. You've worked on my website for two weeks, and I haven't cooked dinner for you yet. So I only thought it fair that—"

"Okay." Rodney relaxed his hold on the steering wheel. He preferred to pay, but Caroline's broad smile showed him that this was important to her. "Did you have anywhere in mind?"

"Your choice. Fast food, truck stop, wherever you'd like to go."

"Well, there's a good soup and sandwich shop not far from here. How does that sound?"

Surprise registered in Caroline's expression. "Appropriate in this weather."

❧

Caroline chose a booth over a table when the hostess asked their preference. They perused the menu while they waited for their coffee.

"The clam chowder sounds good. Have you ever had it here? I'm fussy about my chowder." Caroline peered over the menu.

"No, I haven't, but I've never been disappointed with anything I've tried here."

"Still"—Caroline returned to her menu—"I think I'll play it safe and have the creamy tomato and a grilled cheese. Have you decided?"

Rodney closed the menu. "The vegetarian chili and turkey breast on whole grain."

Once they placed their order, Rodney intended to use the opportunity to get to know Caroline better. Had she lived in Riverside her entire life? Did she have siblings? But before he took the initiative, Caroline pulled the notebook from her tote.

"I'd like your opinion on shipping costs. I'll talk to Mark about them also since he often makes online purchases."

A pang of disappointment caught Rodney off guard. What caused that feeling—the mention of Mark's name and valued opinion, or that she was definitely looking at this outing as a business trip? At this rate she could write their lunches off on her taxes. He tapped his spoon lightly on the side of the mug before laying it back on the table. He gripped the handle to lift the mug. "I'm probably not much help in that area, but go ahead and bounce your ideas off me." He raised his mug for a swig of decaf coffee.

"Of course, this may be presumptuous of me because I haven't received any inquiries from my website or ads I placed in magazines, but I'd think potential customers would appreciate seeing shipping prices on my cost page since that's not included in my pricing."

"Good idea."

"I plan to keep it simple, either certified mail with a return receipt or United Parcel Service. Both of those methods provide a way to track a package."

"Does cost go by weight on those shipping methods?"

"I think so." Caroline rubbed the spot between her brows before the worry divot formed. "So maybe that won't work."

Caroline slid her notepad to the side as their waitress placed their orders on the table. "It sure smells good."

"Yes, it does." *Thank You, Lord, for this nourishment.* Rodney lifted the soup spoon from the saucer. "Perhaps you'll have to build shipping into your pricing. I'm sure Mark can shed some light on the shipping problem."

"Speaking of Mark shedding some light on a problem"—Caroline swirled her soup with the corner of her grilled cheese sandwich—"I described your quilt to him, and he thinks he knows the name of the quilt block." She bit the soup-softened corner of the bread.

"Great, one mystery solved. Two more to go." Rodney stirred his soup to cool it and slid the sandwich plate in front of him.

"Two?" Caroline dunked the sandwich half in her bowl.

"The fabric match and the origin of the quilt."

"No replies from family members?"

"Oh, they've e-mailed back but not with any information I wanted. My aunt's reply was vague. She thought she'd seen it before but couldn't be certain. She hinted that Mom received a quilt for a gift once. She's going to look through old pictures and ask around. It seems everything revolving around this quilt is mysterious, including answers from my family."

Caroline nodded and let the conversation drop. Quiet settled over the table as they enjoyed their lunch. When Rodney finished, he put the empty soup bowl on his plate as he popped the last of his sandwich into his mouth.

Caroline picked up her fork and scraped up the cheese that had oozed from her sandwich onto the plate. "Have you always eaten such a healthy diet?"

Finally, the perfect opening to tell her about his heart health. He shook his head, then held up a finger to indicate he had something to say.

"Well, I'm glad to see you do now. You won't have a heart attack like Ted." Caroline ate the bite of cheese off her fork. "Although I don't take my own advice." She shrugged as she placed the fork on the plate.

"But I have—," Rodney managed to get out before the fresh bread stuck to the roof of his mouth. He took a sip of coffee to loosen the bread's adhesive hold so he could finish his sentence when the waitress approached the table.

"Can I get you anything else?"

"I'm good." Caroline smiled and raised her brows in question to Rodney. Not a hint of tension marring her beauty.

"Nothing for me, thanks."

"Thanks and have a nice day." The waitress slid the bill toward Rodney.

Rodney cleared his throat, ready to explain about his mild heart attack. "Caroline, let me—"

"You said it was okay for me to pay for lunch." The familiar worry lines were back in place on Caroline's face as she reached for their check.

". . .say thank you." Where did that come from? He'd meant to say *explain*.

Caroline laughed. "You're welcome. I thought you were going to insist on paying. Are you ready?" Caroline shouldered her tote bag, slipped from the booth, and headed to the cash register.

He was ready to confess his health issues, but he wasn't ready to squelch her happy mood. He slid out of the booth and waited while Caroline paid their tab.

ঽ

"This is a good-sized store." Rodney pulled into a parking space and pushed the gear shift into PARK. "I thought it'd be a smaller boutique-type shop." Rodney opened his door and slid from behind the wheel.

Caroline gathered her tote and the shopping bag that held Rodney's quilt. She heard the click of the door release and felt a blast of cool air. No one had opened a car door for her in a very long time.

"Thank you." Caroline descended from the cab of the pickup.

"My pleasure." Rodney bowed slightly. "It's the least I can do for the Queen of Quilts." His brown eyes danced with mischief.

A sudden thrill surprised Caroline and forced out a high-pitched giggle. Rodney sidestepped her to get to the store entrance. Pulling the door open, he continued the charade. Bending stiffly at the waist, he said, "My lady," as she stepped through the door. Caroline burst out laughing.

Mark looked up from behind the counter. "Well, listen to you, Caroline Baker, laughing like a schoolgirl."

"It's his fault." Caroline pointed to Rodney, telling on him like the schoolgirl she'd been accused of being.

"Keep it up." Mark nodded to Rodney. "She needs to lighten up more." He extended his hand. "Mark Sanders."

"Rodney Harris. Nice to meet you."

"Now tell me how you pulled a laugh out of this serious gal."

"He treats me like royalty because I'm the Queen of Quilts." Caroline threw her scarf over her shoulder and raised her nose in the air in a mock pose of being socially above the men.

"You do have a God-given talent. No arguing that."

Mark's statement ended her fun. Caroline relaxed her stance. God only gave her insecurity. Her own hard work honed her quilting abilities.

"We both know your mom and my mom shared that title. I'm more of a lady-in-waiting." Caroline's voice was no longer lighthearted.

"Don't sell yourself short. You've mastered techniques that neither of them used. Speaking of which, the quilt you donated for the charity raffle brought in two thousand dollars."

"That's pretty impressive." Rodney whistled for emphasis. "I don't suppose you snapped a picture of it."

Rodney's flair for business never ceased to amaze Caroline. She knew he wanted to use the picture on the website. Why he gave up his career in advertising was beyond her, but then again, so was the fact that he'd never married. He was a keeper—good-looking, smart, ambitious, and fun.

39

"I did." Mark motioned with his head. "It's on the bulletin board with the winner holding up the quilt." Then he turned his attention to a young woman browsing the store.

Caroline caught the slight grimace of Rodney's mouth and followed him over to the bulletin board. He pulled reading glasses out of his shirt pocket to study the picture. Caroline was happy to see an elderly woman had won the wall quilt depicting a freehand design of a decorated Christmas tree. She was holding the quilt to her side, making the entire blanket visible but not its detail, such as the multicolored thread, the stitching shaped like old-fashioned Christmas lights, and the triangle block pattern that formed the tree, all of which blended into the colors of the picture. Caroline sighed. That quilt up close would have made a great example of her work.

"What?" Rodney looked at Caroline.

"The picture doesn't show all the detail in that quilt."

"Like?"

"The quilting, the blocks' formation, or the fabric's pattern."

"Here all I wondered about was if we could crop the winner out of the picture." Rodney rubbed the back of his neck.

Caroline felt her eyebrows involuntarily draw together. Her expression must have shown her confusion because Rodney didn't give her time to respond.

"Written permission is needed if a photo with a person is used."

"You can take people out of the picture?"

"With the right software and depending on the quality of the digital camera used, I may be able to bring out some of the detail, too. Too bad you don't make practice quilts." Rodney removed his glasses and stuck them back in his shirt pocket.

"I do practice the stitch pattern before I use it on the quilt." Rodney's smile at her statement brought out one of her own. "Would that help?"

"Sure! We'd only have to photograph a small portion to show the detail. No one will know it's not of the actual quilt."

Once again, Rodney impressed her with his business sense.

Rodney and Caroline waited beside the counter while Mark finished ringing up his customer. After the woman exited the store, Mark turned to Caroline. "She's a new customer." Mark motioned his head toward the door. "She's interested in taking quilting classes. I've had other inquiries about classes, too, and wondered if you'd like to teach some."

Caroline sucked in her breath. "Me? Teach a quilting class? I don't know." She bit the corner of her lip.

"You *are* the Queen of Quilts." Rodney nodded his encouragement.

"Not only that," Mark said, "but you taught home economics until you had Jason."

"To borrow Rodney's phrase, another lifetime ago." Was Mark planning on paying her to teach? The extra income could help during the slow time with her business. She searched for a tactful way to ask. "What were you thinking?"

"To start, two classes a week for six weeks. One during the day sometime and one during the evening because many of my customers work. You set the days and times."

That didn't tell Caroline anything about the money involved. Caroline cleared her throat and tried another angle. "Are you charging for the classes?"

Mark laughed. "Of course—I am a businessman. I just don't know if I should charge a flat rate for the entire six weeks or per session. I thought we'd split it fifty-fifty."

Rodney broke into the conversation. "Why don't you charge a flat rate per course up front? If people pay prior to the class, they won't miss sessions. Also, you should split the course fee sixty-forty. I'm assuming you plan to profit from the sale of the supplies for the class?"

Not another one. First Ted, then Jason, and now Rodney. Did all men think they knew what was best for a woman? A lump formed in Caroline's throat. Though she admired Rodney's business acumen, all her life she'd known Mark and his generous nature. She couldn't tolerate hurting his feelings over money. Not to mention this decision should be between her and Mark. "I think an even split is fair."

Mark shrugged. "Not really. Rodney made a valid point. I hadn't factored in the sale of supplies. I can even give a 10 percent discount on all supplies purchased here and still come out ahead. Do we have a deal?"

Caroline looked from one expectant face to the other. "Deal." She held out her hand to shake on it.

Mark pretended to spit on his hand before clasping Caroline's. "Who knew all those years ago when you were babysitting the neighbor boy that he'd form a partnership with you."

"I think you left out a few adjectives." Caroline ended the handshake and turned to Rodney. "He meant *annoying* younger neighbor boy who pestered me and my friends when we were out in the yard."

Rodney wore a strange look before he laughed at their banter. Was it relief mixed with enlightenment?

"Don't feel bad, buddy. The girls I grew up with would describe me the same way." Rodney slapped Mark's shoulder in camaraderie.

"Okay, enough bonding or you'll be ganging up on me! Back to the reason why we're here." Caroline lifted the quilt from the bag.

"Let's take it back to the work area." Mark led the way to a large room in the back of the store.

As Caroline began to unfold the quilt, Rodney grabbed two corners and stepped back so Mark could view the entire blanket.

"Pretty good condition, considering the age. This flour sack pattern was popular in the forties."

"Do they make replica material that matches it?" Caroline asked while Mark continued to assess the damaged block of the quilt. "We plan to restore the quilt, if possible."

"I don't know, but now that I've seen it, I can check with my distributors. Is there a deadline for the restoration?"

"Not at all. Why?" Rodney asked.

"I may be able to get ahold of an actual flour sack with this pattern from some of my online sources. But it may take awhile and"—Mark looked up from the quilt—"it could be costly."

Caroline furrowed her brow and looked to Rodney for an answer.

Rodney shrugged. "I'll trust your judgment. If the price seems fair, buy it. You'd know if the seller was price gouging before I would."

"Okay." Mark walked to a file cabinet and took out a camera. "I'll take a close-up shot of the back so I can be sure I've found a match."

After taking several shots, Mark put his camera away while Caroline and Rodney folded the quilt.

"Here are the tops and backs that need to be quilted." Mark pulled a large plastic sack from the top of the file cabinet and laid it on a cutting table.

Caroline removed the first of three separate sacks. "I thought you said two over the phone." She peeked inside. "This looks like the red Nine Patch you told me about."

"I thought this heart fabric for the back would make a great display for Valentine's Day or a great Valentine's Day gift for a special quilter in someone's life." Mark pulled the backing out for a better view.

"How do you want it quilted and finished?"

"A continuous heart pattern with various-sized hearts. There's coordinating binding in the bag. Can you finish it by February first?"

That deadline didn't leave her much time, but if it was the only project she worked on, she could finish it. "It shouldn't be a problem." Caroline tucked the material back into the sack while Mark removed a stack of loose blocks from the next one.

"This one's not finished. I found it at a flea market. All the fabric's there. It looks like a kit. Just finish it and use whatever type of quilting stitch you'd like."

"Okay." Caroline glanced at Rodney, whose bored-to-tears expression pulled at her heart. "You're not having fun. We're almost finished."

"I admit I have no idea what you two are talking about, as far as kits and binding, but"—Rodney winked at Mark—"the jester must wait for the queen."

"I could get used to that title." Caroline flipped her scarf.

"I may have created a monster."

"Believe me," Mark interjected, "you didn't create a monster. She's been a monster for years."

"Hey now," Caroline said over both men's laughter. She shot Mark a stern look before grinning from ear to ear. How long had it been since she'd teased or been teased? Then her heart twisted a little and she knew—since she and Jason began to disagree about her quilting business. She felt her natural smile begin to droop with the ache of financial fears that had been her constant companion for so long. She forced her practiced smile to her lips. "Think you can stop laughing at me long enough to tell me what's in the third bag?"

"It's a surprise and maybe a challenge, depending on how you look at it." Mark pulled small bundles of fabric decorated with various kinds of candies—jelly beans, fancy chocolates, candy corn, kisses, suckers, and ribbon candy. In addition, there was a small amount of red and a larger amount of brown. "A fellow Chamber member who runs a candy store asked if you'd make her a wall quilt that looks roughly like this." Mark unfolded a piece of paper that revealed a rough sketch of six blocks with an old-fashioned candy jar in the middle of each block.

As Rodney peeked over her shoulder, Caroline studied the sketch. "So the fabric with the candy on it is the body of the jar—like candy showing through the glass—the jar lid is red, and the brown's the backing?"

"How on earth did you get that out of those pieces of material and that drawing?" Rodney sounded amazed.

Caroline's answer consisted of a shrug and a smile. "Kind of comes natural, I guess."

"Will you do it?" Mark asked.

"I'd rather appliqué the jar than try to piece a pattern." Caroline bit the corner of her lip. "Is there enough fabric to make a practice block first? I'd hate to make the entire quilt and disappoint your friend."

"There should be," Mark said.

"Okay, I'll give it a try." Caroline slipped all the fabric back into the sack, then placed all three small bags into the larger one.

"And the last order of business for the day," Mark said as he folded a soft-backed book open and pointed to a color picture of a quilt whose blocks matched the blocks in Rodney's quilt.

"You found it!" Caroline's voice squeaked with excitement. She clapped her hands and turned to Rodney. "That solves one mystery surrounding your quilt."

Rodney smiled. "It sure does. So what's it called?"

Caroline and Rodney looked at Mark. He held the book open to show the entire page spread. "The name's from my mom's favorite Bible verse. God's reminder that He takes care of us." Mark drew a circle with his finger around the flower in the middle of the block. "The block's name is Lily of the Field. 'Who of you by worrying can add a single hour to his life? . . . See how the lilies of the field grow. They do not labor or spin.'"

Chapter 4

For the fourth time, Caroline read the trout almandine recipe, checking the ingredients off in her head. Just like the last three times, she accounted for every item in her cupboards or refrigerator. Perhaps she should measure out the ingredients to make sure she had the correct amounts. She didn't want to overlook anything for this meal.

Rodney had worked hard on her website, and while she was showing her appreciation by making him a meal, for some unknown reason, she also wanted to impress him with her culinary skills. Who was she kidding? She knew the reason—attraction. She almost giggled thinking about it, which seemed childish for a fifty-year-old woman to do, so she held it in until the excitement that buzzed through her forced the giggle out. Mark nailed it last week when he called her a schoolgirl. She felt carefree, hopeful like a schoolgirl.

Her pressed outfit hung in her closet, and the baked-from-scratch chocolate cake waited in the refrigerator. She'd prepared it yesterday so she'd have time to whip up another one if her first cake fell.

Was she crazy to feel this way? The more she was around Rodney, the more she wanted to be around Rodney. Caroline laughed out loud as she remembered how she'd debated what to wear to church last Sunday. She finally gave in to the urge to dress up for church, wearing a brown pantsuit, green blouse, and dress flats. In addition, she curled her hair and applied her makeup with a careful hand, topping it off with a new shade of lipstick. Why? Because she knew she'd see Rodney. She'd gone from spending church time reflecting on how bad her life had turned out to trying to impress a handsome man.

Caroline tapped the recipe card on the counter. She didn't know why she bothered going to church anyway. It wasn't like she really believed in or relied on God anymore. However, she'd begun to look forward to joining the singles group for breakfast, which she'd done the last three Sundays.

The click of the back door startled her from her deep thoughts. She wasn't expecting anyone.

"Mom? Or should I say Grandma?"

"In the kitchen." Caroline heard Jason's boots thud on the entryway floor as he removed them. "What brings you here?" she asked as he entered the kitchen.

"Day off." His nylon coat swished as he shrugged out of it, then hung it over the back of a kitchen chair.

"How's Angela feeling?"

"Good—tired but not sick. The doctor says everything's how it should be at this stage. What are you up to?" Jason stood by her and hugged her shoulders with one arm.

"Just going over a recipe. Want a cup of coffee?" Caroline reached for a mug.

"Sure." Jason pulled the recipe card closer. "Trout almandine. Kind of a fancy entrée for one."

Caroline inhaled deeply, dreading Jason's response to her being involved with a man other than his father. Not that she and Rodney were anything more than friends, but still, she'd gone over this conversation in her mind many times. Every scenario she imagined didn't turn out well. "Actually, I'm cooking dinner for a friend."

Jason sipped his coffee, then opened the cupboard where she kept cookies. "Yum, mint ones."

Caroline received a peck on the cheek for stocking his favorite cookies. She followed him to the kitchen table.

"So who's your friend? A church or quilt lady?"

"Actually. . ." Caroline cleared her throat. "I met my friend at church, but, um. . ."

Jason removed a cookie from the package. "What?" he asked, then popped the cookie in his mouth.

"Well. . ." Caroline braced for a bad reaction. "It's not a lady. It's a gentleman. Do you remember Clara Harris from church?"

"The church pie lady."

"Yes." Caroline's grin at Clara's title grew as she thought of the nickname Rodney had bestowed upon her. "It's her son, Rodney."

Jason finished his coffee and pushed the empty mug from one hand to the other. "So, you're dating?" he asked, focusing all his attention on the sliding mug.

"No, we're not dating. Rodney commissioned me to repair a quilt." Caroline caught Jason's eye roll at the mention of her business. She paused for a moment, waiting for the pang of hurt to subside.

"Do you fix dinner for all your customers?"

Even though Jason kept his voice conversational, his eyes communicated defiance, and it angered Caroline. "No, I don't make dinner for all my customers. I'm making dinner for Rodney because he's helping me update my website." Defensiveness made her voice shake as she stared him down. "He's impressed with my business."

Jason snickered.

Caroline cut him off. "Jason, other than glancing at my long arm machine and going off on a tangent about wasting money, you've never even looked at my work."

The ticking of the kitchen clock kept time with Caroline's pounding pulse as she waited for the argument to begin. To her surprise, Jason sighed, and her tension-pinched shoulders relaxed.

"Mom, I know you're a good seamstress. I remember all the church play costumes, not to mention clothes you made for me over the years, but why do you have to start your own business? You know how Dad felt about commission jobs. If you think you need a job and want to make your living sewing, can't you work for a tailor where you'd get a steady paycheck?"

She did remember how Ted felt about careers that earned a commission, not a reliable income to pay the bills. That opinion might be right. She couldn't argue with a valid point like a steady paycheck, especially having experienced a slow time just after the holidays. She'd been excited to get Rodney's business, as well as the quilt for the candy store, but what would she do after that? Would the new website and blog bring in business? Maybe she should apply for the part-time cashier position she'd seen an ad for in the weekly paper. But would she like that kind of work? Shouldn't she enjoy what she did for a living? In the midst of her self-doubt, she remembered the supplement to her income.

"I'm teaching two quilting classes at Mark's store."

She blurted out her news louder than she'd planned and gave Jason a start. His eyes grew wide.

"Sorry, I didn't mean to shout that at you."

Jason bent his head from side to side while weighing her news, a trait he'd inherited from Ted. "I'm guessing Mark is paying you."

Caroline raised her eyebrows and nodded her head. "Right now, it'll depend on class enrollment, but he has quite a few customers interested. I'll get sixty percent of the class fee."

"Well, teaching a class is more like it. After all, you were a teacher once. You should contact the community college in Sioux Falls and see if they'd let you teach one of those recreational classes on quilting."

"I don't know." Caroline pursed her lips. *Wouldn't I be too busy to run my quilting business?* She didn't voice that concern, eager to keep Jason interested, not to mention positive, about her career choice. "Wouldn't I need a teaching certificate for that? I let mine go years ago."

Jason shrugged. "I wouldn't think so for those"—he lifted his fingers in air quotes—"just-for-fun classes. I think you just have to be an authority."

"More coffee?" Caroline blinked back tears as she retrieved the coffeepot. It was obvious by his "just-for-fun" comment that Jason lacked respect for her and her craft. She'd disregard the comment, though, because she'd grown tired of fighting with Jason.

Caroline picked up her trusty notepad. After she filled their mugs, she scribbled a note on the tablet to check out teaching classes at the community college.

"What's that?" Jason asked, then blew across his mug.

"Just notes about what I want Rodney to include on my website and what I need to do to promote my business."

"So this Rodney designs websites for a living?"

"No, he runs a lawn care and snow removal business in town."

"A yardman savvy in web design?" Jason snorted. "Mom, this guy's scamming you."

Her defenses already alert from his previous comment, Caroline pointed her finger at Jason. "Enough. Rodney retired from his former career in advertising."

"So he's an old guy."

"No, only a couple of years older than me."

"Then why'd he retire from that occupation?"

Good question. All Rodney really said was that that career was another lifetime ago. Had he planned to retire early, or did he quit his job to take care of Clara after her cancer diagnosis?

"I'm not sure why he ended that career. Come with me." Caroline stood. "You can't criticize something you haven't seen."

As she headed out of the kitchen, Caroline heard Jason's chair scrape the tile floor. By the time he arrived in the den, her web page filled the computer screen.

Jason read the content before clicking on a link. A picture of Mildred's quilt popped up along with a short description of the work Caroline put into it. After trying a few other links, he looked at Caroline. "It's impressive, but do you think a fancy website makes your business venture less risky?"

Caroline sighed. "No, but I think it will help draw in business. Jason, I have to earn a living somehow. Your dad didn't want me to work, and now I have no job skills."

"Mom, Dad loved you. He wanted to provide for you. You act like he had a massive heart attack and left you alone on purpose. Stop being mad at him. It's not his fault he died. You of all people should know that. To quote your favorite psalm, 139, 'All the days ordained for me were written in your book before one of them came to be.'" Jason scanned the room and held his arms out. "You don't even have one picture of him out anymore. It's like he never even had any ordained days."

The computer screen saver kicked on, hiding Rodney's hard work. There was no doubt Rodney believed in her ability to succeed. Why couldn't her own son? Jason swiveled the office chair and left the den.

Caroline hated that Jason was right. It wasn't Ted's fault he'd died. It was God's fault, and the scripture Jason had quoted backed up that fact. As for the pictures, Caroline had tucked them in drawers. With her financial troubles, she didn't need her once carefree life mocking her.

Caroline found Jason in the kitchen, leaning on his hands and facing the cupboards. She walked up behind him and put her hands on his shoulders. "I'm not angry at your dad." *I'm angry at God.* "I'm sorry if that is how it seems to you."

"I don't want you to work, either. You wouldn't have to if you'd invested the insurance money and not purchased that quilting machine." Jason spat out the words.

"Even if I hadn't made that purchase, the money wouldn't have lasted twelve years until I could draw Social Security."

Jason twisted his shoulders until she removed her hands. She leaned against the counter next to him. Her son had Ted's personality traits and hair color, but he was his mother's son in build, eye color, and disposition. They used to be on the same wavelength, but in the last few months, they'd spent their time together butting heads.

"I need you to understand my situation. Can't we talk this through?"

Jason's silence indicated his unwillingness to solve their problem. He shook his head as he pushed back from the counter. He grabbed his coat as he passed the chair on his way to the entryway. Caroline followed him and stood in the doorway, the ticking of the clock the only noise as Jason slipped on his coat and boots, then grabbed the doorknob. He met Caroline's gaze.

"Bye." He turned and opened the door. As he started to leave, he looked over his shoulder. "I'm not happy about you dating, either."

The rattle of the door glass echoed through the kitchen.

❧

Anger more than hurt from Jason's comments moistened Caroline's eyes. She'd expected a negative reaction about Rodney but thought they could come to an agreement like they used to when they didn't see eye to eye. But she and Jason hadn't been able to overcome their disagreements in the last few months. After this confrontation, she'd make a lousy hostess tonight. Maybe she should cancel dinner? Caroline rubbed the tears from her eyes with the back of her hand. The recipe called for fresh trout, which she'd bought yesterday. With her financial problems, she couldn't afford to let food spoil because of a difficult son.

Caroline marched down the stairs to her workshop, still fuming at Jason's closed mind. The empty long arm machine proved Jason's negative remarks right. The website hadn't brought in any business. Would it? Or was her business venture a waste of money and time?

With Mark's Valentine quilt finished and delivered on time, she planned to make a practice block for the candy jar quilt to show Rodney, who'd had trouble visualizing it.

Ready to spend the rest of the afternoon working on the appliqué block, Caroline pinned the pattern she'd designed from the drawing to the appropriate material. She carefully cut around the pieces. This block might be an example of time wasted if it didn't measure up to the candy store owner's vision.

Why did Jason pick today to visit? His attitude had her in a dither. First she'd considered canceling dinner. Now her doubts about her quilting business might defeat the project. Caroline fretted as she fused the candy jar and lid to the background block and began the tedious task of machine appliqué. She figured it would take most of the afternoon, but to her surprise she finished in just over an hour. She loved the finished product, but if the candy store owner disliked the block, at least Caroline hadn't invested much time into the sample.

With hours left before her efforts were needed in the kitchen, Caroline decided to disassemble Rodney's Lily of the Field quilt.

As she snipped the string knots that held the quilt together, she noticed the geometric shape of the blocks—squares, rectangles, and triangles—that formed the pattern. It appeared to be a variation of a Nine Patch. The quilter used the patterned fabric from the flour sacks for the flower petals in the center of the block as well as the corner blocks. White rectangles bordered the sides, and yellow fabric separated the petals. The design of the block and use of fabric colors made the flower stand out.

A simple lily just being, not working or struggling to grow, trusting God to provide soil, sunlight, and moisture so it can develop into a blooming flower. Caroline smiled at the thought, no doubt planted with Mark's quote of the Bible verse, as she continued to clip the strings that held the quilt top to the back. While Caroline worked, her mood shifted. Each time she snipped the thread, it seemed to cut through the hold she had on her anger and hurt. Calm replaced the aggravation left from her confrontation with Jason.

Caroline checked her watch. Time to start dinner. She caressed the quilt top, then flicked off the worktable light.

In the kitchen, she prepared the trout, then pushed the roaster into the oven. While the trout baked, Caroline changed her clothes and touched up her hair and makeup.

She ran into a problem with their place settings at the dining room table. She placed Rodney at the head of the table and her across from him, but even with her small table, passing items would be difficult. Leaving Rodney's setting at the head of the table, she moved her place setting to his right. She preferred this arrangement, but it seemed intimate. She thought that might make Rodney uncomfortable, so she moved the place mats, dishes, and napkins so they sat opposite each other across the width of the table. Standing back, Caroline viewed the table arrangement. They still seemed far away from each other, but at least they could easily pass the salt.

The light blue place mats and cloth napkins accented the darker blue in her china pattern. The small flowers that decorated the napkin rings were a close match to the flowers that ringed the edge of the plates. Three small crystal votives allowed them easy view of each other and gave the room a cozy feel.

Returning to the kitchen, Caroline placed asparagus in a foil packet. She drizzled it with olive oil, sealed the edges, and stuck it in the oven. All that was left to do now was wait.

Anxious energy kept Caroline on her feet, checking glasses for nonexistent spots and arranging the whole-grain rolls in the basket. Since Rodney ate healthy, she'd purchased healthy groceries for this meal, except for that chocolate cake that had been calling her name since Jason left.

She was glad she hadn't canceled dinner. A peaceful feeling had stayed with her all afternoon as she worked at separating the back from the front of the quilt. When she'd completed the task, the serenity lingered instead of the anger and hurt. Joy filled her, not the exuberant excitement from earlier in the day, but a more contented feeling.

Caroline realized her thoughts distracted her from the task at hand. She covered the filled basket of dinner rolls, then placed them on the dining room table.

☙

The door glass rattled with each thump when Rodney knocked on the back door. He'd sat in his pickup a few minutes, deciding which door to use. Caroline used the side door for business, but should he use it tonight? No porch light brightened either door, but the kitchen window's inviting glow lured him to the back door. The entryway and outside light popped on at the same time.

Caroline swung the door open wide, her broad smile the only acknowledgment he needed. "Come in." She motioned toward the kitchen with a tea towel. "You know the way."

Rodney followed Caroline up two steps to the kitchen, relieved to see he'd made an appropriate wardrobe choice. She also wore jeans. Her oxford shirt, multistriped in earthy greens, blues, and browns, complemented her strawberry blond hair. He slipped off his stocking cap, gloves, and coat, then stuffed the hat and gloves down the arm of his coat.

"I'll take that." Caroline laid the tea towel on the table and reached for his jacket.

"Just a second." Rodney pulled a shiny bag from his coat pocket.

"What's that?" Caroline asked, looking at the bag as she took his coat and hung it in a closet at the other end of the kitchen.

"I know you told me not to bring anything, but I wanted to contribute something. So. . ." Rodney flipped the foil bag so the label faced the front, then rested the bottom on one hand and gently held the top with two fingers as if it were a bottle of wine. "A half pound of Daily Jolt's finest decaffeinated coffee aged to perfection. And ground in the event you don't have a grinder."

"Thank you. It will go perfectly with my homemade chocolate cake." Caroline removed the bag of coffee from its perch. "Unless you'd like some with dinner?"

"No, I prefer water with my meals." Rodney made an exaggerated sniffing motion. "I'm thinking the Queen of Quilts might earn a new nickname, like Duchess of Dinner. The trout smells incredible."

Caroline's face beamed with pleasure. "I'm glad you think so. I'm a little rusty at this."

The beep of the oven timer turned her attention away from Rodney, much to his dismay.

He watched Caroline lift a roasting pan from the oven. "Do you need help with that?"

"No, but you could fill those two glasses with water and take them to the dining room. I'll plate the trout and be right in."

Rodney rounded the corner of the dining room and saw a beautifully set table. When was the last time he had dinner like this that didn't involve a holiday at Michelle's? Since he was so tired of eating his dinner while he perched on the arm of his sofa, he'd have been happy sitting at the kitchen table. He felt spoiled. There was one problem, though. They weren't sitting close enough. He set the water glasses down. Probably a bold move on his part, but he moved a place setting to the head of the table so he could sit closer to Caroline. He finished rearranging the other place setting just as Caroline rounded the corner, carrying a tray that contained a platter and two small bowls filled with fruit.

"I hope you don't mind." Rodney took the bowls from Caroline that held orange sections, maraschino cherries, grapes, banana slices, and apple slices. He put them in the middle of their dinner plates.

Caroline set an attractive platter arrangement of trout almandine, long-grain rice, and asparagus on the table between the two settings.

She began to chuckle, which turned into a full-fledged laugh. The laugh lines at the corners of her eyes deepened, much more attractive than the pesky crevice that appeared when she worried.

"I changed our place settings three times." She motioned for Rodney to sit at the head of the table. "I liked this arrangement best but thought it might be too"—pink tinged her cheeks; then she shrugged in it's-too-late-now fashion, never letting her bright smile fade—"intimate. Please sit down."

"Not for me." Rodney moved closer, then reached around her and took hold of the chair back.

"Oh." Caroline sat and let Rodney guide her chair to the table. "Do you know how long it's been since someone's done that for me?"

Rodney slid his own chair closer to the table. "A long time?"

"Yeah." Caroline sighed the word. She reached for the serving spoon. Rodney stopped her hand in midair by covering it with his own.

"I'd like to say grace." He squeezed her delicate hand.

"Please do." Caroline wrapped slender fingers that felt like silk around Rodney's hand and bowed her head. Rodney's family folded their hands in prayer when saying grace, but had he known Caroline's tradition was to hold hands, he'd have prayed out loud versus silently at every meal they'd shared together. He'd longed to touch her since their first meeting when their simple handshake left a faint tingle on his palm.

"God in heaven, thank You for the bounty of Your love that You bestow on us each and every day. You are a faithful Father, letting us cast our cares upon You and providing for all our needs. Bless the food we are about to receive. In Jesus' name, we pray. Amen."

"Amen." Caroline gave his hand a gentle squeeze before releasing her grasp. "Better dig in before the apples and banana start to turn brown."

Rodney gave her a short salute, spread his napkin in his lap, and scooped a spoonful of fruit. Caroline shook her head as if annoyed by his antics, but her blue eyes twinkled with amusement.

"How was your day?" he asked.

The deep sigh and sagging shoulders answered Rodney's question long before Caroline spoke. Worry pushed the happiness from her features. Regret that he'd asked about her day washed through him. Not quite the mood he'd hoped to set.

"Jason visited this morning."

Odd that that would make her unhappy. His mom had been overjoyed when he'd visited. And Michelle seemed glad to spend time with her own sons.

Caroline reached for Rodney's empty fruit dish, stacked it with hers, and set them aside. Caroline efficiently served the main course. "Is this enough?"

"That depends on if I can have seconds."

The corner of Caroline's mouth twitched. He waited for the corner of her bottom lip to disappear. "You might want to taste it before you ask for seconds. I haven't made this dish in years."

"Well, if it tastes as good as it smells and looks, then I'll want seconds." Rodney took a bite of the fish and rice. The nutty rice and flavor-filled fish melted on his tongue, his low growl of pleasure inadvertent. "This is fantastic."

"Thank you." Caroline gave a curt nod and tasted her dinner. "How was your day?"

"Typical. Since last week's snow thawed in yesterday's forty-two-degree temps and this morning it was ten degrees, we made the rounds to all my clients' houses and put ice melt on the walks and driveways."

"You know what they say about South Dakota's weather. If you don't like it, stick around for an hour because it'll change."

"That's the truth."

"Do most snow removal companies check for ice when it thaws?" Caroline sipped her water and blotted the corners of her mouth with her napkin.

"I don't know. I do it because I have elderly clients. Even if they're able to spread the ice melt, they shouldn't be out on the ice." Rodney helped himself to more trout and rice.

"Rodney, that's very thoughtful."

"Well. . ." How could he tell her that guilt drove him to provide that service? The thought had never entered his mind that his mother had needed help with things like that until she insisted he come to her house to recuperate. He saw how much she paid to unreliable service companies that did a mediocre job at best. How long had she struggled with that or relied on a neighbor to help?

"It's part of the job. By the way, I received an e-mail from my mom's cousin."

"An answer about the quilt? Is another mystery solved, Sherlock?"

Rodney mocked removing a pipe from his mouth. "No, Dr. Watson, I don't believe so. In fact, it may have added another one. She seems to think that another of our cousins, who moved to California years ago, made it."

"So you don't have contact information for that cousin?"

"No, because I didn't even know Mom had a cousin in California." *Can't know your relatives if you never visited home much.* "I sent another mass e-mail to see if any other relatives keep in contact with her."

"Guess that's all you can do, and if she is the one who made the quilt, then mystery solved."

Caroline and Rodney finished their dinner in companionable silence.

Rodney pushed his empty plate toward the center of the table.

"I'll get the coffee and dessert." Caroline eased out of her chair.

The quiet that filled the dining room in Caroline's absence surrounded Rodney. He missed eating a freshly cooked meal at a table. He missed sharing dinner with someone. He missed Caroline. Rodney started to gather the dishes on the table.

Caroline stopped pouring coffee into cups when Rodney entered the kitchen, carrying a stack of dirty dishes. "You didn't have to do that! You're my guest."

"I'm your friend." *God, please let her think more of me than a guest.* Rodney sent up the silent prayer, then set the dishes on the counter.

"Yes, you are." Caroline's tender expression and soft-spoken words engaged a flutter of hope inside Rodney. Friendship was a start.

"Shall we go back to the dining room?" Caroline picked up the saucers and balanced the cups.

Rodney picked up the individual servings of cake. "Here is just fine." He turned and set them on the kitchen table.

"I have something to show you." Caroline gently put the saucers and filled cups down. "I'll be right back," she said over her shoulder as she headed toward the basement.

When she returned, Rodney had polished off half of his cake and coffee. "You've outdone yourself," he said and slipped another forkful of cake into his mouth.

"Do you know how nice it is to cook for someone other than myself?"

"I'm guessing as nice as it is to eat at a table and share conversation." He exchanged a smile with Caroline. "What have you got there?"

"It's the practice block for the candy store's quilt. What do you think?"

Caroline laid a large block out on the table, then dug into her dessert.

In awe of her abilities, Rodney whistled. "I'm amazed at how you looked at that drawing and came up with this." She'd cut the jelly bean fabric into a hexagon shape that resembled the old-fashioned candy store jars from years past. A simple rectangle from the red material became the jar lid. Black thread accentuated the jar and lid shape and, he guessed, held them onto the brown square block. It truly looked like candy in a candy jar.

"I think the store owner will be pleased."

"I hope so." Caroline crossed her fingers. "It turned out almost perfect on the first try."

Rodney recognized the pride in her work that settled in her features. He'd seen it on his own face for years and again recently with the work on Caroline's website.

"At least something went right today." Caroline pushed the block to the side of the table. Sadness washed across her features. "Would you like another piece of cake?"

Clearly she was trying to change the subject. Rodney yearned for another piece of cake but guessed the fudge frosting was laced with butter. "Thank you, but no." Rodney patted his stomach. "I've had plenty, but I could use a coffee refill." Rodney rose before Caroline had the chance and picked up the coffeepot and dry creamer. "How about you?"

"Fill 'er up." Caroline scooted her cup toward him.

After pouring her coffee, Rodney turned the kitchen chair sideways and stretched his legs to their full length, crossing them at the ankle. He stirred the creamer into his coffee. His next question could go two ways, but it was worth the risk. He wanted to be trusted with Caroline's cares just like she shared the love of her work with him.

"Do you want to talk about your day?"

Caroline puckered her mouth to the side, but the worry crease never appeared. Her eyes searched his face. For what? Sincerity in the question?

"I really don't want to bother you with my troubles."

"I asked, so how can it be a bother? Besides, we're friends, right?"

"Yes, we are, but. . ." Hesitation filled her voice. "I just don't want you to view Jason in the wrong light. He's a good person, but Ted's death was hard on everyone. We buried him a week to the day before Jason's wedding."

A joyous occasion turned bittersweet by the loss of a loved one. "That must have been so hard. I can't even imagine." Rodney reached over and clasped Caroline's hand, the only comfort their current relationship allowed.

"Hard doesn't even begin to describe it." Caroline sniffed as the memory misted her eyes. "But that's not the problem. Please don't think we're horrible people."

Like Mr. Workaholic, who'd chosen to ignore his biological family and failed to start one of his own, had the right to judge anyone's family dynamics. He tightened his hold on her soft hand as a sign of encouragement to continue.

Her blue eyes locked on his. "Jason doesn't support my business venture. He thinks I wasted my money on the long arm machine." A flash of anger passed over her features. "He doesn't want me to work, just like Ted didn't, but. . ."

Disgust pulled at Rodney. Did he expect her to stop living because his dad died? What was wrong with Caroline's having a career? Who would it be hurting? She was too young to wither away in an empty house, which it appeared she'd been doing for over a year. Rodney purposely kept his voice even. He didn't want his reaction to shut Caroline down. "But?"

Caroline huffed. "I have to work, and I'm tired of him voicing his opinion about it every time I see him. I know it's risky, but after today I'm more determined than ever to make this business succeed." She pulled her hand free of Rodney's and rapped her fist on the table in determined emphasis.

Rodney's heart jumped. Caroline revealed another layer of her personality. "Fired up" became her. Her rosy cheeks deepened to a shade just lighter than her hair, making the blue in her eyes more vibrant. He suppressed a chuckle, understanding now why some men teased a woman to annoyance. "Then now would be a good time to show you an update I made on your website this afternoon."

They went into the den. Caroline sat at the desk and wiggled the mouse to wake up the computer. Her e-mail account popped onto the screen, announcing she had mail. She clicked the button to close that message. "I don't recognize this e-mail address. The subject line says *quilt*."

Rodney watched her open then scan the message. She jumped from the office chair, turned, and grabbed Rodney by the shoulders. "The website redesign worked." Her voice reflected her glee. "I got a quilt job." She wrapped Rodney in a hug.

Rodney closed his eyes and pulled her close. This was the best paycheck he'd earned for his work. Ever.

Chapter 5

Caroline deliberated too long on what to wear to church and whether she should even go. In the end, she slipped into black corduroys and a snowflake-dotted black turtleneck with a black quilted vest. She chose dangly snowflake earrings since she let her natural curls bounce loose.

She hurried up the steps to the church door, certain she'd be creeping into church during the call to worship.

"There you are." Mildred waited in the narthex. "Rodney and I saved you a seat in our pew."

Caroline didn't have the time to protest. But did she want to? Mildred grasped her coat sleeve and pulled her past the choir lined up, waiting for the processional to begin. The first notes of music sounded as she and Mildred turned up the aisle. Rodney craned his neck in a fifth-row pew, his smile instant when their eyes met. He slid from the pew and stood in the aisle to allow Mildred and Caroline's entrance.

Mildred almost stepped on Caroline's toes so she could enter the pew first, leaving Caroline to sit in the middle. Rodney reseated himself beside her. Close beside her. Her body warmed from the knowledge that Rodney sat near enough that their hands might accidentally brush. A shiver of excitement shot through her when her thoughts turned back to their embrace a few nights ago.

Movement to each side of her caught her eye. She stood seconds later than Rodney and Mildred. Caroline chided herself for not paying attention and for what she was thinking about in church. When the leader started the reading, she realized she had no bulletin. She turned toward Mildred, who had her paper close to her nose.

Rodney's elbow bumped her arm. He extended his arm between them, holding the bulletin at a distance. He managed to get through the reading by squinting, since no glasses were perched on his nose. The organist hit a chord, and as the choir sang a choral response, the congregation sat down.

Caroline reached for a hymnal from the holder attached to the pew in front of her. Only one songbook. She looked toward the other holder. Empty. She eyed Mildred, who appeared to be absorbed in the bulletin. The missing bulletin. . .shortage of hymnals. . .insisting she sit with them. . . Mildred had set her up.

Wouldn't she be surprised to find out that Caroline didn't mind at all. In fact, she liked it. She flipped through the hymnal until she found the page for the first congregational hymn. Between the small, italicized print and Rodney's missing glasses, she was sure she'd have to stand close to him. Another fact she liked. And a quick scan of the bulletin told her she'd get to share the hymnal three more times. Perfect.

Not perfect. Caroline felt her eyes grow wide. Lately she'd just mumbled along while others sang out strong, which was probably for the best, because despite all the talents the Lord had blessed Caroline with, singing wasn't one of them.

Her pulse quickened. If she mumbled or didn't sing along, what would Rodney think? If she did sing along, he'd probably step as far away from her as possible without standing in the aisle.

The time to decide ran out. The opening chords of the hymn floated through the sanctuary. As they stood with the congregation, she offered the hymnal to Rodney. He pulled the left side of the book to him and sidestepped closer to Caroline. He moved the book higher and Caroline followed his lead to keep the writing even. Certain the type was difficult for him to read, she considered, then offered the entire book to Rodney.

He frowned and pushed the book back at her. As the congregation started to sing, Rodney leaned over, never taking his eyes from the music, and whispered in Caroline's ear. "I don't sing well." He began to hum along with the song.

Caroline touched Rodney's arm until he looked at her. "Neither do I." She mouthed the words.

Rodney grinned and in a flat baritone sang out strong. Caroline followed his lead off-pitch but trying to sing the alto's harmony part. Luckily for them, Mildred's lovely soprano, still strong after all these years, echoed through the rafters.

Rodney looked handsome in his dark green sweater and black dress pants. He smelled nice, too. Woodsy and spicy. Ted had worn a heavy musk, while Rodney's cologne smelled fresh, light, clean. Sneaking sideways glances, she admired the strong lines of Rodney's profile and the middle-aged etchings that added depth to his face. Before Caroline knew it, their pastor recited the benediction.

As they rose from the pew, Mildred touched Caroline's arm. "Dear, a few of our breakfast group need to attend a meeting now. We decided to meet for lunch today instead of breakfast. You're both welcome to join us."

"Oh." Caroline turned to Rodney to relay the message.

"I know. Mildred told me earlier, but I'm not going to be able to make lunch. I expect my sister about one today."

Rodney stepped out of the pew as the aisle traffic lessened and shook hands with another gentleman.

Mildred squeezed past Caroline. "Will we see you at lunch?"

"I have a quilt I need to start working on."

Mildred looked past Caroline to where Rodney stood conversing. Her smile turned sly. "Okay, I'd better get to my meeting. You have a good week."

Suddenly, Caroline felt awkward and conspicuous. Not because Mildred might be onto her, but because she didn't know what to do now. Should she wait for Rodney? She wanted to. Should she move along with the crowd? Her nervousness kicked in old habits. She scanned each exit to plan her escape route. The best prospect, the side door, required her to reenter the pew and exit from the other side. She tried to step back into the pew without drawing Rodney's attention away from his conversation.

"Caroline, are you ready?" Rodney's deep voice stopped her departure plan.

"Whenever you are." She smiled as she watched him end his conversation and shake hands.

"Thanks for saving me back there," Rodney said as he removed his coat from the rack in the narthex. "I'm glad he's feeling better, but hearing the details of his heart surgery is not my idea of conversation."

A laugh bubbled out of Caroline. "Do you have a weak stomach?"

"It's not that." Rodney rubbed the upper part of his chest. "It's—"

"Snowing!" Caroline had turned toward the glass entry doors.

Rodney zipped his coat. "Guess this wasn't a good day to walk to church."

"You walked to church?"

Rodney nodded.

"Ten blocks?"

"At eight fifteen this morning, it was thirty-eight degrees." Rodney held up a face warmer and his gloves. "I dressed warm." He pushed through the door and held it for Caroline.

"Would you like a ride home?"

"I thought you'd never ask." Rodney cocked his elbow.

Caroline looped her hand through the opening and let Rodney guide her down the church stairs.

"Where's your car?"

Caroline pointed to her black sedan parked half a block away on the side street to head Rodney in the right direction.

Once in the car, Caroline navigated the wet residential streets, noticing the snow sticking to protected areas.

Rodney peered out the passenger window. "I think the temperature dropped. Good thing I got my exercise walking to church. My afternoon and evening could get busy."

"This won't affect your sister's visit, will it?"

"I doubt it, although she lives an hour away. The weather's not severe enough yet to keep her home."

Caroline turned into Rodney's driveway and pushed the gearshift into PARK.

"Would you like to come in for coffee?" Rodney unfastened his seat belt.

I'm not happy about you dating. Jason's voice echoed from her subconscious. Why had that thought jumped into her mind? Did she want to date Rodney?

"What's wrong?"

Caroline saw the concern in Rodney's eyes.

"Nothing."

"Then why"—Rodney slipped a glove off and gently brushed his thumb in between her tensed eyebrows—"is this line so prevalent? It appears when you're worried." His brown eyes lit with concern.

His soft touch sent shivers of warmth through her body and set her pulse at a faster tempo. He kept massaging the line until she relaxed her face. Rodney moved his thumb from her forehead and traced her brow line. He turned his hand and trailed his fingers down her cheek, never taking his eyes from hers.

Emotion pulled the tension from her face to her throat, causing the first syllable of her sentence to crack. "N–n–n–nothing's wrong." She inhaled a deep ragged breath in an effort to regain some control. *Jason definitely wouldn't like this.* "I just don't want to intrude on your time with your family."

"Michelle won't be here for three hours or so." His voice faint, he leaned closer. His gaze dropped to her lips. His fingers teased the skin under her chin. She sucked the corner of her lip under her teeth.

"Another telltale sign." Rodney's fingers caressed the drawn-in corner, coaxing it out. He traced the outline of her lips, leaving a trail of warmth behind. "You have to stop agonizing over everything. I hope you're not worried about being alone with me."

A stronger whiff of woodsy cologne affirmed that Rodney had slid closer. The pleasant scent lured her to lean toward him.

"Caroline." Rodney lifted his eyes to once again look into hers. "You are so beautiful." His breath was heavy, his words barely audible.

Anticipation quaked her insides. Rodney ran his hand up her cheek, resting his fingers at her hairline. He guided her head to a slight tilt and turned his opposite. His breath warmed her skin. She parted her lips.

The crunch of tires on snow and the roar of a vehicle engine pulling in the driveway startled them. Caroline jumped and scooted away from Rodney until the door handle bit into her back. What was she doing? Getting ready to make out in a car? She was a fifty-year-old woman, not a teenager. Mortified they'd been caught, she felt embarrassment burn her face. She couldn't bring herself to look at the vehicle that pulled in beside hers. What if it was someone she knew?

As Rodney turned toward the windshield and flopped back into the seat, his head bounced against the headrest. He snorted. "Michelle's here."

"Are you coming in for coffee?" Rodney reached for the door handle.

"Noooooo, I don't think so." Caroline kept her head bent, not meeting his eyes and letting her hair cover her face. Her curls bounced with each negative shake of her head, daring Rodney to touch them.

"Caroline, please come in for a cup of coffee. I'd like you to meet my sister." With concentrated effort, Rodney kept his desire from his voice, his tone even and light to lift the curtain of worry that he knew fell over her features.

"But we. . ." Caroline raised her head in what seemed like slow motion and looked at him. She waved her hand in the air between them. "She saw. . ." The corner of Caroline's mouth tucked itself in its usual hiding place, and the furrow line indented.

"We don't know what she saw. She *was* driving. Please relax." Caroline flinched at Rodney's touch but didn't brush his hand from her shoulder.

Fingers drumming on the passenger window echoed through the silent car. Rodney breathed in the warm air, stale from the car heater, and turned his head. Michelle smiled through the glass and waved. He pulled the door lock, then the handle. The door clicked open, and Michelle moved into the open space between the door and car. She bent down just in Rodney's view.

"Hi, big brother. I came early because of the weather."

Michelle's lips curled into a mock smile, a sibling signal to Rodney that she'd seen everything and knew she'd interrupted. She was filing away the incident in her memory for future misery making. She leaned over him, pinning him to the car seat, and reached her arm across him.

Please don't say anything to her. Rodney stared hard at his sister's blond hair, hoping if there was such a thing as mental telepathy, she'd pick up this vibe. He didn't need a setback in his relationship with Caroline. Since the night she'd cooked him dinner, they'd climbed a rung up the relationship ladder, talking at least once a day on the phone.

"Hi, I'm Michelle." Her voice lilted with friendliness. He knew her face now shone with a genuine smile. His tightened muscles relaxed, his feet no longer braced and pushing him back against the car seat.

"Caroline."

"Oh, the quilt lady. Rodney talks about you all the time."

"He does?"

"He keeps me updated on the restoration and the website progress. I didn't interrupt you two going somewhere, did I?"

"No." Rodney and Caroline answered in duet.

"Caroline gave me a ride home from church. I'd offered her coffee, but she's not certain she can spare the time." Rodney looked into the all-too-innocent expression on his sister's face.

"Please join us. I'd like to ask you about a quilt idea."

Interest sparkled in Caroline's blue eyes. "I guess I could spare an hour."

"Great!" Michelle backed out of the car, freeing Rodney.

Michelle chattered about the weather all the way into the house. "When I called to tell you I'd be early, I got your voice mail."

Rodney removed his cell phone from the holder on his belt, flipped the cover, and turned it back on. "I turn it off before I go into the church. Look. I have a message and it's from my sissy."

Michelle's eyes narrowed to slits. Before she could protest or set down the bags she carried, Rodney pulled her into a tight hug, pinning her arms to her sides. He'd gotten his revenge for her interruption and antics in the car, although she did get Caroline to come in for coffee, so he'd give her points for that. He loosened his grip on her.

"Let me take your coats."

Rodney gathered both women's coats and hung them on pegs in the hall. When he returned to the kitchen, the coffeepot gurgled its start. Michelle unpacked containers from the plastic bags and began to restock the freezer. Caroline sat alone at the kitchen table.

"Should I leave something out? Turkey meat loaf, chicken enchiladas, or vegetable soup?" Michelle turned to Rodney with a container in her hand.

"Surprise me." Rodney poured three cups of decaf and carried two to the table. He set one in front of Caroline and the other at the chair across from her. What a strategic plan. He'd sit next to her after he added cream to his coffee.

"I can't believe how healthy you eat. I regret not making my family eat a better diet." Caroline studied the liquid in her mug.

Michelle raised her eyebrows at Rodney as she walked past him, then sat in the spot next to Caroline and slid the cup that sat on the table in front of her. "Why's that?"

"My husband died of a massive coronary."

"I'm sorry—I didn't know."

"It's been well over a year now, but my son and I still experience repercussions from it. I wish Ted had known Rodney. He might have followed his good example. Ted didn't exercise or watch his diet."

"Rodney didn't always. It took one good scare to get him to shape up."

Rodney's stomach dropped like he'd swallowed lead. He'd sidestepped this conversation with Caroline far too long. He wanted to tell her. He wanted to be the *one* to tell her. She deserved to know because of the way she felt about Ted's death. He'd missed his opportune moments, and then the timing never seemed right. Just like right now. As he walked to the table, his feet felt heavy, as if the figurative lead he'd swallowed had fallen directly into them. He sat down, prepared for the worst.

Caroline sipped her coffee and looked across the table at him. "Well, exercise and diet do add years to our lives. We boomers are outliving our parents."

She thinks the scare was due to Mom's illness. He needed to tell her.

"You wanted to talk to me about a quilt?" Caroline turned her attention to Michelle.

Confusion shadowed Michelle's face as she looked from Rodney to Caroline.

Obviously misreading Michelle's confusion, Caroline tried to jog the other woman's memory. "Outside you said you had questions about a quilt?"

"Y–yes, the quilt," Michelle stammered, then smiled at Caroline. "I've seen quilts made from old T-shirts and I'd like to have one made for each of my sons. Do you do anything like that?"

"I never have, but I can. I purchased a pattern for one. The blocks are large with sashing in between."

"Okay." Michelle sounded uncertain.

"It's quilter's language. She uses it all the time." Rodney laughed out loud. "Say it in layman's terms, Caroline. God blessed Michelle, just like Mom, with the cooking talent, not the sewing talent."

"It's true." Michelle laughed. "I can secure a button, but that's about it."

"My pattern has ten-inch blocks." She drew a square in the air with her fingers to give Michelle an idea of the block size. "You use the front or back of the T-shirt for that. Strips of fabric or sashing frame and separate the blocks to make the top of the quilt. I believe my pattern uses twelve T-shirts, three across and four down. I can probably adjust the quilt size if you need me to."

"So I'd just need twelve T-shirts apiece and you'd make it?"

"You'd need fabric for the sashing and the back. Most of the pictures I've seen of this type of quilt have the top pieced together with sashing that matches the back fabric of the quilt or a neutral color that goes with all the T-shirts and a patterned fabric on the back. If you'd like, I can work up a yardage estimate of the amount of fabric needed to put it together."

"That'd be great. You are good, Caroline." Michelle reached over and patted her arm. "My next question was about how much fabric to buy. Will you e-mail the estimate to me or Rodney?"

"Better yet," Rodney interjected, "go to her website and contact her. That way her website logs hits, which moves it up on search engine traffic. I'll e-mail you the link."

Caroline tilted her head and raised her eyebrows. "Now who's speaking a foreign language?"

&.

"I like her." Through the picture window, Michelle watched Caroline back out of Rodney's driveway. The snow had stopped falling, leaving the ground a glittering blanket of white.

"I do, too." Rodney peered over Michelle's shoulder, straining to catch the last glimpses of Caroline.

"Then why haven't you told her that you've had a mild heart attack?" Michelle whirled and faced her brother. "She thinks you changed your life because of Mom, doesn't she? Why would you tell her something like that?" Michelle's temper flared, her tone taking on a fierce edge. Sometimes Rodney pitied his brother-in-law and nephews.

"It's complicated. First, she's been so withdrawn and worried."

"So that makes it okay to lie?"

"Can. . .I. . .finish?" Rodney enunciated each word. "I didn't lie. She jumped to conclusions. I've tried to tell her twice, but before I could, she changed the subject. I didn't know how to work it back into the conversation. Besides. . ." He paused.

"You're afraid she won't want to get involved with a man who could have additional coronary issues."

Exactly. Michelle knew him too well. "Yeah, and she's just coming out of her shell of grief, fear, and worry. Well, grief and fear. Worry still plagues her. That's why I'm having a hard time bringing myself to tell her." While he was at it, he might as well confess the rest. "She knows I was in advertising, but she assumes I retired early, like some baby boomers do, and took care of Mom when she was sick."

"Rodney, relationships are hard enough. You have to be honest with her.

She needs to know job stress and lifestyle took a toll on you."

"I know." Rodney hung his head and rubbed the back of his neck. Withholding information like this was a trust breaker, and he knew Caroline was beginning to trust him. She confided her problem with her son and seemed very open to the impromptu almost-kiss.

"And another thing." Michelle pushed his shoulder to get him to look up, then crossed her arms in front of her chest. "What's this about the website? You'd better not be slipping back into your old work twenty-four/seven habits." Sparks of anger flared in Michelle's eyes. Had they been real, her glare would have set his house on fire.

"I'm not becoming a workaholic again, although I do enjoy that type of work. She tried to design her own website. It screamed amateur, so I punched it up. That's all. She is trying to start a new business. I just wanted to help." *Unlike her son.*

"Come and see it; then you can e-mail her about those quilts."

Michelle's stance relaxed. "Lead the way." She hovered over his shoulder, watching him download pictures Caroline had forwarded to be included on the website. One of them was the before picture of Rodney's quilt.

"Oh, I forgot to tell you that Aunt Jenny thinks she has a black-and-white picture with that quilt in it. She's looking for it. Then she said she'd tell me about it."

"Well, I received an e-mail from Aunt Katherine saying she was sure a cousin in California made it. I didn't even know we had relatives in California." Rodney craned his neck and looked up at his sister.

She shrugged. "Me either."

"Of course, no one has contact information for them."

"Figures. Well, at least you've gotten some responses. They may shed some light on the mystery. E-mail me the link for Caroline's website."

"Speaking of which, Caroline's friend Mark, who runs the quilt shop in Sioux Falls, tracked down the quilt block's name." Rodney hit SEND on the e-mail toolbar. "It's Lily of the Field."

Michelle burst out laughing. "Mom couldn't have known that. She'd have never kept the quilt."

"I know. She hated lilies."

≈

Caroline wrestled with giddiness, guilt, and all the emotions in between as she appliquéd another candy jar block.

It felt nice to be wanted. Scary, too. Yet did she know Rodney well enough to kiss him? She had nothing to compare that to. She didn't remember not knowing Ted. They'd attended school together. Turned into high school sweethearts. Their first kiss happened on their first date.

She and Rodney hadn't really dated, had they? So why would she have allowed the kiss?

What was she thinking? Then she remembered the intoxicating smell of his cologne that had beckoned her closer. The look in his eyes, which weakened her knees even now. His concern about her worries. Yet being alone with him just added to her list of worries. Jason didn't like the idea of her dating. Would he ever? She wanted their mother-and-son relationship back to normal, but even then would he accept her interest in men other than his father? She was definitely interested in Rodney. She longed to know him better.

She stopped the machine. Lost in her conflicting feelings, she hadn't paid attention to her work. Fortunately, the stitches and pattern remained straight, but why take chances? She decided to try another quilt that didn't demand precision.

The Lily of the Field lay on her worktable. She hadn't touched it since that first morning she'd snipped the threads that tied it together. Caroline sat in her sewing chair, seam ripper in hand, and began to cut the hem threads, being careful not to tear the fabric of the quilt top.

Mark's quote of the verse in the book of Matthew popped into her mind: *"See how the lilies of the field grow. They do not labor or spin."* Always aware of her inner worries, she hadn't realized they showed themselves outwardly. Rodney named two telltale signs. Were there more? Could everyone see them?

Caroline pinched pieces of the loose threads between her thumb and finger to remove them from the quilt and placed them in a pile on the table. She lightly brushed the block pattern that represented the flower. Lilies didn't have cars or homes that could need repair. Lilies didn't need health insurance. Lilies didn't need more than dirt, rain, and sunshine, all provided by God, to survive. Thrive even. Why couldn't it be that easy for Caroline? When she'd relied on God by trusting Him to provide a long, happy life with Ted, she'd come up short.

She bit the corner of her lip. Thanks to Rodney, she was now aware she was doing it. She plucked a few more loose threads away from the quilt and ran the seam ripper under more, cutting their hold to the fabric.

Lilies were lucky. *"And so are you, Caroline. 'I tell you, do not worry about your life, what you eat or drink; or about your body, what you will wear.'"* The words popped into her head like they'd been whispered in her ear. She shrugged it off. She'd studied that verse how many times over the years in Bible study? The name of the quilt just brought it to the forefront of her mind. *" 'Therefore do not worry about tomorrow, for tomorrow will worry about itself.' "*

Caroline exhaled and her burdensome thoughts rushed from her mind like the stale air from her body. This quilt wasn't perfect. It boasted crooked seams and misalignment of blocks, yet it was beautiful and, by the wear of the fabric, served its purpose. With her help, it'd continue to do so.

There was no question in her mind this was a good career choice. Somehow, some way, she'd prove that to Jason. Caroline ran her fingers over a quilt block and smiled. But that was a worry for another day.

Chapter 6

Rodney hadn't kept his promise to Michelle that he'd tell Caroline about his heart problems. He talked to Caroline one time after Sunday morning, and that was a short chat over the phone. Telling her about his health condition required a face-to-face conversation.

During the phone call, Caroline was all business, never mentioning anything personal, like the foiled kiss. He prayed that she hadn't been bubbling with worry over it. Instead he hoped she found herself lost in a pleasant daydream, the way he was when the thought of their closeness crossed his mind.

Sunday's snowfall kept his crew busy through Tuesday evening. He plowed customers' driveways while his two part-time employees used the snowblower or hand scooped to clear sidewalks and tight spaces. Since the demographic he targeted when he started his business was elderly people, most living alone, who could no longer do the work themselves, like his mom, he tried to prioritize them by need. Mr. Hanson's physical therapy appointments were every other Monday, so Rodney made sure he had a safe, clear path from his house to the curb where his daughter parked. Mildred liked to grocery shop on Thursdays, the first day of the specials. The list went on.

He didn't mind working his schedule around his clients' needs. Either way, the snow had to be removed. The weatherman forecasted the rest of the week warm and dry, so all Rodney would need to do was check for melting and apply salt or sand, whichever the client preferred, to the slick spots.

He spent his evenings tweaking Caroline's website if she provided pictures of her latest project. He also created a website for his own business. He wondered if other small business owners needed this service. Allison, his old intern, would know. The final thing he did last night before hitting the hay was kick off an e-mail to Allison. He could easily manage lawn care, snow removal, and web design.

Rodney dunked a tea bag in hot water and yawned for the fifth time since he got up. Fatigue plagued him today. He'd hit the snooze button three times before rolling out of bed, and skipped his usual treadmill routine.

Must be all of the hard work the last couple of days. Although pushing snow from driveways with the blade on the front of his pickup in the comfort of the warm cab couldn't really be considered hard work, it was still tiring.

He sipped his tea as he headed to his computer, anxious to see if Allison had responded. A reply waited in his in-box. His index finger tapped the mouse twice and he read, "What are you doing e-mailing at two thirty in the morning? Thought you put those days behind you?"

Rodney rubbed the back of his neck, the soft stubble reminding him that his scalp needed a buzz. He hadn't realized how late it had been when he'd sent the e-mail. No wonder he'd had trouble getting going this morning.

Determined not to fall into old habits, he decided that if he hurried, he could exercise, shower, and get his day back on track by ten after he read Allison's e-mail.

He scanned her suggestions and opinions on the topic, responded with his thanks, asked a few more questions, and then began an Internet search to look at competitors and pricing. It might not be a cost-effective endeavor.

The chime of the doorbell pulled his attention away from the screen. He glanced at the time on the corner of the monitor. Ten fifteen! Another chime echoed through the quiet house. He wasn't expecting anyone. Rodney looked down at his faded exercise clothes and shrugged. Maybe it was just the mailman with a letter or package too big for his mailbox. A few more rapid chimes sounded before he rose from the office chair.

He jogged through the short hall to the living room and tried to see through the beveled door window. He caught sight of what he thought was the back of a white parka descending the stairs. He turned the dead bolt and then opened the door. "Caroline?"

The breeze caught her curls and blew them across her face as she turned on the bottom stair. Her gloved hand pushed the hair behind her ears and revealed her smile.

"Come in." Rodney stood in the middle of the threshold, holding the storm door open with one arm and the main door open with the other.

Caroline stepped past him and waited for him to close the door. The pleasant aroma of her flowery perfume lingered in the crisp morning air.

"Aren't you feeling well?" she asked, her voice filled with concern.

"No, I'm fine, well, a little tired, but fine."

Worry settled into the lines on Caroline's face. She gave him a once-over. Had Michelle called and ratted him out? Was she here to confront him about his health?

"Really, I'm just tired, Caroline. Nothing's wrong with me."

Again her eyes glided over him from top to bottom. Why was she looking at him like that? Hadn't she ever seen a man in sweatpants and a T-shirt?

"Well, okay." Her face remained doubtful. "I'm sorry that I'm running late, but I do have good reason for that. If you're ready, I'll tell you my news on the way."

"On the way?" His mind, fogged with website research and lack of rest, wasn't registering what she was talking about.

"It is Thursday, isn't it?" Her lip tucked under but just for a second; then she pursed her lips tight as if to keep them in place. "Are you sure you're feeling okay?"

He hadn't looked in the mirror this morning. Maybe he looked worse than he felt. "Caroline, I'm fine. I just don't know what you're talking..." His memory bank woke up. His body slumped like a balloon slowly losing air. "We're going to the quilt shop today." He'd been so preoccupied with research on creating a website business, he'd forgotten. "I'm so sorry. It slipped my mind."

Caroline's purse strap slid off her shoulders when they sagged. She hooked her thumb under the strap and pulled it back into place. "It's okay. I'll run Mark's finished kit quilt to him," she said, her voice thick with disappointment.

"I am so sorry." He hoped she heard the sincerity in his voice.

A trace of apprehension ran across her eyes. "Rodney, we don't have to go together." She took a sudden interest in her boots. "You can go another day to look at the fabric dealer's catalogue of retro fabric, since Mark's having a hard time finding a flour sack that matches your quilt through Internet auctions."

Did she think he'd forgotten on purpose? That he didn't want to spend time with her because of the kiss incident?

"I can tell you were looking forward to this trip." Rodney stepped closer and lifted her chin until they were eye to eye. "Can your news wait until later when I take you to dinner tonight to make this up to you?"

"You don't—"

Rodney placed a finger on her lips. "Yes, I do. But I want you to know that I consider this a date." Caroline's blue eyes widened, but she didn't speak. "Not a business dinner, not two friends getting together because they're tired of eating alone, but two people who are interested in getting to know each other better. Are you free?"

When Caroline gave a gentle nod of her head, her soft lips barely brushed his winter-chapped finger, sending intense vibrations coursing through his entire body. He leaned toward her. With one fell swoop, their lips could meet. He lifted his eyes to hers. There it was again, that trace of apprehension. He straightened his stance. He wanted to kiss her. But did she want to be kissed by him?

Silent tension filled the area in the entryway. The corner of her mouth disappeared under her upper lip. Not a good sign. He put his hands on her arms just below her shoulders and squeezed. He looked directly into her eyes. *Trust me.*

"I'll be at your house at five forty-five. Since it's short notice, let's make it casual." He dropped his hands, then held one out. "Deal?"

For the first time since he'd met her, Caroline's face held no expression. She looked from his eyes to his hand and back again. She reached for the doorknob with her left hand. She viewed their relationship as business only. With first the almost-kiss and now the date suggestion, he'd messed up his chances with Caroline.

The click of the latch releasing cut through the unspoken tension in the entryway. Her gloved right hand clasped his extended hand. Her warmth penetrated through the leather and ignited the dying vibrations.

"Deal." She pulled her hand free, opened the door, and smiled over her shoulder. "The Queen of Quilts won't stand for being stood up again."

෴

Caroline emptied the clothing bags on her bed. What exactly *was* casual? Jeans or khakis, sweatshirt or sweater? That question gnawed at her the entire drive to Sioux Falls. She almost called Angela for her opinion, but her intuition told her "bad idea," so she relied on the much too young and lithe salesclerk in the *women's* clothing store. To Caroline's surprise, the young woman listened when she explained her shopping plights—legs too long for most women's inseams and, although she remained thin, gravity-created flaws that needed hiding. The clerk showed her several casual yet stylish outfits and to her credit avoided reds, pinks, burgundies, and form-fitting T-shirts.

In the end Caroline decided on a denim skirt with a back vent that hit just above her knees and a slate blue ribbed V-neck sweater. The last time she'd worn a dress was Jason's wedding day. Her inquiry about whether the store carried panty hose garnered a strange look from the clerk. Bare legs might be the fashion for her generation, but not Caroline's and definitely not in the middle of a South Dakota winter. Although they didn't carry hose, they did stock a vast array of tights, so to save time and a trip to another store, Caroline opted for a pair in navy. She had navy loafers, and with the thaw today, shoes versus boots shouldn't be a problem. Caroline passed on purchasing new accessories. The new outfit was a splurge, but she did have reason to celebrate. Besides, the income from teaching quilting at Granny Bea's would offset this expense to her monthly budget. The clerk assured her that a chain and earrings in gold or silver would be the perfect accessories.

Of course, the day when she was on a timeline, her first stop, Mark's store, had had a steady stream of customers, making it difficult to talk about the quilting classes. She needed to know Mark's expectations for the content of each class.

Caroline jotted down a few notes and promised to type up some loose lesson plans, then e-mail them to him. When she finally headed to her favorite women's shop, she'd hit every red light. Those things, combined with the length of time she spent trying on outfits at the clothing store, had put her behind schedule. The digital readout on her alarm clock warned that she had thirty minutes before Rodney would be there to pick her up.

After a three-minute shower to freshen up, Caroline began the task of getting ready for a date. A date at her age! She'd caught herself worrying on and off throughout the day. Would they have things to talk about other than her quilting business? Really, it was the only topic they ever discussed. Nerves caused her hands to shake as she smoothed the tights over her legs. Would there be room for food with all the butterflies in her stomach? And if there was, would the food stay put?

She decided to accessorize with earrings only, since cooperation ceased to exist between shaking hands and small necklace clasps. She eyed the clock. Fifteen minutes left to do her hair and makeup. The former was easy. She smoothed her curls into a twist and secured it with a tortoise shell–colored clip. She twirled the stray wisps around her curling iron for a few seconds and released them, letting them hang in ringlets. She tipped the ends of her bangs under the hot iron, then finger-fluffed them for a natural look.

Sheer will stopped her hands from shaking long enough to apply her makeup. She dropped her lipstick tube in her small denim clutch at the same time Rodney knocked on her back door.

"It's open," she shouted and ran to the bathroom for one last check in the mirror. She walked into the kitchen to find Rodney holding a mixed bouquet of cut flowers.

"Whoa." Rodney gave her a once-over. "You look very nice."

Without thinking twice, Caroline curtsied. "Thank you."

"These are for you." Rodney held out the flowers. "They were to show you how sorry I was about forgetting our appointment today, but now I'm thinking I'm glad I forgot. You look beautiful with your hair up."

Caroline absently patted her hair with her free hand while a blush warmed her cheeks. She smiled. "Thank you." She noted Rodney's attire, glad she'd chosen denim. His winter jacket covered his shirt, but he wore black jeans. "I'll get a vase."

She left the kitchen for a moment and came back holding a white vase edged with silver. "I hope you don't mind. This one was the easiest to get." She laid the bouquet on the counter while she held the vase under the faucet. "It was a gift from Jason on our twenty-fifth wedding anniversary." She pulled the flowers from the flimsy plastic cover and inserted them into the vase, turning the vase so the silver 2 and 5 faced her.

"Twenty-five years. That's quite an accomplishment."

Frowning, Caroline shrugged. "I thought so at the time. I guess it doesn't mean much now."

"Why would you say that? Of course it means something. You pledged your love and built a life and family with someone for twenty-five years. Not many people do that anymore." Rodney stared at the vase while he spoke. He lifted regret-filled eyes to Caroline. "I think you're very lucky. It's a milestone I'm sure I'll never experience."

"I just thought there'd be more." Caroline sighed and considered the regret in Rodney's features. "I guess I never looked at the other side of the coin until now." Her hand covered Rodney's. "Thank you for turning it over for me. Will you humor me for a minute? I'd like to show you something."

The curtain of regret lifted from Rodney's eyes when he smiled and nodded. Caroline laced her fingers through his and led him to the dining room. She opened a drawer in the oak buffet that matched her table and removed a silver eight-by-ten frame. "This is Ted and Jason." She pointed to the men as she said their names. "Of course, that's me in the middle. It was our last family picture, taken on our twenty-fifth wedding anniversary."

"What a nice-looking family. You should be proud. I believe your son resembles you."

Caroline laughed. "I've always thought so."

She moved a crystal bowl to the side and placed the frame in the center of the table. "For a long time, I saw the glass as half empty. What you just said made me see that it was, no, *is* half full." Caroline stared at her happy family for a few minutes before turning her attention back to Rodney. "Enough of my revelations. Let's get this date started."

For a last-minute date, Rodney did a good job. After dinner at Riverside's only family-owned restaurant, where they enjoyed the Thursday night all-you-can-eat spaghetti special, they walked to Daily Jolt.

The coffee shop sported an eclectic array of comfy chairs, board games, and a community puzzle. Caroline perched on a tall chair in front of the puzzle. She studied Rodney while he ordered their herbal tea. His flannel shirt in green-and-black plaid complemented the olive tones of his skin.

"This morning you said you had news to tell me." He set her tea on the table and pulled up another chair.

"Well. . ." A shiver of excitement ran through her. "I'd say the website is working. I've received two more e-mails regarding quilt jobs."

"That's great! Wait, they weren't Michelle's, were they?"

"No, but I did get her e-mail. I sent her the yardage amounts needed and directed her to examples of T-shirt quilt top styles I found on a website. The first e-mail was from an elderly lady who can no longer hand quilt due to back problems. The other inquiry was from a quilt boutique, and the owner, like Mark, purchases tops or quilts at auctions and is looking for someone to do all their quilting or restoration work before they make them available for sale in their boutique. They'd like me to provide a few references and want to negotiate on my fees."

Rodney rubbed the smooth skin on the back of his neck. "Getting references won't be a problem. I'm sure Mark and Mildred will agree to do it. I will, too, since I've seen your work. As for the fees, we researched a good sample of various-sized and experienced shops, and you're in the median. What are they proposing?"

"A flat rate since they'll supply steady business." Which, combined with the classes at Mark's store, would make it hard for Jason to argue her career choice.

"Is a flat rate fair for, say, a quilt like Mildred's or mine?"

Caroline had been so caught up in the idea of steady business she hadn't considered the level of work that might be involved. "Not really—the time involved in those types of projects is much different from quilting a top and back together on my long arm." Rodney had such a good head for business. Guess it was back to hoping for random website hits and word-of-mouth advertising. She felt her brows furrow and mouth draw down.

"Did they say how many quilts per month or year they'd send you?"

"No." Caroline sighed. "I'd best turn down their offer." Guess one of her problems with Jason wasn't solved after all.

"Don't be too hasty. They started the negotiations. You can make a counteroffer." Rodney rubbed his palms together like a brilliant scientist cooking up a scheme.

Caroline brightened and cocked her head to one side. "I'm listening."

"First, I think you should gather your references but also ask them for some. How do we know they aren't looking for someone because they're negligent on paying their bills?"

Again, why isn't he running a big company instead of a mom-and-pop business? Caroline nodded her understanding.

"Second, we need to know what 'steady' means to them. Third, we can provide a schedule of flat fees that seems fair to you per type of service." Rodney held up a finger with each numeric suggestion.

There was no way Caroline would remember all of this. She reached for her purse to pull out her trusty notepad and realized she'd downsized for their date, which seemed to be turning into a business meeting, something that wasn't supposed to happen according to the list of conditions set forth by Rodney this morning. How would they ever get to know each other better if all they talked about was business? It was his condition, so why had he let the date slip back into business?

"You could write our thoughts on a napkin."

"Or"—Caroline cleared her throat—"we could adhere to your earlier idea and not discuss business on our date. You will remember all your suggestions tomorrow, won't you?"

A wide smile broke across Rodney's face. "That's right. We're on a real date." Rodney's brown eyes grew wide, and his smile faded.

Did Rodney's solemn expression mean he wished they weren't on a real date? At first, Caroline thought he'd seemed pleased at the reminder. Had she misread his interest in her? After all, they'd almost kissed. Maybe he just liked the business part of their relationship. She sucked the bottom corner of her lip under, not caring if it was a telltale sign of her inner worry. She was worried. She liked Rodney. A lot.

"Caroline." Rodney took her hand and laced his fingers in hers. "I need to apologize."

For misleading me? Then why are you holding my hand? Caroline's first urge was to pull her hand from his, but his warmth made her feel. . . connected. Not just to him but the world.

"You deserve a better first date than all-you-can-eat spaghetti, sipping herbal tea, and sitting in front of a jigsaw puzzle."

Her concern was released with her laughter, but hurt replaced the sincerity on Rodney's face. She reached up with her free hand and touched the dimple in his chin with her fingers. "Rodney, I'm having a wonderful time. It's just perfect. Had you planned a big, splashy, get-all-dressed-up date, I'd have been very. . ." She paused.

"Worried?"

"No, well...maybe." Caroline laughed. "Nervous is what I was going to say. But this is comfortable. I prefer comfortable."

"Well, then..." Rodney scooted his chair closer to the table. "Let's liven this date up and see if we can add any pieces to the puzzle."

Caroline picked up a piece and tried it in several places close to her. When it didn't fit, she laid it back down.

"What did you think of the pastor's sermon on Sunday?" Rodney studied the puzzle pieces, chose one, and inserted it into an empty space. The corner of a building took shape.

"Well, um..." *I didn't really listen.* "Interesting." That was a safe word choice, wasn't it? Absently, Caroline lifted another piece and tried to push it into several gaps in the picture, with no luck.

"I like that he preaches on verses from the Old Testament." Rodney moved some shapes around, lifted one he liked, and placed it in the puzzle.

"Most people find the messages in the Old Testament less pertinent to our modern lives." What text had he preached about? Caroline racked her brain for an inkling of a memory of that sermon. She glanced at the pieces around the puzzle, then chose one whose color matched the area in front of her. But no matter how hard she pushed, the shape didn't fit into the selected area.

Rodney picked up another piece and placed it into the space Caroline had tried to fill.

"Then they aren't listening. After all, there were many blended or nontraditional families like Joseph and his stepbrothers who sold him into slavery. And King David, look what he did with Bathsheba. But they repented and trusted in the Lord and their lives turned out all right. Actually better than all right—blessed."

"How true." She could take a lesson from those Bible stories. If the Lord helped Joseph turn his slavery into a blessing with his dreams, could He help her get her life back on track, too?

She tried a puzzle piece in various openings to no avail. Rodney worked along one edge of the puzzle, expanding the picture toward the middle. Several more piece choices for Caroline fared the same results—no match. She shrugged. She sure couldn't put this puzzle together, but she was getting good at picking up the pieces.

Caroline marveled at the comparison of putting together the puzzle and her life. She'd started a business, agreed to teach classes, and gone on a date. Those three pieces were starting to form the picture of her future. *And yet...* Her pleasant thought was interrupted. Gaping holes remained in her life, like her relationship with Jason, her financial security, and her involvement with Rodney.

Caroline took a sip of her herbal tea. *"Therefore do not worry about tomorrow, for tomorrow will worry about itself."* She reflected on the Bible verse that had mingled with her thoughts since starting the restoration of Rodney's Lily of the Field quilt. Peace filled her soul. If she gave God the pieces of her life, could He restore it just as she was doing to Rodney's quilt?

Chapter 7

Caroline vowed to herself and God that she'd make a concentrated effort to pay attention in church this morning. Even with the distraction of Rodney sitting beside her, she'd managed to pull it off. The sermon left her refreshed and inspired. She skipped the singles breakfast so she could get ready for a customer appointment that afternoon.

Her original business plan didn't include hours on Sunday, but since it was the day Michelle visited Rodney, she agreed to an exception to save Michelle a trip.

She'd straightened her house yesterday and placed pictures of important moments in her life throughout the rooms. Joy replaced the dread as she remembered the moments in her life the pictures represented. Ted, handsome in their wedding portrait; Jason, a tiny newborn in Ted's arms; the snapshot a stranger took for them on their trip to the Black Hills. These pictures, back out in their proper spots, should ease Jason's concern that she was angry with Ted because he died.

She stuffed remnant pieces of fabric in a drawer to neaten her workshop before she sat down to work on Rodney's quilt.

"What's your story"—she ran her hands over the top of the quilt— "other than reminding me to stop worrying because God's in control?"

She'd separated the top from the back, thrown out the old cotton batting, and cut the worn hemline from the quilt back. The back fabric, now ready for reassembly, lay folded on the corner of her worktable.

The time had come to remove the damaged block from the quilt top. She could rip it all apart and straighten the blocks and seams, but that wasn't what restoration was all about. To her it was about preserving the quilt in most of its original form, and as it was, she had to alter it quite a bit. The thread was intact in most areas of the damaged block; the large, choppy hand stitches were easy to see and cut with the seam ripper.

She found a pattern for the Lily of the Field online, an exact match to this one in size. She'd feared that she'd have to use the old tattered blocks as the pattern for the replacement block. Not that it couldn't be done, but getting the seam measurement right could be tricky. By using the new pattern, she would have straight lines to cut around and sew.

Since the quilt was old, she didn't want to rip or stretch the fabric by pulling the loosened block free. Instead, with the last thread snipped, she plucked at the broken threads until they were free of the fabric; then she gently removed the block from the top.

Engrossed in her tedious process, she jumped when Jason hollered, "Mom, where are you?"

She went to the door by the stairway. "Down here."

Angela poked her head around the landing. "Is it safe to come down there, or will I see something I shouldn't?"

Caroline smiled. "It's safe. What would make you think there was anything down here for you?"

Angela patted her belly and giggled. "I don't know."

Caroline waited at the bottom of the steps as her daughter-in-law held the handrail and descended at a step-by-step pace.

"Sorry, not taking any chances." Angela rubbed her protruding belly.

Caroline wrapped her arm around Angela's shoulders and gave her a hug; then she guided Angela to a chair. "I wouldn't want it any other way. Do you mind if I finish up? I'm expecting a customer."

Angela eased into Caroline's sewing chair. "Not at all."

While Caroline pinned Rodney's quilt top to her project board, she caught the inconspicuous glances Angela made at quilts or fabric lying around the workshop. She'd be surprised to find out that the two baby quilts posted on the website were made with Caroline's new grandchild in mind. But the grandma-to-be had found a different pattern she liked and was now working on a new one, tucked safely away in a drawer.

"Mom!" Jason's shout, followed by thunderous thudding down the stairs, caused Caroline to straighten from her work. Now what was it? Feet firmly planted and her shoulders braced back for confrontation, she exchanged a look with Angela. Caroline really didn't need this just before a customer appointment.

Jason raced into the room, neck turning until he spotted his mother. "What's this?" He raised a family picture in front of her face. Jason held a picture taken by Angela on the day of his college graduation.

"It's a picture of our family, Jason." Caroline remained calm.

"I know that." He spat out the words. "Why is the picture back out?"

"Because, contrary to what you think, I'm not mad at your father." *Nor God any longer, for that matter.* Caroline frowned. That was an odd thought at a time like this.

"They're all over the house, like"—Jason paused and readjusted his ball cap—"like he was still alive."

"Well, he's not still alive, but you were right. He was a part of our lives, and we shouldn't forget it."

"You can still be mad at him dying with pictures out. Did you just put them back out to shut me up?"

"Jason, I am not mad at him," she said firmly. "This is not the reaction I thought you'd have." Caroline turned back to pinning the quilt top to the project board.

"Well. . .what did you expect me to do?"

Her hands shook, and she dropped a straight pin. She remained focused on the board and decided she'd already pushed in enough pins to hold the quilt top. "I thought you'd be happy."

Out of the corner of her eye, Caroline saw Angela stand and take the frame from Jason. "Are you okay?"

"Yeah, yeah." Jason shrugged, then turned to Caroline. "I am happy you put the pictures out. Sorry for my outburst."

Caroline caught a glimpse of the real Jason in his sincere expression.

"I guess it just took me by surprise."

I'm guessing it'll be the first of two surprises today. Rodney and Michelle, due to arrive any minute, will be the second. Would Jason be polite when meeting Rodney?

As if on cue, Caroline heard a knock on the door before it creaked open. "Anyone home?"

"Down here!" Caroline hollered, comfortable enough with their relationship to let Rodney find his own way down the stairs.

Caroline stepped in front of Jason and in a firm whisper said, "This is Rodney and his sister."

Jason bristled at the mention of Rodney's name.

Caroline continued. "Please be polite. Both of these people are my friends, not to mention customers."

Rodney entered the room first, carrying a large shopping bag in one hand and a plastic fabric store sack in the other.

"She's been to see Mark." He held up the plastic bag with Granny Bea's logo on it. "You should get a kickback for all the business you send his way."

"I think we're even on that." Caroline smiled at Rodney, then looked past him at Michelle.

"Hi, Caroline."

"It's nice to see you again, Michelle. Come in." She motioned with her hands. "I'd like you both to meet my son and daughter-in-law."

Rodney set the bags on Caroline's worktable and removed his gloves.

"Jason and Angela, this is Rodney Harris and Michelle Combs." Caroline made the appropriate hand gestures while stating their names.

"Nice to finally meet you both." Rodney held his hand out to Jason. "Your mom talks a lot about you."

Jason shook the hand Rodney offered. "She talks about you often, too.

Seems you're a jack-of-all-trades." His raised eyebrow spoke the sarcasm not reflected in his voice. Since his tone was civil, Caroline chose to ignore the innuendoes in his comment and gesture.

Rodney shook Angela's hand. "She's quite excited about becoming a grandma. You should see what she's been working—"

"Rodney!" Caroline stopped him before he spoiled the surprise.

"I wasn't going to tell; I was just trying to build suspense." Rodney flashed a sheepish smile at Caroline.

Michelle rolled her eyes. "Nice save, big brother."

"I've made coffee." Caroline pointed to the card table. "It's decaf if anyone would like some." She turned her attention to Michelle. "I'm anxious to see what you chose for fabric."

"Well, I have one very sports-minded son." Michelle pulled a stack of folded T-shirts out of the shopping bag and laid them on the table. "So I went with this." She pulled out black fabric with all types of sports equipment printed on it. "It pretty much covers all the sports on his T-shirts."

A quick flip through the shirts showed hockey, baseball, basketball, and football teams. "Good choice, not just for the symbols in the fabric, but the colors all coordinate, too. Did you decide on what style you want?"

"Yes, I want. . .what do you call the connecting rows on the front?"

"Sashing."

Michelle smiled. "I want this fabric as the sashing and the backing."

"Got it. What's the other quilt's fabric like?"

"This son collects T-shirts from our vacations." Michelle pulled out turquoise material with postcards, stamps, and postmarks featuring tourist attractions weaved into it.

"Perfect!"

The same broad smile that Rodney wore when pleased appeared on Michelle's face. "Instead of this fabric as the sashing, I bought white. I wasn't sure that the turquoise would look so good right next to some of the T-shirts."

Caroline removed that bundle of T-shirts and saw a vast array of colors—orange, navy, red, olive green, white, and black. "I think you're right. I'll bind the edge with white, too, and that will help deflect some of the non-contrasting colors."

"Whatever you think is best. I'd like the quilts to be their Easter gifts, or would that be rushing you?"

Caroline considered the other paying projects and the dates she'd committed to being finished. Then with Angela's fast-approaching due date, the baby quilt needed to be completed. It might be a tight deadline.

She started to pull her lip under.

Rodney glanced her way. "Don't worry about mine."

She unfurled her lip.

He stood by the project board, sipping coffee, and resumed looking at the gaping hole in his quilt top. "Mark's ordered the retro fabric but doesn't expect it in until the end of February." He traced the open area with his finger before looking back at the group.

"And"—Angela gave Rodney a conspiratorial wink—"since I'm due in April, your grandchild won't need a quilt for at least six months."

"Okay, then." Caroline flopped her arms in the air. "I know when I'm beaten."

Everyone laughed except Jason. Caroline cleared her throat. She put Michelle's items back in the bags. "Speaking of your quilt, did you find out any information yet?"

"Well, I found out that no one has contact information for the cousin who moved to California. Aunt Jenny found the picture and promises to get it in the mail. She says her eyes aren't as good as they used to be, but if she has a picture of it, I'm doubtful the cousin in California had anything to do with it, because they're on opposite sides of the family. So we should be able to compare the picture to the quilt sometime soon."

"I look forward to it."

Jason snorted. Caroline cleared her throat again and shot him her best not-now-young-man look. Michelle joined Rodney in looking at the quilt and slipped her arm around his waist. "And," Rodney continued, "how are the negotiations going? Did you get a flat-rate pricing sheet finished?" Rodney turned his head to look at Caroline. His affection for her sparkled in his eyes.

Caroline's heart fluttered, which brought an immediate heat to her cheeks since Jason stood just to her side. She didn't want her son to see something stronger than a friendship between her and Rodney until she had a chance to talk to Jason about it.

"Soooooo. . ." Jason pulled out the syllables, increasing the tension in the room. "You're dating my mother."

Too late. Jason had picked up on their shared look.

Michelle's arm dropped from around Rodney's waist.

"I am, I guess." Rodney walked over and stood eye to eye with Jason.

The desire to push in between the men flared in Caroline, yet her feet stayed firmly planted.

"You guess?" A sarcastic chuckle followed the question. "Either you are or you aren't."

Caroline opened her mouth to intercede, but Rodney held a hand up to stop her.

"It means"—Rodney enunciated each word—"that we've spent time together as friends but only had one date. Although I'm open to many more if it's agreeable with your mother."

Caroline's heart fluttered at Rodney's admission.

Both men turned to face Caroline. Had the anger in Jason's eyes been daggers, she'd have been pinned to the wall like the quilts to her project board.

Jason had been in a mood since he'd arrived today. Caroline wished she knew what was causing her son to act so uncharacteristically these last few months. Where was her easygoing, open-minded son? Did he feel left out or hurt because she didn't consult him before buying the long arm machine? That purchase seemed to be what had triggered all of his anger.

"Well?" Jason forced the word through his clenched teeth.

She looked from Rodney's eager expression to Jason's smug, expectant one.

"Caroline?" A flicker of disappointment crossed Rodney's face at her lack of response.

"Mom?" Jason's tone of voice and expression conveyed cockiness. Was her son making her choose between him and a new beginning? Did he want her to spend her life pining for his father?

She felt the deep crease form as her eyebrows furrowed, the flutters that had lifted her heart now replaced by the beginning of a dull ache. She cleared her throat in order to have complete control of her voice.

"I am agreeable."

Relief covered Rodney's features. The corners of his mouth twitched as he tried to hide a smile. Caroline watched Jason's expression turn more dour as he registered that his mother hadn't given in to his pressure and refused another date with Rodney. The dawning that she chose Rodney over him.

"What is wrong with you?" His teeth and jawline clenched.

Angela came to his side and reached for his hand. "Jason, we should go." Her voice was soft and soothing.

He pulled his hand free and held one finger up in front of Caroline. "I am not going to stand by and let you waste money on this." He pointed to the long arm machine. "Or this"—he pointed to Rodney—"nonsense just because you're mad at Dad for dying. You are acting ridiculous."

"Jason!" Angela pushed her burgeoning tummy between Caroline and Jason. "We. Should. Go. Now." Her commanding tone stopped Jason's tirade. He stalked toward the door.

Angela pulled Caroline to her in a quick hug and whispered, "I'm so sorry. He doesn't mean it." She gave Rodney and Michelle an apologetic smile, then followed Jason through the door and up the steps.

The slam of the door rattled the glass in the door window and echoed through the workroom.

❧

Jerk, jerk, jerk. Rodney berated himself. Why had he puffed out his chest like a rooster to Caroline's son? He never thought her features could display additional worry, but deep lines now etched her face in places the usual day-to-day worries never touched. Her eyelids drooped, and frown lines draped her mouth with its almost nonexistent lower lip. She looked simply mortified.

On the verge of tears, Caroline blinked several times to clear the moisture glowing in her eyes. "I'm so sorry." She placed a shaking hand to her mouth. "This is so unprofessional. And my son, I've never seen him act that way before. Sure, we've been having some problems, but. . ." She shook her head as if the image would disappear like a picture on an Etch-a-Sketch. "I can't apologize enough, and I completely understand if you'd want to take your business elsewhere."

Rodney's heart twisted and he reached for her, but Michelle beat him to it.

"I'm not taking my business anywhere else. Please stop apologizing."

"But Jason's actions—I just don't know—"

Michelle reached for Caroline's hands and held them in hers. "I'm a mother, too. I have sons."

Caroline bent her head to hide her face.

"Their timing is seldom perfect."

Caroline lifted her eyes to Michelle's compassion-filled face. Rodney watched a tear trickle down Caroline's cheek. His heart tightened in his chest, a feeling worse than the pain of his heart attack. He'd hurt Caroline. He'd made her choose. Even the knowledge of winning tugged at his heart, instead of lightening it. What kind of a man would come between a mother and her child?

He wanted to be the one to embrace and comfort Caroline until her pain subsided. After what he'd caused, surely she'd push him away. He couldn't bear that. Instead he stood and watched Michelle salve Caroline's wounds.

"Will you be all right while Rodney takes me back to my vehicle?"

Rodney woke up from his stupor. "You can take mine. I'll walk home later."

"I can't drive a stick shift." Michelle's aggravation was apparent in the glare she shot his way. That probably meant a lecture on the ride to his house.

85

Michelle picked up her purse. "Caroline, e-mail me when the quilts are ready, if I don't see you before then."

A weak smile appeared on Caroline's face, and she nodded to Michelle. He couldn't move, frozen like a yard ornament in the snow cover. She hadn't acknowledged him once since Jason left.

"Rodney," Michelle called from the top of the stairs.

"I'm coming right back." His words to Caroline seemed at full volume in the quiet of the workroom. He lowered his tone. "If that's okay?"

Caroline brushed the wet from her face with the back of her hand, and his feet thawed. He stepped toward her, grasping her tear-dampened hand. He raised it and pressed his lips onto the moisture, then held it against his cheek.

Soft fingers slid down his cheek, resting at his chin. Her thumb kneaded his cleft. "I'll be waiting."

&

Michelle stopped digging through her purse when Rodney slid behind the wheel of the pickup.

"I know you wanted to dress Jason down, but I don't think that would have helped the situation."

Here it comes. Rodney backed out of the driveway and drove toward his house. He braced for Michelle's harsh words, reminding him that had he interacted with his own family, he'd know how to act in these situations.

Instead Michelle reached over and squeezed Rodney's forearm. "Rodney?"

"That boy needs a lecture on how to treat his mother." Rodney spat out the words. "Caroline deserves his respect." *So did your mom.* Rodney's heart sank. He might not have yelled at his mother, but he'd mistreated her in other ways. Never visiting, not really being present when he did visit, and not caring about her day-to-day well-being.

"I know you care about Caroline, but you need to go easy on Jason. A lot has changed in that young man's life in a very short time."

Pursing his lips, Rodney nodded.

"Speaking of caring about Caroline, have you told her about your heart attack yet?"

Rodney pulled into his driveway and parked beside Michelle's vehicle. "No."

"This may not be the best timing, but you need to clear the air about that *today.*"

Although Michelle stressed the last word to emphasize the immediacy of the topic, there was a tenderness in her tone that touched Rodney deep in his soul.

She was right, and Rodney knew it. The protectiveness that surged through him earlier confirmed to him, and obviously to Michelle, too, that he'd passed the attraction stage and developed deeper feelings for Caroline. Judging by Caroline's decision, the feeling was mutual.

Michelle removed her keys from her purse. "Promise me that you'll tell her about your previous health issues?"

"I will." Rodney ached to get back to Caroline. He just hoped in fifteen short minutes, she hadn't changed her mind.

As soon as Michelle was safely in her vehicle, Rodney backed out of the driveway.

The short trip back to Caroline's house seemed endless as he imagined the worst. Doubts tormenting her. Sobbing for her son. Regretting the choice she just made. No, the choice he'd forced her to make. He practically ran into the house.

"Caroline."

"Down here." Her voice held a pleasant lilt.

Rodney found her sitting in her chair, holding the mangled block from his quilt.

She smoothed it across her knees, then looked up at Rodney. Her eyes clear of tears, her features serene, she smiled.

Rodney knelt beside Caroline. "I don't understand. I thought you'd be..." Rodney fumbled for a word. He wanted to choose wisely.

"Upset? Embarrassed? I am, but I've lived through worse, and as silly as this will sound, your Lily of the Field quilt brings me peace." She traced the pattern in the block with her fingers. "Several phrases from the verse in Matthew pop into my head when I work on it. A reminder to me that if God will take care of a lily in a field, I need to stop worrying, because He'll certainly take care of me. I'd sure like to know this quilt's story, why the maker chose this block."

"I'm working on it."

"I know you are."

"Do you want to talk about what happened?"

"No." Caroline rose and laid the block on the worktable. She walked over to the coffee carafe and held it up in question to Rodney. "Shall I pour you one, too?"

"Sure."

She added creamer to Rodney's before she gave him the cup of steaming liquid and motioned for him to sit in the chair. She slipped onto the table with her legs dangling over the side like a child on a bleacher. She sipped her coffee.

"I knew Jason didn't like the idea of me dating. He told me that about

87

a month ago." She laughed. "Before we'd even had a date. What bothers me is how angry he was that I set Ted's pictures back out. I believe now that he's in some stage of grieving. I'll call Angela tomorrow to discuss it."

"I'm sorry I put you on the spot and made you choose. I didn't like Jason's patronizing tone." He rubbed the back of his neck. "Caroline, I'd never want you to choose me over your son."

"I know. And I didn't really." She laughed again. "I mean I did, but I didn't."

She picked him, but not really? What did that mean? Confused, Rodney frowned.

"Tell her." Michelle's instructions echoed in his mind. "I need to tell you something."

"Okay, but I read the confused look on your face, so I want to explain. For a long time now, I've just been going through the motions at church. Not participating, not paying attention, threatening God that I'd stop going. . .but something, habit maybe, kept me attending worship, although I got very little out of it. Then on our date you asked what I thought of the sermon. Remember?"

"Yes. You said 'interesting.'"

"Because it was a safe word. I had no idea what the pastor had spoken about that Sunday. After that day, I made a vow to pay attention. So ask me what I thought of today's sermon." Caroline took a drink of her coffee.

Rodney leaned back in the chair, stretched out his legs, and crossed them at the ankle. He played along. "What did you think about the sermon today?"

"Life-changing."

"Seems to me it was the run-of-the-mill get-ready-for-the-Easter-season type of sermon. One I'm sure you've heard a hundred times before." Rodney drained his cup. "When you were paying attention." He winked.

"You're right." Caroline chuckled. "I've heard it a hundred times before, but I took it to heart today. The sermon was about new beginnings. I felt it was aimed at me. I started a new business. I've met a new person." She grinned when she pointed at him. "And since Ted died, I'll never have my old life back, so it's time to make a change there, too. I didn't choose you over Jason, Rodney. I chose you because it's time for a new beginning for me."

"That's why you're not angry or sad or worried over what happened here today?"

"Well, I am, but I've decided to not let it consume me." Caroline set her mug on the table beside her and rubbed her palms up and down the legs of her jeans. "I've let life's curves weigh me down too long. Now what did you want to tell me?"

Rodney had noticed the signs of worry showed less frequently. Full of himself, he thought he'd brought about her change in attitude. Her admission of the Lord's working in her life humbled him. The Lord had squelched his arrogance once before by sending him a wake-up call in the form of a mild heart attack, which he needed to tell Caroline about.

He searched Caroline's peaceful face. Her eyes full of trust. Her smile beaming, she radiated joy. It was the happiest he'd ever seen her. She raised her eyebrows in a gesture of encouragement.

Rodney knew he had to tell her about his health. But he couldn't do it. Not today.

Chapter 8

Caroline's caller ID flashed Rodney's number as the phone rang. She laid her devotional Bible on the coffee table.

"Hello?" Caroline smiled and hoped it reflected in her voice. She wanted Rodney to know she was happy to hear from him.

"Hi. Mark just called, and my fabric came in today. Since it's not snowing, I don't have to work, so I wondered if you could spare an afternoon and go to Sioux Falls with me."

Caroline mentally checked off which projects she had left to finish and their stages of completion. Taking an afternoon off wouldn't put her far behind.

"That should work fine for me. I have another quilt of Mark's to drop off and the agenda for the evening quilting class for him to review."

"I'll be right over."

"Give me fifteen minutes?"

"Okay, but not one minute more." Rodney chuckled as they said their good-byes.

True to his word, he knocked, then entered the side door in exactly fifteen minutes.

Caroline pushed in the final hairpin to hold her updo in place as she entered the kitchen. Since Rodney's compliment on their first date, she'd begun to experiment with different updo styles. Today she'd twisted her hair into a bun at the nape of her neck.

"You're getting better. You're making it as far as the kitchen now." She'd asked him several times to make himself at home and just walk into her house.

Rodney shrugged. "I don't want to interrupt anything."

"Like a customer's car not in the driveway wouldn't be a huge indication?" Caroline raised her brows to emphasize her point.

"Touché." Rodney bowed his defeat.

She thought the possibility of another confrontation with Jason fueled Rodney's apprehension about just walking into the house, even though the last one had been a month ago. She'd spoken with Angela often, but her conversations with Jason were still strained. However, they were still talking and she knew eventually they'd resolve their differences.

Rodney straightened. "You are the only woman I know who can look great on short notice." Merriment twinkled in Rodney's eyes, but the appreciation in the expression on his face deepened the warmth on her cheeks, making her glad she'd tried a different style with her hair.

Although they had a standing joke about his spontaneity in asking her out, Caroline welcomed his impromptu calls. They made life interesting. Since his standard of dress involved jeans and either a sweatshirt or flannel shirt (today it was the latter in red-and-black plaid), she started each day accessorizing her own jeans with a sweater or fleece top so she'd be ready for any spur-of-the-moment plans.

"Are you ready?" Rodney removed her white parka from the chair and held it up for her to slip into.

"I am." She zipped her coat over her green fleece pullover. It hadn't been snowing, but the early March temps hovered in the twenties.

Rodney picked up a shopping bag. "See, I know the drill. You never go to or leave Granny Bea's empty-handed." He stepped into the entryway.

Caroline grabbed her tote bag, double-checked that her wallet and class schedule were inside, and followed behind.

"My lady." Rodney held the door and bowed as Caroline stepped into the brisk air.

Once they were settled in the pickup cab, Caroline asked, "Did you receive that picture of your quilt yet?"

Rodney shook his head. "She decided to take the picture in and have a reprint made. That way we wouldn't have to send it back. Maybe it'll be in today's mail. Aunt Jenny thinks our great-grandmother made the quilt in the picture."

"So it would be an heirloom quilt."

"Yes." Rodney glanced her way for a few seconds. "The picture is black-and-white. The quilt is folded over a couch like a throw in the picture. That's why Aunt Jenny can't tell. Her eyesight isn't good enough to see detail in background objects, and her memory isn't good enough to recall the quilt's color."

"The idea of it being an heirloom quilt would explain the tattered block." Caroline pulled it out of her bag. She ran her fingertips over the grease marks as she looked across a barren soybean field to a fence line dotted with snow patches. "She'd have used a wringer washer for sure. I brought this along to make sure the fabric was a close match."

"And that, my dear, is why you are the Queen of Quilts."

Joy at hearing her nickname bubbled a giggle out of Caroline. "You know, I thought of that during the pastor's sermon last Sunday."

Rodney smiled. "When he referred to Proverbs 31? 'She selects wool and flax and works with eager hands.'"

"That was it."

"I thought of it, too."

That Bible verse referred to traits found in a noble wife. Occasionally Caroline had daydreamed about being Rodney's wife. A few months ago she'd have worried if that was proper. Now she took it for what it was—a fleeting hope. Caroline traced a triangular shape in the quilt block with her finger, drawing in the peace that came over her when she worked on Rodney's quilt. Was God talking to her through this covering? Crazy as it may seem, these lilies of the field were teaching her to stop toiling and spinning.

"May I share something with you?"

Rodney reached his hand over and wrapped his fingers around hers, his body language the only answer she needed.

"I talked to the pastor and asked if there was a place for me to start helping during service again."

Although Rodney didn't look at her, he smiled and his grip tightened. His Adam's apple bobbed several times before he spoke. "That is wonderful."

"It's thanks to you, you know." She wiggled her fingers until his entwined with hers. "You believed in my business, and. . ." She stopped. She'd shared the calming effect his quilt had over her. Would he understand this quilt was teaching her more than restoration techniques?

"And?"

She couldn't take the risk of Rodney not understanding the lessons this quilt, made many years ago, had been teaching her. It'd be her secret for a while longer. "And my abilities, and that gave me self-confidence," she added in haste. "Not to mention all the help you've given me on my website."

The change of subject was intentional. She'd been bursting to tell him her news anyway. "Without that I'd never have snagged the contract from that quilt boutique."

"So congratulations on negotiations are in order?" Rodney removed his hand as they entered Sioux Falls' city limits.

"Yes, thank you for your suggestions. We settled on a flat rate for standard long arm quilting fees. Three different flat rates for restoration projects, and they promised two quilts a month. They're sending me a one-year contract. I wasn't going to make any announcements until I had the contract in hand." Caroline shrugged. "But I just couldn't keep my happy news to myself any longer."

"I'm glad you couldn't, and congratulations." Rodney's face beamed with the same pleasure that she was sure hers wore.

"Thank you. They told me that they like to help start-up quilters because that's how they got their business started, by displaying and selling independent quilters' projects. You know, I'm not the only quilter they do business with. I guess their shop is popular and in a high-end tourist area."

"It is."

"How would you know that?" Caroline sighed and turned, as far as her seat belt would let her, toward Rodney. "Did you do an Internet search?"

With a quick glance her way, Rodney raised his brows up and down. "You have me figured out, Caroline Baker."

"How long have you known?"

"Um. . ."

"Since they first contacted me?"

"No, after you told me the name of the company."

Miffed, Caroline pursed her lips together. She knew he meant well, but. . .

As if reading her mind, he added, "I didn't contact them. All I did was check them out to make sure they were reputable. The rest was all you."

Her aggravation was fleeting. Not surprised by his confession, Caroline just shook her head. Business-mindedness was second nature to Rodney, so it made sense that he'd check things out. Besides, it was a good feeling to know someone looked out for her business's well-being. She was a entrepreneur and, quite frankly, naive to some things, like negotiating instead of agreeing to their first set of terms.

This contract and teaching Mark's classes provided a steady income with time to spare for taking on other quilting projects. A fact she hoped would please Jason.

Rodney guided the pickup into a parking space in front of Mark's store. He pushed the gearshift into PARK and turned to her. He raised his hand and caressed her cheek with his finger backs, then took her hand in his, only holding on to her fingers. He raised it and pressed his lips to the back of her hand. The quick gentle kiss surged her pulse.

"I am so proud of you." His eyes conveyed his belief in her abilities.

Caroline's heart filled with emotion. Glad a verbal response wasn't required, Caroline knew her words would have cracked if they'd have even come out. Rodney's actions supported a fondness deeper than friendship. She felt it, too, and thought a discussion of the topic would take place in the near future.

Not waiting for her to answer, he released her hand, then slipped from the pickup, rounded the front, and opened her door. She stepped from the cab and managed a thank-you. Their eyes met, and she knew fondness or admiration wasn't what either of them felt. It was love.

Happiness bubbled through her, making her feel light as air, yet weak knees made it difficult to walk into Mark's store. Granny Bea's door jingled their entrance.

Mark looked up. "Perfect timing. I was answering some questions about your evening class. Caroline Baker, this is Sarah Buckley."

Rodney wandered to the corner where Mark kept his display of sewing machines. Caroline hoped this distraction would steady her racing heart. Was Rodney's interest in sewing machines his attempt to regain control over his emotions as well? She walked over to the cutting counter where Mark and Sarah stood and held her hand out to Sarah. Troubles masked Sarah's lovely features. Caroline recognized the look. Not long ago, her own mirror reflected the same distress. Was it grief? A broken heart?

"Nice to meet you." Sarah's warm smile didn't chase the gloom from her face.

"Sarah's wondering what quilt block you'd be making at the evening class. She's partial to Job's Tears."

Sarah's surprise showed in her widened eyes.

Mark pointed to his temple. "A good shopkeeper knows what his customers like, and you keep picking up that pattern."

Job's Tears was a block Caroline had yet to make. Her class synopsis revolved around the Log Cabin block. They'd complete either a wall quilt or table runner with this popular block by the end of the sixth class.

Judging by the emotion she saw in Sarah's eyes, there was a reason that Job's Tears appealed to her. Based on Mark's comment, he must have sensed it, too. Flexibility was the mark of a good teacher. Certain that the Job's Tears pattern would make a wall hanging or table runner just as nice as the Log Cabin block, Caroline smiled and said, "What a coincidence. That's the block I like to use for the evening class. It's one of the things I'd came to talk to Mark about today."

Mark turned his full attention to Sarah. "Can I put your name down on the sign-up sheet?"

Caroline was quite sure she'd never seen Mark smile so sweetly at a customer before. She moved to the side while Sarah signed up for the class. After Mark conversed with her a few more minutes, his eyes followed Sarah as she left the store.

Turning his attention to Caroline, Mark pulled a bolt of fabric from under his cutting counter. "Here is the special-order fabric. And thank you. What block were you really going to use?"

"Log Cabin. I'll have to buy a Job's Tears pattern from you and make a few practice blocks." Caroline pulled the damaged quilt block from her tote bag and laid it on the bolt.

Mark walked over to a shelf and came back with a packaged block pattern. "This is the one she looks at. It's on the house. Use the practice blocks to make a wall quilt and I'll buy it from you for display."

"You don't have to do that."

"But I will." Mark's attention went to the plate glass window. Caroline followed his gaze. Sarah was easing her car from a parking space.

Young people didn't corner the market on love like society convinced people. She looked from Mark to Rodney. It seemed middle-aged men's fancy turned to love come springtime, too. Well, almost springtime.

"That fabric doesn't match Rodney's block at all." Mark's voice jarred her from her thoughts. His attention back on the matter at hand, he folded the block in half so the yellow fabric lay flush on the bolt of retro material.

Rodney joined them. "The flower pattern's the same."

"But the color's off." Mark pointed between the two fabrics. "Even though the material used in your quilt block is faded, it was always a pastel yellow, not vibrant like this one. It sure didn't look this golden in the book."

"It's close enough, isn't it?" Rodney looked to Caroline.

Before she could answer, Mark interceded. "I think we can do better. I know the name of the pattern now, so I'll do another search for a softer yellow."

Caroline smiled. She knew Mark wouldn't stop until he was satisfied that he'd done all he could for a customer.

"Can you return this? If not, I'd like to pay you for it. I'd hate for you to have invested in a bolt of fabric that we didn't use."

Mark and Caroline laughed at the same time. Rodney looked from one to the other.

"What's so funny?" Rodney rubbed the back of his neck.

"He runs a fabric store," Caroline said.

Sheepishness crept into Rodney's features as what he'd said registered.

"I invest in bolts of fabric all the time. Someone will buy this." Mark smiled. "Don't feel bad. You're just out of your element. I don't know anything about lawn care. I just mow the grass."

"Would you keep a yard of this fabric back, just in case we can't find anything closer?" Caroline rubbed the new fabric between her fingers, feeling the soft texture of the weave.

Mark turned over the bolt. Two times it clunked against the countertop as he flipped it to unwind the fabric from the bolt. He measured the length against the built-in yardstick on the table. Razor-sharp scissors separated thirty-six inches of fabric from the bolt. "Your wish is my command."

"My lady," Rodney added.

Caroline shook her head and giggled. She placed the shopping bag with the finished quilt in it on the counter. "Our business here is done. Now that there's been a change of plans, I can't give you the class synopsis today, so"—Caroline looked to Rodney—"how about that movie you promised?"

๛

Slush covered Rodney's boots as he stepped from his pickup onto the street. The sun peeked out through the parting clouds. Clearing driveways and sidewalks was the last thing he wanted to do today. He'd worked into the wee hours of the morning on a website design for an author. His website was as effective as Caroline's in drawing business and hits. Allison gave him the heads-up on how to use keywords that would pull up in Internet search engines.

When he discovered today's blood pressure pill was his last, he decided to stop by the pharmacy before starting his workday. The late March snow, though wet and heavy, wasn't deep, and the mild temperatures had turned it into an icy mess.

Rodney wiped his feet on the mat in front of the store door and made his way toward the back of the building. The pharmacist glanced up from the elderly gentleman explaining his ailment and smiled a greeting at Rodney. The pharmacist stepped over to his filled prescriptions and leafed through the narrow sacks, answering all the man's questions as he multitasked. Rodney mouthed, *thank you,* as he took the bag of pills the pharmacist offered and turned right into Jason.

Jason's eyes narrowed and he let out a grunt. "You should watch where you're going."

"Excuse me." Rodney kept his voice polite even though he suspected Jason had stood directly behind him on purpose.

"I thought you spent all your time preying on old widows."

Rodney clenched his jaw and straightened his back. "That comment was uncalled for. I believe you owe me and your mother an apology."

"Why, it's true." Jason reached around Rodney for the bag the pharmacist held out while still answering the other customer's question. "Last I knew you spent most of your time with her. Dating." He added air quotes as he said the last word.

Jason's smug smile and sarcastic tone flared Rodney's temper. He didn't mind what Jason thought of him, but Caroline deserved better. She was his mother, after all. Yet Rodney sensed Jason was deliberately trying to goad him.

One of the first lessons Rodney learned in the ad game was not to show your anger. He'd dealt with several critical clients from time to time. He drew on that experience now.

"I guess it's partly true. I don't spend all my time with Caroline, but we are dating. Maybe all four of us could get together for dinner sometime." Rodney knew how to turn the tables of anger to his opponent.

It worked. Jason gave a little snort.

"Fat chance of that happening. You are not company I want to keep. I had a father, and I know how to change my mother's mind." Jason stopped himself before he stabbed Rodney in the shoulder with his finger.

"Look, I don't want to be your father, but I do enjoy your mother's company," Rodney whispered through clenched teeth, hoping not to draw attention to them.

"I'm sure you do. What's your angle? Lawn care, snow removal, working at an ad agency, designing websites—none of that adds up. I think you're a conman who preys on widows. She doesn't have any money, if that's what you're after."

Rodney had been nothing but honorable where Caroline was concerned. Barring the one time they almost kissed, the most he'd done was kiss her hand. Jason's goading was getting to him, along with indigestion from his breakfast. He rubbed his chest and swallowed hard. Had they not been in a public place, he'd have dressed this young man down. Instead he chose his words carefully. "I'm not going to stop dating your mom because you're threatening me and acting like a spoiled brat."

Anger snapped in Jason's eyes. He straightened to his full height, which Rodney realized gave him two more inches on Rodney. "I'm sure Mom will appreciate that you called her only child a brat. Doesn't say much for her parenting skills, does it?"

Caroline. The thought tamped down Rodney's anger. He hadn't considered her feelings on that point. She'd be disappointed in both of them, and the last thing he wanted to do was come between a mother and son. "I'm sorry. I shouldn't have said that. I really do want to get along with you." Rodney relaxed his stance in a concentrated effort to back up his words and offered his hand to Jason.

"Yeah, well, leave Mom alone and I'm sure we could be best friends." Jason remained erect. One hand held the prescription, the other now tucked in his pants pocket. Rodney could almost see the chip on his shoulder, waiting to be knocked off.

"Rodney." Surprise filled Angela's voice. She came from behind Jason. "How are you?" She wrapped her arm around Jason's left arm and pushed her weight into him until he took a step back, opening the space between them.

Rodney tipped his head to greet her. "Fine, thank you, and how are you feeling?"

"Great." She ran her hand over her protruding stomach. "Not long now, but I ran out of my prenatal vitamins." She glanced toward the pharmacist, but Jason rattled the sack he held to draw her attention.

"Looks like we're all set, then. It was nice to see you, Rodney." She pulled on Jason's arm until he turned around, slipped his hand in hers, and headed to the checkout counter.

"What's wrong with that boy?" Mildred.

She came around the corner of an aisle where a tall display of reading glasses stood on the end. She must have been there the entire time. Close enough to hear everything.

Damage control. He'd managed it thousands of times in his previous career. "Good morning, Mildred." He purposely inflected a happy lilt in his greeting.

"Good morning, and I'm not giving up that easy. I introduced you and Caroline. I have a right to know what's going on."

Not really. Though he wanted to, he couldn't say that out loud since Mildred was a client of his and Caroline's. He blew out a long breath, not sure himself what was really going on. He'd never experienced someone disliking him personally, without really knowing him. He gave the safest honest answer he could. "He's not happy that Caroline and I are dating."

Mildred clapped her hands together. "You're dating! That's wonderful. I suspected as much, since you always sit beside each other in church, but neither of you said it was official."

Rodney smiled at her enthusiastic response. It felt nice to have someone rooting for him—no, them. It felt great to say out loud, "*Caroline and I are dating.*" As in a couple or—what was the term his nephews used? *An item.* "I wish Jason shared your opinion."

Mildred waved her hand in dismissal. "He's a good kid. He'll come around. You know how it is with family dynamics."

He nodded his head, but in truth, he didn't know. Living on his own since he was seventeen, he'd missed that.

"These things all work out in the end. He'll come around; you'll see." Mildred slipped her hand through his arm. "Why don't we go pay for our medicine and get a cup of coffee? You can tell me all about your new relationship."

❧

Somehow, during his long workday, Rodney missed a call from Caroline. He listened to the message. She'd finally finished the candy jar quilt and was going to run to Sioux Falls to deliver it to the store owner. She wouldn't be back until late. He'd hoped to have dinner with Caroline. If he'd checked his messages earlier, he'd have treated his crew to burgers and fries. Now his dinner would consist of leftovers and eating alone.

Rodney scanned the contents of his freezer. His earlier heartburn lingering, he avoided the spicy chili. He took out the turkey meat loaf that Michelle had left on her last visit, warmed it up in the microwave, then ate it while standing by the kitchen counter. Afterward, he flopped down in his office chair, then rubbed his chest. The indigestion just stayed with him today. Nothing he took helped. He continued rubbing his chest while wiggling the mouse to clear the screen saver. Good thing he'd skipped his workout this morning, or he might be too tired to work on the author's website.

He opened his e-mail, hoping the author had responded with his first round of editing suggestions. A knock and the rattle of the doorknob interrupted his activity. Caroline. Since she'd insisted he enter her home unannounced, he made her promise to do the same, except he'd locked up for the night after listening to her message. She must have stopped on her way home. Thank goodness he'd installed a timer on his porch lights, providing her with some sort of welcome.

A visit from Caroline—his day just improved. He'd thought about the look they shared a few days ago, his unspoken admission of love. He was sure she felt the same strong pull on her heart. Since he'd spilled the beans to Mildred that he and Caroline were dating, he'd decided to voice his unspoken feelings to Caroline.

Rodney hurried to the front door. A pang of indigestion caused him to wince on his way. He clicked the dead bolt with his left hand and turned the doorknob with his right.

Bone-chilling air and Caroline blasted through the door. "Do I owe you another apology on behalf of my son?"

"No." Rodney rubbed his palm across his breastbone.

"Why didn't you call me?" Had she even heard his response? She stopped in front of him. "Didn't Jason make a scene in the pharmacy today?"

"Yes, but you don't need to apologize. He does." He cleared his throat in an attempt to clear the pain from his chest. He needed to sit down.

"I would have rather heard this from you. Instead I found out from—"

"Mildred." They spoke her name at the same time.

"Caroline, would you like to come in and take off your coat?" Rodney closed the door when she paced a few steps away. This wasn't going to be the night to declare his love.

"I thought this would blow over. Really, Rodney, he's a good man." She slipped out of her parka and hung the hood over the knob of a closet door.

She smoothed her black sweater over her jeans.

"Maybe he's scared of his new responsibility of being a father?" Rodney offered as he led the way to the living room. He sat on the arm of a chair. This might not be heartburn. He flexed the fingers of his left arm. Nothing felt numb.

Caroline continued to pace when they got to the living room. Front view. . .back view. "Could be; I just don't know." Front view. "Angela says he clams up whenever she approaches the subject." Back view. "Really, Rodney, he was raised better."

He didn't doubt that, but the intense pain in his chest made it hard for him to focus, let alone answer. He felt sweat bead on his forehead and upper lip. He slipped from the arm of the chair to the cushion. Had his arm gone numb? He squeezed his eyes shut and doubled over, pulling his knees to his chest, the pain now constant. He tried to hold in a moan but failed.

His eyes fluttered open when Caroline screamed his name. He saw her heading to the phone caddy; then she knelt in front of him.

"What's wrong?" Fear iced over the sparkle of her blue eyes. Michelle was right. He should have told her; then she'd have known and called an ambulance by now.

Caroline reached out to touch him as another red-hot pain shot through his chest. His low groan increased to a loud moan that echoed in the now quiet room. She pulled her hand back and a tear trickled down her cheek. It was too late to break this to her gently.

God, please let her forgive me for this. "Caroline," he rasped. "Call 911. I think I'm having another heart attack."

Chapter 9

Rodney woke up to Michelle's concern-mixed-with-anger face hovering over him. Her hand held his.

"I thought you were waking up."

Groggy, Rodney looked around the room. "I'm in the hospital?"

"Right. Do you remember what happened?"

He moved his hand to his chest, pulling IV tubes with it. "Heart attack?"

"Not this time. Gallbladder."

Bits and pieces came back to Rodney. Never-ending indigestion, collapsing in the chair, then EMTs lifting him to a gurney, their barrage of questions directed to his wife. No, not wife. Caroline.

Caroline. Now the memory was clear. She'd stood beside the chair, the corner of her lip sucked in, her brow furrowed as she tried to answer the EMT's questions concerning his health. Running to the bathroom cabinet when they asked what medicines he took. "Where's Caroline?"

"In the waiting room."

"Can't she come in?"

"No, you're still in recovery."

"But you're here."

"I'm allowed because I work in this hospital."

Even groggy from the anesthesia, he heard the sisterly "duh" in her voice.

"I had surgery?"

"Yes." The concern melted from Michelle's features, but anger remained. He could tell by how the lines formed around her mouth. "They removed your gallbladder."

"Are you mad at me because I had to have surgery?" His eyelids were so heavy. He'd just shut them for a minute.

The bustle around Rodney aroused him from his medicine-induced slumber. Michelle stood beside his bed while another nurse started the process of taking his vitals. His mouth was dry, his throat parched. He licked his lips and swallowed. No relief. The nurse stuck a thermometer under his tongue, making it worse.

When the nurse recorded the information and left the room, Michelle asked, "Do you need an ice chip?" She scooped ice fragments out of a Styrofoam cup with a plastic spoon. She held them to Rodney's lips. The moisture that trickled down his throat felt like heaven. Michelle offered another spoonful.

"Thank you. You're a good nurse." Rodney held his hand out to his sister. She gave it a squeeze.

"It's about time you realized someone else in the family was good at their job," she said, her words tinged with anger.

"Why are you mad at me?" Rodney instinctively reached for his chest. It wasn't as sore as last time. "I didn't mean to have a heart attack." Michelle grinned.

"Now I'm funny?"

"No, lots of people have memory lapses when coming out from under anesthesia." She ran her soft hand over the smooth skin of his head just like his mom used to do when he was sick as a child. "You didn't have a heart attack. Your gallbladder burst, so they took it out." Her voice no longer held the angry edge.

"Oh." Rodney closed his eyes. Caroline's worried features appeared. His eyes popped open. "Is Caroline okay?"

"Yes and no. She's pretty shaken up. Why didn't you tell her about your heart attack like I told you to?"

"I don't know." He squeezed his eyes shut tight in concentration. "No." He shook his head. "I do know." He opened his eyes. "She'd stopped worrying. I don't know why or how, but one day her features relaxed and she stopped fretting over every little thing. She seemed happy. She'd been sad so long, I didn't want to spoil it for her. She's so pretty when she's happy." Rodney's voice cracked. It had nothing to do with his dry throat.

Michelle's laugh filled the room. She patted his cheek. "Rodney, even sleepy from surgery, your love for Caroline is written all over your face." She held another spoonful of ice to his lips.

"Is she here? Can I see her?" Rodney pulled the ice from the spoon with his lips, losing the last one. It tinkled against the tile floor.

Michelle grabbed a towel from the sink area in his room, then wiped the wet spot on the floor. "She's here. I'll ask her to come in. I can't guarantee anything. She followed the ambulance and waited until someone came to cover my shift. She wanted to leave, but I insisted she stay, using the excuse I didn't want to be alone. But really it's because I knew you'd ask for her. I'll go see if she'll come in." Michelle turned when she got to the room door. "Rodney, you should know the worried look is back."

Rodney watched sunbeams filter through the window. How far was the waiting room? Rodney fought his heavy eyelids. It seemed like forever since Michelle left. It wouldn't hurt to rest his eyes while he waited for Caroline.

When his eyes fluttered open, the sun's rays had shifted to dusky shadows in his room. He'd fallen asleep while waiting for Caroline.

He heard breathing. Was she here? He strained his neck to see over his shoulder. The bed rail blocked his view. He thought she was in the chair at the head of his bed. He pushed the button on the bed and adjusted it to a more upright position. The noise roused Caroline from her chair.

"Are you okay? Can I get you anything?" She gripped the bed rail with both hands, knuckles turning white from the pressure.

"I'm okay." He reached his hand out to her.

Her hands remained fixed to the rail. Her eyes focused on the IV bag. "I'm glad," she said, then chewed at the corner of her lip.

He moved his outstretched hand to rest beside hers. His fingers overlapped her knuckles. "Please look at me."

A veil once again covered her blue eyes, the worry lines prominent in her forehead in addition to the deep furrow between her brows. He'd hoped to lighten her burdens but had added to them instead. He wanted to pull her to him and hold her tight until all her doubts and fears subsided.

"I'm sorry I didn't tell you about my health when you jumped to the conclusion—"

Caroline cut him off. "You led me to believe. . ." Her voice trailed off. She sniffed and pulled her hands free. She brushed at her eyes with her fingertips. "It doesn't matter." She waved her hands in the air.

"It does matter." Rodney tried to sit upright, but sore incisions forced him to lean back into the pillows, meek instead of strong. "I was a workaholic who thrived on the stress my job created. Or so I thought. My body had other ideas. The heart attack was my wake-up call. I had to change my entire way of life."

Her stance stiffened.

"I know honesty is the most important thing in a relationship, but I don't have much experience in that area either. Just ask Michelle. Not only does a workaholic's health suffer, but his family life does, too. I want you to know I was honest about everything else, and I won't ever withhold anything again."

Caroline closed her eyes and pursed her lips, shaking her head the entire time. She drew a ragged breath before she opened her eyes and for the first time looked directly into his. Sadness and fear mixed with hurt greeted Rodney's gaze and pulled at his heart.

"I put my relationship with my son in jeopardy for you and your lofty ideas about my business. The least you could have done was told me you'd had heart problems. You know how I felt about Ted and the lack of care he gave his body."

He wished he wasn't tied to tubes. He wanted to drop to his knees, tell her he loved her, and beg her forgiveness. "Caroline." His voice pleaded for him. "I've been taking better care of myself. My cardiac doctors are pleased. This health issue"—he waved his hands to circumference the room—"had nothing to do with that."

Resignation flickered in her eyes. "I can't do this again. I can't care for someone and then lose him."

"But what happened wasn't life-threatening." Despite the pain he leaned forward and reached toward her.

She stepped closer to the foot of the bed, out of arm's reach. "It could have been. I thought it was, and so did you." Her rapid blinking indicated she was on the verge of tears.

A lump formed in Rodney's throat, and his chest ached. None of it a side effect from surgery.

"Rodney, I think it's best we don't see each other again. I know I owe you something for working on my website, and I'll finish your quilt. . . ."

"Caroline, don't say that. Let's not talk about this now. Go home and get some rest and give it some time." If only he could get out of this bed. Frustrated, he punched the mattress. The IV tube slapped against the bed frame.

Michelle came into the room. "What's going on in here? I can hear you down the hall. Both of you calm down, especially you." She ran to Rodney's side. "Ease back." She guided his body back into the pillows.

"I knew I shouldn't have stayed." Caroline looked at Michelle, then back at Rodney. "I knew I'd upset you when you need to get rest. But I can't"—she backed away from the bed, her hands shielding her eyes—"I can't do this. I've got to get out of here." She ran to the door. "Good-bye, Rodney," she called over her shoulder.

&

Michelle played her registered nurse card and insisted Rodney recuperate at her house. At first he argued; he had a business to run. She rebutted that even if it did snow, his crew could handle all the snow removal. He needed to rest and get his strength back. Michelle promised that Caleb, home from college for spring break, could lend a hand to Rodney's crew if the need arose.

Rodney sensed Michelle knew the real reason he wanted to go home—to be near Caroline. He'd hoped she'd forgiven him. He'd hoped her feelings hadn't changed. He'd hoped that maybe she wanted to nurse him back to health. However, she hadn't visited or called since she'd run out of his hospital room. He tried calling her, but all he ever reached was the answering machine. In the end, he relented and went to Michelle's home.

Caleb provided a distraction during the day while everyone else was at work or school. The first day was awkward. Rodney didn't have much in common with either of his nephews, nor did he really know them. After topical small talk, he and Caleb struggled for conversation. Caleb suggested they watch movies and they discovered that they both preferred comedies.

By evening, the household bustled. Everyone seemed to talk at once. No quiet dinners on the arm of the sofa, watching the weather. Rodney sat at the kitchen table and watched everyone buzz around Michelle while she prepared their dinner. How did she keep track of what she was doing while participating in three separate conversations that took side turns at any given moment? He felt like an outsider peering through a window like he always did when he was around his family.

Then a memory came to mind. His apron-clad mother stood at the Formica kitchen table, rolling piecrust. Michelle flanked one side of her, rolling a small circle of dough. He hovered on the other side, waiting for the small rolling pin Michelle used, both of them chattering about their day at school as they were making their after-school snack. His, a strawberry jam–filled tart; Michelle's a cinnamon-sugar crisp. A standard activity in their household up until the time his dad took a different job in a different town. At seventeen, Rodney stayed behind to graduate with his class. He missed his family members so much when they moved. He missed being a part of a family and filled that void with work. He saw it now, not before.

"Hey, where are you?" Michelle waved a hand in front of Rodney's face. "And why aren't you over here helping out?"

"Don't you have enough help?" Rodney stood and wiped his palms across his jeans.

"Never."

"What she means is, she needs another person to boss." Caleb looked up from scrubbing potatoes.

Rodney smiled. "I got a lot of that growing up." He joined Caleb by the sink.

Michelle snapped a towel, missing both of them by inches. "Get to work. Rodney, core those apples," she commanded in a low voice, then giggled.

"So where were you a minute ago?" Michelle arranged pieces of chicken in a baking pan.

"Making after-school snacks out of piecrust." Rodney smiled. He'd eaten fancy strawberry tarts made by world-famous chefs in his lifetime, but none of them tasted as good as those childhood pastries.

Michelle's eyes lit up. "I haven't thought about that in years. It was so much fun." She arranged the chicken, scalloped potatoes, and baked apple pans in the oven and closed the door. "We could do that for dessert tomorrow night if you'd like."

"I would." Rodney walked over to Michelle and wrapped her in a hug. "I'm sorry I put my career before family. I missed out on so much. I've been a terrible brother and uncle. Not to mention son, especially to Mom after Dad died. There were so many things she needed help with, and after all the things she did for me, us, well, I let her down."

Michelle cupped her hands around Rodney's face. "A terrible son? Let her down? You were there when it counted. Despite your own health issues, you made her last wish come true, to stay in her home until the end." She hugged him tight. "We all loved you very much, even in your absence."

"Hey," Caleb shouted so his dad and brother who'd moved to another room could hear, "Mom and Uncle Rodney are getting mushy. Someone save me."

Rodney held Michelle at arm's length. "Thank you for everything." He raised an eyebrow and made a slight nod of his head. She nodded back. They ran and embraced Caleb in a big bear hug. "Too late, buddy. I've got quite a bit of lost time to make up."

"Sentimental old people." Caleb didn't return their embrace, but Rodney noted he didn't try to break it either.

"Speaking of which," Michelle said, breaking her hold, "I swung by your house and picked up your mail. The letter from Aunt Jenny came."

Rodney patted his nephew on the shoulder and went back to the table to sit down while Michelle dug through her tote bag. She pulled a rubber-banded stack from her bag and brought his mail to him.

"So, looking through my mail, are you? What else did I get?" Rodney raised his brows.

"Bills, magazines, junk." Michelle stood over his shoulder, waiting for him to open the envelope Aunt Jenny finally got into the mail.

He tore a flap corner and ran his finger under it. The seal popped open without much effort. The picture was tucked inside a tri-folded letter written on notebook paper. Rodney drew his reading glasses from his shirt pocket and slipped them on. The image showed two children posed on their knees in front of a couch that a quilt was draped over.

Rodney brought the picture closer, hoping the detail would be clearer. "I don't know. The flower pattern in the fabric is close, but the blocks aren't right." He held the picture up for his sister to take a closer look.

After Michelle studied it, she handed it to Caleb, whose outstretched hand waited for it.

"What are we looking at?" he asked.

"The quilt," Michelle said. "It's definitely not the same block. It looks nothing like Mom's quilt."

"We've hit a dead end, then. I can't locate any relatives in California, either. I guess we'll never know." Rodney sighed, removed his glasses, then scrubbed his face with his hands. What was the story with this quilt? It didn't just magically appear in his mom's trunk. "Caroline would probably be interested in looking at the quilt in the picture."

"Never know what, and who's Caroline?" Caleb laid the picture on the table.

"When Uncle Rodney was rooting around Grandma's trunk, he found a quilt that he's having restored. We thought it might be a family heirloom. Caroline is the lady who restores quilts." Michelle sat down on a chair and rested her chin in her hand.

Rodney copied Michelle's stance and stared at the picture as if that would turn the quilt on the couch into the one at Caroline's house.

"Is the quilt yellow with white flowers and torn?"

Rodney and Michelle turned their heads in sync to look at each other. The astonishment he felt seemed mirrored in Michelle's features. They both turned toward Caleb.

Caleb's eyes grew wide. "What?" he asked as if he were in trouble.

"Do you know where Grandma got that quilt?" Rodney asked.

"Yeah, I was with her." Caleb narrowed his eyes and shot them both an "are you crazy?" look.

Michelle reached out and touched his wrist. "Where'd she get it, Caleb?"

"We found it. We'd been walking in that preserve area close to her house. Your house." He corrected himself and looked at Rodney. "A thunderstorm came up. The wind came first. We ran toward a shelter and got there just as big huge raindrops started falling. I thought once we reached the shelter we'd be safe from the storm, but then lightning flashed. Grandma was sure it'd strike the shelter. By that time it started pouring. We knew we'd be soaked by the time we got back to her car. Then she spotted the quilt lying on the floor of the shelter. We held it over our heads as we ran for her car."

Caleb laughed. "After we got into the car, it rained so hard we couldn't see. But that's not what's weird. While walking the trail a few days later, Grandma found out that lightning had struck a huge tree and it fell on the shelter. Smashed it flat. Grandma insisted God sent that quilt to save our lives." Caleb shrugged in a no-big-deal fashion. "Must be why she kept it."

Rodney's chuckles grew into a laugh. "I guess we asked the wrong people."

"So, Uncle Rodney, are you interested in that quilt lady?"

Rodney shot a narrow-eyed look at Caleb. "Why would you ask that?"

Caleb shrugged. "Why else would a guy want a quilt fixed?"

Rodney grinned. Maybe he had more in common with this nephew than he thought.

❧

Caroline had turned off the ringer on the phone when she'd come home from her visit to the hospital a week and a half ago. The only indication that the phone rang was when the answering machine message clicked on, startling her every time. She returned the business calls and played Rodney's messages over and over. She should have deleted them, but she savored the sound of his voice. His sincere apologies were a balm for her aching heart but not the cure. The cure, she guessed, was to continue seeing him, but then her anger flared. Had she known he'd suffered a mild heart attack, the EMTs would have arrived ten minutes sooner. He could have died in that time, had it been his heart instead of his gallbladder.

At first, she worried that Jason's confrontation with Rodney had brought on the attack. She'd been half sick all the way to the hospital, thinking her son had contributed to Rodney's supposed heart attack. That worry turned to anger when she realized Jason just might have been right about Rodney all along.

What if they had committed to a serious relationship and this had been fatal? She'd be lost again, just like when Ted died. Trance-walking through life, scared and wondering, always wondering, how she'd face the future. Could she pay the phone bill, the light bill, and buy groceries? What if she got sick or needed a new roof?

Aware her previous thoughts had caused her to pull the corner of her mouth in, she released her lower lip. Oh, what did she care if her face showed her internal concerns? They were valid, after all.

She pushed away from her sewing machine. She'd pieced both T-shirt quilt tops together, trying to finish any projects that tied her to Rodney. She glanced at his quilt still pinned to her display board. Would that fabric never come in? She huffed up the stairs to the freezer to see what weight-conscious frozen entrée would be her dinner.

A knock on the side door startled her, and she bumped her shoulder on the freezer door. She slapped the freezer door shut. Who could that be? It was her business door, and she hadn't made any client appointments. The stretched and worn light blue jogging suit she wore showed brown coffee stains from an earlier spill. Rubbing her shoulder to alleviate the pain, she went down the two steps to the entryway. Mark stood at the door.

She swung the door open.

"Whoa, I hope you don't greet all your customers with that scowl." Mark stepped inside.

"You scared me and I hit my shoulder on the freezer door. Excuse me if it hurts." Sarcasm dripped from her voice.

"Sorry, I didn't mean to." Mark's eyes narrowed as if he suspected her of a crime.

"You and everyone else." *Ted, Jason, Rodney. They all hurt me and didn't mean to.* Caroline's tense shoulders relaxed. That wasn't Mark's fault.

"No, I'm sorry I snapped at you."

"It's okay. Makes up for the time I hid from you while you were babysitting."

One corner of Caroline's mouth twitched until she grinned at the memory. She'd been frantic. Her mother finally came over and called Mark out of hiding with threats of telling his mother.

"That's better. I have something you need." He held up a Granny Bea's bag. "I found a flour sack, exact match for Rodney's quilt. Too bad about his gallbladder attack."

Caroline raised her eyebrows. "So you've talked to him."

"Yeah, I had to get approval to buy this. It was pretty pricey." Mark continued as if he hadn't noticed the snippiness in her statement. "He's still at his sister's but is coming home this weekend. But you probably already know that. He's really thankful you were there that night. I offered to drop it off because I had another errand to run. He suggested I bring it to your house. Guess he's getting anxious to have the quilt completed."

"I guess." Caroline shrugged. "Rodney was thankful I was there, huh?" *Bet he wasn't after the surgery.*

"I don't know why that surprises you. We always want the people we really care about close to us when we don't feel well. Rodney told me about the quilt's history. I think he'd hoped for a better story. Don't you?"

Rodney knew the story behind the quilt? Had he mentioned that in any of his phone messages? Of course not. He had no idea if she'd forgiven him.

"Whoops. Judging by the look on your face, I probably spoiled a surprise. I bet he wanted to tell you the story in person."

Caroline knitted her brows together. She really wanted to know the story. She knew Mark though. He could keep a secret.

"Well I need to get on my way. See you Tuesday night." Mark offered the bag with the flour sack to her.

"Bye." Caroline closed the door behind him, then, through the door window, watched him back out of her driveway.

She sighed. Guess she'd never know the story behind the quilt. Yet that wasn't entirely true. If she asked, Rodney would tell her. But she was going to try not to have an opportunity to ask. Caroline peeked into the bag. The fabric, though brighter from lack of washings, was pastel yellow with white flowers. A perfect match.

After eating her low-calorie spaghetti from the cardboard packaging while leaning against the kitchen counter, Caroline slipped the flour sack from the plastic bag and headed downstairs. She took the cardboard pattern she'd made from the computer-printed block out of her sewing box. She looked over the flour sack for holes, rips, rust marks, or flaws. One area was faded but not damaged in any way. It must have been exposed to direct sunlight. Caroline turned the sack inside out and removed the thread that made the seam. The faded spot should be just big enough to cut the needed blocks from. That way it would match the quilt's fabric even closer.

After steam-pressing all the wrinkles from the cloth, Caroline laid the blocks over the faded fabric. One corner hung over to the brighter part of the material, but most of that would be hidden by the seam allowance. She traced and cut out the blocks, then basted them together by hand. Not her standard method but easier to rip apart in the event she pieced the block wrong. She'd machine sew all the quilt top's seams together to fortify them once this block was inserted back into the top.

In no time, Caroline looked down at a completed Lily of the Field block. She pinned the quilt block into the gaping hole of the quilt top on the display board. *"O you of little faith."* Caroline shook her head as if she could shake her thoughts out. She stepped back and looked at the quilt from several angles. The new block was just a tad bit brighter than the original blocks. Something only a trained eye might catch. *"See how the lilies of the field grow. They do not labor or spin."*

Was her faith small? She'd never thought so before Ted's death. She'd participated in church and all its activities, but now she could see that at her weakest, she turned from God instead of welcoming Him with open arms.

Yet God hadn't given up on her. He'd sent Rodney and this quilt. Caroline took a deep breath and released it along with her tension, anger, frustration, and fears. The only emotion burning in her heart was curiosity. She needed to know the story behind this quilt, because it seemed to be His messenger to her. *"Stop worrying, Caroline. Your heavenly Father knows what you need.*

'See how the lilies of the field grow. . . . Do not worry about tomorrow.' " Her shoulders relaxed for the first time in over a week as she walked back to the quilt. She unpinned it from the board and held it to her face, the fabric cool, soft, and comforting against her skin. And as if it could answer her, she said, "You seem to know my story. Will I ever know yours?"

Chapter 10

Three weeks after his surgery, Rodney's doctor released him so he could resume normal activities. At Michelle's insistence, Caleb accompanied Rodney when he went home. Rodney argued Caleb had better things to do on a weekend than care for his bachelor uncle. He'd lost the fight when Caleb shrugged and said he didn't mind at all.

It turned out his sissy knew what was best for him. Quiet surrounded him from the moment he unlocked the front door. He immediately missed the hustle and bustle of her busy household, noisy video games, the din of constant chattering and clanking of pots and dishes—the noise of a family.

During Rodney's recovery, temperatures warmed into the low sixties. Spring seemed just around the corner, but a Canadian clipper dropped the temperatures back into the thirties and brought with it a storm front. Although snow was forecasted to hit north of Riverside, sleet pinged against the windows. Rodney's crew members promised they were on top of it.

"Do you want to go check your customers' driveways and sidewalks?"

Rodney continued to stare out a window. He rubbed the rough stubble on the back of his neck. "I trust my crew to handle it."

"Then why are you pacing between the windows and door?" Caleb held Rodney's coat out to him.

"Cabin fever, I guess." Rodney took his coat and slipped it on. Not a lie entirely. He was tired of being cooped up in a house. However, it had more to do with Caroline. Did she know he was home? Should he call her? Stop by?

"Let's go." Caleb pulled on a hooded sweatshirt with the USD Coyotes logo on the front. "I'll drive."

Right now the roads and sidewalks were just wet, but at sundown with lower temperatures, they'd freeze. Rodney verified with his crew members which houses they'd covered, then split the rest between them and him. Rodney directed Caleb to the first of five customers. Together they spread melting compound on his customers' driveways and sidewalks.

His customers greeted them both with enthusiasm. Caleb never tired of repeating where he went to college and his current course of study. Michelle had done a fine job of raising her boys. At that age, Rodney had focused on his career and stepping one rung higher on the ladder of success. He'd have never stood in the bad weather and visited with anyone, unless he or she could boost his career. In that retrospect he and Caleb were nothing alike. That dichotomy gladdened Rodney's heart.

Back at home, his mind wandered to Caroline. She never did return his phone calls. Michelle suggested he give her space, time to work through her emotions. It tore at his heart to know that he'd thrown her back into a life of worry and isolation. More than one person in Riverside tattled on Caroline, stating he must have given her quite a scare. She'd reverted back to her old way of life. Mildred's report was what laid Rodney's heart wide open. Just when she'd shared with him her interest in participating in the church services again, Caroline had been absent from church since Rodney's gallbladder attack. At least after Ted's death she still attended church. What had Rodney done to her?

Caleb went back to college early Sunday morning. Good thing, because the weatherman missed his mark on the forecast. The storm took a turn for the worse by early afternoon. Rodney moved a curtain to the side to check out the weather's progress. The heavy wet flakes of spring snow floated from the sky at a rapid pace. His lawn, just yellow-brown grass this morning, sported an inch layer of snow that, of all things, reminded him of quilt batting. Caroline, in a few short weeks, had infiltrated his thoughts in ways he never dreamed a woman could. He sighed and dropped the curtain. No sense going out to move snow yet. He'd be fighting a losing battle at the rate it was falling.

Rodney sat down at his computer. He'd long ago finished his business website and the one he'd contracted for the author. Allison sent him some leads for other small business owners, but he'd left the corporate world for a reason, his health. Looking back over the last few weeks, he'd become obsessed with running two businesses. How easily he had slipped back into the rigors of corporate business, putting in late hours with no room for exercise but lots of room for stress. As he hit the button to send his no-thank-you and I-wish-you-well response to Allison, his doorbell rang.

Rodney tucked his blue flannel shirttails into his jeans as he hurried to the door. Looking through the window, he caught sight of a black sedan in his driveway. His heart leapt. Caroline. What was she doing out on a day like this? He all but ran through the short hall to the front door. He swung it open, not even considering she might not be as happy to see him as he was her.

"Hi." Caroline smiled brighter than the snow accumulating on the hood fur surrounding her face. No sign of worry or anger etched her features like the last time he'd seen her. "I finished your quilt." She held up a shopping bag by the twisted paper handles.

"You should have just come in." Rodney stood to the side, leaning against the door for support, afraid the internal tremors Caroline created would show on the outside, too.

"Well"—Caroline shrugged as she raised her eyebrows—"I didn't know?"

Rodney knew what she meant, but she hadn't worn out her welcome.

"It's really coming down out there." Caroline brushed the snow from her shoulders and tramped her boots on the rug in front of the door before stepping aside so the door could be closed. "Must be close to three inches now. Bet you're happy. It might be the last snow of the season."

Rodney stared at his guest. Rude though it was, he was dumbfounded. This was not the Caroline who had left the hospital, nor the one he'd first met. The hood surrounding her carefree features gave her the appearance of a fresh-faced schoolgirl.

Caroline laughed as she slipped the hood back and water droplets fell onto her face. Rodney's entire body responded to the joyous sound. He felt his features give way to a broad smile. When their eyes met, they shared the same unspoken message they did that day in Granny Bea's parking lot. He couldn't leave the message unsaid anymore. He loved her, every part of her, and he needed to tell her that, even if she didn't want to be tied to a man with health issues. She needed to know how he felt. For a consummate adman, whose words flowed smoothly until he gained an account, these words stuck in his throat, damming up his vocal abilities.

Caroline broke the silence. "We need to talk."

Tell her—tell her you love her. Rodney nodded his head in agreement. *Ask her to take off her coat.* His tongue, thick and heavy, didn't seem to work.

"First, I owe you an apology. . . ."

The notes of a lullaby interrupted Caroline. She pulled off her glove and fished through her purse. "It's Jason and Angela's ring."

Rodney expected her to turn her back to him for privacy. Caroline's demeanor might have changed, but he was certain Jason's attitude about him remained the same, especially if Caroline had told him about Rodney's health.

Instead Caroline continued their previous eye contact and smiled as she said hello. In an instant Jason's voice tones boomed from the phone. Rodney couldn't make out the words, but the worry crevice between Caroline's brows warned him of disaster. How could Jason possibly know Caroline was at his house?

Terror registered in Caroline's eyes just before tears glazed them over.

"I'm on my way." She clicked her cell phone shut. A tear trickled down her cheek as Rodney stepped closer and wrapped her in his arms. He suspected this time the worried look on her face held merit.

"The baby's in trouble," she croaked out. Sobs bounced her shoulders against his chest, and he increased the pressure of his embrace.

After a minute or so, Caroline pushed away from Rodney. "I'm sorry, I have to go to the hospital."

"You're not going alone in this weather."

"I don't know." The corner of Caroline's mouth disappeared.

Rodney grasped her by the shoulders. "Look, if Jason has a problem with it, I'll wait in a different area of the hospital. Now, is your car blocking my pickup in the garage?"

Caroline shook her head no and let Rodney guide her to the back door, where he bundled up for the weather, slipping his stocking cap over his bare scalp as they went out the door.

"Which hospital?" Rodney asked as he guided Caroline to the pickup and assisted her into the seat.

"Vermillion." Caroline reached for her seat belt.

Once inside the truck, Rodney realized that Caroline still held the bag with his quilt in it. "You can put that behind the seat," he said as he pushed the button to activate the four-wheel drive feature.

Instead she removed the quilt from the bag and hugged it. Peace relaxed the pain in her expression. She sighed. "Rodney, your quilt has quite an effect on me."

The wipers squeaked across the windshield as they swatted the snow from the center, leaving it packed at the bottom and sides of the glass as they cycled back and forth. The deepening snow pulled at Rodney's pickup tires, and as he had suspected, the rapidly falling snow created visibility problems once they left the city limits.

"Mark said you found out the story of this quilt."

Rodney, fighting the urge to look at Caroline, remained focused on the road since he was pushing their luck doing fifty in these weather conditions. "More like we found out a story about the quilt."

"Was it the quilt in the picture your aunt sent?"

"No," Rodney said with a slight shake of his head. "But the picture did help us figure it out."

"So there was another clue in the picture?"

Out of the corner of his eye, Rodney saw Caroline unfold the quilt and tuck it around her legs.

"Are you cold?" Rodney reached to adjust the heat.

"No, your quilt brings me comfort, and right now I need that."

She just gave him the perfect opening. He wished he could look at her, but the weather situation didn't permit it. "I hoped I could be the person who brought you comfort."

A gasp broke through the swish of the wipers on the windshield and the buzz of the heater blower.

"I know, I blew it. You'll never know how sorry I am that I wasn't forthcoming about my health issues." Nerves caused Rodney to speak the words too rapidly.

"Rodney." Caroline rested her hand on his forearm. "The comfort I need, which your Lily of the Field quilt provides, is the reminder of God's care. How He loves and provides for His children. 'Therefore do not worry about tomorrow, for tomorrow will worry about itself. Each day has enough trouble of its own.'"

Relief eased through him. At least his actions hadn't destroyed her faith.

"Please go on and tell me about this wonderful quilt of yours. I've been bursting with curiosity since Mark dropped off the flour sack for you. What was in the picture that gave you a clue? Was someone sewing a block?"

"No, the picture held no information; however, my nephew Caleb did. I guess we should have forwarded the digital pictures to the youngsters in the family, too. We'd have solved the mystery right away." When Rodney hit a deep pocket of snow, the pickup lurched toward the ditch. He gripped the wheel tight, guiding it back to what he thought was his lane. The county plows hadn't bladed the road yet.

"So?" Despite her casual conversation, worry filled Caroline's voice.

She was obviously trying to occupy her mind with something other than the terrible conclusions that worrying caused. He could help with that.

"Well, it seems Caleb was visiting Mom and they took a walk in the nature preserve just outside of town. Halfway through the walk, a thunderstorm blew up. They made a run for a shelter and, once inside, found the quilt lying on the floor. Mom changed her mind and decided they'd use it as a shield from the rain and make it to her car. It's a good thing they did, because lightning struck a tree that then fell and smashed the shelter. Caleb said Mom told him the quilt saved their lives. I guess that's why she kept it."

Rodney didn't look over, but by the rustle of fabric, he could tell Caroline was rubbing her hands over the quilt blocks.

"It's not an heirloom, then."

"I'm sure it is for someone, just not for our family."

"So I guess we know the story about how and why your mom had the quilt, but we don't know the quilt's story. Why it was made, I mean." Caroline sighed.

Rodney lifted his foot from the gas as they passed the business bypass exit for Vermillion. The truck slowed, making braking easier as he made his way through town. At the red light he turned to Caroline. Before she faced whatever situation awaited her at the hospital, he wanted her to know that he loved her and she could count on him. He opened his mouth to speak, but Caroline lifted a gloved finger to his lips to hush him.

"Thank you for keeping my mind occupied on the way to the hospital." Knowing blue eyes searched his face. "See, Rodney, I do need you in my life, because I love you, too."

Her declaration of love fortified his heart in ways medicine, surgery, or exercise never could.

❧

Rodney released his grip on their entwined fingers as soon as she saw Jason leaning against a hallway wall, head down. She ran but let her fingers run the length of his hands until their brushed fingertips ended their small embrace.

"Jason." She held her arms out. He lifted his head, then wiped his forefinger across his eyes before moving into her arms.

"Oh Mom," he whispered.

He laid his head against her shoulder just as he'd done so many times in his life. She stroked his hair and kissed the top of his head.

"How's Angela?" She rested her cheek against his head.

"Scared but okay." His words were muffled as they bounced off her parka.

"What happened?" Caroline pushed on Jason's shoulders. He eased back. Caroline placed her palms on his cheeks, stroking her thumbs back and forth to wipe away the tears, leaving her own tears to trickle freely down her face.

"Her back's hurt all day. Then all of a sudden she had intense shooting pains in her abdomen. That's when we came to the hospital." He covered Caroline's hands with his, removing them from his face but holding them tightly between them. "I guess she'd been in labor all day. We just didn't know."

"And. . ."

"And your granddaughter was born about twenty minutes ago. Angela was dilated to ten centimeters when they examined her, so they broke her water and she delivered the baby."

"Why didn't you call me?" Caroline changed their hand positions. This time it was her doing the squeezing from excitement. "I'm a grandma."

"I knew you'd be on the road, and I didn't want you answering the phone while driving."

Caroline pulled Jason into a tight hug. "I'm so happy for you. I mistook your tears of joy."

Jason pushed free and took her hands in his. "My tears weren't tears of joy."

"Does something about being a father scare you?" She searched his face for a sign.

He shook his head and lowered his eyes. When he lifted them to meet hers, dampness glazed them. "No, I'm mad that my daughter doesn't have a Grandpa Baker."

It's a good thing she had ahold of Jason, because his admission knocked the wind out of her.

"Remember how I accused you of being mad at Dad for dying?"

Caroline nodded her head but remained silent.

"Well, I'm the one mad at him. He died too soon. How could he do that to us? He's missing everything. Everything. I managed to keep that anger under control until you started to move on, build a career, and see other people." Jason's eyes moved to a spot over her right shoulder. She braced for the worst, but instead he looked back at her. "When you put his pictures back out, I knew you'd moved on but I hadn't, so the anger turned to rage. I guess I lashed out at everyone for something that no one can control, not even Dad." Jason stopped.

"Jason, you should have said something sooner."

"I'm so glad you came." Jason pulled her into a hug. "I worried that you wouldn't."

Caroline savored the moment with her son before she pushed him to arm's length. "Jason, I will always be there for you. That's one reason I started my own quilt business. I can adjust my schedule for babysitting." They'd experienced sadness and anger. It was time to let joy sneak back into their hearts.

Caroline laughed at the lightbulb-just-switched-on look on Jason's face. He laughed, too.

"You're a father." She squeezed his hand. "I'm a grandma. Rodney." Caroline twisted her neck to see over her shoulder. "I'm a grandma."

"I heard." Rodney joined them and pulled Caroline into a side hug. She laid her head on his shoulder. He offered his hand to Jason.

"Congratulations."

Jason's eyes lowered to Rodney's hand; then he looked at Caroline. She hoped her eyes conveyed her message to her son. She watched as his eyes moved to Rodney's.

"I'm sorry for everything I said and the way I acted." He grasped Rodney's hand. "Thank you for coming with Mom. You're taking good care of her, I can tell. Please forgive me?"

"Bygones are bygones."

"Can we see Angela and the baby yet?"

"Sure."

Rodney released Caroline's shoulder. "I'll be in the waiting room. Take as much time as you need." He smoothed a stray ringlet behind her ear.

"Aren't you coming, too?" Jason asked.

Caroline's chest burst with pride. She slipped one hand in Jason's and the other in Rodney's as they walked down the hall.

Angela looked up from marveling at her newborn daughter and smiled at the chain of people that walked into her room.

Jason gingerly lifted the pink bundle from her arms. "Mom, meet your granddaughter, Brooklyn Mya." Caroline knew her face reflected the same love that Jason's radiated as she looked from her "baby" to the new addition to her family. She gathered their bundle of joy from Jason with practiced ease.

Rodney stood to her side and peered over Brooklyn's head. "She's so tiny." He reached to touch her but pulled his hand back.

Joy bubbled through Caroline, and she laughed. "You can touch her. She won't break, you know."

Rodney stepped around Caroline and brushed the backs of his fingers on Brooklyn's face. She grunted. He jerked his hand away. "Did I hurt her?" Concern filled his eyes.

"No." Caroline shook her head, then rocked back and forth sideways.

A flush crawled up his neck and colored his cheeks. He turned to Jason and Angela. "I don't have much, well, any experience with this."

Caroline noticed Angela blinking her heavy eyelids, tired from childbirth. Caroline bent and kissed the top of her granddaughter's head, then handed her back to Jason.

"Are you leaving?"

"Just for a while." Caroline nodded to Angela. "Someone needs her rest." She walked to the bed, then took Angela's hand in hers. "Thank you for the beautiful granddaughter. You rest now." She straightened. "We'll be in the waiting room."

❧

Rodney twisted the cap from the bottle of water he bought Caroline from the vending machine and handed it to her.

She sat on the edge of a waiting room chair.

She pulled a long drink from it, thirstier than she thought. Rodney sat beside her, lifted her hand, and clasped it between his. His eyes conveyed the message. She knew what he was about to say.

"I love you, Caroline."

She might have known what he was going to say, but she wasn't prepared for the response it evoked within her—overwhelming happiness threaded into every cell of her body.

"I don't want to cause you further worry, but I can't guarantee I won't have future health issues."

"I know that now. And I can't promise you I won't worry from time to time, but I'll try to keep it to the events of the day."

Rodney put his arm around her and eased her back into the chair cushion. She rested her head on his shoulder.

"This is a much better reason to be at the hospital than our last trip," Rodney said.

"Yes, it is," Caroline agreed.

"Correct me if I'm wrong, but didn't the EMTs call you Mrs. Harris?"

"Yes." Caroline giggled at the memory.

"How'd you feel about that?"

Caroline rose up and palmed Rodney's cheek. "Truthfully, I kind of liked it."

Rodney slid her hand to his shoulder, leaned close, and pressed his lips to hers, not once but three times.

"Me, too," he whispered and wrapped his arm around her shoulder, squeezing her closer.

She rested her head back on his shoulder. Contentment washed through her. She'd worried all those months for nothing. Just like the lilies of the field, God took care of her. His plans for her future were better than any she could have imagined.

Epilogue

Is my girl ready?"

Rodney's voice boomed through the closed door, causing six-month-old Brooklyn to kick her legs, making the buckling of the small patent leather shoes a harder task. She cooed and stretched her arms toward the door.

"Which one?" Caroline called back and smiled at her granddaughter's reaction to Rodney's voice. She managed to tuck the small trap through the buckle. Angela stood Brooklyn on her lap while Caroline adjusted the quilted yoke of the small dress before she pulled the white satin skirt into place.

"The little one who doesn't talk back to me." Humor infused Rodney's response.

Caroline imagined his brown eyes twinkling with teasing merriment.

"Yet," Michelle added, and all the women in the small room laughed.

Caroline stood behind the door as Michelle opened it, and Angela slipped her wiggling daughter through to Rodney's waiting arms.

"There's Grandpa's girl," Rodney said in a tone an octave higher than normal. "Let's go find Daddy."

Brooklyn sputtered excited gurgles and coos in answer.

Happiness ensconced Caroline's heart from all directions. Jason and Rodney had become friends as they spoiled the same little girl. It was Jason who first referred to Rodney as Grandpa.

"Time for the finishing touches." Angela carried the quilted jacket to the bride.

Caroline slipped the ivory jacket over her satin sheath. She'd designed and sewn all the dresses for her wedding. She'd quilted a small flower pattern similar to the daisies on Rodney's quilt back into ivory satin using gold thread. Her collarless jacket matched the dress's knee-length hem. Hooked over center buttons, a gold chain fastened the jacket together. Michelle's and Angela's jackets, quilted with the same pattern, served as a blouse, with skirts from the same satin fabric as Caroline's sheath. At her age it seemed silly for only the bride to wear white.

Jason knocked on the door before entering. "The men are in place."

Caroline took one last look in the mirror. She smoothed her jacket and strained to see if her French twist remained intact. "Did I mess up my hair?"

Michelle adjusted a few ringlets around Caroline's neckline and checked that the jeweled hair combs stayed secure.

"I think you're ready." Angela handed her a bouquet of white peace lilies.

Caroline smiled. She was definitely ready, not just for the ceremony or becoming Rodney's wife, but for whatever lay ahead of her in life. That was why she'd chosen lilies for her wedding bouquet, her reminder not to worry but to trust God.

"Mom, you look beautiful." Jason gingerly kissed her cheek so as not to mess up her makeup, then held out his arm.

"Thank you." She slipped her hand through his elbow and they followed Michelle, then Angela out the door.

Caroline surveyed the sanctuary as she waited her turn to walk down the aisle. Ten-inch quilt blocks of every color with the Double Wedding Ring pattern decorated the pews where most brides placed bows. The Lily of the Field quilt draped the altar where the unity candle stood flanked by mixed flower bouquets like the one Rodney had given her the night of their first date.

The music cued her entrance, and as she and Jason took the first step, he whispered, "I love you, and I'm glad you're happy again."

She gripped his arm tighter and nodded, unable to speak through the tightness in her throat. She scanned the smiling faces looking her way, but when her eyes fixed on Rodney, handsome in the traditional black tux, everyone else became a blur. The tightness in her throat slipped down into a swell of love in her chest. She blinked and a warm tear imprinted a path down her cheek.

Jason squeezed both of their hands as he placed her hand in Rodney's and took his seat beside his daughter in her infant seat. Brooklyn's coos continued after the music stopped and through most of the ceremony.

Unlike earlier in the year, Caroline savored every precious moment of the service. She cherished each word the pastor spoke, bathed in the tenderness of Rodney's voice as he pledged his love to her, and felt the joy conveyed on his face as she promised to love him in sickness and in health.

JOB'S TEARS

To Gert and Tom Stevens,
a real life MS heroine and her hero. Thanks for
your research help. Your friendship means the world to me.

Chapter 1

I don't know. Managing a business building may be too stressful with your recent..."

Sarah Buckley watched as Karla Ward, her best friend since grade school, swallowed hard. A lump of emotion no doubt. Even though the doctor had diagnosed Sarah with multiple sclerosis almost eighteen months ago, Karla still seemed to be taking it harder than Sarah.

Had Sarah known this was where their conversation would lead, she'd have chosen a corner table in the rustic coffeehouse chain versus this table in the open area where their discussion could be overheard.

Karla stared into space and tapped her paper cup on the high-glossed wooden table. Finally, her water-filled eyes close to brimming over, she looked at Sarah. "I just mean maybe now's not the best time to try a new career."

Sarah sighed, her good mood now dampened like her friend's eyes. Sarah had hoped for a little girl talk, wanting Karla's opinion on a man she'd recently met. Sarah thought he might be interested and wanted to bounce his actions off Karla. She shouldn't have agreed to meet Karla at the coffee shop before the evening quilting class that she'd looked forward to all day.

After two months, Sarah had a few doubts about her new career choice, but Karla's pessimism made her determined to maintain a positive outlook on all the changes in her life.

Maybe there was still time to turn the conversation around. "No time like the present." Sarah shook her fist in the air in a "go forth and conquer" fashion to show enthusiasm about the changes in her life and hoped it'd rub off on her friend.

Sarah earned a frown for her efforts.

"You are way too flippant about this. I think you need to go to counseling."

"Flippant about and counseling for what?" Sarah raised her eyebrows. "You can say it, Karla. Multiple sclerosis. I have MS. Dancing around the disease's name won't make it go away."

"I know that," Karla snapped. "I just don't know how you can be so accepting of your fate."

"What else can I do? We have to take the good with the bad." Sarah sipped her iced green tea. She wasn't ecstatic about her diagnosis, either, but since there was no cure for MS she had to find a way to live with it.

"Whatever." Karla's eye-roll answer didn't surprise Sarah. Her friend wasn't as grounded in faith as Sarah, who believed that if God brought you to it, He'd get you through it. At least she believed that most days.

"I have to earn a living." Sarah's MS forced her to quit the job she loved as a UPS delivery person. She couldn't tolerate going in and out of eastern South Dakota's hot, humid summer weather. It worsened her muscle spasms.

"That's just it, you don't. There are government programs."

"Stop." Sarah held up her palm. She'd had enough. "I'm not quite forty and only in the first stages of MS. Someday I may need assistance, but right now I just need a job that doesn't aggravate my symptoms."

Karla opened then closed her mouth. She pursed her lips and gave her head a shake, letting Sarah know she didn't share that opinion.

"I wish you were as excited about my new career as I am. The company I'm working for has excellent benefits. I'm in a temperature-controlled office, and I get to dress up. After wearing brown uniforms and comfortable shoes for twenty-two years, having wardrobe choices is a real treat." Sarah smiled before taking another sip of her tea.

"Congratulations," Karla said with a halfhearted shrug. She reached across the table and rested her hand on Sarah's arm. "You know I'm only concerned because I care about you. Right?"

"I know." Sarah placed her free hand over Karla's and squeezed.

Karla's concerned-filled eyes bored into Sarah. "I don't know that you're seeing the big picture with your disease. You need to take it easy."

Sarah did see the big picture. People in all stages of MS attended the support group she'd enrolled in. Many of the people in advanced stages of MS still led very active lives, just like Sarah intended on doing. She wasn't going to cower away in a room and watch life pass her by like Karla seemed to want her to do.

When Sarah didn't respond, Karla added, "I do have your best interest at heart."

I'm not so sure about that. Since her diagnosis, the one thing she thought wouldn't change was her friendship with Karla. Karla, usually supportive, saw only the negatives where Sarah's MS was concerned.

Sarah cleared her throat. "I need to get going. I have to pick up supplies before my class."

Karla released her grip. As she stood, she picked up her cup and said, "I never thought I'd see the day when you'd be sewing. At least you'll have something to fill your time when you find managing a building is too much for you with *MS*," enunciating the last two letters as if to prove she could say them. Karla then walked over to the waste can and dropped her empty coffee cup through the center opening.

Outside the building, Karla gave Sarah a loose hug. "I'll call you, and we can do this again."

Maybe, Sarah thought as she waved good-bye to her friend. Sarah needed optimism, but it was hard to maintain a positive outlook around Karla anymore. Idle minds were truly the devil's workshop. Sarah's own mind had hosted a few pity parties since her symptoms were diagnosed, which was the second reason she enrolled in the quilting class.

Please, Lord, change Karla's attitude concerning my illness and help me to adjust to the new challenges in my life. Sarah sent up a silent prayer as she walked to the other end of the strip mall that housed Granny Bea's quilt shop.

As the door buzzer announced her arrival, Sarah looked around. The quilt store appeared unmanned. Sarah's heart sank a little. She stepped forward and scanned the room's corners. Surely, *he* was here. Somewhere.

"Sarah, you're early." Mark Sanders, the store owner, came from the back of the building, his warm smile waking the butterflies in her stomach. "I was just getting the classroom set up for Caroline. Come on back and keep me company while I test machines."

The butterflies' fluttering wings lifted her heart and blew away all the negative energy from her visit with Karla. Reason number one for taking a quilting class—Mark. Sarah thought she preferred tall, lean men, but this shorter, stocky man sparked her interest. He'd been so welcoming on her first visit to the store. The way his eyes lit up when he looked at her made her feel special. Something she needed right now.

Now when the blues threatened her sanity, she found a reason to visit the store. Even after the briefest conversations with Mark, she left uplifted.

"I came early because I haven't purchased the fabric I need for my class project yet." Sarah held out the letter Caroline Baker, the class instructor, sent out with yardage requirements for either a table runner or a wall quilt. "I intend to use this coupon." Sarah pointed to the bottom portion of the letter that advertised 10 percent off supplies purchased at Granny Bea's.

"Don't worry about it." Mark waved his hand through the air. "You can get that after class. I read Caroline's synopsis, and she's going over quilting terms and sewing methods tonight. She gave me strict orders to have practice fabric available, so I don't think you'll need the project fabric until next week."

Mark led the way to the workroom in the back of the store.

"I'll be just a second." He turned to the right and went into a darkened room.

Sarah took a couple of steps past the threshold. The workroom stretched the length of the store. Three rows of folding tables roughly four feet long made up the classroom. A sewing machine sat at the ends of each table. *Mark must offer sewing classes in addition to quilting classes.*

"Have a seat." Mark rolled a plush office chair out of the darkened room and pushed it over by the first table. He held it steady until Sarah sat down.

"Thank you." Sarah smiled up at Mark as she took a seat.

"You're welcome." Mark continued to smile at Sarah for a few moments. His short light brown hair, combed straight back despite some receding on each side, accented her favorite feature—his eyes. The dark green polo shirt he wore today brought out the emerald highlights in his hazel eyes.

"You look like springtime tonight. Yellow is a good color for you." Crinkles formed by Mark's eyes as his smile widened.

Sarah's cheeks warmed. "Thank you." She'd bought the pastel crop pants set as her Easter outfit. Although it proved to be a little too summery for early April in Sioux Falls, South Dakota, she'd garnered many compliments at church, so she chose it to wear tonight because she wanted to look nice for Mark.

"You're welcome." Mark walked to the last plastic-topped table. He plugged a sewing machine into a power strip and pressed a button then repeated the action on the second machine.

Sarah lifted her left hand. Her fingers glided up and down the length of her dangly earrings. Shouldn't Mark be moving the sewing machines out of the way?

"How many people signed up for the quilting class?" Sarah smiled when Mark looked up from his work.

He moved to the second table in the row. "Five. One machine is for Caroline." Mark pressed a button and a machine lit up. When the second machine on that table didn't respond, Mark scowled and wiggled a power cord where it attached to the machine. He flicked a switch, seemed satisfied, and then walked to the front table.

"What type of sewing machine do you have?" Mark asked as he prepped the last two sewing machines.

"Um. . ." Sarah felt her eyes grow wide. She hadn't considered needing a sewing machine to make a quilt. She'd inquired about the classes to have a reason to talk to Mark. After a bout with the blues, she'd decided a hobby was a needed distraction. "I don't have one. I thought quilts were hand stitched."

Mark knitted his brows. "Not too many people quilt by hand these days. The first day you came into the store you purchased quite a bit of material, so I assumed you knew how to sew."

"My church was collecting sewing kits for a mission project." He remembered her purchase from three months ago? Of course he did. He picked up on her interest in the Job's Tears quilt block. What did he tell her that day? *"A good shopkeeper knows his customers"*—yet he made her feel like more than a customer. Was that his intention or her hope? She wished she could have discussed this with Karla, instead of the ongoing saga of her MS.

Satisfied that all the machines were on and in working order, Mark slipped his stocky frame onto the corner of the table closest to her and swung his legs. "I see. Do you know how to sew?"

Sarah dipped her head. She'd signed up for the class to give her a reason to be in the store. She'd been so focused on the feeling that bubbled inside her whenever she was around Mark that she hadn't considered needing or knowing how to use a sewing machine.

"No." She lifted her eyes like a child asking forgiveness. "Do I need to know how to sew before I can quilt?"

Mark laughed. "I think it would help, but Caroline used to teach home economics back in the day, so it shouldn't be a problem. If Caroline gives you quilting homework or you want to practice, feel free to come into the shop and use one of these."

"How sweet of you!" Relief that she could stay enrolled in the class infused Sarah's response, revealing a little more enthusiasm than she'd intended.

A deep crimson colored Mark's light complexion, but his eyes sparkled as he grinned.

"I me—meant to say that was nice of you." The warmth of Sarah's cheeks was an indicator that her face mirrored Mark's.

"I hope you take me up on the offer." Mark's complexion regained some of its normal color as he crossed his arms over his broad chest. "If you don't know how to sew, what prompted you to sign up for a quilting class?"

"Well. . ." Sarah stopped. Although she didn't agree with people who tried to hide their MS, she was tired of being pitied, so she phrased her response without making a reference to her disease. "I decided that I needed to fill some free time. I noticed all the beautiful quilts on display in your shop and thought quilting might be a good hobby. Then you offered evening classes, so I thought I'd give it a try."

Plus you make me feel special. Thank goodness that thought stayed in her head. Sarah fought the urge to fan the intense blush from her cheeks.

"I think you'll enjoy it. Job's Tears is a fairly easy quilt block, so you shouldn't get too frustrated with it."

"Can I hold you to that statement?" A storm cloud of doubts threatened Sarah's plan. Would she really be able to stay in the class if she knew nothing about sewing? Seeing Mark wasn't the only issue; without the class, how would she fill her free time? Guess it was a good thing that she waited until the last minute to purchase her supplies.

Sarah rested her hands on the rippled seersucker fabric of her crop pants. "Some of the quilts you have on display are so intricate. I can't imagine making one of those."

"Depending on the quilt size, block detail, and quilted stitch pattern, some quilters log hundreds of hours on a quilt."

"Wow." Sarah shook her head in disbelief. "I had no idea."

"It really is an art form."

Sarah nodded in agreement. A few silent moments passed. She tried to think of something else to say.

The deep breath Mark drew broke the quiet in the room. He rubbed his hands down his khaki pants.

Sarah noted Mark's body language. *Is he nervous, too?*

"I could show you how to work the sewing machine."

"You know how to sew?" Sarah's astonishment coaxed a chuckle from Mark.

"Just enough to demonstrate the sewing machines I sell." He slipped from the table and patted the seat of a folding chair in front of one of the machines. "But knowing how to work the machine might give you a step up in class."

"Really, you don't have to do this, I'm sure you have work to do." Although she hoped if he did that it could wait until class started.

"Nothing that can't wait until later." The legs of a folding chair squeaked across the tile floor as Mark pulled a second one over to the machine and sat down. He patted the seat of the empty chair.

Sarah's hands trembled and not from a tremor brought on by her MS. She arose from the office chair then hooked her fingers behind her back, hoping to conceal her nervousness as she walked over to sit beside Mark. Once seated, she clasped her clammy palms together and rested them in her lap.

Mark slid his chair closer to hers. "I'll show you the basics. Now these machines are older models and very simplistic." Mark reached in front of her and flipped a toggle switch. The light on the machine turned off. "Obviously, this is the on/off switch." Mark flicked it, and the base of the machine glowed with light.

He leaned back just a little. "Back here is the lever to raise and lower the presser foot, which holds the fabric together while you sew." The metal piece that surrounded a needle moved up and down.

As Mark pointed to a broken-line symbol on the machine, Sarah tried to concentrate on what he was saying and demonstrating, but their close proximity goosefleshed her skin. The hint of pine she inhaled with each of his movements fogged her mind, making it difficult to process his instructions.

"Now you try." Mark switched off the sewing machine's power and scooted back on his chair. He folded his arms over his chest. "Turn the machine on."

Aware of her rapid breathing, she inhaled deeply then reached up and flicked the ON switch.

"Choose the stitch option."

Sarah stared at the panel filled with colorful stitch symbols. What had he said the standard stitch was? Straight? She thought it was the single broken line. She wrinkled her nose, closed one eye, and turned a knob until an arrow pointed at that symbol.

"Right. You're an excellent student. Now lift the presser foot."

The position of that piece on the sewing machine made it hard to see from the front. Sarah reached her left hand behind the machine and ran her fingers up and down the slender area of plastic. "All I feel is a screw of some type." She tried to peer through the opening of the machine.

"It's at the bottom of the arm." Mark reached up and put his hand over hers. His palm cupped her knuckles as he rested his long fingers over hers. The softness of his skin surprised her as he guided her fingers down the back of the sewing machine arm.

"Feel that?"

Nervous emotion clogged Sarah's throat. She nodded her response when Mark applied gentle pressure with his fingers as he escorted hers down a break in the plastic.

"That's the lever's track."

He continued the slow descent of their fingers to the bottom of the plastic cover. Sarah felt the blunt end of the lever tucked close to the bottom.

Sarah cleared her throat. "There it is." She stole a quick glance at Mark then swallowed hard to clear from her throat the giggle of happiness that his touch inspired. "I thought it was higher."

"I could tell." Mark removed his hand from hers. "Go ahead and lift up the presser foot."

Sarah raised the lever up with one finger. The presser foot rose to its upright position. She pulled her hands back to her lap and laced her fingers together, an attempt at composure. Her hands had trembled before, but now she was afraid of full-fledged shakes. She didn't want Mark to see how his touch affected her.

"Want to try sewing a seam?" Mark reached for some material that lay in the center of the table.

The door buzzer echoed through the store before Sarah had a chance to answer.

"Excuse me." Mark stood and walked from the room.

Fear wrestled with relief inside Sarah. If that was a customer, Mark wouldn't be back, and she'd lost her chance to spend more time alone with him tonight. Sarah had only felt attraction this immediate and strong one other time. She needed to get a grip on her racing pulse and come up with conversation topics. She couldn't let desire rule her heart and head again. She wanted to know Mark, not just be attracted to him.

Muffled laughter drifted through the workroom door. Sarah wished the room had a window in the wall, like the one in the short wall that separated the darkened office from the workroom. The laughter grew louder as Caroline Baker entered the room. She smiled over her shoulder at the tall man who followed her, laden with shopping bags. Caroline pointed, and he entered the office.

"Hi." Caroline smiled at Sarah.

Sarah stood up and walked toward Caroline. She extended her hand. "I don't know if you remember me—"

"Sarah Buckley." Caroline squeezed Sarah's extended hand. "Of course, I remember meeting you, here at the store earlier this year. You were wavering on whether you should enroll in my quilting class. I'm glad you decided to sign up, and I hope you'll enjoy it."

The tall, handsome gentleman came into the room and handed Caroline a canvas tote bag.

"I don't think you met my fiancé, Rodney Harris. Rodney, this is Sarah Buckley."

"Nice to meet you." Rodney grasped her hand, his rough, dry skin a contrast to Mark's soft touch.

"It's nice to meet you, too."

"Right this way." Mark stepped aside when he reached the door-frame. A teenage girl and an older gentleman entered the room.

"I believe this is my cue to leave." Rodney pecked a kiss on Caroline's check. "See you at eight-thirty."

The door buzzer beckoned Mark back out to the main store.

"Have fun." Rodney waved to the quilters as he followed Mark through the door.

Sarah tried to focus on introductions and small talk, but every few seconds she glanced toward the door, hoping to catch another glimpse of Mark.

Mark led two more ladies into the room. "Your class is complete."

Sarah's steady pulse quickened when he glanced her way before he turned back to Caroline.

"Let me know if you need anything," he said as he closed the door of the workroom.

Sarah wished that she could have talked to Karla about this. She'd never had much luck with relationships, but she thought Mark seemed as interested in her as she was in him.

But she'd been wrong about that before.

❧

Like a needle inserted through fabric, dread pierced Mark's heart as he walked to the cutting counter in the center of the store. He thought he had at least six weeks to get to know Sarah better. Since Sarah lacked sewing skills she might not stick out the quilting class.

Mark unrolled the last bit of fabric from a bolt. He measured the piece of material, cut it, and folded it into a fat-quarter square. If she quit the class would she still come to the store? Probably not since she didn't know how to sew. It made his day whenever her petite frame graced his quilt shop. She'd thought he was sweet to offer the use of one of the sewing machines. Would she think so if she knew he had an ulterior motive?

Mark looked up from his work when he heard the door.

"Here's your coffee." Rodney handed him a paper cup from the franchise down the block.

"Thank you for offering to bring me a cup. What do I owe you?" Mark reached into his front pocket for his money clip.

"My treat." Rodney sipped at a lime-colored cold drink.

"Is that green tea?" Mark grimaced and exaggerated a shiver.

Rodney chuckled at Mark's antics. "It is. It's good for you. Want to try a sip?" Rodney waved his cup close to Mark.

Mark smiled. "I'll pass and stick to the hard stuff. Thanks for taking the quilts to the back room."

"It's the least I could do. You looked pretty peaked when Caroline and I arrived. I thought you might be feverish. Your face was flushed. But then when I went into the workroom, I knew why." Rodney winked at Mark.

The heat worked its way back up Mark's neck and onto his cheeks as he remembered the silkiness of Sarah's ivory skin as he cupped his hand around her delicate fingers. He shrugged and sipped his coffee.

"Thanks for letting me hang around your store while Caroline teaches class."

"It's not like you're in the way." Mark looked around the store. "Business is always slow on Tuesday nights. That's why I scheduled a class tonight. I thought the activity around the store might bring in more traffic. Judging by the sales floor it doesn't look like that theory works."

"Maybe you should run a Tuesday night special. An extra discount after seven or a 'buy one yard of a fabric, get one yard for half price' deal. Or would that cut into your profit base?"

"The discount wouldn't. The fabric might, but I guess I could run it on certain fabrics or clearance fabric. I might just give that a try." Mark emptied another bolt and began to measure the fabric.

"Gonna ask her out?" Rodney shook his cup, bouncing the ice against the plastic.

Mark ran his sharp shears down the grain of the fabric, separating it into two pieces. "I plan to, but I don't know if she'll accept. She's a little out of my league."

Sarah was a classic beauty. Long dark lashes fluttered over coal-colored eyes. Her small pug nose with the slight upturn at the tip led down to plump lips. He even liked how her short black hair was cut to show off her dainty ears.

Mark laid the scissors down and folded the fabric pieces.

Rodney scowled at him. "What do you mean by that?"

Mark pointed his index fingers at his body and waved them up and down. "I'm not exactly Mr. GQ. What would a petite beauty like Sarah want with a middle-aged guy built like me? That's what I meant." Yet she did seem interested.

"You're solidly built inside and outside. That's an asset, buddy." Rodney gave a curt nod to punctuate his belief.

"Thanks." Mark knew Rodney meant well trying to build his confidence, but Mark was a Sanders. Sanders men were solid on the outside but not so much on the inside where it really counted.

"At least you know you'll see her five more times. You can build up to asking her out." Rodney peeked over the counter. "Got a trash can?"

Mark motioned for Rodney to hand him the cup and pitched it into the trash under the cutting counter. "Maybe. I'd hoped to speak with Caroline before class, but everyone seemed to arrive at once. I found out tonight that Sarah doesn't know how to sew."

"And she enrolled in a quilting class?" Rodney frowned.

Dread poked at Mark's heart as if it were a pincushion.

"She thought all quilts were sewn by hand. I know Caroline won't kick Sarah out of class and will try to teach her to sew, but I'm afraid she might get frustrated and quit the class. Job's Tears isn't a hard quilt pattern, but for a beginner it might be."

Rodney rubbed the back of his neck with his hand then smiled. "I guess if she does, you'll have to offer basic sewing classes. I know a really good teacher."

"Does Caroline pay you a commission to be her agent?" Mark finished folding the last of the fabric before he grinned at Rodney.

Rodney laughed at Mark's teasing. "Guess my pride in Caroline overflows."

"Sure does, but that's a good thing." Mark wrapped a paper strip with the Granny Bea's logo printed on it around a square of fabric. He pulled the protective paper from the adhesive on the strip and secured the ends together.

"That's why I'm encouraging you to ask Sarah out."

Mark stuck a price sticker on the fat quarter and picked up another square to package. He didn't really need encouragement. He planned to ask Sarah out. Would she accept was the question.

"I'm not looking for a serious relationship." History proved Sanders men weren't good at commitment.

"Are you sure? Having the love of a good woman makes life complete." Rodney pulled a weekly ad-filled paper from his pocket. "I'll just sit over there and leave you to your work."

Rodney and Caroline were the quintessential happy couple. Like all couples in love they wanted everyone else to be in love, but sometimes attraction was enough.

Sarah said she'd enrolled in the class to fill some free time. He'd seen her features darkened when she thought no one was looking as she browsed the store. Something troubled her. It didn't take much to put two and two together—a bad breakup.

He'd been the interim guy many times. It worked for him. Mark told the ladies up front he wasn't looking for anything serious. After he helped rebuild their self-esteem and he refused to get serious, they'd break it off with him. It was a win-win situation for everyone involved. The ladies regained their self-confidence, and he dated a beautiful woman for a few weeks before they went their separate ways. No strings. No hard feelings. No broken hearts.

He glanced over at Rodney studying the paper. A stand-up guy like Rodney wouldn't understand Mark's dating philosophy. Mark wasn't a love-them-and-leave-them type, but he was his father's son, so short, no-strings-attached relationships were in the best interests of both him and the ladies he dated. He'd never been wrong about that before.

Chapter 2

Sarah gathered all the handouts Caroline gave the class, tapped them to straighten them, and then laid them on the end of the table in a tidy pile. Hopefully this stalling tactic would ensure Sarah would be the last to leave the workroom. She needed to confess her inability to sew to Caroline. After a few polite good-byes and see-you-next-weeks among fellow class members, attendance finally dwindled down to just Caroline and Sarah.

"Did you enjoy the lesson?" Caroline picked up papers and the Job's Tears quilt block templates and tucked them into her tote bag.

"Very much." *When I could stop worrying about not being able to sew or see Mark again.* "I do need to talk to you, though." Sarah walked to the front of the room and stood beside Caroline.

Caroline stopped gathering her supplies and devoted her attention to Sarah.

Sarah bent her neck to look up at Caroline. She almost came to Caroline's shoulder. Sarah moved back a step to allow for a more comfortable conversation.

"Shall we sit?" Caroline slid a folding chair away from the table for her student then grabbed the office chair and rolled it closer to Sarah.

After they were seated, Sarah looked Caroline in the eyes. "I have a problem."

"What is it?" Caroline's blue eyes searched Sarah's face before returning to Sarah's gaze.

"I don't know how to sew."

Caroline's jaw dropped.

"I thought quilts were hand sewn, like in old movies that show quilting bees." Sarah hurried through her excuse, not giving Caroline a chance to respond. "Will my inability to machine sew mean I need to give up this class?" Sarah fingered the earring on her left ear.

Caroline pursed her lips together, not in an angry or annoyed way, but more like she was trying to stifle a giggle.

Embarrassment snapped out and wafted down over Sarah's heart like a blanket being thrown on top of a bed. How could she have been so naive about this? *Because, Sarah, you weren't really doing it for the right reason.*

Caroline gave into her grin. She reached over and squeezed one of

Sarah's hands. "I guess I have an authentic quilter in my class. I don't run across many of those anymore."

Sarah knitted her brows together but smiled back at Caroline, some of her discomfort fading. "I don't know if I can be called authentic or a quilter, right now."

"In six weeks you'll be both. I promise you. Now, if you're more comfortable sewing your quilt together by hand that's fine with me. Sewing quilts on the machine is so much faster that it never crossed my mind that someone might want to make a quilt the old-fashioned way. I may offer that option to everyone."

Caroline withdrew her hand and rose from the chair.

"Keep in mind, though, that sewing the blocks by hand takes longer, so you may fall behind during class and have to catch up on your own at home."

Sarah stood then pushed her chair under the table. "Mark did offer to let me practice sewing on one of these machines." A small thrill shivered through her as she remembered his touch during the demonstration of the sewing machine. "So I'm not sure which way I'll go with the project, but at least I know I can sew the quilt by hand, and I don't have to drop out of the class. See you next week."

Sarah practically bounced out of the workroom. Things seemed to going her way, and it showed by the spring in her step. Whether she sewed by hand or came in and tried to learn to machine sew, both would occupy her free time. *And I'll get to see Mark.* Sarah's thought widened her smile.

"What did you do that the teacher punished you by keeping you after class?" Mark stood by the cutting table in the center of the store.

Sarah chuckled at Mark's teasing and walked over to his work area. "Staying after was my choice. I wanted to make sure that I wouldn't be holding the class back with my lack of sewing abilities. Caroline assured me that I could be an authentic quilter and sew the blocks by hand if necessary. So I'll need to get my fabric picked out."

"No time like the present." Mark held his arms out wide. "You can have your own private shopping spree."

"Don't you close in fifteen minutes?" Sarah asked as she noted the only person in the store was Rodney, who rose from a chair in the sewing machine display area and walked to the back of the store.

Mark glanced at the clock that hung above the full glass door. "Yes I do, but if you know what you want, you can pick it out, and I'll get it measured and ready for you to pick up another time."

"Well. . ." Sarah paused, weighing her options. She did have the fabric narrowed down to two different patterned pieces and the solids to coordinate, but she hadn't quite decided between the two. "I think I'd better wait until I have more time to decide. I'll stop by after work some night this week."

"I'll be here. Unless it's Thursday. I'm on a men's bowling league that night."

Was that a subtle hint to come in the store when he was working? "I'll probably stop in tomorrow night after work, then."

"Where do you work?" Mark slipped a pair of scissors under the cutting counter.

"I'm employed by Card Leasing. I manage an office building in the new development area close to the junctions of Interstate 229 and Louise Avenue." Sarah adjusted her purse strap over her shoulder. "My office is in that building, not their downtown location."

"That area built up fast, didn't it?"

"Yes, Sioux Falls's landscape keeps growing and growing."

"Maybe if you stop by tomorrow night you'd—"

The door buzzer sounded, interrupting Mark. Sarah turned to see a frazzled-looking woman rush into the store.

Mark stepped around the cutting counter. "May I help you?"

"Thank goodness you're still open. Do you carry crochet thread? One of my children just told me they need it for a project at school tomorrow."

"I have a small supply over here because some quilters use it to tie their quilts together." Mark pointed to an area that held various types of thread.

He turned to Sarah with an apologetic expression, as if he'd broken a date, not left a thought dangling.

Sarah waved him off with her hand. "I'm sure I'll see you tomorrow. Good night."

"Good night." Mark's eyes held hers for precious seconds before he turned to follow his customer. Had disappointment flickered in his eyes? She'd been reluctant to leave, and now that reluctance was magnified by the emotion Mark conveyed with his eyes. Had he wanted to tell her something important?

Even though she didn't want to, Sarah knew it was time to go. It was too late to choose fabric, Mark had a customer, and he needed to close the store. Pivoting on one heel, Sarah turned and walked to the exit. She pushed through the door, triggering the buzzer that became muffled by the traffic noise as she crossed the threshold.

Pressing her key fob, her compact's headlights welcomed her as she walked toward the parking space. Once she opened her car door she couldn't resist one last glance at Mark through the plate glass windows of Granny Bea's.

To her surprise he stood by the door, visiting with Caroline and Rodney but watching her. He lifted a hand and waved good-bye.

She'd definitely stop by Granny Bea's to purchase her fabric tomorrow night. Slipping into her car, Sarah began to choose or eliminate outfits that she could wear tomorrow, a mental activity that still occupied her thoughts when she arrived home.

ª

Sarah managed to make the early bird Bible study at church even though she changed outfits three times before leaving her house. She'd settled on a short-sleeved royal-blue sheath that she accessorized with a black-, royal-, and white-striped silk scarf. Her black pumps polished her look and added height to her five-foot frame. Her wardrobe indecisions left her feeling rushed, and she couldn't shake it even though she'd pulled into the office parking lot with minutes to spare.

As Sarah walked toward the entrance, the mock-cherry trees surrounding the office building greeted her with their soft pink flowers. The light spring breeze wafted the petals' fragrance through the air, and their pollen-filled centers buzzed with activity.

She entered the building and unlocked her office door. The plush carpet cushioned each step as she walked across the short space to her cherrywood desk. After dropping her tote bag onto her office chair, she hurried to the adjacent room and worked her way down the wall lined with office equipment. She turned on the photocopy machine before checking the fax for any messages received after business hours. She straightened the staplers, paper clip holders, and pens on the counter then readied the postage meter for use that day.

The workroom doubled as a kitchenette. Once the business machines were ready, Sarah turned to the opposite wall and prepared a pot of coffee. Her company provided a photocopier, postage meter, conference room, coffeemaker, and a vending area for the business suites housed down the hall from her office. Of course, the cost to use the office machines was in addition to their rent, but for some start-up businesses this was a very attractive service since it kept their equipment costs down.

Sarah usually arrived about fifteen minutes early to get these tasks completed before the eight o'clock workday started for her clients. She had barely gotten everything up and running and her tote bag and purse into her desk drawer when Ashley Vetter burst through the door.

"Is the coffee ready?" Ashley stopped short and teetered on her stiletto heels. She inhaled. "It is. Remember those case study articles I told you about? My deadline is today at noon, and I was up half the night trying to finish them. I'm not complaining. Those writing gigs are paying the bills while I get established and start attracting clients. I just need to stop procrastinating until my deadlines."

"I think you mean socializing."

Ashley grinned over her shoulder as she strode toward the workroom.

Sarah followed her and stopped beside the coffeepot. "Has any of your advertising worked?" she asked. Ashley's lease was the first one Sarah landed in her building manager position, so she hoped Ashley's business would succeed.

"Not yet, but I am networking." Ashley poured the fresh coffee into Sarah's cup and then into her own insulated mug. She stuck the pot back on the heating element and clicked the lid on her cup. "People have told me that I'm crazy to be a freelance paralegal, but I want to be my own boss. Last night at the chamber event I think I made some good contacts. Plus I met a really cute guy."

Fresh out of college, Ashley had an idealistic outlook on life in general. "You seem to meet a cute guy once a week." Sarah laughed but she could see why the tall, lithe, and leggy Ashley was so popular.

Ashley shrugged her shoulders. "Well, as you know, most of them don't amount to more than one date. You're always so great to listen to my lovelorn tales." She put her arm over her face in fake distress. She peeked under her arm. "*Lovelorn* is an expression from your generation, right?" Her lips curled into a sly smile.

"Aren't you the funny one this morning. You know it's a little before my time." Sarah grinned before she took a sip of coffee.

Ashley leaned against the countertop in front of the coffeepot. "I hope this latest guy calls like he said he would. Not only is he cute, but he seemed to have substance, and I caught him glancing my way from time to time. That's usually a good indication that he's interested."

"Do you really think so?" Sarah sat down on a folding chair beside a small table. She smiled, remembering several of Mark's lingering looks the night before.

Ashley wrinkled her brow and narrowed her eyes. "Your voice sounds, I don't know, dreamy. Sarah, are you holding out on me? Is there a man in your life?"

Since she wasn't able to ask Karla's advice, maybe she should bounce it off Ashley. She'd been dying to talk about Mark. The occasional glances her way that turned into longer looks. The way his eyes shone when he looked at her. Feelings of happiness wanted to bubble out; still, she held them in.

Ashley's laugh bounced around the room. "There is someone. You're blushing just thinking about him."

"Well, there's someone I'm interested in, and I think he's interested in me, but I don't know for sure." Adolescent feelings of insecurity rushed back. She'd been younger than Ashley the last time she felt this way about a guy.

"Spill it, girlfriend." Ashley sipped her coffee.

Sarah hesitated. Ashley was almost twenty years her junior. Sarah had been a bad judge of character at that age.

"Is he someone in the building?" Ashley raised her eyebrows, prompting Sarah to answer.

"No." Sarah shook her head with more force than necessary, causing her dangly earrings to bounce against her jawbone. Somehow it didn't seem ethical to date one of her tenants.

Raising her cup and taking another sip of coffee, Ashley held Sarah's gaze. "Then who?" she asked, lowering her cup.

Sarah cleared her throat. She had to tell someone, and Ashley had confided in her. "His name is Mark Sanders, and he runs Granny Bea's quilt shop."

"That's why you enrolled in quilting lessons!" Ashley smiled wide.

"Kind of." Sarah shrugged but knew her own smile matched Ashley's. She'd save the other reason for another conversation.

Ashley made no move to head to her office. "Tell me about him."

Sarah checked her watch. She still had a few minutes until her official start time. "He's close to my age with brown hair."

"And?"

"He's about five foot eight or nine, wide shoulders, stocky frame."

Ashley kept smiling. "Is he cute?" Her voice raised a few octaves as she said the word *cute*.

"Yes." A thrill ran through Sarah, raising her voice to the same height as Ashley's. It felt good to express her feelings.

"So, I take it since you know his name, you've spoken with him." Ashley took another sip of her coffee.

"Of course, several times but nothing much more than small talk. However, I've caught him looking at me and his gaze lingers, and"—a flush crept onto Sarah's cheeks—"when he demonstrated a sewing machine, he held my hand to guide me through one of the instructions." The skin on Sarah's hand where Mark had touched her tingled. She shrugged. "I don't know, though. Maybe it's just me hoping I have the same effect on him as he does on me."

Ashley rolled her eyes. "Women know when a man's interested. We just need reassurance from our friends. You consider me a friend, right?"

Sarah nodded. The click of a door handle cut through the silence.

"Sarah?" Karla's footsteps padded across the carpet.

"In here," Sarah called.

Ashley straightened. "Time to get to work." She walked toward the door and nodded a greeting to Karla, who stood just outside the threshold. Ashley paused at the doorway and turned. "Sarah, he's interested in you."

In the second it took Ashley to disappear down the hall, Karla's jaw dropped. Her astonished expression caused Sarah's heart to plummet to her stomach. "Who's interested?"

Lifting her cup to her lips, Sarah gulped the last of her coffee, stalling for time.

As Sarah polished off the coffee, Karla crossed her arms over her chest and pursed her lips in disgust.

Sarah waved a dismissive hand in the air as she stood. "Nothing really."

The raised eyebrow and glaring stare told Sarah that Karla wasn't buying that explanation.

"Ashley and I were just trading girl talk about guys we've recently met and the signals they send that shows they're interested." Sarah smiled at Karla as she squeezed past her and walked over to her desk.

"When did you meet a guy?" Karla followed Sarah and seated herself in a guest chair.

Easing down in her office chair, Sarah slipped on her phone earpiece. "I met him while I was shopping." She tried to keep her tone casual, not filled with the giddiness she'd let slip when talking with Ashley about Mark.

"So, you're picking guys up at the mall now?" The sarcasm oozed from Karla's remark.

"No, I'm not picking up guys at the mall. Actually, you more than anyone know that I've never picked up a guy in my life." Sarah's response was clipped because she was tired of Karla's attitude.

Karla shrugged. "The old Sarah wouldn't have, but now it's like I don't know you anymore since your diagnosis."

I could say the same about you.

"Why didn't you tell me?" Karla leaned forward in her chair.

Sarah sighed. "I planned to talk to you about this last night but—"

"We had more serious matters to discuss," Karla interrupted. "That's why I'm here. I don't think you fully understand my concern for you."

Sarah's shoulders tightened. The tension crept up her neck. She rested her right elbow on her desk and massaged the muscles over that shoulder blade. The last thing she needed today was to deal with numbness in her right arm. She was so tired of this same conversation with Karla. Not to mention this wasn't the appropriate time or place to have it *again.* "I understand your concern."

"I don't think you do," Karla interjected. "You don't take anything I say seriously." She scooted to the edge of her chair and rested her forearms on her knees. "I googled MS and discovered it makes you fatigued. You need to rest. You're doing too much. A new job. A new hobby. And now I find out a new boyfriend." Karla rolled her eyes.

"Enough." Sarah raised her voice and rolled her right shoulder to keep the muscles loose. "This conversation is over. If you haven't noticed, I am at work. You might not think I need to work but I do. I'm managing my fatigue with medicine and it's working." *Most of the time.* Sarah paused, not for drama but to calm the burning anger her friend ignited.

"I'm very sorry to say this"—Sarah's voice now non-confrontational— "but unless you want to rent office space, you're going to have to leave. I have work to do."

Karla practically jumped out of her chair. "You're kicking me out?" She grabbed her purse and huffed over to the door. She opened it, paused, then glanced over her shoulder, all traces of her anger gone. "Sarah, be careful," she said, her tone now conversational. "Most guys have a hard time committing to a healthy woman, much less one who has to deal with health issues on a daily basis. I know you don't believe me, but I have your best interests at heart." With a small shrug of her shoulders and a weak smile, Karla closed the door behind her.

❧

Every car that pulled into a parking space caught Mark's eye. He'd been watching for a familiar black compact since five o'clock even though he knew if Sarah worked eight to five it'd take a good half hour or longer to get to Granny Bea's through the rush-hour traffic.

Mark replayed their conversation from the previous night as he reshelved bolts of material. He was certain she said she'd stop by after work, but six o'clock came and went. Still no Sarah.

Ding-dong. Mark jerked his head up, hoping it was Sarah that walked through the door. Disappointment tamped out his initial hope.

"What brings you to my store?" Mark pushed a bolt of fabric into place as he tried to get a grip on his feelings.

"It's that time of the year again." Diane Wall held up a large manila envelope. "How have you been?"

Mark met her halfway in the main aisle of the store. He admired the cut of her expensive business suit as he extended his hand. "Great. Once a sharp dresser, always a sharp dresser. You've never looked better."

Diane smiled at his compliment and shook the hand he offered. "Thank you. As cochair of the MS walk, I'm dropping your packet off for"—she tilted her head as she read the team's name written in black marker on the outside of the envelope—"Gert's Gang. I'm glad you continue to do this each year in honor of your mom."

"Well"—Mark took the information and peeked in at the contents—"old habits die hard, I guess." He'd considered stopping when his mom passed away, but she'd provided such a good life for him, all on her own, he decided to honor her memory by continuing to raise money to fight the disease that left her a struggling single mom.

"I guess." Diane shrugged. She twisted the pointed toe of her shoe. "I'm glad you're doing okay."

"Thanks." Mark knew that when Diane broke it off with him six months ago that she really thought they'd get back together. "How are things going for you?"

Diane held up her left hand and wiggled her ring finger. A large princess-cut diamond sparkled under the fluorescent store lights.

"Congratulations." His dating theory did work—she'd found her true love.

"Thank you." Diane held her hand out and admired her ring. "Well," she said, putting her hand down, "I'm sure I'll see you at the walk." She headed to the exit, her high heels clicking on the polished gray tiled floor.

Mark folded the flap of the envelope closed and held it between his fingers. "Thanks again for dropping this off." He walked to the cash register.

Diane stopped and glanced over her shoulder. "Are you seeing anyone special?"

Mark shrugged. Diane shook her head and pushed through the door. She held it open so another customer could enter. Relief swirled through Mark.

"Thanks." Sarah smiled her gratitude to the woman then snagged a cart and stashed her purse where a child should sit.

"There you are. I thought you were going to be a no-show." Mark greeted Sarah with a wide smile.

Pushing the cart with a slow pace, Sarah stopped in front of the cash register. "I made up some time at work."

"Long day?" Mark asked. Although Sarah's attire remained wrinkle-free, her body seemed to have lost its starch. It looked as if it took all her energy to take the next step. Instead of maintaining her usually erect posture, she leaned on the cart. Dullness replaced the usual sparkle in her eyes.

"That is an understatement." She raised tired eyes to meet his. "How was your day?"

"Pretty busy up until an hour ago." Mark tapped the envelope on the counter by the cash register to give his hands something to do. "Unhappy renter? Would it help to talk about it? I'm a good listener."

A slight twinkle appeared in Sarah's eyes at his offer. "It was a personal matter, nothing to do with work." She sighed, her mouth turning into a frown. "I'm pretty sure a longtime friendship is ending."

He knew it. A bad breakup. He could read the signs from a mile away. Who would let a good-looking lady like Sarah get away? *I would.* Mark sobered at the thought that was surely brought on by Diane's visit. "That happens sometimes."

"I guess." Sarah shrugged with what looked like great effort.

Mark could fix this. Maybe not tonight, but in the near future. He'd bring her self-confidence back so she could go out and face the dating world and find the elusive fairy tale all women seemed to believe in as exampled by Diane's recent engagement. She'd apparently found true love.

"Well, you're here now, and among friends, well, friend." Mark grinned.

Sarah managed a crooked smile. Some of the normal sparkle returned to her coal-colored eyes. "Yes, I am." She sighed. "I should probably pick out my fabric."

Mark abandoned the envelope beside the cash register and rounded the end of the counter. "Mind if I tag along while you pick out your material?"

"Company would be nice. I could use a distraction." Sarah's stance straightened as she pushed the cart, but her pace remained slow as she made her way down an aisle.

Her flowery fragrance lured Mark closer to the cart as they walked to the back corner of the quilt shop. "Are you making a wall quilt or table runner?" As they passed by the section with heavier-weight material, Mark straightened a bolt of denim someone had pulled forward.

"I planned on a wall quilt, but since I might be doing all the sewing by hand, I'm thinking maybe I should go with the table runner." Sarah stopped the cart in front of patterned cotton fabric.

"What did I tell you?" Mark waited for Sarah to look at him. "You can use my extra machines anytime."

"I know." Sarah pulled the paper with fabric requirements for the class from her purse. "And that's very generous of you, but. . ." Sarah's voice trailed off.

"No buts about it. Those machines sit in the workroom and only get used during quilting class, so don't worry about it."

Sarah pulled her pretty mouth into a pucker. Was she considering his offer to use the machines or thinking about telling him to back off? Her grip tightened on the cart. "Here's the thing. Will it really help to use the machines, if I don't know how to sew? I mean, I don't want to ruin my fabric, ripping out mistakes."

Mark crossed his arms over his chest and rocked back on his heels. "I see your point."

"So it's settled. I'll sew my quilt by hand and make the table runner."

"Hmm. Tell you what." Mark dropped his arms and crossed the sales floor to a book display. He couldn't let her get out of coming into the quilt store so easily. He pulled out a hardbound book and returned to the spot where Sarah stood. "I happen to have in my possession a manual on sewing basics." He held it out for Sarah to see.

Sarah took the book and turned it over. Her eyes focused on the bottom left-hand corner.

"You don't have to buy it. Use it when you come into the store to practice on the sewing machines. And you can practice on remnant fabric."

"You're making it hard for a girl to say no." Sarah lifted her turmoil-filled eyes to search his face. It appeared as if she wanted to say yes, but something was keeping her from it, something other than the fact that she lacked sewing skills.

The last thing he wanted to do was scare her away. "I'm just saying, if you want a wall quilt, make one. Don't let a tiny obstacle like not having expert sewing skills get in the way."

Sarah laughed. "Tiny obstacle?"

Mark shrugged. "It's all a matter of perspective."

For a few seconds Sarah drew her brows together, and then a smile lit her face. "Okay, I'm convinced. I'll make the wall quilt." She handed the book back to Mark.

The jangle of the door alerted Mark to another customer. He shelved the sewing book and greeted his customer. By the time he turned his attention back to Sarah, she and her fabric bolts were waiting patiently by the cutting center.

"Ready?" Mark slid a bolt of light blue paisley fabric toward him.

"Yes." Sarah ran her finger down the paper with the fabric requirements for the wall quilt. "I need three yards of that one."

Mark flipped the bolt over several times, releasing the tightly bound fabric before he grabbed the cut end of the cloth and stretched a length of material over the yardstick attached to the Formica-topped cutting counter. His sharp shears whooshed down the material, cutting it loose from the bolt.

"A yard of each of the light blue and white." Sarah pushed the solid bolts of cotton to Mark.

"This will make a pretty quilt. The paisley's the back and part of the block pattern, right?"

Sarah nodded her head. "Is that the name of the fabric's pattern— paisley? I just thought it was tear shaped and fitting for a Job's Tears quilt."

"Guess I never saw that in the paisley pattern. But you're right. Some of the print is tear shaped." Mark slid the cut fabric to the side. "That it?"

"No." Sarah handed Mark another bolt. It was from the clearance area with preprinted Christmas pillow panels. "The printed instructions on the fabric make this pillow project sound easy. Would a project like this help me learn to sew?"

"It would." Mark cut on the solid black line to cut the panel from the bolt.

"When is a good night for me to come in and practice?" Sarah's eyes shone in spite of the dark circles that underscored them.

He bowled tomorrow, and Friday at four started the first weekend he'd had off in six weeks. Mark wanted to be in the store when Sarah came in to practice.

"Monday?" Some of the glow started to diminish from Sarah's face. Mark added hurriedly, "I'm sure you're busy Friday night."

"No." Sarah shook her head.

"Friday it is." Mark didn't really have any plans anyway. He could hang around the store.

Chapter 3

Mark sat in his office, surfing the Internet, when the workroom illuminated. He swiveled in his chair and caught a glimpse of Sarah through the glass window. Dressed in hip-hugger jeans and a white T-shirt, she carried a denim tote bag. Sarah walked to the demonstration machine Mark showed her how to work on Tuesday night.

Sarah laid her tote bag on the table and studied the sewing machine. She reached a finger out and touched the power button. Light reflected on the arm of the sewing machine, and Sarah pulled a fist back and forth in a victory fashion.

When she looked up, Mark waved. Sarah wiggled her fingers. Her sheepish smile conveyed her embarrassment at being caught celebrating her success at remembering how to turn on the sewing machine.

Mark rounded the corner of the door. "Hi."

Sarah giggled. "No one was supposed to see that."

"What else do you remember?" Mark watched the extra flush on Sarah's cheeks brighten the sparkle in her eyes as he crossed the room. No sign of the smudges of darkness that half-mooned her eyes on Wednesday.

Sarah lowered to the chair. "This is where I choose the stitch I want to sew with and this"—Sarah expertly lifted the lever behind the arm of the sewing machine—"lifts the presser foot."

"A quick learner."

"Remembering how to work the machine isn't really sewing." Sarah gave the machine a good once-over. "For example, how do you make it work after you turn it on?"

They hadn't gotten that far the other night. "You run the machine with the foot feed on the floor, or some people put it beside the machine and use their forearm. Would you like me to demonstrate the machine for you?"

"I would, but do you have time? I don't want to take you away from your business."

"Actually, my sales floor shift ended at four. I stuck around to do some special orders." Not a lie. He'd placed two special orders while he waited for Sarah to arrive. Mark held up a finger. "I'll be back in a minute."

On the sales floor, Mark grabbed some lavender fabric from the remnant bin and a spool of black thread. He'd found when demonstrating the machines that dark thread on light fabric allowed the customer a better view of the stitches.

"Mark, didn't you want to take this to your office?" Terri, one of his part-timers, held the MS envelope in the air.

"Thanks." Mark took the envelope from Terri.

Back in the workroom, Sarah had apparently pulled her Christmas project out of her tote bag while she waited for Mark to return.

"Do you have scissors in your bag?" Mark asked, dropping the envelope on the front table.

"Yes." Sarah peeked in her bag and retrieved them.

"We'll practice on this fabric." Mark took the scissors Sarah offered. He cut the wrapper off the lavender material then scooted another chair close to the sewing machine and patted the seat. "Mind switching?"

"Not at all." Sarah slid from one chair seat to the other.

Once seated, Mark ripped the cellophane covering off the spool of thread. "This is how you thread this machine." Aware of his adeptness at this task, Mark took his time putting the thread on the spool holder and pulling it through the necessary path to the needle.

Sarah stood so she could have a clearer view. "Looks easy enough." She smiled at Mark.

"Since you just want to practice a straight stitch, that's all I'm going to show you."

Sarah leaned forward and peered around Mark. "That is the stitch the machine is set to sew." The light scent of her perfume teased him to move closer.

"See, you are a quick learner." Mark closed his eyes and breathed deeply, filling his memory with the flowery scent. Sarah's scent.

Sarah sat back, and the pleasant fragrance drifted away from him. Mark wanted to follow the fading bouquet the same way hungry cartoon characters used to follow an animated cloud of food aroma into trouble.

As if on cue, Mark's stomach rumbled. He cleared his throat. "Excuse me."

"Am I keeping you from your dinner?"

"Not really, I just had an early lunch." Mark reached for the lavender cotton material. A long, low growl cut through the silence in the room.

Sarah placed her hand on his, stopping his movement. "Mark, you're hungry. You don't have to stay and demonstrate the machine. I'll get the manual and try to figure it out myself."

Her concern showed not only on her face but in her voice. It melted Mark's heart. Why would any man lucky enough to be Sarah's type break it off with her? Anger toward her unknown ex-boyfriend sparked in Mark. The unexpected emotion shocked him back to the moment.

"I'm serious." Sarah's silky hand patted his before pulling away.

"Okay, I admit it. I'm hungry but. . ." He should have run out for an afternoon snack before she arrived. He didn't want to leave to go get dinner now because it was evident that Sarah planned to stay and practice. How would he explain leaving and coming back when he already told her that his shift had ended? Plus on Wednesday night he'd intended to ask her to dinner, but his last-minute customer had interrupted and Mark had lost his nerve.

"But what? I'm sure I can figure this out." Doubt flickered through Sarah's dark eyes as her gaze left his and rested on the sewing machine.

"I promised to help you." Mark didn't intend on breaking this promise. After all, Sanders men only broke big promises, not little ones. "Have you eaten dinner yet?"

"No." Sarah never took her eyes off the sewing machine.

"I could order a pizza." Mark hoped Sarah would go for his idea. "We could continue the demonstration while we wait for it to be delivered."

Happiness skipped through Mark's heart when Sarah's eyes met his and she nodded. "I'd like that."

The squeak of the folding chair's legs reverberated through the room as Mark stood. "What do you like on your pizza?"

"Anything and everything."

"I'll be right back." With a quick flick of his wrist, Mark pulled the thread off the sewing machine and handed it to Sarah. "Try rethreading the machine while I'm gone. If you succeed, go ahead and celebrate."

Sarah gave him a lopsided grin as she took the thread.

Once back in his office, Mark, looking through the wall window, watched Sarah thread the machine as he ordered the pizza. When she looked up and saw that he was watching, she smirked, fisted her hand, and pulled it back in victory. Mark erupted in laughter, confusing the pizza place employee on the other end of the line.

Mark came back into the workroom. "Pizza is ordered." He checked the machine. "Victory celebration deserved. Now I'll show you how to wind the bobbin."

By the time the pizza was delivered, Sarah had practiced sewing a straight stitch several times. Mark placed the pizza on the first table in the workroom, along with two cans of soda and napkins.

"I think I'll do a few more practice runs then start on my pillow." Sarah moved from the folding chair in front of the sewing machine to a folding chair across the table from Mark.

He lifted the lid of the pizza box.

"That smells great. What'd you order?"

"All meat." Mark used a plastic fork to serve Sarah a piece of pizza. She placed it in front of her then clasped her hands and lowered her eyes. Mark hadn't prayed before meals since his mom passed away. Not because he wasn't a believer. He'd just gotten out of the habit. Following Sarah's good example, Mark bowed his head.

Thank You, Lord, for this nourishment and the blessings of new friends. Amen.

That felt good. He'd have to remember to say grace more often. Mark lifted his eyes to find Sarah patiently waiting for him to finish.

She smiled. "Next time we'll have to say grace out loud." She lifted her pizza to her lips.

Mark retrieved a piece of pizza for himself. *Next time.* That was a good sign.

"What's Gert's Gang?"

He raised his eyebrows in question as he chewed a bite of pizza. Had he been daydreaming and lost a thread of conversation?

Sarah used her pizza slice like a pointer, motioning toward the envelope lying on the table.

"Oh." Mark sipped his soda before he continued. "That's a team packet for the MS walk. My mom had MS. A few relatives and friends still participate to raise money in her honor. Her name's Gertrude Sanders."

"Your mom had MS."

Sarah's comment was barely audible. Or was it a question? Mark couldn't tell. Her eyes focused on the envelope, and her expression sobered.

"Pardon me?" Mark searched Sarah's face as she turned her attention back to him.

She cleared her throat. "You said she *had* MS."

"She passed away two years ago from"—Mark looked down, breaking Sarah's compassion-filled gaze—"natural causes."

"I'm sorry." Mark's forearm warmed where Sarah rested her palm.

"Thank you." He lifted his eyes.

Sarah patted his arm. "Tell me about her."

Disbelief swirled through Mark. None of the other women he'd dated since his mother's death had asked that question. They talked about themselves, and he let them. It was all part of his dating system.

"It's okay if you're not ready." Sarah had apparently mistaken his silence as reluctance.

"No, it's okay. I don't mind talking about her." Mark smiled.

Sometimes Sarah reminded him of his mom. Not in looks or stature but in her gentle caring way. The Christian way, his mom always said—putting others first.

Sarah slid a slice of pizza from the box and offered it to Mark. His previous thought and her action widened his smile.

"We moved in with my grandma Bea when I was five, and Mom opened a tailor and sewing business in the basement. She was a good seamstress, and it didn't take long until she had quite a clientele list."

The lilt of Sarah's laughter filled the room. "I'm sorry to interrupt, but no wonder you looked so shocked when I said I didn't know how to sew." The crinkles around Sarah's eyes deepened when she laughed, and merriment shone from her dark eyes.

Mark chuckled. "I have to admit most of the women I grew up around sewed—my grandma, my mom, our neighbors Caroline and her mom. I was literally surrounded."

"Is that why you run a fabric and quilt shop? Because of the ladies in your life?"

"Actually, I inherited it from Mom. When her tailoring business grew, she opened a fabric store."

"Where did the quilting come in?" Sarah crinkled her napkin in her fist and lifted her soda can.

"Mom decided she needed a quiet hobby to help her cope with her MS. She ended up with lots of scrap fabric from her tailoring business, so she began quilting."

Sarah's eyes widened, then she began to cough. She lowered the soda can and covered her mouth with her napkin.

"Are you okay?" Mark pushed his chair back and started to rise.

"I'm fine." Sarah spoke through the napkin. "Just went down wrong."

"Are you sure?"

Sarah nodded. Mark lowered to the chair.

"Do you mind my asking how old your mom was when she was diagnosed with MS?"

"Not at all. Twenty-five. Tell me about your parents." Mark grabbed another piece of pizza from the box.

"They live in Brookings. Dad's a retired professor at South Dakota State University and Mom's a legal secretary. Three more years and she'll retire, too. Believe me, she's counting the days. They plan to do a lot of traveling."

"Good for them."

"I think so, too. My older brother and his family live in California. Do you have siblings?"

Mark shook his head as he stood. "Would you like any more pizza?"

"No, thank you."

He closed the lid on the pizza box and slid it to the end of the table. "I'll put it here so I remember to take it home." He gathered their used napkins and the soda cans and walked to the waste can.

"What's your dad like?"

Mark stopped midstep. He never got used to answering this question. He turned and shrugged. "I don't know. He left when I was five."

❧

Sarah leaned back to avoid the steam as she poured boiling water into her china teapot. In seconds the clear water turned pale brown and fragrant as the liquid released the flavors and aroma of the dried tea leaves. Her mom would be here any minute with their once-a-week calorie splurge—bakery cinnamon rolls.

After transferring a wicker tray filled with her pansy-patterned tea service from the counter to the kitchen table, Sarah yawned and stretched. She'd spent a fitful night reliving her question to Mark. Not because of the answer she'd received when she asked about his dad—that he'd deserted his family. It was the timing involved.

It didn't take a genius to do the math. His dad must've left the same time Mark's mom was diagnosed with multiple sclerosis. Karla's cruel remark about men not committing to a woman with health problems had instantly echoed through her mind at Mark's admission. Karla's haunting statement kept Sarah wary of her and Mark's actions the remainder of the night. Was it flirting or friendly banter? She didn't want to mislead him like she'd been misled so many years ago. When she told him that she had MS, would he prove Karla right? Would his interest in her wane?

"I hope not. I like Mark." Happiness tickled her heart at her verbal acknowledgment.

Sarah smiled and traced the lettering on the Granny Bea's bag lying on the table. She trusted God just like Job had, that good could come out of her situation, and that might include Mark. She hoped it included Mark.

The roar of a car engine overtook the chirping birds and neighborhood sounds filtering through the open kitchen window, announcing her mom's arrival. Sarah opened the back door and waved a welcome to her mother.

Dressed in skinny jeans and a long blue T-shirt, her mom appeared ten years younger than her actual age. She pecked Sarah's cheek as she passed through the doorway. "How are you, dear?"

"Fine, a little tired. I didn't sleep well last night." Sarah looked down at her grungy but comfortable exercise outfit, wishing she'd inherited her mom's casual dress style. Sarah closed the door and took a seat at the table.

"Is it from your MS?" Her mother set the bakery box in the center of the table, slid her purse from her shoulder, and stashed it on an empty chair as she sat across the table from Sarah.

"No, something was bothering me. But if I don't take a nap the loss of sleep might aggravate my symptoms."

"I worry that you're doing too much." Her mom added a lump of sugar to each cup and poured the hot tea over it.

Sarah reached for the saucer and carefully placed it in front of her. "Not you, too." Sarah punctuated her sentence with a sigh as she reached over and snagged a cinnamon roll.

Her mother scooted back into her chair. "What do you mean?"

Sarah leaned forward, resting her elbow on the table and her chin in her hand. "Karla's against my job, my hobby, and. . ."

Her mother's raised eyebrows prompted Sarah to continue.

"My interest in a gentleman." Sarah pinched a bite off the cinnamon roll and nibbled on it while she watched her mother's reaction.

Her mother pursed her lips and narrowed her eyes. "We'll get back to him later. How against everything is Karla?"

"Enough that it's straining our relationship."

"That's too bad. You've been friends since kindergarten. Is it really a strain or just a difference of opinion?"

Sarah watched her mother bite into her roll. "It's a vehement difference of opinion, and she just won't let the subject matter die. She wants me to agree with her and I can't. She thinks I shouldn't be working and wants me to quit my job."

"Well"—her mother nodded her head—"she has a valid point there. It's stressful and tiring learning a new job. You should have considered that when you were searching for a different career."

"What?" Although every fiber of her being wanted to jump up from her chair, Sarah remained seated. "You agree with Karla?" Her tone reflected her outrage; then it clicked. Sarah narrowed her eyes. "Did Karla call you?"

Her mother held up her palm. "Hear me out. She's concerned about you, and so am I. You should have looked for part-time office work so you'd have more time to rest."

"I already have too much free time to think about my future with MS. That's why I took up quilting, to occupy my mind with something other than my illness." Sarah took a drink of her tea. The lukewarm liquid did little to calm the anger shaking her insides.

"I don't understand why Karla's upset by that one. It's a nice sedentary activity."

Sarah rolled her eyes and pushed her roll away, no longer excited for her weekly treat. "I didn't choose quilting because it was sedentary. I wanted to create something beautiful. I think you and Karla should attend one of my MS support groups. They encourage you to remain active as long as possible."

Her mother answered with a shrug then sipped her tea. "Now, what's this about a love interest?"

"He's not a love interest." *Just a possibility.* "Mark is an acquaintance that I'm getting to know better."

"Well, don't rush into anything." Her mother's features softened as she reached across the table and clasped Sarah's hand. "Promise me that you'll really get to know him before you get involved."

"I promise." She'd never repeat her past mistake when it came to love.

"And be honest about your MS." Her mom pulled her hand away.

Sarah sighed then nodded.

"I'm your mother, and I love you and don't want to see you hurt. Now probably isn't the best time to get involved with someone. Some men can't handle being a caregiver, at any age." Concern shone in her mother's eyes.

Maybe "some men," but Mark seemed different. After all, he helped his mother. Sarah looked at the Granny Bea's bag at the other end of the table. She'd been drawn to the Job's Tears quilt pattern because she wanted a visual reminder that if you accepted the good from God, you must accept the bad. She hadn't planned the people closest to her would expect her to give up, just like Job's friends and family.

❧

Mark squinted to read the thread number on the end of the spool. *Probably should invest in some cheap readers.* He pushed the thread into the display holder. First his hairline receded, now his eyesight was getting bad. What would be next—his knees?

On Saturday afternoon, he'd toyed with the idea of calling Sarah for a last-minute date. The gorgeous April temperatures beckoned him outside. He'd heard the falls were rushing from the spring snowmelt and thought maybe Sarah would like to take a walk through Falls Park with him. She'd listed her phone number on the class registration, but that was for emergencies, like a class cancellation. In the end, Mark felt it might be an unethical use of the form. Besides, it was easier to say no over the phone, so he planned to ask her tomorrow night before or after class, whichever time worked better.

The jangle of the door buzzer echoed through the room. "Be with you in a minute," Mark called as he shelved another spool of thread. He lifted the empty thread box and turned. Sarah stood at the end of the aisle.

Delight replaced Mark's dismay of the aging process from seconds ago.

"Hi. I came to practice before tomorrow night." Apprehension dotted Sarah's features as she held up her tote bag. "I'm going to start my pillow."

The soft pink blouse she wore complemented the rosy glow of her skin. The hoops of her dangly earrings and sandal straps matched the color of her shirt, dressing up her denim crop pants.

"As good as you did on Friday night, I'm sure you'll finish the pillow tonight." He used the empty box to motion toward the back of the store. "After you."

"I don't really think I'll need your help tonight." Sarah glanced over her shoulder.

Mark's balloon of happiness popped. He liked being in the same room as Sarah. He liked being able to help her learn something new. He liked being needed.

"That didn't sound quite right. I appreciate the instructions you gave me on Friday." Sarah stopped in the darkened workroom doorway and turned to face Mark. "I'd just like to try this on my own tonight." Her voice held a determination that didn't match her expression.

"Excuse me." Mark reached around Sarah and flicked the light switch. He momentarily closed his eyes to savor her flowery perfume before backing up to allow her entry into the room. "You want to test your skill?"

"Exactly." Sarah smiled. "I feel confident when you're right beside me, but you won't be in class with me tomorrow night."

Mark followed Sarah into the workroom. "I understand." He did, too, but that didn't stop the searing disappointment of not being able to stay close to Sarah. Have a conversation with her. Ask her out. Mark watched Sarah turn on the sewing machine and pull her project from her bag.

Aware of his hesitation, he turned to take the box to the garbage can when he saw the Gert's Gang envelope that he'd forgotten to take home. He walked over to the table and picked it up.

"Mark." Sarah stepped closer to the table. "I meant to ask you the other night if you accept new members in Gert's Gang. I'm going to participate in the MS walk and thought it might be more fun to have people to walk with."

"Sure! The more the merrier." Joy fueled Mark's exuberant response. Why hadn't he thought of inviting her to join their group last Friday night? This meant more time to spend with Sarah. Mark opened the envelope to pull out an individual pledge sheet.

"Thanks for doing this, Sarah." He handed her the paper. "The money that walkers bring in goes a long way in helping with MS research."

"That's good." Sarah took the offered paper. "I have a personal interest in multiple sclerosis."

"Me, too, but you already know that." Mark smiled at Sarah.

"Do you mind if I ask you another question about your mom?" Sarah's dangly earrings swayed with a slight tilt of her head.

"Not at all." Mark put the envelope and box on the table. He crossed his arms over his chest and rocked back on his heels.

"How did MS affect your mom's quality of life? Obviously, she worked." Sarah looked around the room. "But did she work full-time?"

As soon as she asked the question, Sarah's stance changed. Oddly, she looked braced, as if she expected Mark to deliver devastating news.

"Yes, she did. Mom stayed very active despite her symptoms. They didn't have all the treatment options available then, either. She started a quilting circle at our church, was a room mother when I was in school, and was involved in a businesswoman's association, in addition to running the house and business." The more Mark talked the more elated Sarah appeared. She placed her hand over her heart and sighed. Her smile was so wide that it narrowed her eyes. Mark felt himself scowl at Sarah's strange reaction to his answer.

She didn't seem to notice. "That's wonderful." She looked at the ceiling and sighed again. "Just wonderful." Then she closed her eyes.

Aware that his scowl deepened, Mark quickly relaxed his face before Sarah opened her eyes. The last thing he wanted to do was offend her.

When Sarah opened her eyes, serenity replaced the apprehension that had lurked in her features. "That really is very encouraging to hear."

"Granny Bea and I did help her quite a bit, but she was very courageous handling her disease." *Unlike the coward who left her alone to struggle.* Mark caught himself before he snorted to emphasize his thought. That might be hard to explain to Sarah.

"She was lucky to have you two."

"Well"—Mark shrugged—"that's what family does, I guess." *Blood family, that is.* He hated thinking about the man that walked out on his mother when she needed him the most. It reminded him that he was a Sanders man and, if he was tested, might find out he had a yellow streak, too. A test Mark never planned to take.

"Are you okay?" Sarah's smile faded.

Mark pushed the depressing truth from his mind. "Yes, it's just that some memories are not always good ones."

Sarah shook her head absently, her dangly earrings shimmering in the light. "I'm learning that."

Great. He'd made her think of her recent breakup. He'd never understand why some guy would dump Sarah. This was an excellent opportunity for him to step in and start building her self-confidence. "Sarah, I had a nice time on Friday night, and I was wondering if you'd like to go out with me sometime." The practiced words tumbled out as nervous tension kicked in. Why had that happened? Nerves never came into play when he asked a lady out, because he never took it personally if she turned him down.

Sarah's eyes widened at the surprise turn in conversation. Her face softened and her eyes sparkled. "I'd love to."

Who would give up a woman that beamed with happiness? "Great. Does Sunday afternoon work for you?"

"It does." Sarah affirmed her answer with a nod and ran her fingers over the sign-up form she held.

"I almost forgot." Mark pointed to the paper. "Fill that out and, as captain of the team, I'll give you a packet for donations."

"Okay. Can I bring it back tomorrow night?" Sarah studied the form.

"Sure. Do you mind if I ask you who it is you're walking for?"

Sarah raised her eyes and stared straight into Mark's for a few seconds. "I'm walking for me. I have MS."

Chapter 4

I have MS." The quiet of the workroom ate up Sarah's admission, yet her words jumbled in Mark's mind as if he stood in a canyon, trying to decipher an echo.

Sarah has multiple sclerosis. The words started to register. Mark knew he should reach out to her. Pull her into a tight hug. Tell her everything would work out, but in true Sanders men fashion, his feet remained planted to the floor like a dead tree's roots in fertile soil.

Wide eyed, Sarah searched his face. He needed to say something to break the awkward silence that ensued after her statement. Should he say it'd be all right, when he knew the long, sometimes pain-filled road ahead of her?

Two deep lines formed between her brows. Panic forced the air from his lungs. No wonder she'd asked so many questions about his mother. How had he missed the signs?

Stupid question. He allowed himself to give in to attraction, that's how.

He hung his head. *Look at her.* He snapped his head back up. He didn't want her thinking that her disease made her unattractive because nothing could make Sarah unattractive. *Say something.*

"I'm, um, s—s—sorry to hear that."

Sarah blinked rapidly at his stammered response. He didn't see tears, but that was a sure sign they'd be coming. What would he do if she started to cry? He strained his ears, listening for the door buzzer. He needed a valid excuse, like a customer, to leave the room. His gut twisted. Why was he born a Sanders?

Sarah continued to frown; then she pulled her puckered mouth to the side as if she were contemplating a response.

Mark cleared his throat. He crossed his arms and rocked back on his heels. This time the Sanders genetics wouldn't win. He'd stay and face this difficult conversation. Mark forced reassurance into his voice.

"Sarah, I know your diagnosis may feel devastating, but they've made great medical strides in the treatment of MS, thanks to contributions from activities like this walk." He tapped his fingers on the heavy paper of the envelope. The contents rattled, emphasizing his point. "You'll have a better chance at managing the disease than my mom."

Sarah's gaze dropped to the envelope. She nodded before raising her eyes to his. Her black eyes bore into him. Could she see through his facade? That it was in his genetics to cut and run in times like these?

"And that's why it's great that you continue to support fund-raisers like the walk." Sarah smiled as she stepped closer. She laid her hand over his crossed arms. "I'm sorry that I dropped my diagnosis on you like that. I didn't even consider it might bring up memories of your mom."

What? She thought she'd hurt his feelings? The moisture that formed in her eyes wasn't from anguish over her diagnosis but empathy for him.

Sarah's kind words and silky touch started a reverberation deep in his heart.

"Don't be sorry." Emotion rasped his voice. He didn't deserve the apology. She did.

The jangle of the door announced the arrival of a customer. Sarah squeezed his forearm and slid her hand down his skin, releasing their contact. "I'd better get started on my project."

Mark nodded, not trusting his voice. His emotions had betrayed him once already. He turned and left the workroom.

As he walked to the cash register area, an older lady smiled his way. He watched his customer pick through the fat-quarter bin as Sarah's workroom confession played over and over in his mind like a skipped record.

"I have MS." "I have MS." He'd missed so many signs. The dark half-mooned eyes mirrored his mom's whenever she'd powered through the fatigue caused by the disease. The shuffling of Sarah's feet when she pushed the cart the other night. And then she thought—

"I'm ready to check out."

The impatient tone shocked Mark from his thoughts. The elderly lady stood in front of the cash register. Her pinched brows and pursed lips emphasized her irritation. How long had she stood right in front of him?

"Sorry." Mark pushed his thoughts of Sarah to the back of his mind. He picked up the elderly woman's items that lay on the short counter, ready to be rung up.

Shaken by Sarah's revelation, he'd failed to greet this customer when he came back to the sales floor. Not good business. "Did you find everything all right?"

"I did."

"We have a new special on Tuesdays after five—buy one yard of clearance fabric, get the second yard half-price." Mark slipped a pink flyer advertising his Tuesday night special into his customer's bag as she swiped her card and entered her PIN.

The register spit out the store receipt. He handed it to the customer. "Thank you. Stop in again." He said the words automatically, knowing they were void of his usual sincerity when dealing with a store patron.

He pinched his eyes shut as the door jangled the customer's exit. Sarah's face filled his memory. Why did God keep striking good women with this disease? The concern she showed for him, although undeserved, twisted his heart. He should have been comforting her. He wanted to comfort her, but something held him back. Something beyond his control—his heritage. He clenched his fists in anger.

When he opened his eyes, Sarah stood beside the checkout counter. "Don't let a cranky customer get to you." She pulled at her left earring and looked out the plate glass window, trying to catch a glance of who might have been in the store.

Unbelievable that Sarah was worried about him. "It's not that." Mark shrugged. "Long day."

"Too long to give me your opinion?" Sarah smiled as she held up a twelve-by-twelve square panel. "How'd I do?"

Mark took the fabric square from her. "Well, you sewed the right sides together and left an end open to stuff it. That's a good sign."

"Only because"—holding up numbered instructions that she'd cut from the panel, Sarah pointed and giggled—"the instructions show it that way. I'd never have given a thought as to which way the fabric should face when sewn together."

Mark chuckled. Sarah's face glowed with merriment as she admitted her ineptness as a seamstress.

"I wanted you to check my seams."

Mark whacked his head with his palm. "I forgot to show you how to follow the guide by the presser foot." He held the pillow top at eye level and inspected the seams.

"I followed the straight line on the fabric." Sarah pointed to a strip on the outside border of the printed picture of an old-fashioned ice-skating scene.

"Good job." Mark turned the square and looked at the next section. "Really, Sarah, you did well for your first time. Just a few swerves from the straight line, but once you stuff it with a pillow, I doubt anyone will notice."

"The corners were hard."

Mark smoothed the fabric on the counter. "It looks like you tried to round them." He glanced up at Sarah.

She shook her head.

"All you needed to do is stop in the corner,"—Mark pointed to the fabric—"leave your needle in the fabric, lift the presser foot, and turn the fabric like this." Mark used his finger to demonstrate the turn. "Next time you come in to practice, I'll show you."

"I thought you didn't know how to sew." Sarah's eyes narrowed as she grinned.

"Just enough to demonstrate the machines I sell." Mark winked at Sarah and handed her the pillow top.

Sarah turned the panel right side out and finger pressed the edges. Intent on the task at hand, she cleared her throat. "I know we'll see each other before Sunday, but can we firm up the time for our date?"

The date! Pink painted Sarah's cheeks when she lifted a tentative gaze to Mark, waiting for his reply. He'd been so focused on Sarah's condition that he'd forgotten he'd asked her out. Was her diagnosis the reason her previous love dumped her? Anger prickled Mark's insides at the thought. Who'd do that? In an instant his mind answered his question. *A Sanders man.*

Mark's eyes met Sarah's. He should stop this now. Tell her that he was out of line, asking her out. Explain about his dad. His heart pounded at the thought of hurting her feelings, but better now than later. He drew in a deep, steadying breath. He had to break the date.

Anticipation sparkled in Sarah's dark eyes, melting Mark's resolve.

"Sure, what time works best for you?"

Sarah stuffed her pillow top into her denim tote bag. "Early afternoon?"

"I'll pick you up at one."

"Okay." Sarah looked around the counter. "If you have a pen, I'll write down my address."

Mark slid a pen and paper toward Sarah, even though he had her address on the class sign-up sheet.

Sarah wrote out the relevant information then pushed the paper and pen back to Mark. "All set, then." She pulled her car keys from her bag. "I'll see you tomorrow night."

Mark stepped around the counter. "Not so fast. I'll walk you to your car."

"My car is right there." Sarah pointed to her compact parked in the spot in front of the quilt shop door. She held her key fob and pressed a button.

"I know." Mark pulled the door open. His bell and Sarah's car horn clamored for attention. He held his palm up, indicating to Sarah to pass through the door.

"Thank you," Sarah said then stopped by the bumper of her car.

"You're welcome." Mark stepped off the curb, opened her car door, and waited for Sarah to slip into the seat. "Now you can say it."

"See you tomorrow night." Sarah giggled as she inserted the key into the ignition.

"Can't wait." Mark closed the car door and stepped back onto the curb. Before heading back into the store, he watched Sarah back out of the parking spot and turn into the street.

He lined up carts then walked through the store, straightening fabric bolts. He'd fully intended on breaking their date, but Sarah looked so happy and beautiful, he just couldn't bring himself to hurt her. *Besides, it appears that she's been hurt enough.*

And maybe, just maybe, his dating theory could do double duty for Sarah. He could give her self-confidence in moving on to a new relationship and insights on how to deal with everything that MS threw at her. In six short weeks, by the time the MS walk ended, she'd be taking better care of herself and ready to spread her wings to find her true love. And once again, his interim-man work would be done.

Chapter 5

The clock told Sarah that she was running behind on Saturday morning preparations. She grabbed her teakettle, stuck it under the faucet, and twisted the cold-water lever.

Managing the building, attending church committee meetings, and working on her quilt kept her too busy to have downtime. She'd slept late, hoping to relieve some of the fatigue that plagued her all week. She certainly didn't need her MS symptoms to act up on Sunday afternoon.

A thrill shivered through her as she thought of spending uninterrupted time alone with Mark. She couldn't wait. She hoped the weatherman's prediction proved accurate: a warm spring day in eastern South Dakota, God's reward for the frigid winter winds.

Mark's reaction the night she told him that she had MS puzzled her. His face drained of color, and panic flashed in his eyes. She never dreamed that her simple statement would bring a flood of memories of his mother's struggle. That had to have been what happened. Not that she had much practice or luck reading people, as her past could testify. The remainder of the night, although polite, he seemed distracted.

Yet Tuesday night, before and after class, he charmed her with playful teasing about his anticipation of their impending date. His text messages and e-mails throughout the week brightened her days. He seemed anxious to get to know her on a deeper level.

Happiness warmed her heart and brought a smile to her face. Like Job, she trusted God enough to take the bad with the good. She'd embraced her MS diagnosis, and now God rewarded her by bringing Mark into her life.

Sarah placed the filled teakettle on the stove at the same time a car pulled into her driveway. Her mother was an angel for not insisting Sarah drive to Brookings every Saturday morning. Wouldn't her mom be surprised to find out that Sarah had a date tomorrow? Sarah unlocked the back door and swung it open wide.

"Good morning."

"Well, you are chipper this fine April morning. You're almost beaming." Karla carried a bakery box and stepped through the door.

"Surprise!" Sarah's mother followed behind.

Sarah's heart fell, and the narrow-eyed glare she gave her mom as she passed by could not be described as beaming. Her mother stopped and placed her hand on Sarah's shoulder. She leaned in and pecked a kiss on Sarah's cheek. "Have an open mind, dear," she whispered.

How many times would Sarah have to tell her mother that she, Sarah, was the open-minded one? Karla practically had her in a nursing home by the age of forty.

The whistle of the teakettle broke the silence and called for Sarah's attention. She stepped around her mom. She deliberately kept her back to the two women as she filled the teapot, adding that and another cup to her serving tray while the tea brewed. How dare they gang up on her?

"I'll carry that." Karla voice startled Sarah. She nudged Sarah away from in front of the counter and lifted the wicker tray.

"I am capable of carrying a tray," Sarah mumbled. Her mother shot her a narrow-eyed stare as Sarah followed Karla to the table.

"*Tsk, tsk, tsk.*" Karla clicked her tongue as she set the tray on the table. "You don't have to do it all. Now sit."

Although the words sounded bossy, Karla's tone was light, so Sarah ignored the double meaning and slipped into a chair. Karla arranged the teapot and cups on the table as Sarah's mom served the cinnamon rolls.

"Thank you." Sarah smiled.

Karla carefully poured tea into their cups.

First Mark saw her safely into her car, and now she was being served. Sarah had to admit it felt nice.

"Hasn't the weather been beautiful?" Her mother smeared butter over her roll. "I've been watching the birds gather supplies for their nests."

"Yes." Karla's cup rattled against the saucer as she set it down. "It's helping my flower shoots get taller with each passing day. How's it affecting you?"

Again, Karla's tone held a friendly lilt, but the pointed look she aimed at Sarah emphasized the comment's double meaning. "I'm feeling fine, if that's what you're getting at. The temperatures aren't nearly warm enough to aggravate my MS. However, stress is a big trigger." Sarah kept her voice conversational and looked wide eyed at Karla as she delivered her double entendre response.

Karla's shoulders stiffened. She set her mouth and jutted out her chin.

"Well," Sarah's mom interjected, "that didn't take long."

Sarah tilted her head toward her mother. "Which one of you planned this little intervention?" This time she didn't hold back, her voice shaking with anger.

Her mother raised her hands in a stick-'em-up fashion. "I did. I just couldn't stand aside and see a long-term friendship dissolve over something as minor as a difference in opinion about a job."

"So you think that by ganging up on me, I'll cave and quit my job?" Not that the thought of resigning hadn't crossed her mind several times this week. The solitude of the building management job wore on her nerves. She missed her former job's hectic pace of delivering packages and having sporadic conversations with the customers on her route. She had way too much time to contemplate the grim future her disease would eventually bring. But she'd never admit that, especially to these two.

Her mother reached across the table for Sarah's hand. "We love you and we're concerned about your well-being. Plain and simple, you're doing too much."

"Yes, it's like you have something to prove. If you won't look out for yourself, then we, as people who care about you, have no choice but to do it for you." Karla reached for Sarah's other hand.

Sarah pulled her arms from the table and crossed them over her chest just like Mark's familiar gesture. Sarah grinned at the thought.

"What is so funny?" Karla snipped.

"Absolutely nothing. I just had a nice thought. Or is that against *your* rules now, too?"

"Really, Sarah." Her mother pursed her lips. "Of course we want you to be happy, but you need to listen to reason. You may be doing more harm than good to your body by keeping a busy schedule. You just said that stress triggered symptoms."

"And this"—Sarah waved her splayed fingers palms down in small circles—"isn't stress?" She paused to check her anger. "I used to enjoy getting together with both of you, but now I dread it. All we talk about is how I shouldn't do anything, yet I'm under a doctor's care and he's pleased with my progress."

"Touché." Her mom took a sip of her tea.

Karla exaggerated an eye roll. "I guess you made your point. No more badgering from me."

"Me either." Her mom cut a bit of her roll and stabbed it with her fork. "So then, tell us what's new."

"Funny you should ask." Sarah looked from her mom to Karla then slipped from her chair and rummaged through her purse. She returned to the table. "I'm taking part in the upcoming MS walk. Would either of you like to sponsor me?"

"Of course." Her mother reached for the form and pen. "Do you *have* to walk or can you just collect contributions?"

"Mom, I thought we were done with that conversation." Sarah sighed.

"It was just a question. But I am your mother and have a right to be concerned."

"I plan to walk the entire route. If I need to stop halfway I can, and if my MS flares up, I don't have to walk at all."

"Fair enough." Her mother marked the form then passed it to Karla.

Karla glanced at the form before laying it on the table. "How are you doing in that quilting class?" She didn't even try to hide her smirk.

"Well. . ." Sarah stood and retrieved her denim tote bag from the hall closet. "I'll let you two be the judge of that." She pulled out her three completed quilt blocks.

"I like the colors." Her mom picked up one and inspected it. She picked up the second one and knitted her brows.

Sarah began to laugh. "Yeah, you can say it. They don't quite match."

Karla reached over and grabbed them. "Are they even sewed the same?" She turned one at a different angle.

"No. The one you're holding I tried to sew on the sewing machine."

"But you don't know how to sew." Karla looked at the back of the block.

"Exactly. I thought all quilts were sewn by hand. Turns out that's not true."

Her mom snatched the quilt blocks back and turned them over. "These two look the best."

"They're the ones that I've sewn by hand. There are still mistakes but nothing like the one I tried on the machine. However"—she pulled the pillow top from the bag—"I didn't do bad sewing the pillow panel."

"Pillow? What does that have to do with a quilt?" Her mom passed the quilt blocks back to Karla and took the sham from Sarah.

"Nothing. I needed something to practice sewing on and that's what I chose."

"Are you renting a machine?" Karla lay the blocks on the table.

"No, Mark told me I could use the demonstrator machines at the quilt shop to learn to sew." Sarah gathered the quilt blocks and set them on top of the tote bag. "I've been stopping in about three nights a week to practice."

She caught the raised-eyebrow exchange between her mom and Karla. "What?"

"You practice sewing after a long day at work?" Her mom topped off their cups.

"Yes."

"How long do you stay and practice?" Karla crumpled her napkin then placed it on her plate before pushing it away from her.

Sarah knew better than to say until closing time. "Not that long."

"You go directly from work?" The terse tone and pursed lips were back.

"Yes." Sarah braced. Didn't they just promise to drop these lectures?

Karla gave a little snort. "I told you. She does too much. She isn't taking care of herself."

Tension thickened the air. Sarah watched her mother and Karla exchange another look as if they were talking to a five-year-old.

"I hope you're not skipping meals, because you need your stamina."

Was her mother serious? Of course she was. Authority dripped from her voice. Had the entire situation not been so maddening, Sarah might have laughed at the statement.

"Obviously, you don't really understand my condition." Sarah purposely infused her response with sarcasm. "It doesn't matter if you eat. Stamina's one of the first things to go with MS."

Sarah watched her mother's cheeks begin to flame with color, a telltale sign of anger. If they were going to treat her like a kindergartner, then she might as well play the part.

"Since you didn't answer the question, we can only assume that means you're skipping meals." Karla picked up the discussion and nodded toward Sarah's uneaten cinnamon roll.

Defiance surged through her, and her chest tightened. "I can't eat when I'm being badgered," she snapped back at Karla. "But to answer your question, Mother, I do eat. Sometimes I stop before I go to the quilt store, and sometimes Mark and I have dinner in the work. . ." Sarah stopped. She heard each thud of the dirge before her pulse beat out the rhythm. She'd just given them more ammunition. She should've kept Mark out of it.

"Sarah." Her mother's voice softened. "Now is not the time to get involved with a man."

"I already told her that. No man is going to want to be a caregiver."

"Karla, stop talking about me like I'm not sitting right beside you."

"I know you don't believe me, but you are setting yourself up to get hurt. Again."

Salty tears stung Sarah's eyes. She squeezed them shut, trying to will the tears away, but instead forced the warm moisture out onto her lashes. Did one bad mistake in her youth mean she shouldn't ever try love again?

Another surge of hurt leaked from the corners of her eyes. She sniffled. This relationship wasn't one-sided like the last one. After all, Mark asked her out.

Sarah opened her eyes and reached for her cloth napkin. She dabbed at the moisture on her face, leaving mascara streaks on the eggshell linen. "This is different. Mark *is* interested in me."

Her mother's audible sigh increased the cloud of tension in the room. "Sarah, I hate to ask this but what are you basing his interest on? Helping you with purchases in his store?"

"Or by talking you into paying for quilting classes when you don't even know how to sew?" Karla patted the Job's Tears quilt block lying on the table. "That only shows his interest in profit, not in you."

The muscles in Sarah's shoulder grew taut. She rolled her right shoulder to alleviate the strain. *God, please don't let this flare the numbness in my right arm. I want to feel good for my date.*

"He's interested because he asked me out on a date." Sarah spoke through clenched teeth. She raised her shoulder and rested her ear on it. No relief.

"Have you been honest and told him that you have MS?" Her mother rose from her chair and stood behind Sarah. Her grip firm, she kneaded Sarah's muscles, helping to relax the tightness.

Sarah straightened then shook her right arm. God answered her prayers—no numbness. "Yes."

"What did he say?" The side of Karla's mouth curled up and she leaned forward, resting her chin in her hands. It was obvious to Sarah she was hoping for the worst.

"Nothing. I sort of blurted it out when I asked if I could join his team on the MS walk." Sarah leaned back in her chair as her mother continued to massage her neck and shoulders.

"Does he have MS?" Her mother stopped rubbing Sarah's shoulder and upper arm muscles.

"No." Sarah shook her head. "His mother did. The team walks and raises contributions as a memorial to her."

"Well, I guess he's used to dealing with someone with MS." Her mom patted Sarah's shoulders and slid back into her chair.

Finally her mother was seeing her point of view. Mark was used to someone with MS. He knew what to expect of the disease and how to handle it.

"When did you tell him you have MS? Before or after he asked you out?"

Karla just wouldn't let the subject die. Now maybe her mother would see what she'd been dealing with for months.

"After. Why?"

"I thought so." Karla smirked. "I doubt that he'd have asked you for a date had he known before that you were sick."

"You're wrong." Sarah looked to her mom for support but received a slight head shake instead.

"Sorry, honey, I think Karla's right. Had you disclosed your MS prior to him asking, that'd be different."

To give her mother credit, her face showed her remorse in her belief, but that didn't stop Sarah's heart from crumbling like a cinnamon roll, the bits of which now littered her empty plates.

"But he didn't cancel after he found out." Sarah whispered her response as she remembered Mark's strange reaction. Was he wondering how he could retract his offer of a date instead of thinking about his mom? That couldn't be, because he'd been texting her all week, telling her how much he was looking forward to Sunday afternoon.

Sarah mustered all her bravado. She cleared her throat and sat up straighter. "He didn't cancel after he found out." This time she said the words with certainty. "As a matter of fact, he sent me a text yesterday, telling me how much he's looking forward to it."

"Okay, so he's not a jerk. He'll go through with this date. Then what? Are you really going to want to continue with quilting class or be on his walking team when he doesn't want to see you on a personal level anymore?"

Karla reached for Sarah's hand, but Sarah yanked it away and rested it in her lap. How could she make them understand that she wanted to live, no, *needed* to live as normal a life as possible? She looked down at her Job's Tears quilt blocks. Like Job, she'd cried out in anger to God after her diagnosis, but since she'd found the quilt shop and Mark, her anger concerning her MS disappeared.

She couldn't let them rob her of the good in her life. In time she'd prove them wrong. Mark wasn't the shallow type, she could tell. Sarah drew a deep breath, but before she could answer, her cell phone rang.

"Excuse me." Sarah jumped from her seat. Happiness inflated her chest as "You've Got a Friend," the tune she'd assigned to Mark, cut through the tense silence in the room. Sarah ran for her purse, glad for the distraction from the conversation.

"Hello, Mark." Joy softened Sarah's voice as she flashed a triumphant smile toward the table.

"Hi, Sarah."

The edge in Mark's voice told her bad news would follow.

"I'm sorry to do this on such short notice, but I have to break our date."

Chapter 6

After church Sarah changed into her gray yoga pants and matching gray-and-pink T-shirt and settled on the couch to work on her Job's Tears quilt blocks. She spread the contents from her tote bag onto the adjoining cushion for easy access. Holding a block, she maneuvered the seam ripper through the machine stitching on the seams, cutting the small stitches and being careful not to tear the fabric. The one thing her mom and Karla had been right about yesterday was that the hand-sewn blocks looked much better.

They weren't right about Mark, though. He had a good reason for canceling their date this afternoon. One of his two part-time clerks quit without prior notice. He had to cover her shift. After his call, Sarah had found it hard to swallow her disappointment. She'd managed to keep her voice light and her answers generic until her mom and Karla said their good-byes.

The last thing she needed to hear from Karla yesterday was "I told you so." Her friend had planted enough doubts that, at first, Sarah worried that Mark was trying to get out of their date. But the more she thought about it, the more she realized her concern was unfounded. She dropped by the store often enough and spent enough time with Mark that if he were lying, she was fairly confident she'd pick up on it. Besides, he'd insisted that they reschedule as soon as he could get a new work schedule in place.

Sarah smoothed out the loose pieces of fabric before pinning the edge together. She threaded her needle then inserted it into the cloth. Her hand sewing showed improvement despite some faint numbness in her upper arm.

The rhythmic movement caused her mind to wander to the verse from Ecclesiastes the lector read in church this morning. *"When times are good, be happy; but when times are bad, consider this: God has made the one as well as the other. Therefore, no one can discover anything about their future."*

She wished her mother and Karla had attended this morning's service at Sarah's small country church. Then they'd see the goal she was striving for in her life—acceptance that God was in control. Right now she was happy, unlike a few months ago. Her life seemed full of hope again since meeting Mark, starting a new job, and finding a hobby. Sarah didn't know if Mark was a permanent fixture in her future. She hoped and prayed he was, but only God knew for certain.

Engrossed in her sewing, she jumped when the doorbell rang.

"Ouch!" Sarah dropped her sewing. As she walked to the front door, she rubbed the finger she'd poked with the needle. She hoped this wasn't a surprise visit from Karla. She wasn't up to another conversation like yesterday's.

She peeked out the window and saw a florist delivery van parked behind her car. Sarah opened the door.

"Are you Sarah Buckley?"

"Yes."

"These are for you." The teenage delivery boy shoved a vase of cut flowers toward her then turned. "Have a great day," he called over his shoulder.

Sarah balanced the heavy glass vase against her side as she closed her door. The sweet scent of irises delighted her nose. She set the large vase on the end table and admired the spring bouquet of daisies, irises, tulips, and crocuses. Slipping the card from the plastic holder, she dipped her nose into the arrangement and inhaled the flowers' bouquet. Was this her mom's or Karla's way of saying, "I'm sorry"?

Sarah opened the envelope and read the card.

I hope these flowers brighten your day. Sorry I had to break our date. See you tomorrow night, Mark.

Happiness fluttered through Sarah, forcing out a giggle. She read the card again and savored the joyous feeling. She knew she was right about Mark. A man who wasn't interested would never send a girl flowers.

She removed an African violet from the stand in front of the picture window and set the plant on the floor. She placed the flowers on the mosaic-topped stand that was right in her line of vision from the sofa where she planned to be the remainder of the afternoon, sewing quilt blocks.

Sarah lifted her cell phone from the end table and sat down cross-legged on the couch. She nervously fingered a throw pillow with one hand as she hit the programmed number in her cell phone. She smiled as the connection began to ring. She definitely hoped God included Mark in her future.

❧

The tissue paper Sarah wrapped around her flowers to protect them in the car worked. Not one flower petal was broken or missing. As she stood back and admired the bouquet sitting on the corner of her desk, she shivered with giddiness.

"Hoo-wee, someone's been a good girl." Ashley strode up behind her then whistled. "That's one beautiful bouquet."

"You won't get an argument from me." Sarah giggled.

"Tell Mark he did good."

"How did you know he sent them? I haven't shown you the card yet."

"Sarah, where Mark's concerned you haven't a poker face."

Sarah shrugged and giggled again. She reveled in the lighter-than-air feeling.

"Judging by the flowers, I can tell he's just as smitten with you as you are with him." Ashley squeezed Sarah's shoulders.

Surprised by the happy tears that welled in her eyes, Sarah swiped away the moisture with the back of her knuckle. It felt so good to have someone share her happiness about her relationship.

"Let's get some coffee, and you can tell me all about your date."

Ashley headed for the adjoining room. Sarah grabbed her cup and inhaled deeply as she passed her flowers. The spring fragrance tickled her senses. Mark's gesture delighted her heart.

Sarah held her cup steady while Ashley poured.

"So spill it." Ashley set the carafe on the warming element.

Ashley pulled a face when she saw Sarah pretending to spill her coffee. "I didn't mean that and you know it. Tell me about your date."

Sarah sipped her coffee. "There's nothing to tell."

"What?" Ashley frowned and looked out toward the flowers.

"One of Mark's employees quit with no notice. He had to cover the shift. The bouquet is part of his apology for canceling our date, and he promised to reschedule, so. . ." Sarah zigzagged her fingers over the textured surface of her gold-toned earring. "I'm sure he really does want to date me."

"What is that supposed to mean?" Ashley's frown deepened. "Of course he wants to date you—he asked you out."

It took a minute for Sarah to realize exactly what she said. She waved her hand in the air. "Well, my mom and friend seem to think now that Mark knows I have—" She stopped. She'd never told Ashley that she, Sarah, had MS.

She cleared her throat. "Ashley, I have multiple sclerosis. The people closest to me seem to think now that Mark knows my medical condition, he won't want to date me."

"Really? Why would that make a difference? Don't they want you to be happy? I don't understand that line of thinking at all." Ashley slipped down into a chair by the break room table. Her nostrils flared and, as she frowned, deeper creases lined her forehead. She seemed to have skipped right past Sarah's illness to anger in defending Sarah's rights.

Sarah furrowed her brow. "You think it wouldn't make a difference to a man if a woman were sick. If he wanted to date her, he would."

"Absolutely. Don't they trust your judgment in men?"

They didn't, and Sarah couldn't blame them. They'd helped her pick up the pieces once. Sarah swallowed hard in an attempt to clear her throat of the bitter pill of past mistakes as she responded to Ashley's question with a slight shake of the head.

"Besides, you look healthy. What does having MS mean, exactly?" Ashley gave Sarah a once-over before taking a drink of her coffee.

"Right now, it means that I lose muscle control in my right arm from time to time. Lots of things can bring on an attack, like the weather, stress, or fatigue. When that happens, I go get a steroid shot and the symptoms usually clear right up."

"Here's to modern medicine and a hope for a cure." Ashley held her travel mug up.

Sarah lightly tapped it with her coffee mug in agreement with the toast. "Speaking of that, I'm taking part in the MS walk. I have a sign-up sheet at my desk if you'd like to sponsor me."

"Sure."

Ashley followed Sarah into the office area. As Ashley wrote down her pledge, the office door opened.

Sarah looked up, ready to give her pat "good morning" or "may I help you." Her heart fluttered. "Mark! What are you doing here?"

Dressed in blue jeans and the green polo shirt that emphasized the emerald flecks in his eyes, Mark held up a box of doughnuts. "Peace offering."

❧

After polite introductions and small talk, Sarah's tenant excused herself.

"I won't get you into trouble just stopping by, will I?" Mark hadn't realized how much he'd looked forward to his date with Sarah until she'd called to thank him for the flowers.

Sarah shrugged. "My bosses are located in the downtown office, and I'm supposed to get breaks, but I usually work through them. Sometimes my lunch, too, so I think I can take a short break now."

Mark wrinkled his brow. Sarah should take her breaks if for no other reason than to ward away the fatigue that accompanied MS.

She started across the room and waved for Mark to follow along.

He hadn't expected such a formal office. The plush carpet and bulky cherrywood desk screamed dignified. No wonder Sarah's attire was always accessorized and polished.

Today was no different. A lavender linen jacket topped her floral-print dress with a formfitting skirt. The back slit in the skirt might have been designed for easier movement, but it showcased Sarah's slender, shapely calves. Her spike-heeled sandals, a shade darker than the jacket, added at least three inches to her height.

"Are you coming?" Sarah peeked around the door.

Mark entered the long room. A stark contrast to Sarah's office area, the office machine room that appeared to double as a break room was decorated in white-and-gray run-of-the-mill counters and clapboard cupboards. He set the doughnuts on the white plastic-topped folding table.

"You look lovely today. You do justice to every color you wear." Mark took the cup of steaming liquid she offered, savoring the flush that deepened the color of Sarah's cheeks.

"Thank you." Sarah's black eyes glistened. "Why did you call the doughnuts a peace offering? I'm not angry with you."

Mark chuckled. "For my conscience. I really hated standing you up yesterday."

"Well, many thanks to you and your conscience for this treat." Sarah removed a doughnut from the box and held it up. "And for your surprise visit. You've made my day."

"Likewise." Mark smiled. Should he tell her she'd been making his day every time she stopped into his store?

"I hope you didn't go out of your way."

"Actually, I didn't. I live in the condos not far from here." Mark pointed to the southeast.

"In the new development?" Sarah nibbled at her glazed doughnut.

Mark nodded his head. "You sound surprised." Only two-thirds of his doughnut was left after his first bite.

"I guess I assumed because you were a lifelong resident of Sioux Falls that you'd live in a more established neighborhood."

"We did, but after Mom passed away I downsized. Unlike Caroline's fiancé, Rodney, I dislike yard work and snow removal especially after a long day of work, so I sold Grandma's house and bought a condo."

"Makes sense. I don't enjoy those activities, either. I rent my Kiwanis Avenue duplex. The owner and his wife live in the other side. He is very particular about his lawn, so he takes care of those things for me."

Good, because you shouldn't be doing that kind of work anyway. Mark broke a sugar-coated doughnut in two and dunked one end into his coffee.

"Thank you again for the treat." Sarah wiped icing from her fingers.

"I should thank you for indulging me. I thought it'd be nice to have friendly company before I start a long day." Mark popped the last of his doughnut into his mouth.

"Another one?" Sarah's dark eyes clouded. "If you want to talk about what happened and why your clerk quit, I don't mind."

Was she a mind reader? As soon as it had happened, he'd almost called Sarah to talk. It was the first time he'd wanted to talk to someone other than his mom when he had a problem. He'd actually picked up the phone then reconsidered.

He wiped his mouth and hands on his napkin. "Rachel's daughter ran into some trouble with the law, so she's moving her grandchildren to her house."

"Sounds like Rachel's family needs our prayers." Sarah twisted her earring as she shook her head.

"I'd say so. It's a sad situation, but Rachel's doing the right thing for the children. She hated to quit with no notice, but given the circumstances she just didn't feel like she could leave them with a sitter while she worked for two weeks."

"So now you're shorthanded."

"Yes. I'm covering her shifts this week until Terri and I can work out a schedule. I'm heading in to work early so I can get some special orders placed before it's time to open." Mark sighed. "Compared to what Rachel's going through, a few long workdays is nothing, but. . ."

"You're not looking forward to it." Sarah's eyes conveyed sympathy.

"As much as I like running the quilt shop, I'm not looking forward to several eleven-hour days."

"It does get tiring. I delivered for UPS for twenty years and pulled long shifts during holiday times." Sarah's expression changed to wistful.

"You had to change jobs because of your MS?"

"Yes, the heavy lifting and summer heat made my symptoms flare, so I opted for a climate-controlled job." She held her hands up, but sadness showed on her face.

"I can tell you miss your old job."

"I miss being busy and chatting with a variety of people each day. It's hit or miss most days here on both accounts. Although I'll find out later today if a large company decided to lease the third floor. If they do I'll be overseeing the remodeling project." Sarah's face brightened.

Mark frowned. He knew how stressful it could be working with contractors, not to mention lessees. She'd be right in the middle of trying to please everyone. Not a good position for an MS patient to be in. "That sounds like a lot of work."

"I prefer to think of it as a challenge." Sarah rubbed her palms together.

Mark smiled at her enthusiasm but made a mental note to make sure she took care of herself if the remodel deal went through. "Speaking of challenges, I have my own to handle today. I'd better head to the store and place those orders before it's time to open." Mark stood. "And I'm sure I stayed longer than I should have."

Sarah waved his comment off. "Don't worry about it. I'll eat my lunch at my desk. And as you can tell, the phone hasn't rung once since you arrived." She put their coffee cups into the kitchen sink and followed Mark into her office area.

Mark slowed his steps to stretch their last moments together. He reached for her hand and cupped it the way he had the night he demonstrated the sewing machine. He felt the familiar curves where the back of her hand met her knuckles, her short, plump fingers, the feathery softness of her skin.

He stopped by the door and searched her face. The soft curve at the corner of her lips beckoned to him. He licked his lips in an attempt to stop the nervous quiver that urged him to kiss Sarah. It didn't work. He leaned toward her. When their eyes met, hers widened.

He'd never wanted to kiss any woman more than at this moment. He'd never wanted to hold any woman close and feel her warmth like he wanted to do with Sarah. He never wanted to protect any woman like he wanted to protect Sarah.

Her hand trembled in his, reminding him that their surroundings weren't the appropriate place for a first kiss. He squeezed her hand before lifting it to his lips and pressing a kiss in her palm, never breaking eye contact. He folded her fingers over the spot he kissed.

"Hold on to this for me." He knew his kiss would be safe with Sarah.

⁂

"You are the prettiest sandwich-delivery person I've ever seen." Mark pulled a foot-long sub from a plastic bag.

Sarah giggled. Since Mark kissed her palm she'd been floating in a bubble of happiness.

"Aren't you eating?" Mark lifted the bag and shook out the napkins. "I can share."

"It's all yours. I ate mine on the drive over." Sarah turned on the demonstrator machine. "I need all the time I can get to try and sew a quilt block on the machine before the class starts. I ended up ripping the last one apart and sewing it by hand."

Mark brought his sandwich and drink to the middle of the worktable as Sarah spread out her supplies. "Will it bother you if I sit here and watch?"

"No, but it may bother you to watch a woman who has absolutely no idea how to sew since you're not used to that," Sarah teased Mark.

He gave her a weary smile. "It won't bother me. You're so thoughtful to bring me dinner."

"I told you I know what it's like to work long hours. Little things matter." Besides, she wanted to touch his heart the way he melted hers with the surprise visit to her office.

"I saw the Help Wanted sign in the window. Has anyone applied?" Sarah lined up two pieces of contrasting fabric then tucked them under the presser foot.

"Not yet. I did have a lady inquire, thinking that her daughter may be interested in it. However, Terri's daughter is home from college in a week. She has a summer internship lined up, but that doesn't start until the first of June, so Terri's going to see if she'd like to fill the open position to earn some extra money." Mark raised the straw to his mouth.

The simple gesture warmed Sarah's palm where he'd placed his sweet kiss. "That sounds like the perfect solution. Then you can take your time finding the right person for the position."

Mark nodded as he chewed a bite of sandwich.

The machine whirred as Sarah guided her fabric toward the needle. "Darn."

"What?" Mark looked over.

"My fabric keeps slipping." Sarah lifted the presser foot and pulled the pieces free.

"You need to pin it together." Mark wiped his hands on his napkin.

"Then how will I sew it? Won't pins break the needle?"

Mark shook his head as he stood. Sarah forgot her quilt project as she watched him walk around the table and stop beside her. His navy-striped polo shirtsleeves stretched tight across his biceps. The sharp crease in his navy trousers, a shade lighter from consistent pressing, led down to athletic shoes.

"I knew I'd be on my feet all day." He lifted one foot. "I wanted to be comfortable in case the Tuesday night special works. My timing wasn't good concerning the start of that, but. . ."

"I was just thinking what a smart man you were, wearing practical shoes on a long day." Sarah thought she saw the circumference of Mark's chest increase a little as his instant smile pushed all the weariness from his features.

"You"—Mark tapped the end of her nose with his forefinger—"are just what I needed today."

His intense stare made Sarah hold her breath. Would he kiss her?

Mark leaned toward her, closing the gap between them. The emotion conveyed in his hazel eyes caused a rapid pattering of her heart. His warm breath tickled her cheek. Sarah leaned forward and tilted her chin, ready to receive his kiss.

A light rap on the workroom door broke their eye contact. "Sorry to interrupt your dinner, but it's time for me to leave." Terri threw her boss an apologetic look.

Sarah caught the slight tremble of Mark's hand as he glanced at his watch. Was attraction surging through him, too? Numbing his thoughts and putting his senses on high alert?

"Go ahead and leave." Mark's baritone held a bass edge. He cleared his throat. "I'll go out to the sales floor as soon as I show Sarah a sewing method."

"Thanks. I'll see you tomorrow at noon." Terri gave them a wiggle-finger wave as she left through the back door.

"Let's start with two new pieces of your pattern." Mark held out a steady hand.

Sarah lifted two pieces of her quilt block, hoping Mark didn't see her own hand shake from her palpitating heart, and laid them in Mark's outstretched palm. How had he gained control in such a short time?

Mark lined up the raw edges of Sarah's quilt blocks. "Slide your straight pins over to me." He pinched several pins out of her plastic pin container and scattered them on the table. "This is what you need to do." He poked each of the pins into cloth so that the sharp end was even with the raw edge of the fabric. He handed it back to Sarah.

She studied the pins lined up a few inches apart. "Do I take the pins out as I sew?"

"You could, but I think you'd have better luck leaving them in until your seam was finished. Don't worry. The machine will stitch right over the pins. Try it."

Sarah lined the fabric up with the seam-measurement marker on the sewing machine. She lowered the presser foot and slowly pushed down on the foot feed. Concentrating on her sewing, Sarah began to regain control of her emotions. After a few minutes, she was finished. "That worked so much better!"

Mark's eyes crinkled from his wide smile. "Have fun practicing." He scooped his garbage up from the table and headed toward the door.

"Are you sure you don't know how to sew?" Sarah started pulling pins out of the material.

"Only enough to demonstrate the machines I sell." Mark winked then walked out the door.

Although the edges weren't even, Sarah had one block sewed by the time Caroline and her classmates started arriving. She wasn't sure if it was faster to sew by hand or the machine. Both took arm control. Yet MS tingled her arm as if it were asleep—more times than she cared to admit by this time of the day.

Once everyone was seated, Caroline began the class. "I just want everyone to work on their projects tonight. I'll walk through and check your progress or answer any questions that might have come up since you worked on your projects last week." She held up a table runner. "I finished this during the week. I'll pass it around so you can see how the blocks look when they're finished and sewn together."

Caroline handed the table runner to Sarah, who ran her fingers over the Job's Tears blocks. Caroline had sewn the quilt's pattern pieces crisp and even, creating distinct angles that added to the beauty of the block. Sarah's heart sank a little. Even her hand-sewn blocks were jagged in spots, giving her block a choppy look. Karla was probably right—Sarah was wasting her time.

"While you're looking at the table runner, don't use it as a measure for your project. I've been sewing and quilting since I was teenager."

Sarah slowly lifted her eyes to Caroline.

"Your wistful expression gave you away. The very first quilt I ever made was four-by-four-inch blocks, in pink and orange, sewn in rows. Some had wide seams and some had narrow seams. At ten, I wanted to do whatever my mom did, so while she made a double wedding ring quilt for my grandparents' fortieth wedding anniversary, I stitched a psychedelic twin-sized quilt for my bed, which brings me to something I'd like to discuss tonight."

After examining the front and back of Caroline's table runner, Sarah passed it to one of the elderly ladies then resumed pinning more pieces together as the other machines' purrs mocked her lack of abilities. Yet the last block she sewed was her best work so far.

Caroline examined everyone's stacks of blocks and returned to the front of the room. She pulled a chair to the center. "I'm sorry I didn't bring my hippie quilt, as my grandmother donned it."

"You still have it?" the teenage girl asked.

"Yes, I do." Caroline laughed. "It's a little worse for wear but still serves its purpose. That brings me to what I want to talk about tonight. Every quilt has a story. You just heard the story of my first quilt. I made it because I wanted to be like my mother. Tonight, I'd like you to share with the class why you wanted to make a quilt so we'll all know your quilt's story."

Caroline smiled wide. Her laugh lines crinkled, emphasizing the love of her work. "Who wants to go first?"

Sarah's machine whirred as she tried to keep her fabric pieces lined up with the measurement guide. Between no sewing experience and a numbness interfering with her arm's control, she had to stop occasionally to realign the material. This required too much concentration for her to talk about her reason for enrolling in the quilting class. Plus, did she really want to disclose the number one reason she was here? She wasn't ashamed of her multiple sclerosis, but was it everyone's business? Sarah continued to try to get a fluid motion to her sewing.

After considerable silence, the elderly gentleman said, "I'll go first since I'm probably the least likely person to enroll in a quilting class. My granddaughter, Brystol, and I enrolled in the quilting class because our family voted last Christmas that this year's gifts would be homemade, so I'm making my wife a table runner for Christmas. I'm sure she thinks she'll get something made from wood since woodworking's my hobby."

"Won't she be surprised!" the second elderly lady interjected.

Sarah stopped sewing and turned to look at the gentleman. His face beamed with apparent love for his wife.

"I think so." The man winked at his granddaughter.

"And you sew so well, too. She will love it." The lady nodded her assurance to him.

"Grandpa ran a car upholstery business for years so he knows how to sew." Brystol smiled at her grandfather.

"So, does that mean you're making a family member a Christmas gift, too?" Caroline looked at the young girl.

Brystol stopped sewing. "Yes, for my older sister." She shrugged before refocusing on her work.

"I'm Mary and I'll go next." The chatty lady smoothed a finished quilt block with her fingers.

Sarah took a deep breath. She had sewn together only half a block in the time it took Mary to finish one. She continued to stitch while she listened.

"I'm selling my house and downsizing to a smaller apartment, so I decided to give myself a housewarming gift of a wall quilt."

Sarah cut the thread, releasing her cloth from the machine. She noticed a shade of sadness in the woman's expression. "What a wonderful way to celebrate a positive change in your life." Almost the same reason Sarah had enrolled in the class.

Mary brightened. "Thank you, dear."

"My table runner will be donated to my church bazaar," Mary's friend piped up.

"Sarah, you're up." Caroline shot her a sly smile.

What was that all about? Sarah left her pieces half-sewn in the machine and began to pin others together while she spoke. "About eighteen months ago, I was diagnosed with MS. I had to make some changes to my life, which ended up giving me a lot of free time." Sarah's voice cracked and the last few words came out in a whisper.

Sudden emotion welled up in Sarah as she visualized those first few months of bitterness. She cleared her throat, hoping the rush of feelings didn't shake her voice again. What was wrong with her? She'd moved forward months ago. "So I decided I needed a hobby to fill up my time. I thought I'd better do it right away because who knows how long I'll be able to do intricate movements." The immediate flush of embarrassment burned her cheeks. Where had that come from? It might be true, but that was never a conscious reason she enrolled in the class.

"Grandpa, our quilt stories are kind of lame compared to everyone else's."

"No, they're not," Caroline said. "Because they're all made with love for a special reason—be it happiness, service, or healing. Recently a quilt not only brought me healing but happiness. As I restored a Lily of the Field quilt, I relearned the lesson of the Bible verse, Matthew 6:28–34, that the block was named for and remembered I need to trust God with my life. In addition, I fell in love with the quilt's owner."

"What a wonderful story about your quilt," Sarah said, remembering the number one reason for her enrolling in this class. Mark.

"Actually, that is all it is. A story about a quilt, although Rodney and I tried to find out the *real* story behind the quilt, the reason it was made, but we weren't successful."

Caroline stood and began to walk around her students. "I'd just like you all to remember to never underestimate the power of a quilt."

When Caroline patted her shoulder, Sarah jumped. Her knee-jerk reaction caused her to stop guiding her fabric but not lift her foot off the foot feed. As the needle buzzed up and down, the piece of fabric turned sideways. Sarah frowned and looked up at Caroline. Had she made an error while sewing?

Caroline's eyes met Sarah's. Her mouth curved in slyness that could match the Grinch's. "Healing and happiness. Quilts have a wonderful way of bringing people together."

Chapter 7

An electrician cracked Sarah's office door and stuck his head in. "Miss, the other contractor is tied up and won't make it out here until around six."

Sarah sagged in her chair. It was the third time this week. She rubbed the bicep of her right arm, knowing that it wouldn't relieve the symptoms. Six really meant seven, or not at all. On Wednesday night, she'd waited for a carpet person to come and measure the room. At seven, he'd finally called and canceled.

At least today she was smart enough to bring along her quilt blocks and a can of soup. She didn't know if it was acceptable or not to work on her project in the office, but she had to have something to do.

Sarah shook out the sewing supplies from her tote onto her desk then dropped her bag to the floor. For the millionth time, she mulled over what Caroline had said in class. Sarah had ripped the sentence apart and sewn it together so many ways, but the end result always seemed the same—Caroline saw through her where Mark was concerned. Maybe Mark mentioned something to Caroline?

Tired from the long working hours of the last three days, Sarah wished she could rest her head on her desk while she waited, but that would be unprofessional. Yet she knew a quick nap would do her a world of good since her MS had deadened her right bicep just after noon.

As Sarah struggled to thread her needle, she reminded herself that, like Job, she must take the bad—in this case long hours and the effects from MS—from the Lord, as well as the good.

At least the construction project filled her working hours and then some. The last two days, she'd played intermediary between the building managers, the construction people, and the new tenants. It was impossible to keep everyone happy, but she was trying.

Sarah wiggled her fingers, attempting to remove the frozen feeling from her right arm. After several attempts she managed to push the thread through the small needle eye. Her hand sewing would be difficult tonight. She pushed the needle into the fabric, trying to use the fingers of her left hand to guide the implement back up and into the material.

"Ouch!" Having poked herself with the needle, Sarah rubbed the tip of her middle finger with her thumb. She glanced at the clock. She really wanted to stop at the quilt shop tonight to practice sewing and see Mark. She'd almost called him earlier to see if she could bring him something for dinner. However, because of her arm tingling, she doubted she could guide the fabric through the machine any better than she could hand sew.

Sarah tried another way to control the needle, but it was no use. She could barely feel it between her fingers, let alone guide it into her fabric.

Ashley breezed in from the hallway. "What are you still doing here?"

"Waiting on a construction person so they can give me a bid for the remodel." Sarah began to gather her quilting supplies with her left hand.

"You look beat."

"I am. Fatigue is a major symptom with MS." Sarah unsuccessfully tried to put fabric in her tote bag.

"What's wrong?" Ashley dropped her briefcase and purse to the floor and stepped closer to Sarah.

"It's just my MS. It affects my right arm."

Ashley frowned as she snatched Sarah's bag from the floor and held it open. "You need to go home."

"I can't. The new client wants the bid first thing in the morning." Sarah sighed and dropped her sewing supplies into the tote. If she could just lie down for a few minutes, she'd feel much better.

"Do you have any medicine or anything to take?" Ashley put Sarah's tote on the floor beside her own.

"I do, but I'd rather wait until I get home." Sarah glanced up at the wall clock and wished the contractor would hurry.

"Understandable. Should you be driving?"

Sarah heard the genuine concern in Ashley's voice, unlike the tone Karla used with Sarah. "I'll be fine." She forced happiness into her voice and smiled at Ashley. Sarah would be fine if she just rested a few minutes while she waited for the contractor to arrive.

"I don't know about that. Listen, I don't have any plans for tonight. I can wait around and drive you home." Ashley dropped into the reception area's guest chair.

The contractor stuck his head in the door once again. "They're here. I'll take them up so they can get started."

"I'll be right there." Thank goodness they came at the time they said they would. "Ashley, thank you for your offer, but I don't want to impose. Go home. I'll be fine." Sarah stood, but as soon as she put weight on her legs, the sensation in her right leg felt like tiny pins poking her muscles. She stamped her foot, trying to wake it up. "Great. My leg fell asleep."

She leaned against the desk and wiggled her ankle. No relief. Dread pulled at her heart. Maybe she'd just sat wrong, blocking the flow of blood to her leg. She stamped her foot again. Some improvement but a niggling sensation remained.

"Do you need some help?" Ashley stood.

Sarah took a tentative step. Better. "No, I'm fine, but maybe I shouldn't drive since I'm so tired. This shouldn't take long."

"No problem. Like I said before, I don't have plans."

❧

Still half asleep, Sarah glanced at her digital alarm clock. When her mind registered the time, she sat straight up in bed. Her mother would arrive for their Saturday morning visit in a few minutes.

Sarah flexed her right arm. It was amazing what a good night's sleep would do to lessen the numbness. Tentatively, she stepped out of bed. Sarah smiled, relieved that her leg felt normal. She must have just sat in the same position too long yesterday.

Sarah padded to the kitchen to start a pot of tea, smiling all the way. Today was the day. Anticipation shivered through her as she considered outfits for her date with Mark.

Just as she started to add water to the teakettle, the doorknob rattled.

"Just a minute, Mom." Sarah put the kettle in the sink before heading to the door. Unlocking the door with one hand, she twisted the knob with the other. Before she swung the door open, she drew a deep breath in case another surprise visit from Karla awaited her. Even that wouldn't dampen her spirits today.

"Good morning." She returned her mother's bright smile and sighed with relief that her mom was traveling alone this Saturday.

Her mother's smile faded as she gave her daughter the once-over. "Are you all right?"

Her mother's appraisal of Sarah's appearance as she entered the kitchen annoyed Sarah. So she was still in her pajamas and slippers at nine thirty in the morning. "I've been putting in long hours at work this week, so I slept in."

"Sarah, I'm telling you that you are taking on too much." Her mother pursed her lips before setting the bakery bag on the table. "I told your father that he needs to have a talk with you."

"What did Dad say to that?" Sarah removed two mugs and luncheon plates from the cupboard.

"He said you always sound fine and *happy* on the phone and that you were a big girl and could take care of yourself." Her mother took the mugs, filled them with water, and placed them in the microwave.

"Good, because he's right." Sarah shot her mother a grin as she placed the cinnamon rolls on the plates and grabbed some napkins.

"I don't think so." Her mother pulled the paper covering from two tea bags. When the microwave timer went off, Sarah headed into the living room.

Her mother followed carrying the steaming mugs with a steady hand. She carefully set a mug on each end table.

Sarah waited for her mom to sit down then handed her a plate and napkin.

Her mother slipped off her sandals before tucking one leg under the other. Sarah joined her on the couch.

Sitting cross-legged, she faced her mother. Balancing her plate on her legs, she broke off a piece of her roll. The spicy burst of cinnamon followed by the sweet creaminess of frosting brought out a hum of appreciation from Sarah.

"Thank you for always bringing my favorite." Sarah smiled at her mother.

"You're welcome." Her mother cocked her head and studied Sarah. "Actually, your father may be right. Perhaps Karla has planted seeds of doubt in me. I don't think the sun will shine brighter today than the twinkle in your eyes. You must really love your job."

Happiness erupted in Sarah's heart. Her job had little to do with her beaming joy. That could only be attributed to Mark and the appreciation that flamed in his eyes when he looked at her. The internal quiver inspired by his touch. The zap of electric current that, days later, still tingled her palm where he'd kissed her. Sarah swallowed her bite of roll and drew a deep breath. She hoped her mother would share her excitement. "It's not my job. Today's my first official date with Mark."

The dropped gaze and pursed lips told Sarah that her mother didn't share her enthusiasm.

"Why can't you be happy for me?" Sarah hated the pleading sound of her voice.

"I don't want to see you get hurt again." Her mother placed her plate with the half-eaten roll on the floor beside the sofa. "I know that you don't think so, but you are vulnerable. I don't want someone taking advantage of you."

"Tell me, Mom, how is Mark taking advantage of me? He's never been anything but a gentleman."

"For one thing, you're not thinking clearly. You haven't been for months now. I'm sure he can sense that. People aren't always what they seem. You know that from experience." Her mother's raised eyebrows emphasized her point.

Sarah couldn't argue with that. But would that one mistake in love haunt her for the rest of her life? "This relationship is entirely different. I'm an entirely different person. I *know* that Mark's interest is genuine."

"Really? You are sure that he's not a married man?"

Now they could both see the elephant in the room. "Yes."

"Absolutely?"

"Why are you so against this relationship? I've dated several men since then, and you've never discouraged me. Is it because of my MS diagnosis?"

"No." Her mother lifted the plate from Sarah's legs then placed it on the floor atop her own. She slid closer to Sarah and grasped her hands. She searched her daughter's face before meeting her eyes.

"I am not against the relationship because of the MS. I believe that you can lead a very active life with your disease, but you are going to have to make adjustments. I never disapproved of your other relationships because I could tell that you weren't that serious about those men."

"How can you say that?"

"Because, Sarah, you have a certain look when you're falling in love. I saw it when you were in your twenties when you mistook signs from a professional acquaintance. I see the same look now."

Was she falling in love with Mark? The thought sparked a surge of happiness in her heart, chasing out her annoyance with her mother. "So, your daughter's being in love is a bad thing?" She'd admit she learned a hard lesson in her twenties, one she didn't plan to repeat. She pulled her hands free of her mother's grasp and rubbed her palm in the spot that had been branded by Mark's soft lips.

Her mother sighed. "See, it's there again. You're going into this relationship blindly. Are you going to be able to handle it if your heart gets broken? The last time it took you several years to bounce back. Now, with your medical condition, a depressive state like that could be, well, detrimental. The experience left you wary, but I just feel you've let that guard down with this man."

That was true. She'd allowed herself to trust Mark, ever since seeing his warm smile that first time she entered his store. The more she got to know him, the surer she was that his values were solid and his actions sincere. "Mark is different."

"We'll see." Her mother stood and paced to the window.

You will see. Mark is different. Just one more thing she had to prove to the world.

&

Mark pulled into Sarah's driveway about twenty minutes earlier than he was supposed to be there. If he hadn't driven around the neighborhood three times, he'd be thirty minutes early.

He slipped from his four-wheel-drive pickup. Sticking his hands in the front pockets of his khaki cargo shorts, he surveyed her home. The tan-sided duplex shared a driveway but provided privacy by having the double garages as the connecting point.

Mark didn't have to look at the house number to tell which side was Sarah's. A large wreath comprised of various pastel-colored flowers with a welcome sign in the center hung beside the door. Judging by her clothing choices, Sarah was partial to pastels.

The light breeze swayed the planter hanging by the corner of the garage, sending the sweet fragrance of petunias through the air.

Should he text her or just knock? He swiped his fingers over the nervous beaded moisture on his brow.

Mark wandered to the end of the driveway and looked up and down the street. Women liked to take their time getting ready, didn't they?

It was ridiculous for Mark to be so anxious. He didn't know what to expect since he hadn't seen Sarah since attempting to kiss her in the workroom. It had just felt so good, being with her, he'd gotten a little carried away by the moment.

The weather was perfect for their outing, seventy degrees with a light breeze. He leaned against the back rubber bumper. Sarah hadn't been back in the store since the night they'd almost shared a kiss. Each evening he'd waited for her to walk through the door. When she didn't, the night seemed endless even if he was busy. Although she did text him, saying she'd taken on a project at work and had been putting in long hours. He hoped it was true and she wasn't uncomfortable and avoiding him.

"Mark?" Sarah stood beside the pickup. "What are you doing?"

Lost in his thoughts, he hadn't even heard Sarah approach the vehicle. He straightened and felt beads of moisture dot his forehead and upper lip. "I was early." He knew his grin was sheepish.

Sarah laughed. "I've been ready for an hour." She picked at a white thread on her lime-green-and-white-striped T-shirt that matched the cuffs on her green shorts. "So to pass time, I worked on my quilt blocks." She stuck the errant thread in an outside pocket of her purse.

"Guess that means we're both ready to get this date started, then." Mark took her hand, guided her to the passenger side of the pickup, and opened the door.

After sliding into the driver's seat, Mark eased the pickup from the driveway.

"We match today." Sarah waved her finger back and forth between them.

Her pleased expression made Mark glad that he'd chosen the lime-green-and-white plaid shirt.

"I got the dress code memo." Mark winked at Sarah before he pulled away from the stop sign, glad that Sarah lived on the same side of town as Falls Park. If he calculated correctly, they'd be there in fifteen minutes.

Sarah squealed when the opening bars of a pop song drifted through the pickup cab. "I haven't heard that song since high school."

"Me, too." Mark increased the volume a bit. "I pay for multiple stations on my XM radio but seldom change it from the eighties music."

Sarah joined in on the chorus of the song and tapped her hand on her knee. "That takes me back to my high school days."

Mark adjusted the volume to allow for easier conversation. "You do feel up to a stroll through the park today?" If Sarah's MS symptoms were bothering her, she might prefer to catch a movie instead.

"Oh yes, I need some fresh air."

"Me, too. I've been cooped up in the store too much this week. The long hours coupled with the perfect weather, I've been anxious to be outside, connecting to nature."

Once they were parked, Mark quickly exited the vehicle and rounded the back to help Sarah out of the high four-wheel drive, glad he'd purchased the model with built-in running boards since Sarah was so petite. Although it might be nice to hold her waist and lift her out to the ground, Mark held his hand out for Sarah to grasp for balance as she eased from the seat.

"This was my very first indulgence after my mom passed away." The horn on the pickup honked as he hit the Lock button on the key fob. "I'd always driven a van with handicap capabilities to make it easy for Mom." Why had he shared that? It was Sunday afternoon all over again, when his first thought was to call Sarah after his employee quit.

"It sounds like you were a good and dependable son." Sarah laced her fingers in his and gave his hand a squeeze.

I had to be—she didn't have a good and dependable husband. Mark sighed. He was losing sight of his dating strategy with Sarah. Something he couldn't afford to do because he'd never want to hurt her. Yet he was a Sanders man. He'd seen firsthand how reliable they were. He didn't quite understand some of his feeling regarding Sarah, but he had to get back to his original plan. That included getting her to talk about her breakup so she could let go of the hurt.

"Tell me, Sarah, how a beautiful woman like you has managed to be unattached?" Mark steered them toward the roar of water on the falls.

Sarah's shrug pulled their joined hands up. "Never met the right guy, I guess. The older I got, the less I dated."

Sarah's wistful expression of love gone wrong twisted Mark's heart.

"As a matter of fact. . ." Sarah took a deep breath before finishing.

Here it comes, her first step in letting go of the old boyfriend.

"This is hard to admit, but this is the first date that I've had in three years."

"What?" That blew his dating theory out of the water.

When Sarah stopped walking and stared at him, he realized he'd verbalized part of his thought.

Mark stopped short. "I'm sorry, Sarah, but you're gorgeous. I guess I figured you'd have your choice of suitors."

Sarah lifted her right hand to her chest. Her eyes sparkled like the sunshine-kissed water going over the falls. Her features softened with her gentle smile. "Thank you."

Her ragged whisper of gratitude tugged at Mark's heart. It took all of his willpower not to pull her into his arms and kiss her.

Mark followed when Sarah began walking again. "I wasn't dating anyone when I was diagnosed with MS, and at the time, I thought not being in a relationship was for the best. I knew I had to come to terms with the disease before I could commit to anything else."

"When did you find out you had MS?" Mark swung their joined hands.

"About eighteen months ago. It bothered me quite a bit at first because of some of the changes the doctor told me to make, but I have a handle on it now." Sarah sighed. "I just wish my mom and longtime friend thought I did."

It clicked. Mark stopped walking, halting Sarah with a slight tug on her hand. He gazed out at the falls. The rushing waters roared over the rocks then dropped into a foaming pool before continuing on their journey. The breeze lifted the spray, misting the air and dampening their faces. Sarah was upset about a relationship breakup, just not the kind Mark thought.

"Mom's supportive to an extent. My friend Karla isn't at all. She wouldn't even pledge me for the MS walk." Sarah voice didn't hide her disgust with her friend. "They both think I do too much. When I had to change occupations, they thought I rushed into the first job that hired me. They think I should work part-time, not have any hobbies, not be involved in any organizations."

Anger burned inside of Mark. He'd witnessed that so many times with his mother. He'd like to meet those women and tell them a thing or two. Having multiple sclerosis didn't mean you had to quit living. The person fighting the lack of muscle control needed to be supported, not discouraged. Mark checked his anger. "Don't let them get to you." He slipped his arm around Sarah and hugged her close.

Sarah leaned into him. "Sometimes it's hard not to, but I refuse to be defined by my disease."

Mark released the hug and cupped her face in his palms. He tilted her head up and drank in the determination that flashed from her eyes. The breeze ruffled her fringe of bangs as he traced his spread fingers up the soft curve of her cheeks, grazing the silky hair cut just above her ears.

The thunder of his heart drowned out the crash of the water on the rocks of the falls. Sarah shouldn't be fighting this battle alone.

Sarah rested her hands on his forearms. The slight squeeze of her velvet touch signaled her consent to the kiss. Her eyes fluttered shut as he closed the small gap between them and captured her lips.

He'd intended to kiss Sarah today. He'd intended it to be a good-night kiss. He'd intended it to be short but sweet.

However, Sarah needed to know that someone supported her and wanted to protect her from the cynics in the world. An intense emotion welled inside him and, when their lips touched, spilled over into the kiss, surpassing the innocent I-had-a-good-time-today message he'd intended to convey at the end of the date.

Instinct took over as Mark deepened the pressure and dropped his hands from her face and wrapped them around her shoulders. He needed to tell her that he'd be her shelter, the one who'd help handle her problems. *Yeah, right.*

The subconscious thought triggered the realization of what he was thinking. Mark ended the kiss and drew a ragged breath.

Raw feelings showed in Sarah's dark eyes as she searched his face.

That was not a part of his dating plan. What had he done?

❧

The brooding began the minute Mark told Sarah good night on Saturday night. It was the only way he could control his giddy feelings caused by one fantastic kiss.

Mark stopped shelving fabric bolts and pursed his lips to remove the smile brought to his face by the previous thought. A repeat of the afternoon kiss couldn't happen again and it hadn't.

When they'd reached Sarah's door, she turned in an expectant manner. "Mark, this was a wonderful day." The light from the full moon couldn't compare to the radiant happiness shining from Sarah.

He'd known he couldn't repeat the same mistake as earlier in the day. Maybe if he didn't touch her soft ivory skin. It took all his willpower, but he stuffed his hands in the front pockets of his shorts.

As he leaned in, Sarah rested her hands in the exact spot they'd been earlier in the afternoon. The same quaking from her touch vibrated through him. It took all of his willpower, but he managed a chaste good-night kiss, which lasted about two seconds. Who knew love's electrical current didn't need much time to shock happiness into a heart?

The full moon magnified Sarah's beauty as her trust-filled eyes searched his face. She didn't seem to mind the quick peck, judging by the breathless sound of her voice as she said good night.

Mark sighed. It tore him in half trying to ward off the happiness with the brooding. Yet sooner or later he'd let Sarah down. He knew that. It was in his genetics.

On Sunday, Sarah called to thank him again for the nice afternoon and evening. He'd hoped she was stopping by the store to practice sewing, but she had a church committee meeting later in the day. Then yesterday, she ended up having to work late, so she couldn't spend the evening sewing in the workroom.

Here it was Tuesday evening, and no matter how hard he tried, the anticipation of seeing Sarah was bringing out the joy of that kiss.

Mark noticed a bolt with under a yard of cloth wrapped around it. He pulled it from the shelves to cut it into fat quarters.

"I'm back from dinner, so go anytime." Terri walked to the cash register area.

"In a minute." Mark put the fabric bolt under the cutting counter as he glanced at the clock. Sarah should have been here by now. He pulled his cell phone from his pocket. Had he missed a text? They'd planned to share dinner before the class.

Mark walked to the front plate glass windows and scanned the parking lot for Sarah's compact.

"A watched pot never boils."

What was Terri talking about? Surely she didn't know he was worried about Sarah. He turned. "Pardon me?"

Terri laughed. "That's what my grandma would say if we watched out the window for our dad to arrive home. I thought it was appropriate. The customers won't come in any faster for the Tuesday night sale with you watching out the window."

Mark grinned. "I guess not." He'd forgotten about his Tuesday night promotion.

When he turned back to the window, he noticed that Sarah had parked in front of the door and was walking around the front of her car. Really, she was limping while holding on to the hood of the car.

At the jangle of the quilt shop door, she turned before stepping from the curb. The soft light of dusk didn't mask the dark circles under

Sarah's eyes. That, coupled with the limping, told Mark that her MS was acting up.

"Hi." Her voice sounded brighter than he thought it might as she continued to steady herself with one hand on the car. She held her free hand out to him.

Mark ignored her hand and pulled her into a side hug. "Hi." She leaned into him, and the warmth of her body comforted his longing to see her. "Let me get whatever you're after."

"It's my tote bag, purse, and our dinner."

Mark gathered the bags as quickly as he could. He could tell that she needed to sit down. He manually locked the car door before joining her on the curb.

He held his hand out to her, but she waved him off. "Just get the door, okay?" Sarah smiled, but Mark could tell that it took concentrated effort for each small step she made toward the door.

Mark opened the door, and Sarah made it through. She was still dressed in her office attire—a blue ruffled blouse under a short-sleeved white linen pantsuit—and the blue-and-white strappy slip-on sandals weren't helping with her footing.

Once inside the door, he offered his arm, and this time Sarah accepted. "I hope you like chicken. I bought grilled and extra crispy."

Even tired and bothered with MS, Sarah worried about others.

"I like both and it smells really good."

Sarah flicked on the workroom light. She let go of Mark's arm when they were close to the table. "Do you mind taking my stuff to the machine I use?"

"Not at all." Mark set the bag of food on the table and watched Sarah drop onto a chair.

"It feels so good to sit down. I've been running all day." Sarah lifted her right leg with both hands and rested it on the metal support bar underneath the table.

"I hate to tell you this, but it shows." Mark unpacked the food. "Sarah, with MS you need to rest. Mom took a nap almost every afternoon."

Sarah frowned. "I don't have that luxury. Your mom ran her own business." Her answer was clipped.

"Don't you have a lunch hour? You could rest in the break room." Mark dished food onto two paper plates and slid one in front of Sarah.

Sarah dropped her gaze. "I've been too busy to take a lunch the last two days."

"Sarah—" Mark stopped when she held up her hand.

"It's only because it's the start of this construction project. You know with contractors you are at their mercy for time schedules. It's not like I'm not eating. I eat piecemeal in between crises."

"Still, you should get away from your desk for a few minutes, especially since you've been putting in long hours." Mark removed another drumstick from the cardboard container and placed it on his plate before forking a bite of mashed potatoes.

"Can we talk about something else?" Sarah's eyes brimmed with tears. "I spend so much time dealing with renovations that I'm dreaming about them." Sarah tasted a tiny bite of potatoes before pushing them around on her plate.

"Okay, how did your church meeting go?" Mark took a bite of his drumstick.

"Great." Sarah's eyes lit up. "Not only am I leading the summer early bird Bible study group, but I'm also on a committee to review the curriculum for children's and adult Sunday school."

Mark grimaced before he could stop it. Her schedule was too demanding for a person with MS.

Sarah's sigh held a tone of disgust. She placed her fork, which was still holding a piece of chicken on which she'd been nibbling, atop her napkin and worried the hoop earring in her left ear. "What's wrong with that?" Defiance flashed through Sarah's dark eyes.

"Nothing, if you have the time, but do you?" Mark held her gaze. It was obvious she didn't like this conversation, but he knew firsthand the punishment MS could dish out.

"This remodel project won't last forever. Once I get the bids and know we're within budget and the client is getting what they want, then my work hours will go back to normal."

The corners of Sarah's mouth drooped as she narrowed her eyes at Mark. "Excuse me." The metal chair legs scraped across the tile floor as Sarah pushed away from the table.

Mark stood. "Sarah, I didn't mean to make you angry. I just want you to understand that leading an active life is not the same as leading a busy life."

"Active and busy are the same thing." Sarah rose from her chair.

Mark walked around the table. "Please sit down and enjoy your dinner."

"I'm behind on my quilt blocks, so I need to work on them *now*." Sarah started to turn away.

Mark saw the wobble. His stomach clenched. "Sarah, stop." He bumped his hip on the corner of the table, trying to get to her before she tried another step.

Sarah's eyes widened, her left arm reaching, missing the chair and knocking it off balance.

Mark seemed to be moving in slow motion while Sarah moved in real time. Her arms flailed in the air. He wasn't going to get to her in time.

The clang of the metal chair hitting on the tile floor muffled her cry as she started to fall.

Chapter 8

Two quick steps for momentum before Mark twisted his body sideways. He straightened his right leg as he dropped to the floor. His left hip and bent leg absorbed the shock as he thudded against the tile floor. Jarring waves of aftershock traveled up his spine, rattling his teeth.

His right shoulder smacked hard against the floor, and he strained to keep his head from the same fate. His vision blurred. He fought the urge to close his eyes and succumb to the pain.

Mark hadn't slid for home base in thirty years, but the maneuver worked. Seconds after he made contact with the floor, Sarah's head and torso bounced against his chest, knocking any remaining air from his lungs. He wrapped his arms around Sarah and held on tight. He'd done it. He'd cushioned Sarah's fall.

Laying his head against the cool tile, Mark sucked in air that his lungs puffed out as rapidly as he breathed it in. In between breaths, he huffed, "Are you all right?"

"I think so."

The catch in Sarah's voice said differently.

He drew a steadying breath and pushed himself up with one arm. The other arm remained around Sarah, holding her close. When had that happened?

Sarah struggled but with his help managed to guide herself into a sitting position. "My leg must have fallen asleep."

"Sarah, I think it was more than that." Though it pained him to do it, Mark's tone turned stern.

Shrugging from his embrace, a slight pout marred Sarah's features as she turned away from him. The burning pain in his left hip was no match for the agony seizing his heart. He'd hurt Sarah. Yet he wouldn't pull the words back, even if he could. What if that had happened to Sarah and she'd been alone? She needed to heed the warning symptoms of her MS.

Mark grasped the end of the table and pulled himself upright. He bent to help Sarah up, but she flailed her left arm at him.

"Maybe it was my shoes. I've had trouble walking all day." Sarah struggled to lift herself from the floor.

Ignoring the pain in his right shoulder, Mark scooped Sarah from the floor, one arm around her waist, the other under her knees. He set her on the table.

"First things first—did you get hurt?" He patted the arm of her jacket with his fingers to remove some gray dust she collected on her way down. He lifted her chin and looked directly into her eyes. "Be truthful."

Sad resignation crossed her features. "I don't know for sure. All I feel is tingling in my right arm and leg."

"Well, I'm taking you home."

"I want to stay for class. I'm already behind."

"Sarah, you need to rest. You can't keep going on this way. Do you really think that you can sew in this condition?" He'd seen that the control in her right arm wasn't at full capacity when she fell.

She shrugged.

"I'm taking you home. End of discussion." Mark hated to see Sarah's deflated demeanor, but she needed to stop overdoing it. He started to gather up their dinner. Sarah'd barely touched hers, so he'd make sure she heated it up at home.

"You can't take me home. I need my car to get to work tomorrow. I'm feeling much better anyway. By the time I sit through class, I'll have rested and will be able to drive myself home." Sarah slid from the edge of the table.

Tentatively, she put her left foot on the floor and then tested her right foot as if she were dipping it into a swimming pool to check the water's temperature. Taking in her subtle movements, Mark could tell her right leg was leaden.

"I'll be right back." Mark moved a chair closer for Sarah. "I'm going to tell Terri that I'll be gone for about an hour. Is there anything in your car that you need?"

"No." Sarah didn't disguise her terseness. "Really, Mark, I want to stay."

"I know that you want to stay, but you're not going to. You need some rest. While I'm talking to Terri, why don't you call someone to meet us at your house to stay with you tonight?"

Sarah's eyes grew wide, and her mouth gaped open at Mark's commanding tone. He'd hurt her feelings. The thought caused his heart to twist. It took all of his resolve not to cave in with an apology allowing her to stay.

"This is in your best interest." Mark purposely softened his tone. "I'll be right back to help you gather your things and take you home." He kept his eye on Sarah until he passed through the workroom door.

It surprised Mark to find a half dozen customers milling around the quilt store. He waited until Terri finished ringing up a customer, explained the situation, and headed back to the workroom.

Sarah hobbled from table to table. Her eyes met his when he came into the workroom. Mark crossed his arms over his chest and rocked back on his heels.

"My leg feels better, but you're right. I need to go home." She looked down at her pants leg. "Must have happened when I fell."

Mark saw the long rip in the leg of her outfit. "Are you sure you're not hurt from the fall?"

Sarah shook her head. "Only my pride. Thanks for catching me. Did you get hurt?"

"Judging by the burning pain in my thigh, I'm pretty sure I'll have a whopper of a bruise." Mark smiled at Sarah. "But I'll live. My truck's parked in back."

Mark gathered the same load of bags that he'd carried in from Sarah's car. He crooked his elbow. Still unsteady on her feet, Sarah slipped her hand through the opening and gripped his bicep as they made a slow journey to Mark's pickup parked in the back lot.

Mark opened the passenger door.

"I've got it." Sarah stepped onto the wide running board with her left foot and grabbed the handle attached just above the side window.

When she wobbled, Mark gripped her waist and steadied her; then she continued to maneuver her body into the seat.

Moments later, Mark had only driven a few blocks when he realized that Sarah was dozing, her head leaning against the window. What drove her to take on so much? Determination was an admirable quality but not to the extent Sarah was taking it.

At the stoplight, Mark turned to check on his passenger. Her soft, even exhales briefly fogged the passenger window. Her relaxed features showed no sign of stress. When the light turned green, the slight acceleration swirled the cool evening air through his open window. Was it too cold for Sarah?

He brushed her lower arms with his fingers, intending to check her skin temperature. Instead, it roused her from her slumber.

"Are we at my house already?" Sarah yawned and stretched then reclined her head against the headrest, facing Mark.

"Just about. Did you find someone to come and stay with you?"

After a few moments of silence, Mark glanced toward Sarah. Had she fallen back to sleep?

Sarah's eyes were wide open. "No, I didn't call anyone."

"Sarah, someone should be there with you."

"I know my parents or Karla would come, but"—her tired sigh showed her weariness—"I'm not up to the lecture that would accompany their help."

"Lecture?"

"They all think that I'm doing too much. Well, Karla doesn't think I understand the severity of my illness."

Anger flared in Mark, that Sarah's loved ones would lecture her when she didn't feel well. Didn't they understand that someday she might need their help getting dressed or in and out of a car? Mark's knuckles whitened as he gripped the steering wheel.

Sarah sighed as he turned into her short driveway. "They don't understand that, like Job, I'm taking the bad with the good in my life."

That explained Sarah's interest in the Job's Tears quilt block and why she signed up for a quilting class when she didn't know how to sew. Mark's anger at Sarah's support system died down to a smolder of annoyance. He wasn't quite sure that Sarah's interpretation of her problems mirrored Job's struggles. Job did nothing to bring on his suffering, and although Sarah did nothing to bring on the MS, she wasn't being very smart about the management of her disease.

Sarah needed to relax more. He suspected she started the quilting class for that purpose only to find it more stressful because she lacked sewing abilities.

"I wish you'd have called someone, but since you didn't, I'll stay long enough for you to get settled in for the night." As Mark parked, slipped from the pickup, and rounded the front, he chided himself for not staying in the workroom to make sure Sarah made the phone call.

Sarah opened the truck door and, with the help of the dashboard and headrest, turned in the seat. "I will be fine"—Sarah enunciated each word—"tonight, tomorrow, the next day."

She tried to slide from the passenger seat, but Mark blocked the open space with his body. He cupped her face in his hands. "I know you will because I'm going to see to it."

※

Mark arose early the next morning so he could pick Sarah up for work since her car remained in the parking lot in front of his store where it'd stay today. He'd devised a plan after he left Sarah's house the night before.

Slipping the earpiece of his phone into place, he commanded, "Call Sarah."

"Good morning, Mark." Some of the weariness in Sarah's voice had disappeared, probably due to a good night's sleep.

"Good morning. I'm on my way to your house to pick you up for work but just realized that maybe you don't feel like going into work today and want to call in sick."

"Of course I'm going to work today. I'm in the middle of compiling and finalizing remodel bids." Sarah didn't disguise the "duh" factor in her voice.

Mark ignored it and continued with his plan. "Have you eaten breakfast yet? I haven't and thought maybe we could swing through a drive-through on the way to your office." At least he'd know that she ate something.

"Oh, an egg sandwich sounds good." Her voice brightened.

"I should be there in fifteen minutes. Will you be ready?"

"Yes. See you in a few." Sarah giggled before she ended the call.

Instead of lecturing Sarah, like her family, about her overdoing, he'd figured an alternative approach might be more beneficial. Today, by driving her to work, he'd make sure she didn't have to fight rush-hour traffic and ate a good breakfast. There'd be no working late tonight because without a car, she'd be dependent on him to get her back to the quilt store. Since Terri's shift ended at six, Sarah would be forced to leave at quitting time.

He couldn't control her lunchtime for relaxing, but he'd make sure she had a relaxing dinner even if it was eaten in the workroom of the store with her feet propped on a folding chair. He didn't have all the details worked out, but he knew that his work schedule allowed him two days to surprise her with a lunch date. Again, she might not be napping to ward off the fatigue that accompanied MS, but she would be resting.

Mark pulled into her driveway. Before he could exit his vehicle, Sarah came out of her front door. She sported the yellow crop pants outfit that she wore to the first quilting class. She balanced her tote bag on her left shoulder. Mark saw the subtle drag of her right foot as she walked toward the pickup. Her shoe choice, sturdy low-heeled sandals that buckled just under her ankle, suited her disease better.

Mark exited his pickup. "Let me get that for you." He took her bag. The pleasant flowery scent that he'd come to associate with Sarah tickled his nose. He inhaled deeply as he slipped his hand in hers. "Not only do you look terrific, you smell good, too."

"Thank you." When Sarah giggled, light danced in her eyes, even though dark smudges remained under them. Hopefully, his plan would work and fatigue's telltale signs would be gone by the end of the week.

❧

On Saturday morning, Sarah waited for the barista to fill her order. She felt great. The problems with the construction blueprints started to diminish by Friday, which pleased her boss because of building costs and left Sarah's shoulders lighter without that burden of responsibility.

Mark surprised her for lunch two days in the past week and met her for dinner two nights. Sarah rolled her eyes. Being a typical man, he always brought or ordered too much food and insisted she take it home. Which was okay—less cooking and cleanup time involved in reheating leftovers, plus she enjoyed thinking about him while dining on his entrée.

A garden club event kept her mom in Brookings, so Sarah slept late then puttered around her apartment until after lunch. Now she intended to surprise Mark with a sweet treat then work on her quilt blocks.

Carrying a pressed-board tray—loaded with two coffees, a slice each of lemon poppy seed and banana bread—in one hand and her tote bag and purse in the other, Sarah walked to Granny Bea's. She stepped aside to allow a customer to exit and slipped in the open door.

Something was wrong. Mark's hair fell to the side, exposing some thinning on top. His light blue polo shirt was nearly untucked from his cargo pants on his right side, and his reddened face looked, well, harried.

Mark measured then cut fabric as he chatted with a customer. Several other people milled about the store.

Slipping the coffee tray and bag on a shelf under the cash register, Sarah wandered to the middle of the store. When she caught Mark's eye, he did a double take then sent her a weary smile. A disheveled stack of fabric bolts lay at the unused end of the cutting counter.

She turned a small circle on her heel, looking around the store. No sign of Terri or her daughter. Two carts full of patriotic material sat alongside empty shelving near the front of the store. Sarah walked over to it and found one cart actually held two neatly folded quilts.

Waiting until Mark finished ringing up his customer, she strolled toward the cash register with knitted brows. "What's going on here?"

"Illness struck at Terri's house. She and her daughter both have strep throat. Poor gals. Terri's voice is so raspy I could hardly understand her. But that leaves only me on a Saturday, of all days." Mark ran his fingers through his hair, the gesture explaining today's tousled hairstyle.

"Well, I put a treat under the counter for you, if you have time."

Mark lifted a cup of coffee and sipped it. "You might not believe this, but this is only my second cup of coffee today." He peeked into the bag and withdrew the banana bread. "I haven't eaten since breakfast."

Sarah watched as Mark inhaled the sweet treat. "What can I do to help?"

"Nothing. You came here to practice." Mark nodded toward the tote bag dangling from her arm as he handed her the second coffee and the bag.

Sarah pushed the bag back toward Mark. "I think you need that worse than me. Save me the calories."

"You don't have to worry about calories, Ms. Buckley." Mark winked. "But you also don't have to tell me twice that it's mine. I'm starving."

"Look." Sarah leaned on the counter. "I know I can't help on the register or the cutting area without training, but I can finish that display over there."

A hesitant look crossed Mark's features. He popped the rest of his lemon bread in his mouth and ran his fingers through his hair again. "I don't know. This is your day off."

"What does that have to do with anything?" Sarah wrinkled her brow.

Minutes passed before Mark audibly exhaled. "Okay, arrange it however you want."

Sarah celebrated with a victory fist, which brought a gleam to Mark's eyes.

"Hand me your tote, and I'll stow it under the register. But if you get tired, go back to the workroom and rest." Mark gave her a stern look and pointed his index finger at her. "I mean it."

"I will, don't worry." Sarah turned on her heel and headed toward the display area in the front of the quilt shop.

As she studied the pegboard that hung above the three-by-three-foot shelf, she determined that the quilts should be hung on the pegboard above the fabric. It would be easier to hang the quilts before she shelved the fabric bolts. Sarah moved the sturdy step stool to the shelf and began to hang the first quilt.

"Excuse me."

Sarah looked down at an elderly lady.

"Can you help me find this thread?" She held up the end sticker from a spool of thread.

After pushing another pin into the top of the quilt to hold it to the board, Sarah turned to find Mark. He was busy cutting fabric for a lady while another waited her turn. "Sure." Sarah climbed down from the step stool and took the offered spool information.

"Even with my glasses that print is pretty small. I don't want to get the wrong color."

Sarah led the way to the thread display, chitchatting all the way about the lady's quilt project. Sarah located the brand and color family before perusing the spools for the numeric code. "Here you go."

"Thank you."

As the woman walked away, Sarah went back to the display. During the next two hours, Sarah either assisted customers with simple requests or listened to their suggestions about the display she'd assembled. All the conversations warmed her heart and reminded her of the reason she'd loved her UPS delivery job so much—the varied conversations.

Mark approached the seasonal display just as Sarah was putting on the finishing touches. With his hair neatly combed straight back and his polo shirt now tucked into his sand-colored cargo pants, he'd lost the frazzled look from earlier in the day. Sarah thought Mark's hair combed this way complemented his eyes, yet she found him very attractive when his hair feathered across his forehead, as it had earlier in the day. Her fingers itched to ruffle his hair back up so it fell across his forehead in a tangled mess.

"I think you missed your calling. That's a great display." Mark studied both sides of the shelving and pegboard. He crossed his arms over his chest and rocked back on his heels. "This is an excellent idea." Mark waved a finger at all the red, white, and blue sewing accessories Sarah had arranged across the top of the flat framework of the shelf.

A thrill of pride bubbled through Sarah at hearing Mark's praise of her work. "I was going to ask your permission to add all the patriotic-colored thread, yarn, and quilt binding over here, but you were busy with a customer at the time. I figured if you didn't like it, I'd just put it back where I found it." Sarah shrugged.

"Whew, we've been busy today. Murphy's Law. I guess I should be shorthanded all the time. It's pretty quiet now, though, so you go practice your sewing and relax. Help yourself to a soda in the small fridge in my office."

Sarah glanced around the store. Two customers perused the fabric. She'd had so much fun helping out in the store that she hated for it to end, but she needed to get to work on her Job's Tears quilt blocks. "I probably should. I'm really behind on assembling my quilt blocks."

She followed Mark to the register area where he gathered her bag from under the counter. "Can you stick around until dinnertime? I'd like to buy you dinner, that is, if you don't mind eating in the workroom again."

"I can and I don't." Sarah flashed a broad smile over her shoulder as she walked back to the workroom. She grabbed a soda and Mark's office chair from the darkened room adjacent to the workroom.

She arranged a folding chair so she could put her right foot up while she sewed. She'd have to try running the foot feed with her left leg.

A slight tingle had started in her leg as she'd finished up the display.

She'd visited her MS doctor during the week, and he confirmed her suspicion—her MS now affected her right leg, too, a fact she planned to keep secret. She'd accepted her fate and knew that God was sending all her extra activities as the good to counterbalance the bad. She wished her family members felt the same way. She hated keeping secrets from them, but in a way she was sparing them, and herself, from more disagreements. What others didn't know wouldn't hurt them.

Chapter 9

Late Tuesday afternoon, Mark balanced on his haunches, storing extra thread in a lower cupboard. The door buzzer signal sped Mark's heart. Could it be Sarah? He glanced at his watch. Five o'clock. His heart rate returned to normal.

"Be with you in a minute!" Mark called, intent on finishing the task at hand. When all the boxes were stacked away in neat rows, his knees groaned with midlife stiffness as he pushed himself up onto his feet. He scanned the store but couldn't see anyone.

Mark walked toward the front of the store and saw a stocky, white-haired gentleman beside the patriotic display, leaning on a cane. "Uncle Walter?"

Mark held out his hand as he approached his father's brother.

"Mark."

Walter's hand met Mark's, his uncle's handshake firm, his uncle's eye contact deliberate, a holdover from his army days. Then Walter pulled Mark into a loose hug. Arm's length affection. It ran in the family.

"Nice setup you have here." Walter nodded toward Sarah's hard work. "Looks like something Gert would have put together. You must have inherited her artistic talents as well as her sewing skills."

Mark held his palms up. "I only sew enough to demonstrate the machines in the store. A friend of mine assembled the display, but I have to agree, it reminded me of Mom's work, too."

Walter met his eyes. "She was a good woman, your mom. Deserved better."

Mark's heart twisted, and instant moisture misted his eyes. He knew Walter wasn't referring to her MS. He swallowed hard but ended up answering his uncle with a nod. Walter patted Mark's shoulder then looked back at the display.

"I'm glad to see America being proud of her soldiers again. Greeting them at airports, holding celebrations."

Walter's wistful face held regret. Mark knew some of the returning Vietnam vets weren't showered with glory. He placed a hand on Walt's shoulder and squeezed.

"Well, I came here to ask you a favor. Is this a good time to talk?" Walter adjusted his glasses.

"Sure, if you don't mind talking on the sales floor. My sales help is at her dinner break." Mark crossed his arms and rocked back on his heels.

"Here's fine." Walter waved his hand in the air. "It's nothing that private." He lifted his quad cane. "Hip replacement surgery. I'm going to get rid of this."

"That's great. When?" Mark didn't remember his uncle without a limp. During active duty, shrapnel had injured Walter's hip.

"I'm shooting for October, after the busy season at the hotel. I know it's early, but I wondered if you'd take me to the VA hospital and wait while I had surgery."

"You know I will." That was the downside of being a Sanders man— no woman to help them during the hard times. But then again, it was of their own doing. Probably in a few months, Sarah would just be a pleasant memory. The thought clenched Mark's insides. The truth hurt.

"Thank you. Now I'll get the date scheduled with a surgeon and let you know." Walter smiled.

"Excuse me a second." Mark saw Sarah through the plate glass window and walked over to open the door.

"Thank you. I brought dinner." Sarah held up a bag from a grocery store deli.

"Smells great. Sarah, I'd like you to meet my uncle Walter." Mark guided Sarah by the elbow to where his uncle stood.

"Uncle Walter, I'd like you to meet Sarah Buckley." Mark relieved Sarah of her bags. "She's the one who arranged this display. Sarah, this is Walter Sanders."

Sarah met Walter's firm handshake and direct eye contact with a smile. "Do you like the patriotic arrangement?"

"Very much. You did a good job."

"Thank you. It was my first try. Would you like to stay and have dinner with us? There's plenty of food."

"Thank you for asking, but no. I want to get home before dark. You two go on and eat your dinner." Walter's cane rattled as he lifted it then thunked it against the tile floor as he took a step toward the door. "Good to know you." Walter nodded to Sarah.

Sarah reclaimed her bags. "It was nice to meet you, too." She wiggled her fingers at the men before turning and heading back to the workroom.

"Let me walk you out, Uncle Walter." Mark took short steps to keep the same stride as Walter. As they neared the front of the store, the door opened.

Mark and Walter paused as Caroline came into the quilt shop.

"Walter! How are you?" Caroline dropped the bags she carried and wrapped the man in a hug.

"Good." Walter patted her back. "How are you?"

"She's better than good—she's in love." Mark regretted the words as soon as he'd spoke them. Love and Sanders men just weren't a good mix.

Walter chuckled. "Congratulations, Caroline."

Caroline laughed.

"I can't believe you still hang around this guy after all the trouble he gave you growing up." Walter wagged his finger at Mark.

"The tables have turned. Now I give him trouble." Caroline continued to laugh as she picked her bags back up.

"It was nice to see you, Caroline. Mark, I'll be in touch."

Mark grabbed the door and held it open for his uncle. "Good-bye. Call me anytime."

"He looks good," Caroline said as she and Mark walked toward the back of the store.

"He's getting a hip replacement in October. He came to ask me if I'd sit at the hospital during his surgery." Mark sighed.

Caroline stopped walking. "Don't you want to?"

"Of course I do. It's just Uncle Walter's another reminder that Sanders men aren't good with relationships. They either leave or drive away women." Mark looked down at the toe of his scuffed loafers, not proud of the fact the same blood ran through his veins.

"Mark! You can't even compare Walter's situation with your father's desertion. Walter is a fine man."

What Caroline said was true, but what Caroline didn't say was true, too. His dad was a horrible example of a man, and that was whose blood coursed through Mark. His heart no longer pattered with happiness at seeing Sarah. This relationship was doomed to be short lived by genetics alone.

Until Caroline's soft fingers lifted his chin, he'd been so far into self-pity he didn't hear her bags rustle as she set them on the floor.

"Mark"—Caroline's tone now soft, soothing—"you and Walter are both Sanders men cut from the same cloth, fine cloth, good cloth, sturdy cloth. He is nothing like your father any more than you are. Don't ever forget that."

He searched her eyes and gave her a weak smile.

Caroline patted his cheek then picked up her bags and headed into the workroom.

Mark's gaze traveled to the plate glass window, searching for another glimpse of Walter, who was probably long gone by now. Was Caroline right? Walter hadn't shirked his duty to his country, having intended to keep his promise of marriage to his fiancée. He'd stayed solid in times of trouble, unlike Mark's father. Walter's qualities reminded him of denim—tough, strong, enduring—whereas his dad's character was as thin as cheesecloth.

Caroline's words supplied the sunshine Mark's heart needed to let hope grow. He favored Walter's character. Why had he never seen that before? Mark had helped his mother through difficulties with her MS, he rode out tough business times, and, because he loved Sarah, for the past week he'd changed his plans to ensure that she took care of herself by getting plenty of rest.

It took Mark's mind a second to catch up with his heart. He smiled. He loved Sarah, and knowing that she had MS didn't change that fact one bit.

※

Sarah's stomach grumble insisted that it was past lunchtime. In fact, it was thirty minutes past her lunchtime. Interruptions drew Sarah away from compiling and printing out the rent bills, normally a two-hour job. She'd started that task first thing that morning and was now just finishing. As she folded the last rent billing and stuffed it into the envelope, the door to her office swooshed open. Her shoulders sagged—not another construction problem on the third floor. If so, it'd be three for three today. She tentatively raised her eyes.

"Hi, Sarah." Karla crossed the short space to the cherrywood desk.

Not a construction problem but an issue just the same. Sarah felt her shoulders sag further but forced lightness into her voice. "Hi, Karla, what brings you here?"

"Well, I was hoping that you had a minute to talk." Karla started to sit down in the reception chair.

"Wait." Sarah held up her hand to stop Karla. "Can we talk in the break room while I eat my lunch?" That way Sarah could confine the unpleasantness, which she was sure was coming, into a room where a client might not overhear.

"Sure." Karla smiled as she adjusted her purse strap on her shoulder.

Sarah slipped the phone earpiece from her ear and led the way to the adjacent room. "Have a seat." She pointed to the folding chairs beside the imitation-wood-grain table.

Once Sarah retrieved her sandwich, orange, and soda, she sat beside Karla. "How have you been?"

"Good." Karla smiled. "How about you? I haven't seen you in, well, forever."

More like three weeks, but who was counting? "I'm good but tired most days." Sarah saw Karla's instant frown. "I landed a big lease—the entire third floor. It requires a major renovation, so I've been putting in long hours here."

"So, you're finally around people more?" Karla searched her face. "Because you're such a people person, I don't understand why you'd want to work such a solitary job."

Karla's comment struck a chord inside of Sarah. Since she helped Mark that day in the fabric store, she'd really missed the variety of people she saw in her old job. Here, Ashley was the only person she really talked to. Other than saying good morning to other tenants, Sarah's encounters were brief and sporadic.

"Well, it's an adjustment, but then again, there's no heavy lifting and it's climate controlled, which helps my MS symptoms. I guess it's the bad that I have to take with the good." Hopefully, that should convince Karla, although today Sarah had trouble swallowing Job's lesson.

Karla shrugged. "There are lots of jobs that are climate controlled where you'd interact with people all day. But if you like it, I guess. . ." Karla's voice trailed off as she looked around the bleak break room.

"I came here to give you this." Karla lifted her purse and unzipped the side pocket. She pulled out a check and handed it to Sarah. "My sponsorship for your MS walk."

"Thank you." The unexpected gesture cracked the wall Sarah had built around her heart where Karla was concerned. She gasped when she saw the amount. "This is very generous of you."

Karla shrugged. "It's the money I was saving for my trip to Europe. That isn't important anymore. I want them to find a cure for MS." Her gaze lowered, and her voice cracked. "I can't imagine life without you."

The defensive wall around Sarah's heart disintegrated. Had that been the real issue all along with Karla?

Sarah wiped the crumbs of lunch from her hands with her napkin then placed her hands over Karla's and squeezed. Karla finally lifted her gaze.

Sarah smiled. "Thank you very much. I'm sure it will help with research so all people who suffer with MS can lead fuller lives."

Karla nodded. "Now tell me what you've been up to besides working too much." Karla lifted her eyebrow to emphasize her last two words.

Today, the simple gesture warmed Sarah's heart instead of igniting her anger. "I volunteered to head the early bird Bible study through the summer, and in addition to my quilt class, I'm working on a committee to review church curriculum material."

Even as Karla's frown deepened the creases of her brow, Sarah's defenses stayed in check.

"Sarah, you're doing more now than you did before your diagnosis. Are you sure that you aren't overdoing it?" Karla pursed her lips. "Do you allow yourself any time to rest?"

Sarah drew a deep breath. Mark worried about that, too. Couldn't any of them see how much happier she was now versus six weeks ago? When she had too much free time, it turned into a pity party about having MS and she'd have to push herself to leave her house to visit the quilt shop. Now, unless her symptoms flared up, she was so busy she seldom gave her MS a second thought.

"I'm fine, really," Sarah said, certain that reassurance was all Karla really needed.

The skeptical look Karla shot her made Sarah flinch, and defensiveness began to niggle her insides.

"At least the quilt class ends in a couple more weeks. That should relieve some of your stress. How is it going, anyway?"

"Just a second and I'll show you." Sarah left the room to get her tote bag from her desk drawer. She pulled the completed blocks out as she returned to the room. "I planned to make a wall quilt, but I'm behind on sewing my blocks together." She placed six blocks in front of Karla. "I may be changing to the table runner."

Sarah sighed. When she did find the time to work on the Job's Tears blocks, she struggled with the lack of control from the MS in her arm, making the sewing even slower.

"I see improvement." Karla arranged the blocks side by side on the table.

"Thanks. I've found hand stitching the blocks works best for me." She paused, hoping Karla wouldn't say "I told you so" with her next admission. "And I'm also finding that I have to sew in spurts because of the MS in my arm, so it's taking longer than it should."

"Maybe I should have enrolled, and we could have made the quilt together since it seems so important to you." Karla started laughing. "Although my sewing wouldn't look any better than yours, and I don't have MS."

Sarah chuckled. "Remember those aprons we made in that home economics class we both hated?"

"Yes." Karla continued to giggle. "And they made us model those aprons in a fashion show. Embarrassing. That's why, for the life of me, I couldn't figure out why you enrolled in quilting class." Karla wiped at the corner of her eyes with the back of her hand.

"There was a reason." Finally, the conversation she'd been wanting to share with Karla for some time.

Karla sobered. "I know. You like the guy that runs the quilt shop. It's not like before, though, is it?"

"You mean one-sided interest?" Sarah searched her friend's face.

"No, I mean mixed signals. Sarah, I witnessed that married man talking to you, flirting with you, remember. I know your mom never thought so, but he led you on. You weren't wrapped up in some fantasy crush. He was a player. Please tell me that Mark isn't a player because—"

"I have the same look on my face when I talk about him?"

The astonishment on Karla's face pulled another laugh from Sarah. "Mom told me that."

Karla's features softened into a smile.

"One thing I know for sure is Mark isn't married. A family friend of his teaches the quilting class, and Mark introduced me to his uncle the other night."

"Okay, so he's not married, but that doesn't mean he's not a player and when your class is over you'll never see him again."

"Well. . ." Sarah wanted to jump to Mark's defense, but really, this was what she'd wanted Karla's reassurance on for a long time. "You tell me. He's always happy to see me. He's polite and treats me with respect. He compliments me, introduces me to people. We've only had one official date, but we spend a lot of time together. He drops by and brings me lunch and calls and text messages me throughout the day. He's always where he's supposed to be and, like you and Mom, he expresses his concern that I'm doing too much." Sarah stopped when she realized that she'd hardly taken a breath while she was ticking off Mark's attributes. Sheepishness stirred in her. "Sorry, I might have gotten a little carried away there. What do you think?"

"I think the only thing you left out is if he's a good kisser." Karla winked.

Sarah smiled broadly. "I don't kiss and tell."

Karla returned her smile. "He sounds like a great person. I hope to meet him soon, maybe at the MS walk?"

"You're coming to the walk?" Sarah clapped her hands together.

"Yes, to support you, encourage you, or just cheer you as you finish." Karla stood. "I'd better let you get back to work."

Sarah walked her friend to the door. What an unexpected joy God sent her today.

Karla stopped in front of the door. She pulled Sarah into a tight hug. "I still think that you are overdoing things a bit, but Mark is good for you. Happiness surrounds you like a halo when you talk about him. I really hope he loves you as much as you love him."

There was no time to respond to Karla's statement before her friend disappeared out the door. Where did Karla get the idea that Sarah loved Mark? Sarah never mentioned it to anyone, even though it was true. She loved Mark.

❧

"Am I glad to see you." Mark's expression showed his relief as he relocked the main door to the quilt shop. "I couldn't face another Saturday working alone."

"It's my pleasure, although I'm not sure how much help I'll be." Sarah stashed her purse and tote on the shelf under the cash register.

"Terri's family is sure having a run of bad luck. First strep, now food poisoning." Mark sighed and jerked his head toward the HELP WANTED sign. "I guess it's just coming at a bad time for me."

"Well, I'm here now. Just show me what you need me to do." Happiness bounced through her since Mark phoned early this morning. As soon as he'd hung up with Terri, he'd called Sarah. His first choice. He needed her.

"I think you're here in plenty of time for some training. Measuring and cutting the fabric isn't that difficult, but there are some other things I'd like to run through."

"Okay." Sarah adjusted the ruffled collar of her light pink top. Glad she'd chosen it along with the white crop pants and flat tennis shoes. On the phone, Mark had said to dress casual, but she thought the tennies might be pushing it. To her relief, Mark also wore athletic shoes, jeans, and a white polo shirt with GRANNY BEA's stitched across the left side.

"I know it was hypocritical of me to ask you to come in and help me out in the store today when I'm telling you all the time that you overdo it. So, I'm insisting that if you get tired, you go rest in my office. I don't care how many customers are milling around the store."

Sarah's heart swelled with pride and love that she was the first person Mark turned to in his time of trouble. That seemed like a good sign. "I promise I will. But I feel great today. Obviously, you haven't had any luck hiring someone." Sarah pointed to the HELP WANTED sign in the store window.

"I'm getting a lot of people who want to work certain part-time hours like afternoons or evenings. But the people who are flexible don't feel like a good fit for the store." Mark grimaced. "Sadly, I've been down that road, and it's easier to be under the stress of working alone."

Sarah closely watched as Mark demonstrated how to lay, smooth, and hold the fabric to cut it to ensure the accurate yardage. When it didn't take long for Sarah to catch on, Mark left her with instructions on cutting fat quarters while he ran down to the coffee shop for their breakfast.

After an hour of practicing cutting while Mark wrapped and marked the fat quarters, she felt confident she'd be an asset in the store. Time would tell, sooner rather than later. Mark flipped the door sign to OPEN and clicked the dead bolt.

Sarah continued to work on the fat-quarter task since Mark had fallen behind on that job in the last week. With each empty cardboard bolt she stacked in the cart beside the cutting table, a sense of accomplishment filled her. Similar to when she delivered parcels, and the piles became smaller and smaller.

Sarah's first customer test came about thirty minutes after the store opened. While Mark was busy showing a young woman the difference in the sewing machines, Sarah assisted a lady by cutting several yards of three different fabrics.

"What are you making?" Sarah wrote the number of yards on the preprinted form along with the price from the end of the bolt.

"This is backing for several quilt tops my church circle made. We're raffling one as a fund-raiser and giving the other two to the family that lost their home in a fire."

"What a wonderful idea. Will you get them quilted that fast?" Sarah measured a length of the fabric against the yardstick built into the counter. She repeated the process six times then smoothed the fabric and ran the scissors down the crevice in the countertop.

"We're tying the top to the back. That goes fast, and with many hands we'll get them finished in a couple of hours."

Sarah slid the folded cloth to the woman who then laid it in her cart.

"I'm not in a circle at my church, but I might steal your idea and see if the ladies in our circle will make a quilt and raffle it for a mission we sponsor in the fall." Sarah smiled. "We could choose a simple pattern."

"A nine patch sews fast."

"A nine patch." Sarah hadn't realized that she expressed out loud her mental note for the next committee meeting. Not knowing what that quilt design was, Sarah smiled at the lady. "I'll keep that in mind."

"Our circle made a pretty nine patch in red and green and backed it with poinsettia-printed fabric. We raised quite a bit of money with that quilt." The elderly lady's wide smile and twinkling eyes showed her love of quilting.

"Sounds lovely. Is there anything else?" Sarah smiled back at the lady.

"No thank you, dear."

"Good luck with your projects."

As the lady walked toward the cash register, Sarah rolled the bolts to tighten the remaining fabric. She heard Mark excuse himself from other customers so he could ring up the elderly lady's purchases.

Sarah looked up in time to see both Mark and the lady looking her way. The lady waved and headed for the door as Mark walked toward the cutting table. Sarah's stomach dropped. Had she done something wrong?

Mark shook his head as he crossed his arms over his chest; then he smiled. "That customer just told me that I should give you a raise." He gathered the bolts of material.

"What?" Sarah giggled. Then she knitted her brows. "You're teasing me. She didn't really say that."

"Yes, she did. She comes in here a lot and told me that even though you don't know what a nine patch quilt pattern is, you're a very nice person and you'll learn." Mark chuckled.

Sarah laughed out loud. "Guess my expression showed my lack of knowledge."

Mark shrugged. "All that matters is she left happy. Keep up the good work."

Sarah watched Mark restock the fabric bolts before returning to the customer in the sewing machine area. She liked that Mark had shared his customer's compliment. She liked the cheery atmosphere of the store. She liked working with Mark.

After hanging up the phone with Mark this morning, she'd said a prayer for Terri and her family for better health. But Sarah almost hoped Terri needed another day of rest. It was fun working in the store. Sarah had forgotten how enjoyable work could be.

Chapter 10

Mark added more navy-blue thread to the accessories on Sarah's display. She'd done such a good job helping him out on Saturday and Sunday afternoon.

Unfortunately, he hadn't seen much of her since then. She texted him throughout the day, and they spoke briefly once each day over the phone. Her schedule this week was full. Too full for someone with MS, and he'd added to her burden, leaving her little time to rest.

He really hadn't expected her to come into the store to work last weekend. After he ended the call with Terri last Saturday, he'd dialed Sarah's number without thinking, because he had a problem and he wanted to talk to her. Actually, she was the one he wanted to share everything with these days.

That was selfish of him, because what free time Sarah had, she needed to use it resting, not helping him out.

The jangle of the door buzzer startled him, and he knocked over four spools of thread. He caught three before they hit the floor, but the fourth rolled away from him.

"Hi, Mark."

Mark looked up from his retrieval duties. "Hi, Diane. Did you come for my team information?"

"Yes, and I'll collect donations if you have any."

"I have a new team member for Gert's Gang this year—Sarah Buckley." Mark made a spool pyramid with the navy thread before he zigzagged around material displays to where Diane stood. "The information's in my office. I'll just be a minute."

Diane was leaning against the register counter when Mark returned with the MS walk packet.

She read the list of names on his envelope. "All the regular walkers plus one."

"That's right."

"Is Sarah Buckley a friend of yours?" Diane glanced up from the envelope.

Mark drew a deep breath. Although Diane had no problem telling him she was engaged, Mark found it hard to tell a former girlfriend that he was dating someone else. Generally, he never again saw the women he dated.

"By the twinkle in your eyes, I'd say more than a friend of yours. A girlfriend, perhaps." Diane's warm smile encouraged him.

"We've been dating. Nothing serious." The last two words rushed from Mark's mouth with practiced ease. Why did he say that? This time it wasn't true.

"Right, nothing serious." Diane lowered the envelope then scanned the quilt store before looking directly into Mark's eyes. "Does she know that?"

"What do you mean?" He was always very forthcoming with his dating intentions. Had he been with Sarah?

"I mean, do your actions speak louder than your words? Are you saying you don't want a serious relationship—yet still doing all those little caring things you did while we dated, things that instill hope in a woman?"

Mark noted the slight edge in Diane's voice. Not quite sure what she alluded to, he crossed his arms over his chest and rocked back on his heels. With a grin, he kept his voice tone even and teasing. "Do I need to remind you that you broke our relationship off?"

Diane smiled sadly then shrugged. "No, you don't need to remind me. I thought if I broke it off, you'd have a change of heart—but you didn't." Sorrow infused her words.

She was serious. Is that what the other women had done, too? They hadn't gained self-confidence and planned to move on? Instead, they hoped by breaking it off, he'd come running back?

Diane laughed. "Your expression is priceless. You had no idea, did you? I wouldn't change one thing about my life right now, but Mark, you broke my heart. Just be mindful of this with"—Diane stopped and checked the envelope—"Sarah. Just be mindful of her feelings. They may be stronger than yours and, well. . ." Diane shrugged. "A broken heart's kind of hard on the self-confidence."

Mark felt like he'd walked behind a bowler who, just as the bowler swung the ball back for momentum on his roll, had clipped Mark in the stomach. Mark had broken Diane's heart, hurt her self-confidence. His body deflated. He was a Sanders man, through and through. "I'm s–s–sorry." Disbelief filled his words with the realization that his dating theory wasn't foolproof.

Diane adjusted her purse strap over her shoulder as she jutted out her chin.

The buzz of the air conditioner kicking on broke the thick silence in the store.

Diane fidgeted with the zipper tab on her purse. He'd broken her heart. What could he say to that?

"Well. . ." Diane sighed and turned to go.

Mark needed to say something. He caught her arm. "I am sorry, Diane. You're right. I had no idea that I hurt you like that. Please accept my apology." To how many other women did he owe this same courtesy?

Diane's lip curled into a sad smile. "I forgave you awhile ago, but I do accept your apology. Again, my life is better than I ever thought it'd be, but I've needed to hear that from you. I've needed that closure for a long time. So, thank you. And now maybe you could do me a favor."

"Anything."

"I know this is none of my business, but. . .don't hurt Sarah the way you hurt me." Moisture filled Diane's eyes, and she blinked rapidly before giving him a weak smile. "I guess I'll see you Saturday at the walk." She turned on her heel and headed for the door.

Mark watched Diane leave the store, then the parking lot. He stared blankly through the plate glass store window. What had he done? Followed right in his dad's footsteps, that's what. He might not have been married to the women, but he deserted them in other ways. Was he giving Sarah false hope? When push came to shove would he back away from her?

Mark watched a cloud pass over the sun, blocking out its rays, just like Diane's admission covered his heart with sadness. How on earth did he think his dating plan was fair?

Lord, please forgive me for hurting all the ladies I dated in the past. I've been blind to the feelings of others, and I'm truly sorry.

He didn't deserve Sarah. Maybe he didn't deserve anyone. Sanders men just weren't dependable. Mark turned from the window. Yet he'd helped his mom run this store, and he didn't hesitate when Walt asked for his assistance earlier in the week.

He'd do right by Sarah even if it meant his heart got broken.

❧

Would this light never change? Sarah rubbed her right arm, but it remained dead. Using her left hand, she moved her right arm to a comfortable position on the armrest. With difficulty she guided her car through the intersection, taking it slow for easier steering. Even though it was Saturday, she'd taken the long the way to the park where the MS walk started, to avoid heavy traffic.

She yawned. What a busy week she'd had, but at least after this morning, she could cross one thing off her to-do list. By the afternoon, another item, the last curriculum meeting, would be marked off; then maybe she could get some quilt blocks sewn together. She flexed the fingers of her right hand as her arm rested. Hopefully, her medicine would kick in soon. She'd needed to refill her prescription but just couldn't work a stop at the pharmacy into her schedule this week. So she'd skipped her dosage a few days, to stretch her meds out until today when she could get to the drugstore.

Maybe she should have taken Mark up on his offer of a ride to the walk. The parking lot was packed. Awkwardly, Sarah turned her steering wheel with her left hand. Pulling her compact into one of the few remaining spots was tricky one-handed.

Sarah slipped from her car then zipped her car keys in the front pocket of her backpack. After several attempts to get her backpack in position with a numb right arm, she finally just inserted her left arm in the arm strap and let the backpack dangle at her side.

With each step toward the Gert's Gang gathering spot, Sarah's right leg tingled. She took deliberate and slow steps. Why of all days were these MS symptoms so intense? Mark waved as soon as he saw her. Caroline and Rodney turned and waved, too. Sarah straightened and tried to walk her normal stride but felt like her right foot was sliding into each step.

"Sarah, we were getting worried that you stood us up." Caroline patted Sarah's back as Sarah stopped by the group of people gathered around Mark.

"Here is a shirt for you." Mark held out a red MS walk T-shirt with the corporate sponsors listed on the back.

"I'm glad I wore navy yoga pants." Without thinking, Sarah tried to pull on the T-shirt. Her right arm failed to move in the direction it needed to.

Mark stared at Sarah. "Are you okay?"

"Just a little MS problem." Sarah forced a smile and wrestled with the T-shirt sleeve. "I think it's due to the unseasonable heat and humidity that blew in this week."

"Let me help." Mark took her backpack and guided her arm through the sleeve. He pulled the back of the T-shirt down while Sarah pulled the front. "Should you be walking today?"

Already annoyed with the flare in her MS symptoms, anger surged through Sarah. "I'm fine." She snapped the words as she fought back a yawn.

"Okay." Mark held up his hands in defeat then grinned. "I missed you this week."

His smile and words warmed her heart. "I missed you, too. I'm so behind on sewing my quilt blocks, but I've been working late and had two church meetings." Sarah tried to suppress another yawn but failed.

"Have you been getting enough rest?" Mark's beautiful hazel eyes were hidden as he narrowed his gaze on her.

"I went to bed late last night, that's all." She wasn't about to tell Mark that she'd been up past midnight every night this week. He was beginning to sound like Karla and her mother. She didn't need that today. It was taking every ounce of her strength to stand. She looked around for a bench. "I'd like to sit down."

"There's a chair over there." Mark crooked his elbow.

Praise God that Mark was a gentleman. Having him to lean on made her walking easier. She eased into the chair.

"Would you like some coffee? They have a stand over there." Mark pointed.

"I'd love some."

Sarah listened to the anxious chatter of the other walkers. She'd looked forward to this day, but now she felt too tired to enjoy it.

Mark handed her a cup of coffee then sat on the ground next to her. "They have doughnuts, too. Would you like one?"

"No thanks." Sarah sipped the bitter beverage brewed stronger than she really liked.

"Is any of your family coming?"

Sarah rolled her eyes. "I doubt it. They aren't too supportive of my activities."

"I don't know two of the people who gave you very generous donations. I assumed the couple with your last name was your parents." Mark winked.

"Yes, the other one was my friend, Karla."

"Isn't she the one—"

"That thinks I'm doing too much? Yes, but then that seems to be the general consensus of everyone I know." Sarah looked pointedly at Mark.

His Adam's apple bobbed as he set his jaw. "Sarah, I think their concerns are valid. You don't rest enough. Fatigue is a huge issue for MS patients. You are overdoing it."

Sarah rolled her eyes. "I'm just proving that a person with MS can lead an active life." She let the terseness she felt flow into her words.

"The key word there is *active*. You are leading an *over*active life. I don't think I could keep the schedule that you do, and I don't have MS."

Sarah blinked. She'd never really considered that before. Had she been this involved in activities before her diagnosis? She'd worked overtime on her old job during the holiday season. She'd always been involved in at least one church committee. Really the only thing new was Mark, the quilting class, and the MS walk.

"Discouragement is not what I need today." Her own body's rebellion was enough to handle without everyone else thinking she should give up.

But she'd learned from Job's story that if she trusted God, He'd help her to understand this affliction. See her through. After all, He'd already provided so many good opportunities for her that she shouldn't even be grumbling about her MS symptoms today. "I'm finishing this walk."

Mark pursed his lips. "Well, I'm staying right beside you. You do realize that I recognize the subtle MS signals that maybe your mom and Karla miss."

"Like?"

"The shuffle of your feet to hide the slight limp or sliding your feet along versus taking a step." Mark touched her forearm.

She pulled it away. "You are the one person I felt was on my side. Because of your mom I thought you understood how important it is for me to continue on with life as normal as possible." She tried to push off the chair, but her right arm slid off the canvas arm. Mark's strong arms stopped the chair's wobble.

"Sarah, let me help you." He stood to the side of the chair and wrapped his arm around her. She leaned into his warmth, and as he lifted, she stood.

"Thank you." Her appreciation came out more clipped than she'd intended, but she was tired. She was in pain. She was fed up with all the people wanting her to give up.

"I am on your side, Sarah."

Someone called Mark's name before she could respond. She pulled free of his embrace. "Go, where *you're* needed."

The immediate hurt that registered on Mark's face twisted her heart with regret. Yet the disappointment she felt in the knowledge that he agreed with her mom and Karla justified her remark. Maybe she was wrong that Mark cared for her.

"I'll be right back." Mark let go of her but kept his eye on her as he walked away, no doubt looking for those telltale MS signs.

"A few of us are going to get started." Caroline stopped beside Sarah. "I'd ask you to join us, but I'm sure you're waiting for Mark." Caroline's blue eyes twinkled as she teased Sarah.

Sarah glanced to where Mark stood, his back facing her. "Actually, I'd like to get started. I'll join your group, and Mark can catch up."

With concentrated effort, Sarah bent down and picked up her backpack. Straightening, she brought up the rear of the small group of people. The short rest in the chair eased some of her symptoms. Although her arm ached, she felt she'd regained some of the control in her right leg. Not quite her normal gait, but she was keeping up with the group.

The sun blazed in the morning sky. She prayed that the front that moved into the area, bringing unseasonable mid-May warmth and humidity to South Dakota, would pass by this day. Her prayer went unanswered.

Although the temperature was actually a comfortable seventy-five degrees, the dew point made it feel more like eighty-five. Her sweat-dampened hair stuck to the nape of her neck. She raised her left arm and swiped the side of her face with her T-shirt sleeve. The weather fought against any good her MS meds were doing for her today.

Pain shot up Sarah's right leg with the next step she took. She grimaced but managed to stifle a groan.

"Sarah!" Mark's voice rose above the noisy laughter and chatter of the walkers.

She didn't want Mark to see her difficulty in walking. It took all her resolve to try to take a normal step. Whether anyone liked it or not, Sarah was like Job. She wanted to accept the bad with the good that God sent her way. Why couldn't others see their negative attitudes weren't conducive to her well-being?

"Sarah, wait."

Glancing over her shoulder, Sarah saw Mark jogging toward her. Once again, with concentration, she moved to take a normal step.

Her leg didn't cooperate. She started to wobble. The loaded backpack threw her balance off. She let it fall to the ground and tried to overcompensate, but with the lack of feeling in her leg she had no idea where to find her footing. She tried to throw her weight to the left, but the movement increased the speed of the fall. Her body pulled her backward. She closed her eyes and braced for the impact with the sidewalk.

"Oh." Mark's breath added additional heat to the back of her neck as her body knocked into his sturdy chest. He gently set her down on the sidewalk. "Are you all right?" He panted the words.

"Yes." Sarah's left leg was bent, and her right leg stuck straight out.

Members of the group she'd been walking with turned around when they heard the commotion. As a small crowd began to gather around her, humiliation stirred the embers of her anger into full-fledged flames. "Just help me up," she snapped.

"Not until I make sure you are okay."

Mark's terse tone turned her anger into rage. She struggled to get up, but her body wouldn't cooperate.

"You aren't going anywhere until the on-site paramedics check you out." Mark's firm grip held her in place.

She turned her head and glared at him. "Help me up."

His hazel eyes glared back at her. He clenched his teeth. "It's the walk's rules. I'll help you up after they check to make sure you aren't hurt." He tightened his hold on her arms. "If you're hurt, they'll take you to the hospital. If you're not, I'm taking you home."

Sarah started to retort when two paramedics broke through the small crowd of people. After they shooed the people on, they went through a series of limb-movement checks. All they found was a cement burn on her left leg from her having grazed the cement on her way down.

After the paramedics cleaned then applied antiseptic to the abrasion, they set her in a wheelchair and suggested she let Mark push her for the rest of the walk. Sarah's humiliation deepened.

What a nightmare! She wanted out of this horrible chair. Why of all times had the weather heated up so early in the season and brought her such misery?

Mark sat in the grass beside the wheelchair and allowed the paramedics to clean the scrape that ran the length of his calf. Since the paramedics had first arrived, she'd avoided his gaze, but now she stole a glance his way. His face showed no emotion, and he laughed when the paramedic made a joke about the rescuer's injuries being worse than the rescuee's.

She should reach out, squeeze Mark's hand, and thank him for his help. After all, it was the second time he'd saved her from severe injury. But if she did it would seem like she'd be admitting defeat, especially after his change of attitude toward her active lifestyle. Mark stood and shook hands with the paramedics then turned to Sarah. "Where's your cell phone?"

His question confused her. Had he lost or broken his in the fall? "My backpack. Why?" She dug through the small area where she stowed her keys then held out her cell.

He shook his head. "Call someone—your mom, your friend, anyone, and tell them to meet us at your house."

"What?" Sarah's voice showed her surprise.

"We're not having a repeat of last time. You need someone at your house until you can get your MS under control. They need to make sure that you rest."

"I'm fine. It's just the heat." Sarah started to put the cell phone away.

Mark snatched it from her. "I'll do it, then. Who do you want me to call—your mom or Karla? It's not just the heat, Sarah. You have to scale back your activities. The long days at the office, followed by church committee meetings—they're adding to your misery."

"Give me my phone." Sarah reached in Mark's direction. He handed her the phone.

"And unfortunately, I've added to your stress, too, letting you help me in the store. I'm sorry for that. I knew better, and it won't happen again."

Bitter tears burned in Sarah's eyes. How could he take away the one thing she really liked, helping at the fabric store? "But I was just rescuing you those days, like you just did me."

Mark pursed his lips and shook his head. "Not the same, Sarah. Please make the call so I can get you home."

"What if I don't want to go home? What if I want to stay for the entire walk?" She jutted her chin out in defiance.

"Fine, but you're spending it in the wheelchair." Mark positioned his stocky frame in front of her as if to block her escape. Right now, making a break for it seemed like a great idea.

Her gasp sounded far away and faint, like the last echo bouncing back to its caller. The sad reality snuck in. It didn't matter what her mind or spirit wanted—her body bound her to the wheelchair, holding her captive.

Her anger, instant and intense, caused her hands to tremble. She had no choice. Today she was dependent on Mark and whomever she decided to call. Why had this happened to her?

❧

The urgent slap of sneakers on the cement drew Mark's attention from Sarah and gave him a second to compose himself. Her wounded expression twisted his heart in pain. He hated being stern with Sarah, but she obviously didn't comprehend the effects of MS on her body.

"Sarah, are you all right?" As she ran, the woman's purse swayed from her elbow then slapped into Mark's chest as she bumped into him when she squatted down in front of the wheelchair.

Sarah's lip quivered, but she squared her chin again.

"Did someone knock you down?" The woman grasped Sarah's hand.

Sarah's slight head shake removed the panicked concern from the woman's face. The woman's eyes narrowed, and Sarah took a sudden interest in her backpack.

Mark cleared his throat. "She fell."

The woman stood and raked her eyes over Mark. "Are you Mark?"

"Yes." Mark stuck his hand out.

"Karla." She clasped the hand he offered.

"I think Sarah was just about to call you."

They both turned to Sarah. She sighed and looked from Mark to Karla.

"My MS is really bothering me *today*." Her annoyance showed on the last word. "Mark feels that someone should stay with me for a while. Would you be able to spend a couple of hours at my house?"

"So you don't want to stay for the walk?" Mark wanted to verify her intention, since a few minutes ago she wanted to finish the walk.

Sarah yawned. "No. I want Karla to take me home." She flashed an indignant look at Mark.

"Um. . ." Karla looked at Mark and then Sarah. "I have to pick up my dog from the groomer in twenty minutes, but after that I'd be happy to take you home and stay with you."

Like a half-burned candle melting in a votive cup, Sarah dissolved in the depth of the wheelchair. She needed to get out of the hot, humid weather.

Mark frowned. "I'll take you home and wait until Karla can get there."

"Okay." Her meek voice revealed her reluctance to be dependent on others.

Mark hated seeing Sarah like this, probably just as much as she hated being in this situation. How could he make her see that some of her misery was self-inflicted?

Karla again kneeled in front of Sarah. "I'll stop at my house and pack a bag. We'll have a sleepover, just like old times. I'll pick up some lunch and treats. Is there anything special you'd like?"

Sarah dug through her backpack. She pulled out a pill bottle. "Can you stop and pick up my refill?"

"Sure." Karla took the bottle and put it in her own purse as she stood. "I'm leaving now. I'll see you at your house."

Mark watched Sarah pull a bottle of water from her backpack and struggle to remove the cap.

"I can do that for you." Mark reached for the bottle but backed off at the look Sarah shot him. "Let's get you home, then."

For once it paid for Mark to get to the walk site early. His pickup wasn't parked far from the starting point. He pushed the chair to the truck and angled it so he could open the passenger door.

In the second it took Mark to swing the door wide, Sarah had stood. "I don't think so." Mark admired Sarah's independent spirit, but ever since she'd fallen down, he'd wanted to scoop her into a tight embrace. The two quick steps it took Mark to get to Sarah seemed endless. He lifted her as if he would carry her across a threshold.

To his surprise she wrapped her arms around his neck, buried her face in his shoulder, and began to cry. Mark instinctively tightened his hold around her waist.

"Oh Sarah." He managed to choke out the words around the lump in his throat before kissing the top of her head.

Sarah stiffened. Her hands pushed against his chest as she tried to sit erect in his arms. "Don't. Pity. Me." Each word held a drip of venom like the fangs of a coiled rattlesnake.

What just happened? Mark searched Sarah's face. Though her eyes were red rimmed there was no mistaking the lick of angry flames flashing in her coal-colored eyes. "Sarah, I—"

"Put me in the truck." Even through clenched teeth, Sarah's words were loud and clear. She'd set her features as if she'd been etched in stone.

Mark obliged by lifting her onto the truck seat. He moved forward to assist in adjusting her to a more comfortable position.

"I've got it."

Mark wanted to help her. To defend himself. To protect her.

Instead, he backed away and closed the pickup door. He pulled the wheelchair back to the sidewalk, stopping by the driver's side. The weather was too hot for Sarah to wait in the vehicle while he returned the wheelchair to the paramedics.

He flicked the door handle and inserted his key in the ignition. A quick turn and the truck engine roared its start. He pressed the air-conditioning button and turned the fan to high. Sarah might not take care of herself to reduce her MS symptoms, but he could. He sneaked a glance Sarah's way. She wiggled herself back into the seat and snapped the safety belt.

"I'll be right back."

A snort of air was Sarah's indignant reply.

Mark shut the truck door, grabbed the wheelchair handles, and then hurried along the sidewalk, dodging other walkers, reporters, and onlookers. He'd envisioned this day much differently. A hand-holding, romantic stroll from start to finish, ending with a heart-to-heart talk over dinner, hoping he read her signals correctly and that she, too, wanted to take their relationship to a more serious level.

Obviously, he'd misread those signals. Why was he surprised? Didn't he recently find out that he'd broken many hearts along the dating path? Was the pain ripping into his heart right now payback for all the suffering he'd caused other women?

Mark handed off the wheelchair and thanked the paramedics for their help before turning back toward the parking lot.

Caroline's opinion about him being more like Walter than his father had hushed the warning voices inside Mark, causing him to let his guard down. Sarah's immediate rejection to his words of comfort separated the false happiness he held in his heart from the stark reality. He was a Sanders man. They didn't win in love.

The click of the pickup door roused Sarah from her quick nap. She lifted her sleep-laden lids, saw it was Mark, and then turned her head toward the side window and closed her eyes.

The low volume of the radio and Sarah's even breathing supplied white noise for Mark's thoughts as he drove across town to Sarah's house.

Her self-inflicted exhaustion and misdirected use of her meds had obviously caught up to her. Perhaps that drove her attitude today, mistaking his comfort for pity. His mom's MS fatigue made her cranky but not vehement. Something drove Sarah to overdo. But what? And more importantly, why?

Mark pulled into Sarah's driveway. They'd beaten Karla. He pushed the gearshift into Park, killed the engine, and still Sarah didn't stir.

He knew she'd deprived herself of rest, so he wanted her to sleep as long as she could. Carefully he slid the backpack from her lap. Quietly he exited his vehicle, searched for her house keys, and unlocked the door.

Sarah's head still tilted sideways, her forehead resting against the side-window glass. He lifted the door latch and cracked the opening. He stuck his arm through the small space, held Sarah's shoulder, and then opened the door wide.

His touch startled her awake.

"You're home," Mark whispered. The softness of Sarah's skin invited his hand to stay put on her shoulder even as she straightened her head.

Sarah blinked several times like a sleepy child. The last blink uncovered the deepened anger that shone from her eyes. She'd gotten her bearings.

Her left hand swatted Mark's hand from her shoulder. "I think I can do this on my own." Sarah turned her frame until her legs dangled in the open doorway.

"Let me help you." Mark hovered at the edge of the pickup door, on alert for the first sign that a limb might inhibit her movement and knock her off balance.

"I don't need help." Sarah's voice shook as she spit out the words. She eased herself to the sidewalk and, holding on to the edge of the pickup bed, stood clear of the door.

Mark gave it a push, and the latch clicked its closure.

Sarah braced herself against the body of the four-wheel drive with her left hand and slowly took a step.

Walking a few feet to her side, Mark noted the slide of her right foot versus an actual step, but it was better mobility than she'd had at the MS walk. Her right arm, however, stayed stationary at her side. When she made her way around the vehicle, she stopped. There was about three feet between his bumper and the stair railing to her door.

Tentatively she took a step and wobbled. Her stubborn I-can-do-this attitude had gone on long enough. Mark wrapped her arm around him. "Lean in to me."

"I wish Karla were here." Sarah tried to look around Mark.

Mark's heart sank. He wanted her to wish for his help. Still unclear how she'd interpreted his earlier response as pity, he cleared his throat. "Sarah, I'm sorry I made you angry today. I only have your best interest at heart."

Sarah allowed him to lead her to her door.

"My backpack." She tried to turn, but his firm grasp didn't allow it.

"I placed it just inside the door."

She shook her head and reached for the doorknob. "You can let go of me now."

Mark released her physically, but emotionally he held on. "Sarah, I—"

"Enough." She held up her hand. "I thought you of all people would understand. After all, you told me that your mother led a full life with MS, just like I'm trying to do. Yet you are really like everyone else, full of pity for poor, sick Sarah." She twisted the knob and stepped through the threshold.

"Sarah, being overinvolved and living a full life are two different things." Mark took a step toward the door. Sarah's palm thumped into his chest.

"I'll be fine until Karla gets here. I thought you cared for me, but now I realize you just took pity on me. Have a nice life. Good-bye, Mark."

Sarah hurled her words at him like a fast-pitched softball. Dazed and confused, Mark took a step back just before the door banged shut.

Chapter 11

The insistent rumble of Sarah's stomach forced her to hang up her office phone after being on hold with a carpet warehouse employee while he checked the order mix-up for the new lessee's carpeting. Her boss wanted the issue resolved as soon as possible, but she'd have to call back later. She needed to take her medicine and eat lunch.

Sarah removed her Bible from her bag and headed back into the break room. She'd called in sick yesterday and gone to her MS doctor. The steroid shot she received at her appointment worked wonders for her leg. If she kept her stride slow, she managed her normal gait. Her arm was back to what she referred to as "MS normal." She sighed.

How had she been so wrong about Mark? Why did everyone else think they knew what was best for her? She was glad that Karla had insisted on Sarah's sleeping in and taking short naps for the remainder of the weekend, including Sunday, even though Sarah hated missing church. But the relaxing weekend and sick day on Monday had left her feeling refreshed and almost pain-free, not to mention clearheaded.

She stuck leftover Chinese in the microwave and uncapped her water bottle. Once her lunch was heated, she settled in at the table and opened her Bible. As leader of the summer Bible class, she'd chosen to study the book of Job, mostly for the same reason she wanted a quilt made from the Job's Tears pattern—a reminder that Job accepted his fate. He knew how to take the good with the bad, just like she accepted her MS diagnosis and all the changes that came with it.

"I missed you yesterday. What are you up to?" Ashley breezed past her to the refrigerator.

"Getting the lesson ready for my Wednesday morning Bible study." Sarah turned in her chair as Ashley grabbed an apple from the refrigerator and took a bite.

She walked over and stood behind Sarah. "You're studying Job. I always felt so sorry for him, the way the devil used him as a guinea pig. He endured all the bad stuff the devil inflicted him with, yet he still trusted God. That's the kind of faith we all need."

Sarah smiled, knowing she did have the faith of Job, trusting God, and He'd given her all these wonderful activities to take her mind off her disease.

"How'd the MS walk go?" Ashley planted herself on the folding chair opposite Sarah.

The smile faded from Sarah's face as the feelings of helpless humiliation rushed back to her. It wasn't bad enough that she fell in front of everyone, but then she gave in to her disappointment and weakness, thinking Mark would understand. But instead of consolation she received pity.

"Sarah?" Ashley's brow wrinkled in confusion.

"Well. . ." Sarah sighed then turned in her chair and lifted her crop pants over her knee. "I fell about a block into the walk, so that's as far as I got."

"What? What happened? Did you trip?" Ashley leaned forward in her chair to study Sarah's injuries.

Ashley's concern-filled questions brought hot tears of relief to Sarah's eyes. If anyone would understand, she knew that it'd be Ashley. She actually cared about Sarah's well-being. "My MS symptoms tripped me up."

"I see." Ashley leaned back into her chair.

Her voice lost its previous concern. "Were you doing too much again? I know you put in long, stressful hours last week. I overheard your boss chewing you out about going over budget on the remodel project." She lifted her eyebrows.

Sarah shrugged. "It was just part of my job." It seemed that was really what the job was about, taking complaints from the renters, her boss, and now the construction crew. She missed the days that people were happy to see her bring a package through the door.

"I'm no doctor, but Sarah, I think you need to scale back. I think you should tell your boss that the construction project is just too much for you to handle."

"I can't do that!" Sarah's voice rose with each word. "I'll get fired." Why did everyone think she didn't need to earn a living?

"Well, there are many ways to make a living."

Had Ashley read her mind?

"Don't look at me like that." Ashley laughed. "Take me, for example. I'm a freelance writer and paralegal. Surely you have other options than managing this building."

Young, hopeful, and optimistic—qualities in Ashley that Sarah admired. Yet they didn't really apply to a woman pushing forty who'd been diagnosed with MS. She'd taken the first job offered to her because she feared she'd have trouble getting hired at her age with an illness.

"Don't be such a skeptic." Ashley laughed harder. "I'm making it my goal to help find a better-suited job for you. One with way less stress. Let's see. Maybe a preschool teacher?"

Ashley continued to list obscure professions until Sarah finally laughed. "Okay, okay, if you find any of those job openings, I'll apply."

"Good." Ashley threw her apple core into the waste can beside the wall. "How's it going with Mark?"

Sarah's shoulders sagged.

"I see." Ashley touched Sarah's arm. "What happened?"

A flicker of anger still burned in Sarah at his reaction to her tears. However, it was no longer directed at Mark and his pity, but herself. Over the course of the weekend, she decided that, once again, she'd been a poor judge of a man's intentions.

"It seems I misread Mark's interest in me. He only feels pity for me, not love."

Ashley's eyes narrowed. "Are you sure?"

"As sure as I am that I have multiple sclerosis."

*

Jitters shook her insides as soon as Sarah pulled into the parking lot beside the quilt shop for her last class. She'd tried to arrive as close to class time as possible. She didn't want to see Mark.

If only she could race through the store to the workroom, but she couldn't find her tote bag with the few completed Job's Tears quilt blocks and the remaining supplies to make a wall quilt. The last time she remembered seeing it was the day she helped Mark in the store.

So although she didn't want to see or talk to Mark, she might be forced to. Perhaps she'd get lucky and Terri would be working.

From her car, Sarah tried to peer into the plate glass window to catch a glimpse of the salesperson on the floor. She was familiar enough with the routine of the store to know that someone would be at his or her dinner break.

Sarah fumbled around in her car, picking up trash and straightening floor mats for a few minutes until she saw Caroline arrive. That was when it occurred to her that she wouldn't be staying even if her tote was there.

She'd promised Caroline last week that she'd be caught up to the class with all the blocks completed and sewn into a top, ready to quilt. She didn't even have enough blocks completed to make a table runner. For a moment she considered leaving and cutting her losses. Instead she drew a deep breath and stepped out of her car.

Nervous apprehension knotted her stomach with each step closer to the door. She wanted to see Mark, yet she didn't. Over the weekend her feelings flip-flopped between apologizing to him for closing the door in his face or thanking him for the assistance he gave her, even though it came with a lecture. She'd been flabbergasted when Karla suggested she call him on Sunday evening to let him know that she was feeling better. In the end she decided that it could wait until tonight. And now she hoped to avoid him altogether.

The jangle of the bell seemed amplified as she braced for Mark's normal greeting to customers. However, it was a woman's voice who called, "Be right with you!"

Terri. Sarah's heart wrenched. Tears of disappointment threatened her eyes. She swiped at the dampness with her fingertips. What on earth was that all about? Yet she knew. She'd expected Mark.

Sarah waited by the cash register and watched Terri approach from the clearance section of the store.

"Hi, Sarah. Did you need something before class starts?" Terri eyed the clock above the door.

"I can't seem to find my tote bag with my class project. I remembered having it with me the day I helped Mark." Sarah's voice cracked as she said his name. She cleared her throat. "The day I helped out at the store."

"I know Mark really appreciated your help those two days. We get so many compliments on that patriotic display. I think your tote is in the back room, right where you left it."

As Sarah opened her mouth to tell Terri that she'd never made it as far as the back room, the store's front door opened. Sarah's heart betrayed her as it skipped a beat in hope that Mark would come through the door. The overwhelming disappointment threatened her eyes again as the two elderly ladies returned Terri's greeting.

"I can't believe six weeks have passed. Can you?" The friendlier of the two ladies looked at Sarah and motioned for her to join them walking back to the class.

"Um. . .no." Sarah guessed she should go back and see if her bag was on the table. She wondered if Caroline would allow her to sit and sew a block while the others learned to start quilting their project. If not, she'd make her apologies to Caroline and the class, and leave.

Sadly, Karla was three for three. Sarah's job wasn't right for her. The quilt class wasn't right for her. And Mark wasn't right for her. She wouldn't be in this situation if she hadn't been inflicted with MS. Self-pity began to weave its way through her thoughts.

Sarah allowed the elderly women to walk into the workroom first. Caroline instructed the other two classmates on how to pin the project together for quilting. Sarah's eyes rested on her tote on the table beside the sewing machine she used. The memory of Mark's demonstrating the machine tugged at her heart. A phantom feeling warmed her skin where his hand had cupped hers.

She might have told herself that she didn't want to see Mark tonight, but she did. She sighed as she picked up her tote, ready to make apologies to everyone in the room. The heaviness surprised her, and then she noted the girth of the bag. Slowly she sat down and pulled the contents from the bag.

"Ouch." She flinched as her finger met a straight pin holding the back fabric and batting to the quilt top.

"Wow, Sarah, you were busy this week. Hold your project up for the class to see." Caroline clapped her hands together, as if her voice didn't hold enough surprise.

Confused, Sarah shook her head. "I don't think this is my project." Yet the fabric did match the color scheme she'd chosen for her Job's Tears quilt. Carefully, she unfolded the lumpy square.

"It's beautiful," the young girl exclaimed.

"Yes, it is." Caroline lifted a corner and ran her hand over it then looked up at Sarah with a twinkle in her eye. "I was so surprised when Mark called and asked me to bring a hand-quilting hoop for you tonight since he'd just sold the last one he had in inventory."

"Puts mine to shame." One of the elderly ladies shook her head.

"I. . ." Sarah looked around the room at the class. "I didn't make this quilt. There must be some mistake." She laid the quilt on the table and smoothed her fingers over it.

Caroline came back with a large wooden hoop. "Isn't this your block?" Caroline pointed to a block that's pattern was misshapen. "And this one."

"Yes, but the rest. . ." Sarah's voice faded. She looked at Caroline, who wore a mischievous grin. "Did you finish my quilt top for me?"

Caroline's laughed echoed around the room. "No, I didn't." She winked at Sarah. "Mark must have little elves that come into the quilt store at night, like in the shoemaker story."

Sarah wrinkled her brow in confusion as she took the offered hoop.

Caroline stood close and whispered. "Maybe I shouldn't have said 'little elf.' Maybe I should have said 'a handsome elf.'" When Sarah looked her way, Caroline smiled wide and put her index finger over her lips to shush the conversation.

"I'll get you started with the running stitch." Caroline pushed the needle in and out of the fabric several times. "I'd follow the seam line if I were you." Caroline ran her finger along where she thought Sarah should hand quilt. "You won't get your project hand quilted tonight, but I'll make arrangements to meet you here and show you how to finish the raw edges when you have your project quilted." Caroline started to walk away then turned. "There's no expiration on that offer, so don't feel rushed."

Sarah hardly heard the instructions. Did Caroline mean that Mark had finished the quilt? Before trying it herself, Sarah studied the simple running stitch Caroline had started on the quilt held tight in the hoop frame. Though the layers were thick, Sarah managed the up-and-down motion of the stitch. She rested her arm on the table, which helped ease her control of her right arm.

Mark couldn't have finished her quilt. Maybe Terri or her daughter had. Sarah would definitely ask Caroline after class.

As Sarah found a rhythm to the stitching, something Ashley said about Job popped into her thoughts. *"He endured all the bad stuff the devil inflicted him with."*

Job did nothing to bring on his misery.

But I have been. Sarah gasped. Had she been so intent on taking the good with the bad that she'd been overdoing?

Mark had told her that he couldn't keep up with her schedule, and he didn't even have MS. He'd also told her that overdoing wasn't living a full life.

Sarah stopped stitching and traced the pattern with her fingers. She'd likened herself to Job all these months, and in reality, she was nothing like Job. She took the first job she'd been offered because it was temperature controlled. She volunteered for every church committee she could so her thoughts wouldn't wander to her future. She'd negotiated that lease with absolutely no knowledge of how wrong things could go with remodel projects. She'd filled her days with activities because she hadn't really trusted God to get her through the bad times.

Yet He *was* getting her through the bad times. What would she have done without Mark and Karla this weekend?

Sarah fought the urge to bury her face, pins and all, into the downy quilt and cry. Even after she'd locked him out of her life by closing the door in his face on Saturday, Mark finished her quilt because he knew how badly she'd wanted a wall hanging. Or was it because he felt the same way about her that she did about him?

She'd been so wrong. Mark wasn't like the other man she'd thought she'd loved. How could she have even compared Mark to her past mistake? Could he forgive her? Would he forgive her?

Sarah purposely parked her compact at the far end of the strip mall's parking lot. The pounding of her heart echoed in her ears. She drew a deep breath, thankful for the cool Canadian air that moved the jet stream. The unseasonable heat wave laced with high humidity blew out of the area. Between that and the weekend rest, her MS symptoms were again under control.

Last night in the quiet of her room, she'd had a long conversation with God. Through tears of regret on how she handled her disease and the people in her life, she'd promised to trust Him, just like Job.

As she walked down the sidewalk, Sarah smoothed her hands across her yellow crop pants and fidgeted with the ruffles down the front of her blouse. When she approached Mark's store she peeked into the plate glass window in hopes of catching a glimpse of who was working. Mark stood at the cutting counter, no doubt cutting fat quarters. He wore her favorite shirt, the dark green polo that deepened the emerald hue of his eyes.

Sarah stopped by the window where the large orange-and-black HELP WANTED sign hung. With her heart pounding faster she stepped through the door and angled herself out of Mark's range of vision.

The jangle of the door buzzer prompted Mark's pat response. "Be with you in a minute."

Running her fingers under the tape, Sarah loosened the sign from the window. She held it behind her back and walked toward the cutting counter, her flip-flops slapping against the tile floor then against her heels.

When Mark looked up, surprise etched his features. He laid the scissors on the counter, crossed his arms over his chest, and rocked back on his heels. "Sarah." He glanced at the clock on the wall. "What are you doing here this time of day?"

Sarah wanted to run around the counter, throw her arms around him, stare into his beautiful eyes, and beg his forgiveness. Instead she decided to let the cutting table be a buffer in case Mark didn't share her feelings. "I took a personal day. I needed a break."

Mark started to move his lips then pursed them together. He didn't need to speak. His eyes conveyed the message. Finally.

Fighting hard not to break his eye contact, Sarah cleared her throat. "I came to apologize and to thank you."

Mark dropped his arms, and a slight sparkle shone in his eyes. "Okay."

"I'm sorry that I jumped to a false conclusion on Saturday. Can you ever forgive me?" The fear of rejection sheened her eyes with moisture, but she saw a slight nod of Mark's head.

"I'd like to apply for this position." Sarah pushed the HELP WANTED sign across the cutting counter toward Mark.

"Are you kidding me?" Anger flashed through Mark's features as he dropped his arms. With a swoop of his hand he pushed the sign to the end of the counter.

He strode around the counter, stopping in front of Sarah. Her only line of vision was his thick chest that heaved with his sharp intake of breath. His exaggerated sigh rained hot breath on the top of her head.

She willed her amusement out of her eyes as she lifted them to meet his face.

"You already do too much. You don't need to add a part-time job into the mix." Mark placed his hands on her upper arms just under her shoulders and squeezed. "You have to realize your limitations with MS. Your physical condition on Saturday tore my heart out."

Emotion deepened the green highlights of Mark's eyes. "Sadly, I believe most of your misery was self-inflicted. You might not care about your well-being, but the people who love you do."

Sarah's legs weakened. Not a result of her MS symptoms but from the rapid thump of her heart. Had Mark just said he loved her? She lifted her hands to Mark's biceps and leaned into his strength to steady her shaky limbs.

With her small movement, Mark shifted his arms and pulled her into a tight hug. She rested her head against his chest the same way she had on Saturday. Joy, mixed with regret, weaved in and out of her heart as if it were quilting it together. How had she mistaken his concern for pity?

The sea-kissed scent of Mark's cologne calmed the tides of her emotions enough for her to pull slightly away. She needed to look into his beautiful eyes. She needed to tell him that she loved him.

She drew a deep breath and searched his face then tilted her chin until it was a hairbreadth away from his. Once their eyes met, the joy-filled tightness in her chest expanded, and her need to tell Mark she loved him overtook all of her other emotions.

"I love you, too," she managed to whisper just before Mark's tender kiss stopped her from voicing all the other things she'd planned to tell him.

Sarah jumped at the first tinkle of the door buzzer, putting an abrupt end to Mark's sweet kiss. He squeezed her as he whispered in her ear, "To be continued."

Heat rushed to Sarah's cheeks as she watched Mark approach his customer. She could tell by the shake of his head that whatever the person searched for, Mark didn't stock.

The lady thanked Mark as she walked out the door. A giddy smile lit his face when he returned to Sarah. "Perhaps we should go to the back room." He walked over to her with outstretched arms.

Sarah grasped his hands with hers. "First, while I'm thinking straight, I need to tell you a few things."

Mark interlocked their fingers and lifted his brows.

"On Saturday, I thought you were pitying me, but then I realized that was my emotion. I'd been pitying myself since the doctor diagnosed my multiple sclerosis. Can you ever forgive me?"

"Yes I forgive you, but you have to stop overdoing. I'm not hiring you part-time." Mark's features and tone took on a serious edge, but he never released her hands.

"I'm going to stop overdoing. You and my mom and Karla were right. I've been doing more than I did before my diagnosis. I was trying to prove to myself that I could still lead a normal life. I wanted the good to outweigh the bad, but what I was mistaking for good was actually bad for me. So I decided to make some changes."

Sarah laughed out loud at the skeptical look on Mark's face.

Mark raised his brows. "And those changes would be?"

"First, I'm never enrolling in a quilting class again when I can't sew, no matter how cute the quilt store owner is."

The sparkle in Mark's eyes deepened those gorgeous green flecks. He showed his thanks by lifting her hand to his lips and brushing a kiss to the top before rubbing it gently across his cheek. His clean-shaven skin soft and silky.

"Second, I'm going to limit my extracurricular activities to church or MS committees."

She earned another kiss to her other hand. "Excellent choices. Anything else?"

Sarah drew a deep breath. "I plan to quit my job."

The evident surprise on Mark's features tickled Sarah. She tried to suppress a giggle but failed. "After I worked here in the quilt store those two days, I realized how much I didn't care for my current job. It's too solitary and demanding, so I thought I might try working part-time. That is, if you'd consider a woman with absolutely no sewing skills as an applicant for your job."

Mark's expression went blank. "Sarah."

Her heart dipped. She wasn't really qualified to be a paid employee in the store although she hoped Mark would let her try. "It's okay, you can think about it." She understood if he wanted someone with sewing abilities. After all, it was a quilt store.

"Oh. . .and I need to thank you for finishing my Job's Tears project." Sarah didn't try to fight the impish grin.

A sheepish look settled on Mark's face, and he shrugged.

Sarah laughed. "I thought you didn't know how to sew."

Mark studied the toe of his shoe before raising his eyes to hers. "Just enough to demonstrate the machines I sell."

Sarah cocked an eyebrow. "I have it on firm authority—"

"Caroline." Mark huffed. "Okay, I know how to sew and quilt."

"Why didn't you tell me?" Sarah stepped closer to Mark.

"It's not a very masculine quality."

Sarah marveled at the stocky man before her that made her feel so secure and loved and couldn't believe he worried about being masculine. "That is something you don't have to worry about. So what do you sew?"

With some hesitation, Mark looked around the store. "All the projects on display in the store and some of the quilt tops."

"Well, thank you again for getting my quilt ready to finish. It's beautiful. I'm trying to spend an hour a day on the quilting. So far it's working out well with my MS."

"I knew it meant a lot to you. And you mean a lot to me. That's why I want you to take care of yourself. I've waited a long time to find you. Now about that job." Mark pulled her close and kissed her forehead. A thrill shivered through her as he trailed kisses down her nose. Certain this meant the job was hers, with a slight jut of her chin she positioned her lips to receive his, but he pulled away and smiled at her.

"I don't want you for an employee." Mark's features remained merry, but that didn't stop her gasp.

She opened her mouth but no words came out.

Gently Mark pushed her gaping mouth closed and held one finger over it to shush her in case her words decided to gurgle out. Was he still upset with her? He couldn't be, not with that mysterious grin.

"I think I need a partner rather than an employee."

Sarah's eyes widened. She hadn't planned on investing in a business. She started to protest when Mark's finger again applied light pressure to her lips. "Let me finish." He shook his head, and the sparkle in his eyes grew brighter. "You'd make a great partner, but the problem is this has always been a family-owned business."

A muffled squeak of delight passed through Sarah's lips. Her heart raced. Was he insinuating what she thought?

Mark removed his finger and dropped to one knee. "What do you say, Sarah? Would you like to be my partner for the rest of your life? Will you marry me?"

Sarah sat down on Mark's bent leg. "Yes." She didn't wait for him to initiate the kiss. She cupped his face in her hands. As their lips met, her heart expanded with love, and she finally understood what Job had meant.

God had counterbalanced the one bad thing in her life, her disease, with Mark and all the people who loved her.

ROSE OF SHARON

For all Vietnam Veterans, with thanks
and gratitude for your service to your country.

Chapter 1

Walter Sanders grimaced as the car tires rolled through the ruts in the short gravel driveway. The slight jostling sway of his body pulled at the long incision that ran from his waist to midthigh. He palmed the area, hoping to hold it steady and stave off the pain from his recent hip-replacement surgery. Even the soft fleece lining of his sweat pants, brushing against the tender skin around the incision, sent stinging pinpricks up and down the area of the wound, more annoying than painful.

"Sorry about that." Mark cast a sideways glance at Walt as he eased the car through another pothole.

"Guess I didn't realize that the driveway needed grading until now." Walt placed his hands on the seat and shifted his weight to his palms and his left leg, hoping the slight lift off of the seat would absorb the shock of the next bump. "It's a wonder I have any customers."

Walt looked across the half-acre RV park portion of his hotel business. Years ago, he'd purchased a prime location off of an Interstate 29 exit, built a twelve-room hotel with living quarters and, when Winnebagos came in vogue, poured cement slabs and erected electric poles.

Most of his fall regulars remained in their campsites. A lone fifth-wheel RV sat in the spot closest to the manager apartment of the hotel, with no sign of life. The owners probably ran into one of the nearby communities for supplies after unhooking their vehicles.

As Mark swung the car around to pull as close as he could to the residence door of the hotel building, Walt noticed a combine in the field behind his property.

The green behemoth's blades ate up the sun-dried soybean stalks then belched out a trail of dust into the air. At the rate the farmer clicked along, the ground would be barren before sunset. October had arrived in southeastern South Dakota.

"Wait here while I get your walker." Mark turned off the ignition and popped the trunk before exiting the car.

Walt fisted his hands and swallowed the hard lump of pride clogging his throat. Having relied on himself for fifty years, he had struggled with having to depend on others during the recovery from this operation. Unfortunately, he had another four to six weeks to go.

Sarah, Mark's fiancée, burst through Walt's back door and hurried down the sidewalk to the compact car. Dressed in jeans and a T-shirt, she appeared to be younger than her years. A warm smile lit her face, giving the impression she had not a care in the world. Yet she had health problems of her own. She'd had no business staying in his small apartment and running the hotel and RV park during his hospital stay.

Although he'd prepared for his hip replacement by closing down the hotel portion of his business for the surgery and six-week recovery period, the doctor's office had then moved the operation up a week. Walt had had several reservations during that time, so Sarah insisted that she would fill in rather than have him cancel on the guests. With the large medical bills that would accompany his surgery, he'd relented.

Sarah hugged Mark. Walt averted his eyes. He prayed nightly for Mark and Sarah's relationship to be a success. He'd never wish the pain of a broken heart on anyone.

"Welcome home." Sarah opened Walt's car door then gingerly leaned in and kissed his cheek. "You look tired. Did the ride home wear you out?"

Walt reached for her hand and gave it a squeeze. "The longest hour of my life, but it could have been the driver." He winked, trying to inflect jest in his answer to remove the worry from her eyes.

The drive from the VA hospital in Sioux Falls tired him but wasn't truly the longest hour of his life. A Vietnam jungle held that honor. Eighteen and scared, he'd waited for what seemed like days until the chopper blades cut through the hot, stagnant air.

Metal clinked as Mark locked the sides of the walker into place. "Good thing Sarah let me use her car. The ride in my four-wheel drive would have been bumpier."

Walt's snort echoed through the car. Keeping his knees and ankles together, he used his hands to turn his body toward the compact's open passenger door, just like the therapist had taught him. "I would still be in the hospital because there would be no way I could climb up in that thing."

"As soon as you're healed, I bet you can." Sarah stepped back and Mark placed the walker in front of the car door.

Gripping the handles of the walker, Walt lifted himself from the car and stood not his normal five foot eight inches but as straight as the incision's soreness allowed. The surgery's pain was nowhere near the constant burning of his hip socket for the last forty-four years.

Mark carried Walt's suitcase on one side and Sarah stationed herself on the opposite elbow as Walt took short, even steps on the sidewalk. Consciously he placed his right foot completely on the ground to take a step instead of putting his weight on the ball of his foot, his gait since

Vietnam. This normal stride felt foreign to him after years of limping to ease the shooting pain with each step.

Halfway up the walk, Walt stopped. "You two don't have to hover." The words sounded gruffer than he meant them. He'd relied on himself for so long that having people show concern for him was, well, foreign, too.

"Uncle Walt. . ." Sarah placed her hand on his arm. "We're just trying to help."

The concern on her face softened his heart and moistened his eyes. He blinked. What was wrong with him? He steeled his jaw and pursed his lips. If he spoke now, emotion would crack his voice. He managed a nod and a quick pat of her hand before he continued up the sidewalk.

Good soldiers controlled their emotions. Maybe it was the pain medicine or the relief of being home, but feelings locked in the deepest depths of his heart fought their way to the surface. Clearing his throat, Walt stopped again. "I really do appreciate all you two have done for me."

"That's what family is for." Mark stepped to the storm door and held it open.

First the walker crossed the threshold, then Walter's right foot followed by his left. Ready to relish the essence of his home, Walt drew a deep breath, hoping the familiar mix of settled dust and stale food would feed his soul and calm his rampaging emotions.

Instead, Walt's breath gushed out of him at the greeting of fresh-brewed coffee, spicy cinnamon, and bleach. Not the homecoming welcome he'd expected.

He looked around the kitchen and squinted his eyes against the sparkle. Sunshine burst through clear windows and gleamed off the chrome dinette table legs. The bright whiteness of the refrigerator and stove made them look as if they'd just been delivered and installed.

"You cleaned my house?" Walt turned narrowed eyes to Sarah.

Her eyes rounded, seemingly because of the terseness in his tone.

The plastic-tipped ends on the walker legs squeaked across the linoleum floor as Walt guided the walker to the table. His gaze roamed to every nook and cranny of the kitchen, not a speck of dust or grease to be found.

He turned to Mark, who now had a protective arm around Sarah. "I hope you helped, because you"—Walt pointed to Sarah—"young lady, had no business undertaking a project of that magnitude by yourself."

Sarah smiled. "He did help out, but there is no need to worry about me."

Walt raised his eyebrows.

"Well, okay, you can worry about me if you want to, but my MS symptoms are under control and—"

"I made her take lots of breaks." Mark squeezed Sarah's shoulders.

"Good." Walt smiled. He'd seen the effects of multiple sclerosis on Mark's mother and prayed that Sarah, with the help of modern medicine, could fend off its symptoms for a long time.

"I'm always so busy cleaning the hotel rooms. . ." Walt closed his eyes, inhaled, then held his breath a moment. "I've never had a nicer welcome home."

"And shame on the era."

Walt opened his eyes and met Mark's disgust-filled gaze.

Mark's simple response swept a storm of memories to the front of Walt's mind. He shook his head. No time for that today.

"I believe I smell coffee and cinnamon rolls?" Walt scooted the walker closer to a red vinyl–covered dinette chair and eased down onto the padded seat.

"Sorry, it's coffee cake." Sarah crossed the short width of the kitchen and slid a pan from the oven.

"Don't be sorry; just dish me up some." Walt rubbed his palms together while his tongue brushed against the bristly hairs of his white mustache as he exaggerated licking his lips. "I've been eating hospital food too long."

Mark and Sarah burst into laughter, apparently amused at his antics. He was so caught up in his happy homecoming, his chest heaved in merriment and jarred his incision, but not enough to sober him. The short stay in the VA hospital opened his eyes to his abundant blessings. Many of the veterans' health problems couldn't be fixed with surgery.

Sarah brought the cake pan to the table. After stashing Walt's overnight bag in the bedroom, Mark grabbed mugs from the white metal cupboards while Sarah carried the carafe of fresh-brewed coffee.

Walt's stomach growled in anticipation of the sweet brown sugar and spicy cinnamon treat as Mark plated generous portions of their midday snack. Sarah poured the steaming dark liquid into mismatched mugs advertising various area businesses, and returned the pot to the heating element.

After a week of bland food, Walt's mouth watered for a bite of flavor-filled food. He lifted his fork.

"Do you mind if I say a prayer?" Sarah slid onto the chair next to Walt and reached for his left hand.

He laid the fork down and cupped her hand. Her thumb softly caressed the purple bruise left by his IV on the thin skin of his hand.

When Mark sat and grasped her free hand, Sarah bowed her head. Walt closed his eyes and followed her lead.

"Dear Lord, thank You for Uncle Walt's successful surgery. Restore his body with strength and stamina as he heals and works hard at his physical therapy. Keep his spirits up if the days get difficult, assuring him that You never leave Your sheep alone. Bless this food and family time. Amen."

"Amen." The word came out in a gravelly whisper. Moved by Sarah's heartfelt prayer, moisture built in the corner of Walt's eyes. Keeping his head bowed, he squinted hard, hoping to remove the water before it became a full-fledged tear.

Just when he thought he'd regained control of his emotions, Sarah squeezed his hand. A tear broke through the seal of his lid and lingered in the outer corner of his eye, threatening to slip down his cheek at any moment. He gave up the battle and opened his eyes.

"Thank you for that prayer and"—he waved his hand, encompassing the room—"all of this."

"My pleasure. Now dig in." Sarah lifted her mug. "To health and happiness."

Mark and Walt both lifted their mugs to Sarah's coffee toast.

Walt savored his first bit of the moist cake, letting the sweet, spicy flavors burst in his mouth. "This is the best coffee cake I've ever eaten."

Sarah beamed. "Thank you."

"She's a good baker." Mark patted his husky middle. "Can't you tell?"

Sarah rolled her eyes. "Uncle Walt, would you like me to catch you up on business, or are you too tired?"

"Now is as good a time as any." Walt scraped his fork across the plate, raking every crumb of the sweet treat onto his utensil.

"I had to turn on the no-vacancy sign one night because the rooms were full."

Walt raised his eyebrows and smiled. "Kind of late in the season for that." Being a small roadside hotel, the only time his No-Vacancy sign got a workout was the first two weeks in August as bikers wore out the interstate to get to the Sturgis motorcycle rally. "Either you're good for business or something happened in one of the nearby towns."

Sarah gave a small nod of her head. "A graduating class had its twenty-year class reunion during homecoming week."

Walt didn't bother to ask which class or city. He'd wait to read it in the local paper that was presumably stuffed in the stack of mail on the counter.

"I see some of my summer residents flew the coop while I was away. But it looks like I picked up a new fifth wheel. Did they have any problems setting up?"

"No." Sarah's tone held amused surprise.

"Can't figure out why they'd want to park so close to the drive though. They had better spots to choose from. Besides, that electrical box gives me trouble sometimes." Walt sipped his coffee. Holding the mug steady with both hands, he returned it to the table. "Forgot to tell you that. Going to have to get that fixed one of these days. Hate to have someone all set up and settled in and then have to move even one spot over. Plus that one's a tricky spot to back into. He did a good job though, must be an old hand at it."

Sarah giggled. "It's not a he."

Walt scrunched his face. "Beg pardon?"

"I said it's not a he. It's a she." Sarah's giggles turned into laughter.

He hadn't heard wrong.

"Don't look so surprised, Uncle Walt. Women have been driving for years." Mark chuckled.

"A gal? All alone?" Usually his customers were couples or single men.

"Yes, she's by herself." Sarah grinned.

Walt shifted his weight on the chair and reached for his walker. It was time to change position to relieve the dull ache in his hip. "Guess it's a good thing she chose that spot. Safer."

Adjusting the walker, Walt slid from his chair, wincing just a little at the pressure adjustment to his hip. *Heel to toe, heel to toe.* He mentally repeated his therapist's instructions as he pushed the walker to the kitchen window.

"I'll have to keep a sharp eye on her." Walt sighed. "Although I don't know what help I'd be."

The scuffing of a chair against the linoleum caused Walt to turn his head. Sarah joined him by the window.

"I don't think you have to worry about it. She seems like one capable lady who's never backed down from a challenge. There she is now."

On the blacktop, a bright yellow extended-cab pickup with dual wheels waited for a tractor pulling a wagon filled with soybeans to pass by before turning into the RV park's driveway.

Mark joined them at the window just as the pickup zipped into the driveway, bouncing through the potholes like a monster truck over a line of salvaged cars.

"Whoa, where's the fire?" Walt let out a low whistle. "I'm going to have a talk with that young'un."

Like a race car driver making a pit stop, the driver whipped into the parking spot beside the fifth wheel. A tall, broad woman slid from behind the driver's seat then opened the back door. She pushed at the snow-white curls the wind whipped into her face as she grabbed her purchases and bounded to the camper's door.

"Well. . .she's old enough to know better." Walt huffed. What was it with women of that generation, driving like maniacs? He turned to Sarah. "How long's she staying?"

Sarah's lips curved into a mischievous grin. "Guess that's up to you, Walt." She patted his back. "She's the nurse you hired."

❧

Using a little too much gusto, Lil Hayes dumped the grocery bags onto the miniature countertop. The plastic bags slid across the laminate counter, releasing cans onto the floor. Chasing cans down the short hall that led to her bedroom wasn't her top priority; instead she stashed the milk and eggs in the refrigerator. Slinging her laptop bag over her shoulder, she stepped out the door, almost missing the aluminum step attached to her fifth wheel.

Stopping long enough to push the door closed—she didn't need the gale-force winds springing open her camper's door—she listened for the click of the latch before turning to walk across the gravel driveway.

The whine of semi tires speeding down the interstate, along with the roar of the combine in the neighboring field, gave a new meaning to the phrase "quiet country life."

In her haste Lil kicked up gravel in the driveway. A pebble slipped into the vent hole of her Crocs like a hole in one. She stopped her speed walk to the house to tap the stone back out. As she did so, her bag slid off her shoulder and down her arm, dragging her cardigan sleeve with it.

Rock-free, she picked up her pace to cover the short distance between her campsite and Walt's home.

He'd arrived earlier than she'd expected, or maybe not. She'd dragged her feet leaving for this assignment. Had she known this patient was a Vietnam veteran, she'd have declined the job and been halfway to her winter spot in Texas.

Tiffany, her boss, talked her into one more assignment before she, Lil, snow-birded out of South Dakota. She'd argued that Lil was closer to the patient's age and would be more understanding. After signing the contract, Lil learned Walter Sanders had served in Nam. She felt honored to nurse veterans of other wars back to health. Nam, not so much. Too many bad memories, but maybe caring for Walt Sanders would be her chance for redemption.

Lil sighed. Maybe Walt was a trouper and the assignment wouldn't last the full six weeks that her contract listed. But none of that mattered right now because she was late.

Although the nursing contract didn't specifically state that she had to be present when the patient arrived home, she liked to be there in the event he needed help exiting the car, crossing over the threshold, or lying down, or just to instill peace of mind that he wasn't alone.

Her plastic shoes snapping against the sidewalk, she lifted her head to see two sober young faces alongside a creased face with a clenched jaw and spaghetti-western showdown eyes peering through the window. At her.

Defensiveness rallied every nerve in her body. How long had they been watching? Obviously long enough to see her roar into the driveway. Perhaps that's what caused the sour look on his face. Or maybe he was in pain from the surgery.

Stopping for a moment to compose herself, she realized that in her haste, she wasn't presenting a very professional or competent picture. Readjusting her sweater and laptop bag, she finger-combed the curls tickling her cheek and tucked them behind her ear. That was the best she could do with her mad mess of curly hair most days. Sometimes it even helped to have the wind beat them into submission. She sent up a little prayer that that was the case today.

With her natural stride she walked up to the entrance. Just as she reached for the storm door handle, a young man opened the door.

She stepped backward, expecting to see the pixie of a girl she'd checked in with. "Hi, I'm Lil Hayes."

"I'm Mark Sanders, Walt's nephew." He stepped aside while holding the door open with his outstretched arm.

"They must have raced through your uncle's release paperwork," Lil said as she crossed the threshold.

A gruff baritone barked from behind the door. "Nope. Only one speeding is you."

So pain wasn't the cause of the lemon-sucking look she'd witnessed on her patient's face.

"I have speed limits posted."

She hadn't been driving *that* fast. Lil gulped down the defensive rebuttal on the tip of her tongue. She didn't want to get off on the wrong foot. "I ran late and I like to be here when my patient arrives, so I hurried a little."

"A little." A snort from the senior Sanders echoed through the kitchen.

Obviously she'd already gotten off on the wrong foot. Might as well defend herself. Stepping around Mark, she placed her hand on her hip, pulling herself to her full height of six feet. Practiced at using her extra inches as a towering intimidation device to get her own way, her retort rolled off of her tongue. "You've never been a little late? Driven a little too fast?" *Let he who's not sinned cast the first stone.*

"Nope, always leave on time." Walt's eyes found hers, accepting her challenge, and their stare-down began. His hazel eyes were mesmerizing, daring her to make another remark, of any kind.

The buzz of the refrigerator and offbeat breathing of people cut through the tense silence. Her trained ears caught the respiration of one, two, three people. Someone was holding his or her breath, waiting for the fight to start. She guessed it was Sarah.

"Whoever is holding their breath better release it. I was only hired to care for one person." Her raised eyebrow goaded Walt to draw another gibe from his arsenal.

"Well." The word whooshed as Sarah exhaled. "I think we need to rewind here."

Lil studied her patient. Although he bent over the walker, she guessed his height about five foot eight like his nephew, with the same broad shoulders and husky build, but Walt carried about twenty pounds more than Mark around his torso. Could be the cause of his high blood pressure as indicated in her case file.

Sarah's words reminded Lil that Walt's mind and body had been through the trauma of surgery. Dropping her arm to her side, Lil smiled. Walt proved to be a worthy opponent, not bothered by their height difference.

"Walt, I am sorry that I sped through your driveway. I assure you it will not happen again. Please accept my apology."

His gaze held hers as the walker scraped across the floor toward her, his lips moving as he recited some sort of silent mantra. He angled his path, and when he was beside her he gave a quick nod of his head, the only indication that she was forgiven.

Lil surveyed the living area, something she should have done prior to Walt's arrival. Small, cozy, and uncluttered. Perfect elements for rehabilitation. A paneled living room extended from the kitchen and from this angle appeared to be rectangular.

A soft groan alerted her that Walt had sat down. She turned and smiled at Sarah and Mark before going over to the table. "You have a cozy home. Just the perfect size—"

"For one? That's what everyone says." Walt hung an arm over his walker and laid his other arm on the table, breathing deeply from the excursion.

"I was going to say the perfect size for recovery from hip surgery." Lil pulled out the kitchen chair closest to Walt and sat down. She lifted her bag to the table and pulled out a file. "There are a few things we need to go over."

"Now might be a good time for us to head home." Mark walked over to Walt and patted his shoulder.

Walt twisted the walker into position. "I'll walk you to the door."

"Not this time." Sarah wrapped her arms around Walt's neck in a loose hug. "You sit here and rest."

Walt reached up a hand and patted her arm. "Can't thank you enough for all that you've done. Appreciate it."

Although the words were simple, Lil heard the fondness for the young couple inflected in Walt's tone. Her heart began to warm toward her patient. Perhaps this was the real Walt and what she'd seen so far were the aftereffects of the surgery and meds.

"You call me if you need anything, although I think you're in capable hands." Mark grinned at Lil and shrugged his shoulders as Walt harrumphed at his statement.

If Mark thought his uncle was a hard case, he needed to think again. Her first nursing assignment turned out to be her toughest. He'd been a Vietnam vet, too. Lil shivered. Nothing since had compared to that experience, and that was saying something, considering she had worked the night shift in the emergency room most of her career.

"It was nice to meet you, Lil." Sarah shook her hand again.

"Bye," Mark said.

Walt lifted a hand and gave him a salute. "See ya."

Getting right down to business, Lil began, "Did they send home any prescriptions or did you stop and pick some up?"

Walt nodded. "We picked some up."

"Where are they?"

"In my bag."

Lil looked around the kitchen. "Where is that?"

"In the bedroom." Walt nodded toward the door on the opposite end of the adjoining wall to the living room. He started to stand. "I'll get them."

"I'll get them. You stay sitting." Her authoritative tone drew raised eyebrows from Walt as she slipped off the chair and rushed across the kitchen. Like squealing tires on pavement, her plastic shoes squeaked her halt on the vinyl floor. She turned to Walt. That was the second time he'd tried to stand after having just taken a seat. "Unless you're uncomfortable sitting." Sometimes the pressure of sitting aggravated the incision.

When his tired eyes met hers, she knew. "Would you like to lie down for a while and do all of this later?"

The relief covering his features was the only answer she needed.

"Do you remember when you took your last pain pill?"

Walt held the edge of the table as he stood. "Just before lunch."

"I'll get your room ready and find your pain medication, unless you need help?"

With pursed lips Walt shook his head, but Lil noticed a slight grimace as he put weight on his right foot.

Pride. Male patients, especially veterans, were the worst in that way, wanting to be tough all the time. Lil walked over to the door, glancing over her shoulder every few minutes to make sure Walt was doing okay. Slowly but surely, he was making his way across the ten-foot width of the room.

Entering the bedroom, she found his overnight bag on the bed and began to unzip it. The room silenced. The walker stopped its rhythmic clacking thump against the slick flooring. "Taking a rest?" she called over her shoulder as she grabbed the prescription bottle stuck in the outside side pocket of a carry-on bag that had seen better days.

Her only answer was a vibrating rattle.

"Walt!" Lil dropped the plastic container and ran for the kitchen.

Chapter 2

Slouched forward over the walker, Walt's eyes met Lil's, sending a silent plea. Lil's heels took a beating from the flap of her shoes in the seconds it took to reach her patient. She slipped her shoulders under Walt's right arm and braced as his weight sighed against her body.

"Don't know what happened. I feel real weak." Walt sucked in deep, heavy breaths.

This was her fault. Why had she left her patient alone? She'd only done that one other time and had learned a hard lesson in the process. She knew why she'd left this one by himself. She'd been too distracted with being late, *and right*, that she didn't access her patient the way she should have upon his arrival home.

"Your body's been through a lot. Weakness is not uncommon."

Lil scanned the room. Metal cabinets with Formica countertops ran across the length of the room and ended just before the bedroom door. If he could make it over to the counter, it would give him something to lean against for support while he rested. Then maybe she could leave him alone long enough for her to get a chair.

With her body as security, the heaviness of Walt's breathing lessened along with the rattle of the walker.

"Do you think you can make it over to the counter? That will give you something stable to hold on to or lean against while I get you a chair." Lil bent down further, trying to adjust her height to his to keep from stretching his body at an upward angle. She turned her face to Walt's, his squared jaw set at a defiant angle.

"I think I can make it to the bedroom, if you let go of me."

The words snipped out of Walt, but his head remained down with his body weight still transferred to Lil's shoulders.

His spirit was willing but his flesh was weak. "Don't try to be a hero."

"Too late for that. It's what got me in this predicament in the first place."

The warm breath from Walt's huff of disgust tickled her hand resting on the walker.

"Let go. I feel fine now." Walt tried to shake free of Lil's grasp. She felt a small tremor in his muscles and tightened her hold.

"Nice try. You move the walker, then we'll take a step together." Dampness soaked through his shirt where her hand rested on his waist.

To her amazement, he didn't argue but scooted the walker a few inches, then took a shaky step. She baby-stepped with his pace, mindful of the space between their feet so she didn't trip him.

"You're doing great," Lil encouraged, even though his struggle was revealed in his white-knuckled grip on the walker and the tremble in his leg that brushed up against hers.

Walt stopped. More weight shifted to Lil's shoulder as he lifted his left hand from the walker. Lil watched him swipe a trickle of perspiration from the side of his face by his ear, wishing she could swat her own drops of exertion away.

"Ready?" With his jaw set and eyes focused on his destination of the bedroom door, Walt scooted the walker a few more inches.

Thank goodness for the cozy quarters and a bedroom just barely big enough for a bed and dresser. Just a few more steps to the doorframe. Once they cleared that hurdle, they'd be home free. The bed sat a mere two steps into the room.

Lil's muscles joined Walt's in the shaky rebellion of extra exertion. The pallor of her patient gave her stamina a boost. Minutes passed as their feet crawled across the short span of the kitchen. Two steps, then rest. Two steps, then rest. Walt's body rebelled with a cold sheen of sweat. So did hers.

Stubborn determination showed on Walt's face, and Lil guessed it was what fueled him to continue on.

"We're almost there," Lil said, her encouragement breathier than she'd have liked.

"Yep." Walt's answer was released on a sigh of relief as he eased the walker to a stop in front of the raised wooden threshold.

The walker was wider than the narrow doorway, Walt reached a hand out and pressed his palm against the frame then repeated the gesture with the opposite hand. No instruction necessary, Lil ducked under his arm, turning the lightweight walker sideways to allow entry into the room.

Once inside the door, she righted the walker for Walt to hold and finish the last two steps into the room. She started to smile her encouragement, but when their eyes met, she saw a spark of fear cross his hazel eyes just before they seemed to lose their elevation.

Lil dropped her gaze. Walt's arms shook as he held tight to the opening, weakness taking control and bending Walt's knees deeper and deeper.

"Hold on." In a flash, Lil squeezed between the walker and the door. They'd made it this far. Walt couldn't fall. She couldn't let him.

He released the burden of his weight against her as soon as she looped her arm around his waist. He grasped the walker with both hands.

"Let's go," he said and the walker banged down on the hardwood. One large left step, then a right hitched step and they were beside the bed.

Walt pushed the walker to the side and hopped on his left foot to turn his body. Although this went against her medical training, Lil let this battle go and followed Walt's movement until the backs of their thighs butted against the bed.

Lil released Walt and, knees buckling, he dropped onto the bed in a sitting position. His head hung down, his back heaving as he caught his breath. A sheen of moisture gleamed on the salt-and-pepper hairs of his arms.

"Scoot back a little," Lil instructed as she bent to lift his legs. Once Walt was settled on top of a well-worn, hand-sewn, rail-fence patterned quilt, Lil removed his athletic shoes and raised his legs enough to free a knobby afghan at the foot of the bed to cover him.

With his eyes closed and breathing returning to normal, Lil assessed her patient. Faint pink trickled back to the high angle of his cheekbones. The white ring of shock no longer traced his lower lip. When she removed his eyeglasses, his lids fluttered but never opened. The possibility that he had already dozed off caused her to whisper, "You rest now." She touched his forehead with the backs of her fingers. Cool, no fever.

Lil patted Walt's shoulder and stepped to the door.

"Guess I was wrong. Sometimes there is a reason to hurry. Thanks, Speedy. I wouldn't have made it without you."

❧

Lil closed the bedroom door, fighting the urge to slide down it and let the brimming tears flow freely. "Thank You, Lord," she whispered as she wiped the dampness from her eyes with the buttonholed corner of her sweater.

No doubt God had been with them, giving Walt that extra burst of strength to get to the bed and reminding her that you never leave your patient alone.

Palm to her chest, she surveyed Walt's kitchen. One crisis averted but some safeguarding remained.

A kitchen towel lay loose on the edge of the counter. That could be a problem if Walt lost his balance and sought stability from the sturdy cabinets as he rested between steps. Placing his hand on it with force could slide it back, throwing him off balance.

Lil pursed her lips, marched over to the counter, snatched the towel up by one end, and snapped the loose end against the Formica, punishing it for her imagined crime against Walt.

Walt, what an anomaly. First he chided her for speeding, then he thanked her for speeding. Of course, she'd sped for different reasons a few minutes ago. Walt's life might have been in danger. Then again, she could have endangered someone else's life earlier, driving so recklessly.

Maybe she was the anomaly. Lil shrugged. She had been her entire life when it came to men. Why would Walt be any different?

Opening the cupboard door under the sink, Lil found what she expected, a three-bar hinged towel rack. Tri-folding the terry cloth rectangle, Lil hung it neatly across the top bar and closed the cupboard door.

Speedy? The downy lilt of Walt's voice implied it as a nickname. An endearing one, not like the taunting middle-grade schoolyard names that stuck with her through school—Amazon, Giant, Godzilla. A tingle of pleasure wrapped her heart in a hug.

Maybe this case wasn't so bad after all.

Work. Lil's mentality reminded her heart that that's what she was here to do. She pushed her silly emotions out of the way so she could focus on getting Walt well. She wanted him to get a good report in four weeks so she could head to her winter home.

Returning to her safety inspection, Lil noted shoes lined up, like soldiers waiting for inspection, in a corner by the door. Her knee joints creaked as she bent and tucked the errant laces into the shoes' openings.

Using the wall for leverage, Lil straightened and looked around. Satisfied the kitchen held no malice toward Walt, she entered the living room.

The dark paneling and heavy drapes shadowed the room. Lil sought a light switch before noticing there was no overhead fixture.

Lil walked to the window, grasped the plastic wand, and pulled the rubber-backed drape open. The afternoon sun filtering through the window didn't chase the shadows from the corners but did brighten the center of the room so Lil could see what she was up against.

A pole lamp with three bell-shaped metal shades stood in the corner behind his recliner. Two bright orange lamps sculpted to look like genie bottles, sporting oversized pleated and age-yellowed lampshades, sat on matching laminate shelf end tables.

The three lamps sitting in close vicinity of each other were the only source of illumination for the rectangular room. She huffed. Walt needed a clear, well-lit path.

Rearranging the room wasn't an option. Two doors cut into the far narrow wall, leaving little room for a piece of furniture. There was a closet and perhaps the entrance to the hotel office, Lil guessed, then closed her eyes to picture the outside structure in her mind. The office door faced north. Definitely the entry to the hotel office.

All of the furniture pointed to the opposite wall, where a flat-screen television, a stark contrast to the mid-seventies gold-plaid couch and matching recliner, was mounted to the wall.

Walt needed to update his décor. A trickle of fear ran up her spine as she collapsed onto the sofa. Surprisingly for the age of the couch, the cushions provided support. The short back hitting her at her shoulder blades, she rested her head against the wall.

Many Vietnam vets had trouble moving forward with their lives, preferring the past. Was Walt one of them? Except for the television, it appeared that he was.

❧

Wake up. Walt internally commanded his stuck-closed eyelids while his dream continued in the projection room of his mind.

Open. Asleep but aware, he raised his brows until his forehead crinkled, yet his eyes didn't pop open. Instead he dreamed on. Running toward green eyes that led him through the jungle, promising the safety of home. As he ran on uneven ground, his right foot came down and twisted. He began to fall. An involuntary jerk jarred his body.

His eyes popped open. Sweat beaded his brow and upper lip, his breath and heart still keeping up the frantic pace of his feet during the dream.

As he blinked to clear the sleep-hazed focus, the familiar planes of the plaster ceiling and frosted-glass light cover in the center of the ceiling eased his sense of place.

His finger rubbed across the soft cotton dips and bumps in the quilt he used as a bedspread, a long-ago gift from his sister-in-law, Gert. The afghan that once covered him was hanging off the bed, held to him by fingers lassoed in the loose gaps of the afghan's pattern.

A *night*mare—even though the late afternoon sun peeked through the east window, assuring him he was in the comfort of his own room, not running through a field.

Walt released a ragged breath as his heart rate steadied. He'd been having this same dream for forty-five years. He should be so used to it that it wouldn't ignite his adrenaline anymore.

It was the worst of his two recurring nightmares. Living and dying was a black-and-white affair. Not love. It held too many shades of color and changing emotions. With love, nothing was cut and dried.

Discomfort pulled at Walt's right hip, not the normal burning pain that had become a part of him. He shook his hand to free his fingers from the chain links of yarn. Palms down, he pushed himself up, bearing the weight on his left hip until he was in a sitting position. Holding both legs together, he swung them over the side of the bed.

The coolness of the oak floor provided solid ground, anchoring him in the present, clearing the dream's cobwebs out of his mind.

A clench of emotion filled his chest. He hated reliving the pain of that day. Before Nam, he'd spent hours gazing into those blue eyes. He'd spent every second of his tour of duty dreaming of coming home to those blue eyes. He spent decades running away from them in his dreams.

His Nancy, so sweet and shy when he'd left. The thought of making a life with her got him through the dark days of war. But while he was serving his country, his country and Nancy changed.

Two short years turned Nancy into an outspoken war protestor. Instead of welcoming him home, she hurled his promise ring and insults at him. Yet the names she'd called him weren't as hurtful as the contempt those blue eyes reflected when she looked at him.

Walt rubbed his own stinging eyes with the palm of his hand before running his fingers down his face. He reached for his glasses on the bedside table. His mind flashed to the end of his dream. Green eyes had surrounded him. He couldn't outrun them.

He blinked, now fully awake. He slipped his glasses on as if the prescription lenses could help him clearly remember his dream.

The eyes in this dream had been green. They weren't clouded with disgust but sparkled with something else. Challenge, maybe?

A soft rap on the door interrupted his recollections.

"Walt, are you awake?" Lil opened the door and stuck her head through the crack.

"Yeah," he croaked, his throat dry. He swallowed hard. No relief. It'd been that way since his surgery.

"Sounds like you need a drink of water. Stay right where you are." Lil's head disappeared.

Walt gritted his teeth at Lil's commanding tone before scrubbing his hand through his hair. Green eyes. Nancy's eyes were blue. Could the effects of his pain meds cause a color change in a dream?

Lil swung the door wide, bringing an overflow of the kitchen's sunlight with her. She handed him the glass.

"Do you want to put your shoes on, or do you prefer slippers?"

"Slippers." The second syllable rose an octave, making it sound like it'd come from a pock-faced teenage boy.

Walt took a sip of the water. The cool liquid soaked his throat like the summer rains quenched the sun-dried soil in the field surrounding the RV park.

"They're in my bag." The water restored his voice tone, which came out just as irritated as he felt.

Lil released the closet's doorknob. What was wrong with that woman? She had no boundaries, planning to rummage through his closet!

The mattress gave a bounce as Lil lifted his bag to the foot of the bed. The whooshing clack of the metal zipper filled the room. Before he could say stop, Lil, in her tunnel-vision pursuit of the slippers, moved the top contents to the bed.

He had private items packed in that bag.

Walt gulped the last of his water as he reached for his bag with his free hand. "Scoot that over here. I can do it."

His fingertips grazed the rough tapestry on the side of the bag as Lil, elbow deep in his valise, pulled the bag closer to her.

"You need to save your strength." She paused long enough to shake a warning finger, then returned to her invasion of his privacy.

Walt gritted his teeth as a wave of weakness washed over him. Humbled at not being able to care for himself, his palms ached with the engraved memory of the slick varnished doorframe when his fingers, digging into the grooves of decorative trim work for traction, became no match for his legs, growing limp like noodles in boiling broth.

"Here they are!" Lil's booming voice bounced off the walls of the tiny room. She held up the worn leather Romeos and clapped the slipper soles together as if applauding her victory cry.

Could a woman be any louder and pushier? He shouldn't feel that way. After all, without her broad shoulders to lean on, literally, he'd be zipping north on the interstate, en route to the VA hospital. He preferred a slight slice of a woman like his Nancy, but the sturdiness of Lil's structure was just what he'd needed to take the last few steps to the bed. His body's husky pressure would have laid a slender girl low like prairie grass bucking gale-force winds.

Lil might grate on his nerves, but she'd proved her nursing abilities, earning his respect.

The intruder rounded the end of the bed, knelt down, and held a Romeo steady for him to slide on. "Right foot first?"

"Put those down. I'll slip them on myself."

"No, now lift your foot up." Lil reached down and lifted his heel for him.

He fisted his hands at her clipped words. A man should be able to put on his own slippers.

"I want to make sure they're on secure." She guided his right foot into the soft leather then held out the other Romeo.

Walt placed his slippered foot on the floor and stretched out his other foot.

"Do you feel like Cinderfella?"

A Jerry Lewis fan. At least they'd have that in common. He owned the DVD. Maybe she'd like to watch it tonight. Before he could respond, Lil began talking again.

"Remember that movie? It was a comedy but I can't place the star."

Ready to jump into the one-sided conversation, Walt opened his mouth.

Lil lifted her head, perhaps searching his face for an answer before looking directly into his eyes.

His reply lodged in his throat. His heart started beating at marathon speed as if he was running through that field again. Lil had green eyes. Just like the ones in his latest dream.

Chapter 3

A loud *tsk* stopped Walt in the middle of a hitch step.

"What are you doing?" Lil's megaphone voice sounded behind him.

He flattened his right foot as she quick-stepped around him. Irritated at having to be reminded, he drew his brows together and shot her a look.

She raised a brow and crossed her arms over her chest, catching and tossing his attitude back at him with her deep green eyes. His heart fluttered as his dream scene played through his thoughts.

The upper tips of his ears warming, he dropped his focus to the front bar on the walker.

Heel to toe he stepped, hoping this concentrated effort would halt the wildfire spread of a blush from his ears to his cheeks.

Lil seemed to have lost interest in his every move. When he looked up, she stood in front of the range with her back to him, fumbling with a cast-iron skillet.

"That's better."

Walt frowned. Did the woman have eyes in the back of her head?

Continuing his slow pace, Walt aimed the walker at the bathroom door at the opposite end of the wall from the bedroom door.

Holding up the pan and waving her hand above the electric burner element, Lil let out a snort. "I thought that bathroom was a pantry." She giggled. "Was I surprised when I opened the door! Although it reminds me of the girls' locker room at my high school, the walk-in shower with no tub is a good setup for you."

She held her hand closer to the burner. Obviously satisfied with the heat level, she centered the pan on the burner.

Heel to toe, heel to toe. Walt fumed, repeating his walking instructions faster while his walker clacked, like typewriter keys, on the linoleum flooring. She'd snooped through everything while he rested.

He reached the narrow door and stopped. Why did they make walkers wider than doors?

"Let me help with that."

Fear banged his heart against his chest. It was one thing to snoop through cupboards, but this? Walt placed a hand on the counter for balance.

"I've got it," he declared louder than he intended. He gripped the middle of the upper bar on the walker and gave it a quick twist.

Stepping carefully and using the door for stability, Walt followed the walker through the door, slamming it shut just as the squeak of Lil's footsteps grew closer.

He'd dodged a bullet. Leaning against the door, Walt sucked in air, hoping to calm the panic coursing through him. If the last four hours were any indication, he'd never make it through the six-week convalescent period.

He needed to set some ground rules. He'd have a talk with Lil.

※

"You and I need to talk." Lil pointed the blunt end of a wooden spoon at him.

The hiss of the frying pan called her attention back to its contents. She twirled the spoon like a baton before dipping the rounded end and swirling it around the pan.

"I know we do." Walt hoped she'd heard his I-mean-business tone over the sizzle of the vegetables hitting the pan.

Steam rose and filtered through the air, assaulting his nostrils. His stomach gurgled its approval of the sautéing onions.

"I hope you like veggie and cheese frittata."

"Fra-what-a?" Walt frowned. How could he know if he liked it if he couldn't even pronounce it? "I don't eat fancy food."

Lil turned from the stove, giving him a deadpan look. "A frittata is not fancy food."

The pressure on the ball of Walt's right foot reminded him to flatten his step as his walker and stomach raced to the range.

Bits of translucent onions popped in a greenish oil.

"Legs feeling stronger?" Lil looked over her shoulder at Walt.

He nodded as he inhaled deeply. A low rumble started in his stomach and built to a full-fledged growl.

"Here." Lil stuck the spoon handle out. "Stir these while I add the other ingredients. By the sounds of it"—she jerked her head toward his midsection—"I should have started this earlier, but I didn't know what time you ate supper."

Walt bore his weight on his left leg as he stirred the onions around the pan. "What are you frying these in?"

Lil dropped in a handful of sliced mushrooms. The off-white pieces looked nothing like the golden bits he dumped out of a can.

"Olive oil."

"I told you I don't eat fancy food." His stomach rumbled its plea for a taste. Traitor.

"Stir," Lil commanded.

Walt dragged the spoon around the edges of the pan, then through the center, watching the meat of the mushrooms darken.

The *tap-snap* of eggshells competed with the continued sizzle of the frying pan.

"That's what we need to discuss." Lil rapidly moved a fork through a bowl, the tinkle of metal on glass keeping a steady beat.

She set the bowl on a cool burner. Green specks swirled through the settling mixture then began to float to the top of the frothy beaten eggs.

"That looks fancy."

"They're dried herbs. You need to change your diet."

Walt tapped the spoon on the side of the pan, freeing a stuck cluster of mushrooms and onions. "What makes you say that?"

Apparently oblivious to the gruffness in Walt's voice, Lil added a tight ball of something green to the pan.

"The lard in your fridge. I didn't even know they sold that anymore." Palm up, she wiggled her fingers at Walt, signaling she wanted the spoon back. Walt acquiesced then watched as Lil broke up the green lump, spreading it through the pan.

"What'd you do to that spinach?"

"Squeezed out the moisture so our eggs aren't runny." Lil dumped the contents of the bowl into the pan and gave it a quick stir before sprinkling it with white cheese. Then she covered it with a beat-up pizza pan.

"I hope this makeshift lid works. Your kitchen utensils are sparse, but then again, it doesn't take much to heat up processed food."

Walt jutted his jaw in defense. Obviously, she'd poked around in his cupboards. That was the conversation they needed to have. Respect for others' privacy. "I eat a varied and balanced diet."

"*Of canned, processed food.* You need to eat fresh food, organic if available so you can control the sodium and soak up the nutrients."

Lil waved Walt away from the stove then stuck the pan in the oven to finish the cooking process.

The burst of heat from the oven warmed Walt's pant legs. "I have a serving of each food group, just like they taught in school." *Argue with that one.*

"Fruit laced in corn syrup packs more calories than the sugars in fresh fruit, and if I remember right, you are a borderline diabetic."

Lil beat Walt to the table, where she pulled a file from her bag.

Jaw clenched, Walt gingerly sat down. He narrowed his eyes, focusing on the calendar hanging above the wall-mounted Princess phone.

Six weeks, forty-two days, one thousand eight hours. . .

"Walt."

The soft warmth of Lil's hand on his forearm stopped his calculations and trembled his insides, her plump fingers pillows against his sun-crinkled skin. Those pain meds must have heightened his sensations instead of dulling them.

The slight pressure of her squeeze pulled him back into the conversation.

"What?" He meant the answer to be gruff; instead the word came out husky.

"I'm not trying to be critical. It's just that proper nutrition helps a body to heal."

"Faster?" Walt relaxed his face into a smile, the first since his surgery.

"Can't hurt," Lil answered with the gusto of a person who thought she'd won the argument. Victory dancing through her green eyes, she returned his smile.

Walt's smile widened as his mood brightened. The sooner he could get his solitary lifestyle back, the better—even if it meant eating new-age food.

a

A week later, Lil cut the last petal piece of her Rose of Sharon quilt project from the bright yellow cotton fabric while Walt paced through the living room.

Up and down the short piece of clear walking path he went for what seemed like the hundredth time this hour. He was antsy. They'd watched all his Jerry Lewis movies. Walt needed a hobby to pass the time.

"Walt, does your incision hurt? Are you in pain?"

"Nope." The walker clacked across the living room floor, stopping by the window, also for the hundredth time in an hour. He peered out at the same not-yet-harvested cornfield that Lil could see from her vantage point.

"Anything changed out there since five minutes ago?" Lil picked at the loose threads that had been made by cutting the fabric and were now scattered on her jeans.

Walt leveled her with a look.

"Guess not." She laughed then picked up a piece of dark green material and began to cut around the tracing of the stem pattern. "Want to help?" She held out the scissors and fabric to Walt.

He frowned and shook his head. "Looks like a nice day. I'd like to go for a walk."

"Good idea." Lil put her fabric on the wide arm of the sofa then rocked forward, lifting herself off the couch.

"Can't though. I'm housebound."

"Who said that?"

"The nurse at the VA hospital."

"There's nothing in your file about it," she said, pretty sure the confusion on Walt's face mirrored hers.

"Well"—Walt's voice held a gruff edge—"*I'm* not senile. I know she said that while I recovered at home, I'd have to stay inside the house."

Lil's hackles rose at his inference that *she* was the senile one. "And I'm telling you the doctor's instructions say normal activity as tolerated." Pleased that her tone held just the right amount of authority, she gave a quick nod of her head for emphasis.

Leaning so close to the window that the tip of his nose grazed the glass pane, Walt reminded her of a punished child.

"Why do you make a case out of everything? I'll get the file for proof." Lil started for the kitchen, longing for some fresh air and exercise, too.

The walker thumped behind her.

"Don't get snappy. I'm trying to keep you out of trouble."

Walt's statement threw the light switch in her brain. She stopped short.

Walt didn't. His walker bar grazed her backside, pushing her forward in a trip step. The toe of her plastic shoe sticking to the oak floor caused her to stumble a couple of steps before she could right her balance.

"Whoa there, Speedy. Don't get faster than your feet will go." Walt chuckled.

Ready to retort, Lil whirled around, finger in air, intending to coerce an apology out of him. Instead the merriment that waltzed on his features caused her heart to somersault. *Relaxed and happy, Walt Sanders is one handsome man.* She drew her brows together. Where had *that* come from?

"Sorry, Lil, but you looked a little like Jerry Lewis bumbling around in his movies."

Thinking of the antics in the movie they'd watched yesterday afternoon, she grinned. "I imagine I did."

Her admission gave Walt permission to release the laughter bubbling inside of him. The walker rattled with his shaking shoulders, competing with Walt's baritone guffaws.

The good medicine of laughter eased the tightness in his shoulders. His body no longer tense, his stance resembled his nephew's.

As Walt's last chuckle died, he cleared his throat. "I think I needed that."

"I think so, too. What do you say we try a walk around the inner circle of the RV park?"

Walt grimaced. "I'd really like to, Lil—"

Snapping her fingers, Lil interrupted him. "That's why I stopped. Did a nurse at the VA hospital talk to you about home health care?"

Walt's eyes rounded. "That's *their* rules."

Lil nodded. The private nursing company that she worked for allowed the patients more freedom than the other service.

"Then what are we waiting for?" Walt tipped his head toward the kitchen door. "After you. Just warn me if you plan to stop."

≈

Stopping outside of the door, Walt zipped his jacket to stave off the bite of the breeze. He inhaled, pulling in the crisp air spiced with faint diesel smoke and dry dirt.

Home. He never tired of the roar of eighteen wheels on pavement. He never tired of the tractors and combines manipulating the fertile soil. He never tired of the changing seasons.

Fall's crisp air rejuvenated his soul just like spring's warm breezes coaxed out the buds on the trees and flowers. Summer's heat and humidity were nature's perfect greenhouse for corn crops to flourish, while winter snows blanketed the slumbering ground like Gert's warm quilts on a bed.

He never understood the folks who headed south in the winter. Although South Dakota winters could be harsh and unrelenting, the snowbirds missed so much. The stark red of the male cardinal balanced on the needled branch of a snow-kissed pine tree. The frozen crystal-crusted snow that glistened like sequined costumes under stage lights. The hushed solitude after the vicious blizzard winds died.

"Have a change of heart?" Lil stood at the end of the sidewalk where it met the gravel driveway.

Walt released a breath. "Just enjoying my home. The air is so invigorating. Let's walk the outer loop of the campsite."

Lil's lips made a grim line. "I don't think you have enough stamina for that. You'll need to build it back up. As a matter of fact, our first stop is going to be my camper so I can grab a lawn chair to carry, in case you find you need to sit down."

"Gonna be a waste of your time." Walt rubbed his palms together before placing his hands on the walker and taking a step. *Heel to toe, heel to toe.* When he reached the end of the sidewalk, Lil fell into step with him.

"Careful of the loose gravel." She stopped and tapped the heel of her shoe on the ground.

Walt stepped past her. From the distance of the house, he hadn't noticed her top-of-the-line rig. "Whoa, two sliders. Fancy food and fancy camper."

Lil passed him. Glancing over her shoulder, she raised a brow and gave him a grim look, but her eyes held a glimmer of merriment. Her emerald eyes. Thank goodness he hadn't dreamed about them again. Funny how a dream could change when the dreamer was induced with medicine.

After a few minutes, they reached the camper. Lil reached up to open the door.

"I'd invite you in, but that entry step isn't stable enough. I'll be right back."

Walt grabbed the edge of the door. "Can I peek inside?"

"Sure." A little grunt escaped Lil as she used the door edge to help hoist herself up. "I'll only be a minute."

Maneuvering the walker as close to the opening as possible, Walt leaned into the doorway. Rich brown paneling covered the walls of the living room area where a matching love seat and two overstuffed chairs upholstered with a green-and-brown leaf pattern sat bolted to the floor.

A purple-backed quilt with embroidered blocks rested over the back of the love seat. Sprigs of various-colored lilacs finely stitched onto lavender fabric blended well with the earthy furniture and walls. Her blanket appeared to be as loved and used as the quilt covering his bed.

The kitchenette's counter jutted out about a foot, and with the living room slider out, it created a homey feel of actual rooms, unlike the campers from years ago. A sewing machine sat on the tabletop visible through the open area between the cupboards and the counter.

Scattered in the chairs were several plastic sacks stamped with various fabric-store logos. Walt smiled, thinking of Gert, Mark, and Sarah.

The purr of a plastic roller on a closet door reverberated through the small space. Lil appeared with a blue canvas folding lawn chair in hand.

"What do you think?" She stopped, holding her arm out and slowly turning her body as if she were a showroom demonstrator.

"Nice. Cozy." Walt stepped back to allow Lil's exit. "How long you had it?"

Lil pushed the door shut. "I bought it just before I turned sixty, so almost two years now. Usually about this time I head to Texas for the winter."

Walt pursed his lips and shook his head. "Didn't peg you for a snowbird." He lifted the walker and took a step.

"You say that like it's a bad thing." Lil fell in beside him.

"Don't you miss the change of seasons?"

"I leave in late October and come home at the end of April. The only season I miss is winter."

"Then don't you miss the holidays with your family?" His peripheral vision caught the slight shrug of her shoulders.

"Without a family of my own, I'm kind of like my camper. A fifth wheel."

"I can relate to that, but. . ." Walt stopped to rest a minute. They'd only gone about a third of the way around the inner driveway. "Gert, Mark's mom, always included me even after my only brother, Duane, abandoned them."

He seldom talked about his brother because he was so ashamed of what he'd done. The concern in Lil's eyes prompted him to go on. "He left right after Gert was diagnosed with MS. Mark was five. None of us ever heard from Duane again. One day in 1997, I got word that he passed away. I just hope God forgave him for what he did, because I didn't."

"God is in the forgiveness business if you're right with Him."

Throat choked with emotion and mist forming in his eyes, Walt nodded and stared out at the interstate. He hoped her words were true. He'd been right with God for years, but he'd been to Nam. Terrible things happened during war, and he came back to an unforgiving nation, an unforgiving woman. His hope lay in the promise of the scriptures. It's what got him through his terrible ordeal.

"Do you need to sit?" Lil asked with a whisper of a voice.

Walt sniffed. "No." He moved the walker and took a step. He'd have to cut back on the pain medicine if Lil would allow. He liked his emotions buried in the depth of his heart, not hanging around the surface, spilling out anytime they felt like it.

"Was your brother younger or older?"

"Younger." Duane was a lucky one; his number never came up.

"I have an older sister. By three minutes." Lil giggled. "I never let Lily forget it either."

Gripping the walker, Walt started to angle around the circular part of the driveway. A rivulet of sweat trickled down his back as his breaths came quicker. "I think I'd better sit a minute."

Lil pulled open the chair and placed it behind him. "I'll hold it while you sit so it doesn't tip."

Carefully, Walt lowered into the chair. Not the best support for his sore hip, but it would do. "So there are two of you with the same name?"

Lil scooted around the chair to look at him before she spoke. The breeze lifted her white curls, rearranging them in tangles on the top of her head. She reached up with both hands and smoothed the front edges behind her ears. The natural light of day revealed age's effects—a few brown spots on her hands and vertical creases by her nose—but her ivory skin and twinkling green eyes gave her a youthful glow.

"I have a fraternal twin, so really not two of me. You can breathe a sigh of relief now." The skin around her eyes crinkled with teasing.

Walt exaggerated an exhale then winked at Lil. "But you have the same name? I figured Lil was short for Lily or Lillian."

"Well it's not, and that's my little secret."

Sure, you can rummage through my dresser, closets, and cabinets like you own the place, but it's okay for you to keep a secret. Walt bit his tongue to keep from speaking his thoughts. After a week, Lil handled all the chores around his house like she owned the place.

"Lily is the good girl. She and her husband live in Brookings. They have two sons. My nephews each have two boys. They'll celebrate their fortieth wedding anniversary next May. The quilt I'm cutting pieces for is my winter project and their anniversary gift." Lil sighed then rubbed her reddening nose.

Time to get back inside. Neither one of them needed to catch cold. Walt started to rise.

"Hold on there." Lil slipped under his arm, wrapping her right arm around his waist and holding the walker steady with the other hand. "Don't worry about the chair. On three, stand."

A week ago, Walt had hated having Lil's help, but today her nearness and support comforted him.

"One."

Walt made sure his knees were even and hip-width apart.

"Two."

He fisted his hands in a firm grip around the walker handles.

"Three."

He pushed up with his legs. The metal legs of the chair clinked against the gravel as the wind and Walt's momentum caused it to topple over on its side.

Once he was steady, Lil folded the chair and carried it in the crook of her elbow.

"So you're a quilter?"

"Yes, my grandma taught me."

"Gert was a quilter. She made the one on my bed."

"I wondered where you got that rail fence. It's hand quilted. It's a nice one."

"Thanks. She said it was a manly pattern."

Lil laughed out loud. "Guess I never thought of that. I'm making a Rose of Sharon quilt for Lily and Gale. I always liked the Song of Songs in the Bible, and they've been married so long, I thought it was a good fit."

Walt smiled. "Gert said stuff like that so much it rubbed off on a neighbor girl, Caroline. She runs a machine-quilting business now."

"Gert sounds like a great lady."

"She was." Just like his Nancy, the one he left, not the one he came home to.

"Mark runs the quilt shop that Gert started. He's a quilter, too, and he sews better than most women." Walt cleared his throat and gave his head a small shake. "I was his only male role model. Guess I didn't do a very good job."

Lil tsked and swatted the air. "Don't say that. There's nothing wrong with a man sewing or quilting. As a matter of fact, I could use your help with my quilt. Since you apparently have no hobbies, it'd give you something to do besides pacing."

There she was, bossing him around again. First it was about his diet. Now he needed a hobby. He'd lived sixty-two years without a hobby; he didn't need to start one now. "I don't care if you bring it to the house to work on it, but I'm not going to help." He used his best I-mean-business voice.

"Hmm. . ." Lil hummed her answer. "Do you need to sit again?"

"No," he said, although he didn't remember the inner circle of the driveway being quite this long. They were almost back to Lil's camper.

"Then why are you limping?"

Walt stopped. He hadn't even realized that he was. "Old habits die hard, I guess."

Lil sniffled.

He pulled a red paisley handkerchief from his coat pocket and handed it to Lil.

She hesitated.

"It's clean."

Lil smiled. "Thank you. I think all the harvesting is messing with my allergies."

"Do you want to take your chair back? I can wait here."

"No, I'll take it to the house. That way we have it when we walk tomorrow."

Heel to toe. Walt continued on.

"So I take it you never married?" Lil asked the question in a matter-of-fact way.

"Nope." Walt stopped and surveyed the hotel portion of his land before focusing on the barren fields surrounding it. The solitude of this place saved him after the war, giving him his peace of mind back. He knew that Bible verse Lil's quilt was named after. It was how he felt about Nancy. "I had my own Rose of Sharon before my number came up, but then when I came home. . ." Walt paused, but not for dramatic effect. He'd said too much already. That was it—no more pain medication for him.

Lil placed a soft hand over his. "She didn't wait for you?"

The look of caring in Lil's green eyes melted his heart. "Not like you think. It'd have been easier if she'd fallen for another man. Instead she fell in with the turbulent time. She protested the war and everything about it, including me. I thought she'd be proud of me when I came home, but I was wrong. She acted like I started that war, not went to do my duty. . . ."

Walt stopped talking when something unreadable crossed through Lil's eyes and her touch stiffened on his hand. She was probably as shocked as he was that someone could be that cruel to a wounded soldier.

"We'd better get in the house." Lil pulled her hand away and crossed her arms over her chest as she walked. Her lawn chair dangled haphazardly from the crook of her elbow.

They walked the rest of the gravel driveway in silence. As they started up the sidewalk, Walt glanced at Lil. She looked ahead, but he was sure she was seeing the past. Maybe she'd lost a love in Vietnam. He'd put her in this funk; he'd try to get her out of it.

"So, Lil, you called your sister the good girl. Does that make you a bad girl?" He raised his brows and lilted his voice.

Lil turned wide eyes to him. "I just meant that she did what all girls were supposed to do back then—marry, start a family, and, well, I didn't." The rush of Lil's words matched her nervous dance from foot to foot.

His attempt at humor had obviously backfired, but now he needed to know just who was taking care of him.

"Well then, why did you imply you were bad?"

Chapter 4

I didn't say I was bad," Lil snapped at Walt. Now, after his confession about the girl who jilted him and the reason she did, Lil couldn't tell him why she'd hinted that she was bad. "I said I was different."

Back in the day, Lil and Walt's ex-fiancée were cut from the same cloth. Waiting at airports, spouting out insults, showing contempt for America's finest.

Lil's opinion of the war never changed, but her thoughts about the servicemen did when she'd met Larry. The soldiers returning from Vietnam had tried to do the right thing by their country, just like any other soldier returning from war.

Walt tilted his head a little as he studied her. His hazel eyes penetrated, as if they could read her heart and know what shame hid there.

"Were you a women's libber marching for equal rights?"

Not exactly. Lil bit her bottom lip as her eyes welled up. "It's time to go inside."

No matter how hard she tried to live down those rebellious years, they just kept coming back to haunt her. She had to get Walt nursed back to health in record time and get out of here. She'd been in this dangerous territory one other time in her life and never planned to return to it. Ever.

Once inside the house, Walt removed his jacket and hung it over the back of a kitchen chair. "That wore me out. Think I'll go lay down awhile."

"Okay." Lil studied the scuffed toe of her shoe, afraid if she made eye contact with Walt, her brimming tears might spill down her cheeks.

The whir of the refrigerator motor as it cycled on seemed magnified in the silence of the room.

Walt sighed. Then the creak and rattle of the walker announced his departure.

Sniffing, she lifted Walt's handkerchief to her nose. *Worn out and a sigh. Lil, what kind of a nurse are you?* "Walt, do you need my assistance?"

Keeping her head down, Lil lifted her eyes to check his progress. He stopped at the bedroom door, started to turn his walker, then hesitated.

"Look, Lil." His back remained to her. "I didn't mean anything by what I said. I was just teasing. Being career-minded doesn't make you a bad girl, just an independent one. I'm sorry if I upset you."

Lil's chest rattled like the walker as she sucked in a ragged breath, intending to tell Walt how she vehemently protested the war all four years of college. How she organized rallies. How she treated the returning soldiers.

After all, confession was good for the soul, but would her admission be good for *his* soul? His recuperation was going nicely. That fact, coupled with the slouch of his shoulders and earnest apology, changed her mind. What would it hurt to let him think it was something else?

"And the truth will set you free."

It was obvious Walt was going to stand there with his back to her until she said something. Lil cleared the emotion from her throat and God's nagging reminder from her thoughts.

"It's okay, Walt. I know you were teasing. I'm just a little emotional today, I guess."

She saw his silent nod while he turned the walker and entered the bedroom. The latch softly clicked as the door closed.

Lil slumped onto the kitchen chair that held Walt's jacket. She put her elbows on the table and her face in her palms. Soft curls fell forward, lightly brushing her knuckles. Her favorite fragrance wafted from her wrists, torturing her nose, the sweet, flowery scent hanging like the acrid smell of a dead skunk.

She was a skunk, too, for not telling Walt the truth, but the last time she owned up to her past, it ended in disaster. And for some unknown reason the thought of Walt thinking badly of her pierced her heart.

ॐ

A storm front moved through, bringing gloomy, drizzly days with it that matched the mood inside Walt's home. Between his nervous pacing and window peering and Lil trying to keep everything on a professional level, the tension inside the house was as thick as the rainy haze outside.

Walt gazed out the kitchen window in the direction of her camper. "I thought you were going to bring your sewing machine in to work on your quilt. You can't be getting too much done on it at night."

That was true. Each evening, after making sure Walt took his medications and had everything he needed in his room, she headed back to her camper and tried to cut out the quilt blocks, but her heavy eyelids didn't cooperate. Nor her patient.

"That would be your fault." Lil drummed her fingers on the kitchen table.

Turning from the window, Walt scowled at her. "How's it my fault?"

"Wasn't it your idea to use your hunting walkie-talkies?"

"A person tries to be nice." Walt moved from the window, carrying the walker with him.

After Lil leveled him with a look, he put the legs of the walker back on the floor.

"I didn't say it wasn't a nice suggestion, but you're not using them for emergency purposes only."

"I'm just testing them to make sure they'd work in an emergency." Walt sat down at the table.

In theory, Walt's idea seemed brilliant, so she had agreed since the man didn't own a cell phone. In practice the idea lost some of its dazzle.

He used the walkie-talkies for everything but an emergency. He insisted he talk to her from the time she closed his back door until she was locked securely in her camper. Just in case something might happen, like a rabid animal darting out from under her camper or her falling down. Then if he couldn't sleep, he used the device to carry on entire conversations until drowsiness overtook him. It was sweet of him to be concerned about her; however, it also increased the emotional attachment that she was trying to break.

"You don't want all that mess over here," Lil argued, but in reality she could use a diversion as Walt stood and moved to another window.

The green quilted-flannel shirt he wore today accented his hazel eyes. Lil shook her head. She had too many thoughts like that lately. Another reason she needed to focus on something else.

"Won't bother me. You can sit at the table and sew while I practice walking and building stamina."

That's what you call it. I call it bored, nervous pacing. Lil harrumphed at his statement and earned a pulled face from Walt.

"I'll go get it," she said, rising from the chair, "but you're helping me with it."

"I told you sewing—"

Lil cleared her throat loudly. "Don't you even say it."

Walt snorted. "How'd I get stuck with a women's libber?"

"Lucky, I guess." Without thinking Lil looked right into Walt's eyes, which seemed to shine with appreciation directed at her. Her heart answered by quick-stepping around in her chest. Her heart's happy dancing weakened her limbs. Just the reaction she didn't need. She dropped her gaze to the floor.

"Turn your eyes from me; they overwhelm me." Song of Songs verses kept popping into her thoughts since she'd started that Rose of Sharon quilt,

which certainly didn't help her situation. With her eyes still averted, Lil scurried out into the crisp fall air.

The breeze's icy fingers crept into the neck of her sweatshirt, trailing down her back in a cat-scratch pattern. As flushed as she felt, she was certain steam would rise from her collared fleece at any moment.

She wasn't letting this happen again to her *or* Walt. First, it wasn't professional on her part. Second, they were too old for these types of feelings. Yet Walt's short-cropped white hair not only offset his hazel eyes but emphasized his olive skin tone. It was hard to tell the shape of his lips with a bushy mustache covering the top one, but she wagered they'd favor Mark's.

Lil's eyes grew wide. What was she doing? Crushing on Walt like a schoolgirl. Clenching her fists, she sorted her feelings into the appropriate compartments in her heart and mind. In order to keep those emotions in place, she concentrated on finding excuses for why she shouldn't feel this way. Maybe if she barred the doors on those emotional containers, it would hold them in place, at least until her assignment was complete.

She dawdled as she gathered her quilting supplies, hoping the additional time away from Walt would calm her erratic behavior. Although her feelings didn't seem fickle, Lil guessed her and Walt's close proximity drove their feelings of attraction.

Walt's two-week follow-up doctor's appointment was tomorrow. He was getting around pretty well. Maybe he'd get a good enough report that he wouldn't need a full-time nurse and her agency could reassign his case.

She removed her cell phone from the case clipped to the waistband of her blue jeans, pressed the code for her preset numbers, and hit the SEND button before her heart could talk her out of this.

Her hand trembled as the call rolled into voice mail. Nerves caused her to speed talk so she didn't change her mind. Lil left a message requesting dismissal from Walt's case. Her heart dropped as she disconnected the call. Didn't matter. She'd done what was best for the both of them, even if her heart sagged at the thought.

After snapping and locking the plastic cover onto her portable sewing machine, she hefted the machine off of her table and headed back to Walt's house.

A mud-caked pickup slowly drove by on the blacktop highway in front of the RV park. The driver peered through the windshield, then the passenger window, studying her and the hotel as he idled past. *Must be a local wondering if Walt's home yet.* Since her hands were full, Lil smiled as she jerked her head in a greeting. The man lifted his hand and continued down the road.

Lil squeezed her shoulders toward her ears. No longer under the fever of her blush, she found the air was chilly. She hurried up the sidewalk to find Walt waiting by the storm door.

Standing as far to the side as the walker allowed, Walt opened the door enough for Lil to wedge into the narrow space then use her body to fully open the door.

"Wish I could carry that for you."

Her dancing heart kicked up its heels again. "Well, you can't." Lil snapped the words, angry with her pattering heart, not Walt.

Walt sucked his pursed lips in and out as if he were stopping his retort. Hurt clouded his mesmerizing eyes.

"I'm sorry I snapped like that." Lil lifted the sewing machine to the table, never taking her eyes off of Walt. "The cold is bone chilling; the machine is heavy." *Keep heaping excuses, Lil, to keep those false emotions in line.*

His dejected look twisted her heart. He really was a big help opening the door for her when her hands were full. "It was very nice of you to want to help me. Thank you for opening the door. I don't know how I'd have managed."

The coffeemaker releasing a burp as the last gurgle of water cycled through it woke up her nose to the fact there was fresh-brewed coffee. She glanced at Walt before turning to the table, intending to stash her bags of fabric on the top.

A gasp escaped Lil as the bag's plastic handles slid down her arm. She let them drop to the floor.

Two gold-rimmed cups covered with a lilac pattern sat on matching saucers. Dark chocolate Milano cookies, arranged in alignment with the third saucer's ripple design, sat between the two cups.

Without thinking, she turned to Walt, placing her hands on top of his where they rested on the walker grips. With a slight movement Walter's fingers entwined with hers.

"It's my way of apologizing."

The sincerity in Walt's eyes shamed Lil for taking out her lack of control on him.

He continued. "I know I hurt your feelings or brought back old memories or something the other day, and I'm sorry. I've spent most of my life wishing we could rewind time, but we can't, so I hope you accept my apology."

But it's me who owes you, and many other soldiers, an apology.

Lil searched Walt's hopeful face. She couldn't tell him that now. "As I told you before, no apology was necessary. I'm not upset with you." She smiled. "I promise I'll try harder to fight the melancholy." Lil wiggled her fingers free. "Thank you for this. It's about the nicest thing anyone has done for me in years."

Pride straightened Walt's stance as happiness beamed from every crinkle of his handsome face.

"I'll have to let you pour the coffee."

Lil walked over to the pot and lifted it from the heating element. She narrowed her eyes, the nurse in her overtaking the woman.

"How did you manage this with your walker?"

"I filled the pot with water and scooted it across the counter. Then I leaned against the counter for balance while pouring the water into the coffeemaker."

Lil poured the steaming liquid into the fragile china cups. "Where did these dishes come from?"

"I keep them in the back of that cupboard." Walt pointed to the metal hanging cabinet next to his bedroom door. "They were my mother's. I don't have the entire set, just a few pieces. The quilt I saw in your camper the other day reminded me of them. I thought if you had a quilt with lilacs on them, maybe you'd like the china cups, too."

"I do. They're lovely."

"I'm surprised you haven't seen them while rummaging through my cabinets."

Lil furrowed her brows. "What?"

Walt chuckled. "Put the coffeepot back and let's sit down."

When Lil turned from returning the pot to the coffeemaker, Walt stood with one hand on the walker and the other on her chair back. He'd taken his last pain pill two days ago. Lil couldn't remember the last time he winced while walking or sitting. He was regaining his stamina if he could pull a snack like this together. Lil smiled, confident he'd receive a good report and not need her daily nursing skills.

As soon as she slipped onto her chair, Walt removed his hand and sat down, forcing out a grunt of relief.

Lil bit into a flaky cookie. The dark chocolate center oozed out its bitter sweetness as she chewed.

Walt pushed her sewing machine to the farthest end of the table, giving him more elbow room.

"So what made you decide on a quilt for a gift? Seems to me to be quite an undertaking."

Lil sipped her coffee to clear her palate. "Well," she said, sheepishness crawling through her, "I sort of owe her one."

Walt's forehead wrinkled in confusion.

"When I bought my new fifth wheel, I took my sister's grandsons camping at that Kampgrounds of America south of here just before the Iowa border."

"I know that KOA."

"Well, we decided to go to a nearby nature preserve for a picnic and hike. Even though it was late spring, my great-nephew brought a quilt along. Not just any quilt, but one made for Lily by our grandmother. When we were ten, our grandmother made us each a quilt that had something to do with our names. My sister's quilt was a Lily of the Field block. Lily loves her name and she loved that quilt. One time when Mom laundered it, some fabric caught in the wringer of her washer. You remember those old wringer washers?"

Walt nodded.

"Lily cried for days because it ripped a block. Anyway, it was in my pickup and we needed a tablecloth, so we used it. Out of nowhere a severe storm blew up. We gathered our gear as fast as we could so we could get back to the KOA shelter. I thought the boys had the quilt and they thought that I had it." Lil sighed. "The next day when we went back, there was a fallen tree on the shelter house and no quilt to be seen anywhere."

"Maybe it blew down a path."

"We thought so, too. Several times we went back and searched for that quilt, thinking it may have blown into a shrub or someone might have turned it into the lost and found at the visitor center. But we never found it."

"Was she upset?"

"Just a little bit." Lil pulled out the words as she outstretched her arms as far as they'd go. "I'm hoping this makes up for it." Lil noticed Walt's empty cup. "Need a refill?"

Walt nodded.

Lil retrieved the pot, and on her way back to the table, outside movement caught her eye. It was the pickup that drove past earlier.

"Looks like you've got company."

⁂

Walt kept his knees together and turned in the chair to peek through the window, but the blinds blocked his view.

"That truck drove slowly by earlier. I figured it was a friend of yours wondering if you were home."

Standing up, Walt used the chair back for security and walked a step to reach the window. Using two fingers he parted the miniblinds for a better view.

"It's Bill Grant. He belongs to the VFW and is always trying to get me to be more active. I suppose this has something to do with the Veterans Day celebration." Walt started for the door.

Lil's loud exaggerated clearing of her throat stopped Walt in his tracks. As she hurried to bring his walker to him, her layers of white curls bounced with each step, inviting his fingers to smooth the wisps back from her face.

"Sorry, but until the doctor says you don't need to use this, you need to use this."

Walt frowned. He'd done just fine using the counter as support when he set the china on the table. But he grasped the walker's handles and started for the door. Walt opened the door midknock. Crisp autumn air with just a hint of winter kissed his cheeks.

"Walt, I need to talk to you." Bill removed his Farmers' Co-op cap.

"Is it about Veterans Day?"

Bill's watery eyes met his as he gave his head a small shake.

"Come in and sit down." Walt led the way to the table, while Lil closed the door.

"This is my nurse and *friend*, Lil Hayes." Why had he emphasized the word *friend* like that? True, he was growing accustomed to her snooping and insistence that he eat healthy meals. Their opposing opinions ignited lively conversations over the walkie-talkies. He'd stopped counting the days and hours he thought it'd take for him to heal and be rid of her, but were they really friends?

"Nice to meet you."

When Lil smiled warmly at Bill, a twinge of jealously shot through Walt. He'd been trying for days to coax a smile like that out of her. He ran his hand up and down the slick fabric of his athletic pants as he fought the urge to make a fist. Maybe *friend* wasn't the right descriptive term.

"Likewise." Bill's voice was polite but he remained somber.

"Could I get you a cup of coffee?"

"No, thank you." Bill worried the bill of his cap before placing it back on his head, then removing it again and running his hand over his bald head. "Sam Garrett has passed away."

Walt reached out and placed his hand on Bill's forearm. "I'm sorry to hear that, Bill."

Blinking rapidly, Bill looked at Walt. "He was my best friend." Bill's voice cracked. He cleared his throat hard. "I know he's in a better place with the good Lord and out of pain." He pulled a blue handkerchief from his jacket pocket and wiped his eyes.

Walt patted Bill's arm. "Shall we say a prayer?"

Bill nodded. "I'd like that."

Walt looked at Lil before bowing his head. She'd closed her eyes and folded her hands.

"Oh Lord, how it comforts us to know that Sam is in Your hands, safe and pain free, enjoying his new body and the glory of heaven. However, those of us who knew Sam and loved him here on earth are dealing with a different kind of pain. The gnawing hurt of loss. In the upcoming hours, days, and months, stay close to Jeanie as she mourns the loss of her husband, their children as they mourn the loss of their father, and Sam's friends, especially Bill, easing their pain while guiding them to the solace of Your love. Amen."

Walt looked from Bill's eyes shining with grief to Lil's green eyes filled with pride. She placed her hand to her heart, a silent signal that she'd been touched by his prayer.

"Walt and I are in a men's prayer group at church," Bill said, his voice stronger now.

He must have read Lil's signal, too.

Bill turned back to Walt. "I know this is a bad time for you and the hotel is closed, but Sam's relatives need a place to stay. Is it possible they could stay here?"

Walt knew Sioux Falls was a little too far for grieving family members to travel each day. Campers in the RV park were self-sufficient, but guests staying in the hotel—that was a different story.

"I'm sorry, Bill. I'm just not up to it."

"I know it's a lot to ask, but it would only be a week or so."

Walt rubbed the back of his neck with his hand. "I just don't see how I could do it. I can't lift anything heavy; there's daily cleaning and laundry, continental breakfast to prepare."

"Maybe I can get some ladies from church to help out." Bill's voice held a small smattering of hope.

Running the hotel was hard work. There was no way that, during his recuperation period, he could do all of the work involved. Yet Sam had been a good man, the kind of man who'd stop combining his own crops to help out a sick neighbor.

Bill broke their eye contact and hung his head.

Walt glanced Lil's way. Although they didn't always see eye to eye, he could tell she was the kind of woman who'd pitch in with a project like this. *A Rose of Sharon.* His thought lifted his heart and the corners of his lips. He cleared his throat. Bill looked up.

"I'll do it. I'll open the hotel for Sam's family."

Chapter 5

I 've got a good helper here." Walt raised his fist thumb out like a hitchhiker and jerked it toward Lil. "Tell Jeanie there will be no charge for anyone. This is my memorial to Sam."

Bill's body sagged with relief while, at the same time, every nerve ending tensed in Lil. This was too big of an undertaking for Walt. Had he volunteered her to help? She'd been lost in thought over Walt's wonderful prayer skill and the revelation of another side of this appealing man.

There she went again with the romantic notions. She should have told him that she'd called her supervisor for reassignment. But the tea party he surprised her with blindsided her rational side. It was nice to be pampered. Made her feel loved.

Her eyes bulged at the thought. Lil quickly turned her back to the men until she stopped her astonishment from showing on her face. Where had that kind of thought come from? Wherever it came from was the reason she couldn't stay. Shouldn't stay.

"It was nice to meet you, Lil."

Becoming aware of life around her at the mention of her name, Lil turned back to the men, giving Bill a weak smile. "You, too. I'm sorry for your loss."

"Thank you." Bill stood. "I will talk to the church ladies. See if they'll help with the cleaning and maybe some breakfasts."

Walt and Bill walked toward the door. With good-byes said, Walt, having watched Bill pull out of the driveway, turned from the window.

"Walt. . ." Lil braced herself. She had to tell him about her wanting to leave.

He lifted his head, his face drawn in sadness. "He fought a good fight. Battled that cancer for two years." Walt sighed as the walker clacked across the floor. He slumped into a chair. "Not quite the party I had in mind." He waved his hand in front of the china.

"Sam lived in this community his entire life and I never met anyone who disliked him."

Lil slipped into the chair beside Walt. She needed to treat this conversation with care. "About opening the hotel—"

"Sorry." Walt held up his palm. "I should've asked you first, but you're such a stand-up gal, I knew you wouldn't mind. Besides, it'll give us something to do."

Putting her elbows on the table, Lil rested her face in her palms. Some stand-up gal she was. How could she put this?

"I think after my doctor's appointment tomorrow, we should stock up on a few items. I'll make a list."

Lil bent her fingers, peeking through the slice of space it created.

Walt showed no sign of moving. Instead he stared idly at the china cup in front of him.

Was he talking to her or just talking?

"Maybe the relatives won't stay around for breakfast. Maybe they'll go to Jeanie's." Walt's voice cracked and he wiped his eyes with the middle knuckle on his right index finger.

"Would you like some time alone?" Lil rested her arms on the tabletop, resigned that now just wasn't the right time to tell Walt she wanted to be released from this assignment. Besides, Tiffany hadn't returned her call yet, so she didn't really know if she'd be leaving in a day or two.

Walt sniffed. "No," he said, shaking his head. "I don't want to be alone."

Lil's chest swelled with fear. Those mesmerizing eyes conveyed another meaning to his words as his hand engulfed hers. *Do not arouse or awaken love until it so desires.* It wasn't possible for feelings to develop this quickly, was it? Swallowing hard, Lil knew it was, had lived it. But this wasn't genuine, just fleeting infatuation.

Silent minutes ticked by as Walt stared at the china cup and Lil stared at their hands.

"Sam served in Nam, too. I didn't know him back then since I'm not originally from here. Doctors at the VA think his cancer might have stemmed from chemical warfare over there."

Lil choked back a sob. War never really stopped for soldiers who saw action. Why hadn't she understood that when she was young?

"Guess I was lucky on that account. I wasn't subjected to the chemicals." Walt shivered as his eyes locked onto hers.

"Sam led the Memorial Day services. He always told the story about coming home. It was February 1968. The men in his unit, excited to be coming home, had no idea how the country was reacting to the war until their plane landed in Southern California. Before disembarking, they were told they'd be ushered to a hangar where they needed to change into civilian clothes before entering the airport because protesters waited inside. The superiors were trying to stop a riot from breaking out. They succeeded, too."

Lil gasped.

Walt squeezed her hand. "I couldn't agree with your reaction more."

Lil's rapid-fire pulse boomed in her ears. Walt mistook her reaction. She lived in California in 1968. As a war protester she waited for many planes, wanting to hurl insults and accusations, stealing the soldiers' pride in serving their country and their relief to be home.

"Better go see if anything needs to be done to ready the rooms." Warm tingles remained on Lil's skin when Walt withdrew his hand from hers.

Her confused emotions twisted the past and present together in a tangled mess. She knew this nursing assignment would be tough because of Walt's veteran status. Although gruff at times, he was an honorable soldier and faith-filled man who deserved a better person than her for his caregiver.

Walt stood. "I wish I didn't need this." He grasped the walker and started toward the living room. "Are you coming?"

Hesitating, Lil rose from the chair and followed. "I thought we were going to check on the rooms." Grief must be fogging Walt's thinking, like her emotions clouded hers.

"We are." Walt crossed through the doorway into the living room.

"But the doors. . ."

Walt stopped and turned. "That's the parking entry. The main entry to the hotel is through the office."

Apparently Lil's mind was fogged by past regrets but Walt's was clear. She followed Walt through the living room, then through one of the doors on the far living room wall. Expecting to find a small cubby of an office, Lil marveled at the spacious square room, large, bright, and modern.

Yellow-and-white-striped wallpaper decorated the upper walls, meeting white wainscoting in the middle. The reception counter's light wood, varnished to a high shine, wrapped around a small workstation housing a computer, cordless phone, and rolling chair.

Wooden kitchen cabinets with a sunny-yellow countertop lined a wall. Two toasters, a microwave, and an industrial coffeemaker with a heating element on the top, as well as where the coffee brewed, sat stately on the counter.

Four diner-style tables and chairs sat about four feet from the cabinets. Mounted on the wall opposite the cabinets was another flat-screen television.

Walt stopped by the workstation and removed keys from a drawer by the computer. "Would you check and see what I have for coffee? Top cupboard just above the pot. I might need to call the service."

Lil walked over to the cupboard. Two large boxes, one marked DECAF, sat on the shelf. She tipped each one "You have seven packages of regular coffee. The decaf box is almost full."

A pen scratching on paper sounded as Walt jotted a note.

"Anything else while I'm over here?"

"Don't think so." Walt started down the hallway, opening a door to their right marked LAUNDRY.

Wide-eyed, Lil followed behind. The room housed two industrial front-loading washers and dryers. The washers sat on one side, the dryers on the opposite wall. A long white plastic table cut the room in two. A cart with a large canvas bag inserted into a hollow area sat just inside the door.

Walt opened a closet lined with linens, towels, and cardboard boxes and began inventorying the supplies. "Good on soap. And it looks like Sarah caught up the laundry." He turned. Taking his hands from the walker, he placed them on his hips. "I'll be on laundry duty."

"I can't have you overdoing," Lil argued. "You'll run the desk and nothing else."

Walt raised a brow. "It doesn't take much to throw towels and sheets into a washer and dryer."

The walker clacked past her as Walt headed into the hallway. Lil followed, closing the laundry room door behind them.

"If the laundry's caught up, my guess is Sarah has the rooms clean and in order." Walt stopped in front of the first room's door in the hallway, inserted a key in the lock, and opened the door.

Bleach's bitter scent burned her nostrils, which, in turn, drew water from her eyes. The room, though neat and clean, mirrored most small hotel rooms with low-pile brown carpet, institutional white walls, a multicolored bedspread, and a framed watercolor print centered over a laminated wood headboard.

"Just like I thought. The work won't start until guests arrive. Guess we'll have time to work on your quilt this afternoon."

"I guess." Lil shrugged. She'd wanted to dust or vacuum, any kind of physical activity to burn off the anxiety of her situation.

"You've been awful quiet, and I think I know why." Walt closed the door and started down the hallway to the office.

I don't think you do.

He placed the keys back into the drawer and continued to his main living quarters. "You're worried that I'm overdoing it by opening the hotel to guests."

Lil closed the door to the office and looked up to face Walt, who had turned and was now gazing at her, not fazed a bit by their height difference.

"Don't be concerned. My stamina's coming back, you know."

She did know. It's what she'd been counting on. That after tomorrow he'd lose the walker and gain a quad cane, leaving one hand free and causing him to need her less. Her heart squeezed hard at her last thought. When had she started wanting Walt to need her?

❧

"Do you have an iron and ironing board?" Lil flipped the clasps of the sewing machine cover, the clack of metal against the plastic announcing its release. She lifted off the cover and placed it on the floor.

"Yes, they're in the hotel laundry room. Why?"

"These pieces need to be fused to the back fabric before I appliqué around them," Lil called over her shoulder as she headed out of the kitchen.

Walt fingered a stack of cut fabric. How anyone could turn these odd geometric shapes into anything that resembled a flower was beyond him. Tilting his head to look through his bifocals, he studied the large square block with tracing on it.

"Hmm, she has a pattern to follow." Pulling a square from the pile, he matched the small shapes of fabric to the corresponding pattern on the block.

"Good job."

Walt jumped. "You startled me," he grouched. He'd been so intent on seeing the picture the pieces created that he hadn't heard Lil's plastic shoes squeak against the floor.

Lil put the iron on the table, then fiddled with the lever under the ironing board until the legs released. Looking around, she found an outlet, placed the board beside it, then began unwinding the cord wrapped around the iron's handle.

"I wondered how all those little pieces fit together. Didn't realize you had a guide to go by."

"Well, now you know and you're good at it, so that will be your job." Lil licked her finger and quickly tapped the iron to test the heat.

"I'm not going to sew."

"Who said anything about sewing? I need you to fuse these pieces on the block like this." Lil lifted the green pieces from the table and placed them on the end of the ironing board. She grabbed something flimsy, cut to the shape of stems, and laid it on the large bright yellow block's template.

"Is that tissue paper?"

"No, it's fusible lightweight interfacing. Watch." Lil lined up a green rectangle over the papery fabric and placed the hot iron on top. After a few seconds, she smoothed the iron over the fabric then lifted it.

"See." She lifted the large block with the green fabric stuck to it then set the iron down. "Now when I appliqué around it, the fabric won't move. Think you can do that for me, to help pass the time, or is it too girlie?" She pulled a face, but it couldn't hide the challenge reflecting from those green eyes.

"I guess it would help pass the time in a more constructive way than staring out the window."

Walt lined up another piece of fusing, carefully placed the green fabric over the top, and with a deep breath, pressed the hot iron down.

"Only takes a few seconds." Lil watched over his shoulder.

Placing the iron in its caddy, Walt lifted the fabric and shook it. "It's like magic."

Lil rolled her eyes but smiled. "It is an invention that comes in handy for this quilter. Now, I'll need all the green fabric adhered to the block first. When you're finished, give it to me and I'll start to appliqué around the edges while you work on the next block."

"We'll have a regular assembly line."

"Sort of. The appliqué process takes awhile, so I'm sure you'll get ahead of me. So if you need a break to sit down, feel free."

Lil readied her sewing machine while Walt worked on the quilt block.

"I wonder if Mark sells this stuff in his store." Walt aligned the fabric and pressed the iron down.

"I'm sure he does."

"Want to stop there after my appointment tomorrow? I can update him on my recovery while you look around."

"I'd like that, but you haven't endured a car ride since you came home from the hospital. You already want to pick up some supplies, so you might not feel up to it. And shouldn't someone be around here in case people come to check in?"

Walt's head jerked up. "I never thought of that. I'm going to have to call Bill, tell him my schedule. See if they know when folks might be arriving." He placed another green stem on the fabric.

Finding it hard to carry on a conversation and accurately adhere the pattern pieces to the fabric, Walt and Lil worked in silence.

A soft rap sounded through the kitchen. Walt turned to Lil. "Was that you?"

"No, I think someone's at the door."

Walt glanced at the clock, surprised that almost two hours had passed while he helped Lil with her quilt blocks. Putting the iron in the caddy, Walt walked around the ironing board. "I knew if I stopped watching out the window someone would sneak up on us." He winked at Lil as he passed the table and went to the door, not realizing he'd left the walker behind until the swing of his arm to open the door threw off his balance.

Teetering, he grabbed the wall just as he felt Lil's arm slip across his back to steady him. "Thanks, Speedy."

"You did pretty well, but you need to remember that walker."

The chiding grated on Walt's nerves.

"Now that you're steady, wait here."

A low rumble started in Walt's throat at Lil's firm command. Just as he was ready to release it, the rap grew louder. "Just a minute," Walt hollered, releasing his irritation with Lil on whoever stood on the other side of the door. Instantly aware that he'd just snapped at an innocent bystander, Walt strained to see out the window.

"It's hard to see in the dusk, but it looks like a blue sedan," Lil said as she set the walker beside him and gave him a "what's your problem?" look.

Walt harrumphed and shook his head but bit back his retort as he continued toward the door. "A blue sedan. That would be Sandy's car." Walt opened the door, which wasn't an easy task with Lil shadowing him. He waved Sandy's petite frame in through the storm door.

"Lil, this is Sandy Callahan. We attend the same church."

"Sandy, this is Lil, my nurse and *friend*." Even in his aggravated state, his subconscious emphasized the last word.

"Nice to meet you."

Walt smiled as the women said their polite greeting in unison.

"Bill said that you might need some help readying the accommodations and then cleaning throughout the week. I called the Joy group and we have many volunteers, so just tell me what you need done and when and we'll make a schedule."

"Sit down." Walt motioned with his hand. "Want a cup of coffee?"

"No, thank you. I can't stay that long. What are you making?" Sandy ran her hand over the block Walt had finished.

"Lil's making her sister a Rose of Sharon quilt." Walt sat down at the table.

"Is she getting married?" Sandy turned to Lil.

"No, it's for her fortieth wedding anniversary."

"Almost the same. You know it used to be a tradition to give a Rose of Sharon to a bride because it represents romantic love and the sacrament of marriage."

"Sounds like you know your stuff." Lil smiled at Sandy.

"Well, our Joy group makes quilts for missions every year and we try to do a quilt block named after a Bible verse. Then one of us researches the block and gives an educational session on the pattern's history and how it relates to the Bible verse."

"What she said about the Joy group is true, but she's also being modest about her knowledge of quilting." Walt rapped the table with his knuckles. "Her quilts win first place at the county fair every year."

"Congratulations. That's wonderful." Lil patted Sandy's shoulder before taking a seat across the table from Walt.

"Thank you." Sandy looked at Lil. "I'm sorry to stare, but have we met before?"

"I don't think so. But I've been a nurse for many years, so maybe. . ." Lil shrugged.

"What's your last name?"

"Hayes."

"Lil Hayes. Is that your maiden name?"

"Yes, it is." Lil smiled.

"Even that sounds familiar. Do you ever enter quilting contests?"

"No, can't say that I have."

"Well, I know you from somewhere, those beautiful green eyes of yours and your name. My memory isn't what it used to be, but it will come to me. Now let's get down to business."

❧

"I thought for sure I'd get a good report." Walt stared absently out of the passenger window.

"You did get a good report. The doctor said you were right on track for healing." Lil chided him for putting a negative spin on his prognosis, although she'd hoped for better news, too.

Walt turned toward Lil and jerked his head toward the walker resting against the backseat. "I thought I'd be rid of that and back to using my quad cane or. . ."

"I know you think you're ready to try walking on your own." How many times had she caught him walking around the kitchen without his walker yesterday? "But you've relied on a cane for years to offset your limp. You may have to relearn your body's center and balance."

She earned a frown for her reasoning.

"You know I'd be more help around the hotel if I could use a cane instead of a walker."

Lil nodded. "That's true, but Sandy seems to have things organized, so all you'll have to do is check people in and fold the dried towels."

Walt chuckled. "She's a dynamo in the organization department. Because of her abilities, the soup dinner fund-raisers go off without a hitch and the church rakes in quite a profit."

"Do you usually serve hot breakfasts?" Lil eased off the gas and hit the brake as the light ahead turned red.

"Nothing more than toast or instant oatmeal. You don't mind coming over early and popping the egg casseroles in the oven, do you?" To look at her, Walt turned the best he could in his seat.

The sunshine through the windshield couldn't hold a candle to the light in his eyes. Unable to break her stare, Lil noted how the sun's rays brought out the green flecks in his hazel eyes.

She jumped at the loud honk behind her. "Oops." She felt warmth crawl up her neck as she pressed the gas. Walt's car roared through the intersection.

"Ease up there, Speedy." Walt grabbed the handle above the door with one hand, bracing against the dashboard with the other.

As the car resumed its normal pace, Lil swatted at Walt's arm. "It wasn't that bad."

Walt crossed his arms over his chest and smiled. "You need to turn left at the next light."

"I see it. It's a good-sized store. I thought it might be smaller, more like a quilter's boutique." Lil steered the car into the turning lane.

"No, really it's a full-blown fabric store, not just a quilt shop."

Lil pulled into a handicapped parking spot. She lifted his placard from the console and hooked it to the rearview mirror.

Walt pulled his door handle.

"Just a sec and I'll get your walker." Lil exited the car and rounded the back.

Walt had the door open, turning with his knees together as Lil retrieved, then opened the walker, and locked it into position. She stepped back, allowing Walt the space to get clear of the car door.

"Doesn't seem right, you opening and closing my car door. I should be doing that for you." Walt guided his walker to the slanted part of the sidewalk.

Wind seasoned with a hint of moisture blew a littered plastic store bag along with sandy grit through the parking lot, causing Lil's eyes to water.

"Everyone needs help now and then." Lil stepped from the parking lot to the sidewalk then waited at the quilt store entrance while Walt made his way to her side. "I think we got lucky with the weather today. No rain."

"Considering the forecast, I thought we'd be fighting rain-slicked roads today, but no precipitation nor freezing temperatures yet."

Lil shivered despite her heavy fleece jacket. "But it's getting there."

A bell jangled as Lil pulled open the door to allow Walt to pass through.

"Be with you in a minute," a muffled voice called.

An aromatic mix of lot-dyed cloth fragranced the store. Lil paused and eyeballed Granny Bea's interior.

"This is quite a place." Two tiered shelves covered one wall, filled to capacity with bolts of fabric in every hue imaginable. A large NOTIONS sign hung over a far corner that housed peg boards filled with sewing tools, thread cases, and book racks.

Various styles of sewing machines, cabinets, and chairs lined the opposite walls. A cutting counter divided the room. Circular shelves holding bolts of print fabrics were scattered throughout the store. Like wildflowers that popped up in a field, quilts of all shapes, sizes, and patterns dotted displays all over the store.

"I like this." Lil, having stopped beside a circular shelf not far from the entrance, put her hand on her hip, purse swinging at her wrist.

Walt turned. "Sarah put that display together."

A freehand wall quilt hung suspended above a circular shelf filled with bolts of fall colors and prints. A tree was appliquéd in the center of the quilt. Various-colored leaves fell around it, the machine stitching giving the appearance of a windswept motion. The material for the back matched the leaves.

"Look at that! The quilter cut the leaves from the fabric and sewed them to the top. How clever." Lil reached up and smoothed a corner of the quilt between her thumb and fingers.

"Caroline made that one." Mark popped up from behind a display case of thread.

"I told Lil about Caroline and your mom and you. Well, all the quilters I know. Lil's a quilter, too."

Walt's eyes shined with pride as he looked over at Lil.

A tiny thrill sent a warm shiver through her at Walt's boasting. Lil thought about including Walt in the quilter category since he helped her, but reconsidered. His pride was bruised enough at not being able to run his business on his own.

Mark and Walt walked toward the cash register counter while Lil continued to peruse the store.

"I didn't get a good report today."

"What? Why?"

"Walt!" Lil raised her voice to megaphone decibel as she called across the store. "I told you in the car not to say it that way. You're causing Mark undue concern."

"Stop eavesdropping, Lil, and shop."

The snappy tone turned Lil in her tracks. She started to march to the register counter when she saw a wide smile on Walt's face.

"I knew that'd get you going."

Lil screwed her face into her best don't-mess-with-me-man look as she approached the men. "Your uncle is progressing as the doctor planned; however, he still needs to use his walker." She turned to Mark with a reassuring smile.

Mark put a hand to his chest. "Uncle Walt, you had me worried."

"I want to use my cane."

Lil snorted. "He tries to walk around without any aid. I caught him at it four times yesterday."

"Stop tattling on me." Walt scrunched his face. "I just really wanted to be able to use my cane. It's hard to run a business using this." Walt lifted the walker from the floor and shook it.

"Wait a minute, what do you mean? You closed the hotel for four weeks." Mark crossed his arms over his chest and rocked back on his heels. "Actually, let's start at the beginning. What exactly did the doctor say?"

Walt sighed. "That I'm healing normally but I need to use the walker for at least two more weeks."

"That's good news." Mark released his arms. "Do you need a chair?"

"No, thank you. My stamina is back." Walt peered around Mark. "Where's Sarah? Is she feeling okay?"

"She's doing great. Today is her day off. Now, stop changing the subject. What's this about running your business?"

"A good man went to be with the Lord. He and his wife had just downsized and moved into those new senior-housing apartments. They have four children who need a place to stay. Sioux Falls is too far for a grieving family to drive every day."

"Are you sure you're up to it?" Mark looked to Lil for reassurance.

She nodded. "I think so. Sarah had the rooms all cleaned and ready to go. The ladies' group at Walt's church are donating breakfast casseroles and helping with the daily cleaning."

"We figured breakfast hours would be eight to ten, not the normal six to nine. If the folks don't want to eat at the hotel, they can take the food the ladies donate with them to Jeanie's. With the eight ladies cleaning rooms, Lil and I will only have to do the laundry."

Lil caught Mark's skeptical look. "I won't let him overdo. And it might be good for him. He's been pretty bored this past week."

"So bored"—Walt walked to the counter and leaned on it—"I started helping Lil with a quilt."

Mark burst out laughing. "I can't believe that."

"I am. I'm really good at fusing the pieces to the back. Tell him, Lil." Walt waved his hand in the air.

"He is good at fusing on the quilt block pieces to the fabric, but he's not patient waiting for me to finish my part so he can start again."

"What quilt pattern are you making?" Mark winked at Lil when he addressed the question to his uncle.

"A Rose of Sharon." Walt stood tall and puffed his chest out like a proud child who'd aced a spelling bee.

Mark's low whistle echoed around the store. "That's a detailed but beautiful pattern."

"It's for my sister's fortieth wedding anniversary." Lil smiled at Mark.

"Because that type of quilt represents romantic love and used to be given to new brides."

Lil laughed at Walt's adding the small piece of quilting trivia he knew to the conversation.

"And because"—Walt scrunched his face Lil's way—"she lost her sister's favorite quilt."

Mouth open ready to defend herself, Lil heard her cell phone ring, so she wagged a scolding finger toward Walt as she stepped away from the men. Squinting to see the small numbers, she realized it was Tiffany. She darted down a clearance aisle while the phone jangled in her hand.

Talk about bad timing. Lil hesitated then declined the call. She'd let it go to voice mail. As much as she wanted to leave, Walt still needed a full-time nurse and the hotel guests would be another diversion from her budding feelings.

The men's laughter drifted through the store. From her vantage point she could see Walt. Dressed in dark denim bib overalls and blue plaid flannel shirt, with his face lit with laughter and life, no one would guess that he recently had surgery.

He is so handsome and fun. Lil leaned her arms on the bolts of cloth in front of her.

A loud beep broke her dreamy staring, alerting her she had a voice message. The cell phone noise drew Walt's attention. He looked up. Instinctively, Lil looked down, not wanting him to know she'd been gazing his direction.

Her gasp cut through the store.

Lil couldn't believe her eyes. She gasped again.

"Is everything okay back there?" Mark called.

"F–f–fine." Lil pulled the bolt from the shelving. She found the end and separated the cloth to a single layer, then worked the soft yet grainy fabric between her thumbs and fingers.

The cloth wrapped around this bolt looked and felt like the old-time flour sack material. And not just any flour sack material either. The yellow background was more vibrant, but the white flower pattern, the same as the flour sack fabric, burned in her memory.

"Do you like that?"

Concentrating on the bolt of cloth, Lil's upper body jerked in a jumping fashion. "Oh! I didn't hear you walk over."

"That's apparent. We didn't mean to startle you, Lil."

"It's okay." Lil lifted her face to Walt's rounded hazel eyes filled with concern.

"Are you sure, because you look like you've seen a ghost." Walt's bony hand covered hers resting on the fabric.

"I kind of feel like I have." Lil turned to Mark. "To answer your question, I don't like it. I love it. It's almost an answer to a prayer."

"I special ordered that for a quilt repair job, but it wasn't the right color—"

"Let me guess," Lil said, shock shaking her voice. "The yellow's too dark."

Mark's wide-eyed expression mirrored Walt's.

"What's going on here?" Walt tapped his walker against the floor for emphasis. "Now you're both wearing eerie expressions."

Chapter 6

Lil didn't even glance his way. She hugged the bolt of fabric to her as if being reunited with a long-lost love. Anger and hurt tied together in a knot in Walt's stomach. He didn't like to be left out, especially where Lil was concerned.

"Was the quilt a Lily of the Field pattern made out of flour sack cloth?" Lil's lips quivered as she waited for Mark's answer.

Still wide-eyed, Mark nodded.

Walt reached out and squeezed her shoulder. "Lily's quilt."

Sniffling, Lil wiped her eyes with the backs of her fingers. "That's the quilt I lost that belonged to my sister, Lily."

"Mark, do you know who has that quilt?" Walt kept his eyes fixed on Lil, who cradled the fabric bolt in her arm and lovingly scanned it as if it were a newborn child.

"I do, Uncle Walt."

"Is it a regular customer? Someone we could talk to, maybe get it back?"

Lil's green eyes filled with hope as she looked up at Mark. "I'd pay them, whatever price they want. Do you have their number?"

Mark held both his palms out to stop their barrage of questions. "If you two will follow me to the office, I can show you a picture of the quilt."

Once inside the small office off of the classroom in the back of the store, Mark wiggled his computer mouse and clicked on his Internet browser.

Lil continued to hug the fabric bolt.

"I'll take that if you'd like to have a seat." Mark pried the material from Lil's hands as Lil, trancelike, sat down. "Uncle Walt, would you like a chair?" Mark placed the bolt of fabric on top of a file cabinet beside his desk.

"No, I'll stand right behind Lil."

Moving the keyboard to the side, Mark typed a website address. Walt's heart pounded as he read what Mark was typing.

When the site popped up, Lil gasped. "Caroline Baker. A quilter has it? Do you think she'll sell it?"

"I don't know. It's pretty special to her, too." Mark clicked on the site's before-and-after link as his eyes met Walt's over Lil's head. His probably-not message was loud and clear.

"Lil"—Walt laid a hand on her shoulder—"that quilt has a good home with Caroline. She's the little neighbor girl I was telling you about."

"You two know her?" Lil turned her head from side to side.

"Very well." Mark grimaced. "Lil, she credits that quilt with changing her life."

"Oh."

One short little word infused with more sadness than Walt's heart could handle. They'd dashed Lil's hopes.

Lil studied the monitor. "She did a really good job restoring it. It looks like new." She sniffled as she lifted her fingers and trailed them down the monitor. "At least it has a good home."

Just as Walt's heart twisted with disappointment for Lil, she laughed.

"Actually, Lily will be happy to know that one block isn't torn."

Lil's belly laughs echoed through Mark's office.

Mark shot Walt a questioning look and Walt shrugged. Maybe it was just a way for her to cope, now that she knew the quilt was someone else's and lost for good.

Lil wiped her eyes with her fingers as her laughter wound down. "I probably sound like a nut to you two. Lily is the sweetest person, but if you want to get her in a huff, say something about that quilt getting caught in the wringer." She smiled the way everyone does at their sibling's silly foibles.

How many times had Walt brought up something that he knew got under his brother's skin, just to get him riled up? He never agreed with what his brother had done to Gert and Mark, but through the years, Walt missed him and wished he was still around to needle.

"Thank you for showing me the pictures, Mark." Lil checked over her shoulder for Walt's location before rolling the chair back.

Now standing, she looked at Walt. "Since you're familiar with my project, do you think this fabric matches the colors I chose for the Rose of Sharon quilt? I could use it for the backing. At least that'd be something to remind Lily of her old quilt."

"Let me get a closer look at it. You were holding on to it like it might run away from you." Walt winked at Lil then studied the colors of the fabric. "I think the yellow's a good match to your petals."

"I do, too. Either way, I'm buying the entire bolt." She handed it to Mark.

Mark frowned. "I don't remember any Rose of Sharon quilts having yellow in them."

Walt rolled his eyes. "Lil's does."

She shrugged. "I prefer yellow roses."

&

Wake up. Walt tried to force his conscious mind to take control of his subconscious. *If I could just open my eyes, this would end.*

Vines tangled around his boots, sucking him down. Legs stiff from being motionless so long, slowing him down. The extra weight carried on his shoulders, pressing him down.

His knees bent deeper than they should have, making his steps uneven, throwing off his running pace. The air, hot and stagnant, burned his lungs.

Still he ran, his mouth open, greedily gobbling as much oxygen as he could. His exposed tongue absorbed the jungle's rank odors, gagging him, turning his stomach.

Every inch of Walt's body screamed, *Stop, take a rest*, but the angelic singing of chopper blades cutting through the air lured him forward like a siren's song.

Sweat ran down into his eyes, stinging and blurring his vision. Still he lifted one leaden foot, then the other. He had to get them to open land.

Wake up! His shout reverberated through his semiconscious state, but his subconscious mind couldn't hear him over the *whoosh, whoosh, whoosh* of the blades cutting through the thick air.

Lightning-like pain shocked his body with each step. He had to get to the open field. Branches snapped at his face. He stumbled over something—what, he didn't know. He didn't care.

Then his body rebelled for more oxygen. His stiff legs buckled, and he dropped to his knees. Closing his eyes, he saw her blue eyes, shining with happiness, welcoming him home.

Between each thunderous whoosh of the blades, he heard Nancy calling, *"Come home."* Burden lightened, his adrenaline kicked in. Rising to his feet, he ran on sturdy legs. Eyes closed, he trusted her voice and sprinted with the grace of a gazelle through the last of the jungle snarls, Nancy's blue eyes leading the way to the clearing.

A breeze kissed his sweat-drenched face. He opened his eyes. The chopper hovered a few feet away. Other soldiers ran or crawled toward it. He ran even faster, closing the distance between them and home.

He was within a foot of the chopper when rapid fire exploded around them. Dirt soared into the air and the black pellets rained down as bullets plowed up the ground. He felt the ammunition cut through the air as it buzzed past him. Soldiers inside the helicopter reached under his arms and pulled. With his torso half in the chopper's belly, it lifted off, and so did the weight from his shoulders.

Gunfire pounded down on them. He tried to crawl farther into the gut of the chopper. A second later his body lurched forward. Forced into the helicopter from behind, his face skinned across the rough metal belly of the aircraft as a white-hot pain blasted through his hip.

"Walt."

The lilt of a woman's voice called his name. Nancy was calling him home. He tried with all his might to open his eyes so he could gaze into her blue ones.

"Walt."

Her soft hand surrounded his. He tried harder to force his eyes open.

"Walt. Wake up. You're dreaming."

That's not Nancy's voice. His mind overcame the fog of the dream. *Open your eyes.* Walt's eyes popped open. His heart was racing, his breathing heavy.

Where was he? It took a minute for his eyes to focus in the semi-dark room. Familiar outlines of his living room, shadowy from the lack of the afternoon sun, took shape. His breathing slowed. He was home.

Lil kneeled beside his chair. As she grasped his hand, fear filled her green eyes.

"Walt."

It'd been Lil's voice he heard, not Nancy's.

Lil lifted her free hand and wiped it across his forehead, gathering the moisture beaded there before turning her hand and running its silky back down the side of his face.

"Are you okay?"

"Just a dream." Hoarse, he cleared his throat, fighting his instincts to pull Lil into a hug, feel her warmth as a tangible example of reality.

Lil lifted her brows over concern-filled eyes. "I'd say a nightmare."

Sucking his pursed lips under his mustache, he nodded.

"Want to talk about it?"

He shook his head. Could he talk about it? What would she think of him? They gave him a Purple Heart. Called him a hero, but he wasn't. He'd failed. The only hope he had was God's promise of forgiveness.

"Okay." Lil squeezed his hand as she gave him a weak smile. "Could I get you anything? A glass of water?"

As Walt leaned forward to reposition himself in the chair to take some weight off of his incision, he felt the dampness in his flannel shirt. "Probably should rehydrate." He pushed down on the armrests of the chair as he stood then grabbed his walker.

Lil beat him into the kitchen. Ice tinkled as it hit glass. In seconds, water hissed through the faucet.

"You don't have to hurry." Walt entered the kitchen. "I'm not dying of thirst."

Lil flicked the cold water lever into the off position, her eyes still veiled in concern.

She sighed. "I guess I just felt I needed to do something for you." She handed the glass to Walt as he stopped the walker beside the kitchen sink.

"Thank you." He sipped the water.

Lil stared out the window while Walt stared at her. Tall and broad, loud and pushy, not his type at all, yet where had she been all his life? When he saw the compassion in her eyes, he wanted to share the nightmare with her. Something he'd never wanted to do before. Tell her about the worst moment of his life. His biggest failure. He knew she'd understand.

"I'm sorry if I frightened you, Lil."

She turned when Walt placed his hand on her shoulder. Her smile was still weak, but some sparkle had returned to those beautiful green eyes. "I was frightened for you, not me."

The soft fluff of Lil's fleece top oozed between his fingers when he squeezed her shoulder. She'd have been a woman to come home from war to and build a life with. "My nightmares are always the same, and mild compared to some soldiers."

"I guess that's a good thing."

"It is a good thing." Walt sipped at his water. "Shall we make a pot of coffee and work on your quilt?"

Lil nodded.

"You get the coffee and I'll fill the pot."

Walt dropped his hand as Lil moved toward the refrigerator.

"You know, coffee doesn't stay any fresher in here. It really should be stored in the cupboard above the coffee maker."

"So you've told me." Walt leaned against the front of the sink while he filled the pot with water. "Every day this week," he mumbled.

"What?"

"Nothing." Walt grinned at Lil as she placed the filter into the pot and scooped the coffee into it.

Walt handed the brimming decanter to Lil. "You do the honors."

She dumped the water into the reservoir. "Should I clear a spot in the cupboard to store the coffee?"

"Not today."

Lil pursed her lips and frowned, but she walked the can of ground coffee back to the refrigerator.

"This would be easier without the walker." Walt had his fingers looped through the handles of empty mugs while trying to grip the walker.

"Some guests checked in while you were napping." Lil removed the cups from Walt's grasp, her fingertips grazing his skin and leaving a pleasant tingle.

"I put them in the first two rooms. I wrote the information on a white tablet since I don't know how to run your reservation software."

Lil took a seat behind her sewing machine and flipped on the toggle switch. A light in the machine popped on, creating a soft glow around the needle.

"I'll enter it into the system later. At least that's something I can do to help." Walt sighed. "It's not like these are regular overnight stays anyway."

"They were very grateful." Keeping her head bent, Lil lifted her eyes and her gaze locked onto his.

The emotion conveyed in her green eyes, pride and admiration, warmed Walt's heart.

Self-conscious at how to handle Lil's appreciation, Walt shrugged. "It's the least—"

"You could do. I know. I meant it as a compliment." Lil turned her attention back to a quilt block and adjusted it in the machine. "Walt, you're a very kind man."

A kind man. He was just doing the right thing. Yet that's what he thought when he went to war. When he came home, *kind* wasn't one of the descriptive words Nancy hurled at him. Just the opposite. She'd called him a savage.

Unaccustomed to being held in high esteem, he didn't know how to respond to Lil's statement, so he decided to change the subject.

"Did you get the appliquéing done on any of the blocks so I can fuse the petal pieces?" Walt lifted the walker and started toward the ironing board.

"Put the walker down and use it." Lil didn't even look up from the machine.

"What are you, a teacher with eyes in the back of her head?" Walt placed the walker on the floor.

"I have ears." Lil turned, tucking snowy curls behind her ears, proving to Walt what she said was true. "I didn't hear the scuffing of the walker, and I know my patient isn't patient."

Lil snickered at her play on words.

"That's it. No more Jerry Lewis movies for you." Walt's teasing brought out Lil's broad smile and lifted his spirits, chasing away his self-consciousness.

"You'd better get that iron heated up because you're holding up this assembly line. I'm almost done with the last block."

She adjusted the fabric under the presser foot. The steady purr of the machine's motor scooted the needle back and forth on the fabric with a rhythmic beat.

Walt gathered his supplies, tested the iron, and started fusing the yellow petals onto the fabric. "That black thread really makes the pattern stand out."

"It does make it pop."

"I'm sorry that Mark doesn't think Caroline will part with the Lily of the Field quilt."

The purr of the machine stopped. Lil sighed.

"Well, they have put time and money into it and probably developed a huge emotional attachment to it. Her website said her husband, Rodney, inherited the quilt, so it's not like they're the ones who found it either. There's no obligation to give it back."

"And it does have a good home." Walt pressed the iron down on the yellow fabric. "I can't believe how well this yellow and the background of that fabric"—Walt pointed to the bolt lying across the kitchen table—"match."

"I know. Lily will be so surprised."

"Well, if her reaction is anything like yours, you'd better have the smelling salts handy, Nurse Hayes. I thought you might pass out."

Walt lifted the block from the ironing board, stepping it over to the table. "Ready for you to do your stuff. You know, I should make one of these for Mark and Sarah for their wedding gift."

"It would make a lovely gift, but maybe you'd better hire someone to make it."

Walt studied the small fabric piece to make sure it lined up perfectly on Lil's traced template.

"I'm helping you. You could help me. I think we make a pretty good team."

❧

Lil kept her head down, her focus no longer on her sewing but on Walt's words. They were feeding off each other's feelings in this close proximity. *"Do not arouse or awaken love until it so desires."*

Is that what they were doing? Creating feelings? Or had love decided to be awakened? How was she supposed to tell?

Lil let off the foot pedal and rubbed her temples, her mind and heart grappling in an emotional cage match. "The project is moving along faster than I thought it would."

A safe answer, not really denying they were a good team yet not affirming it either.

"I think Mark felt sorry for me and gave me a good deal on that bolt of fabric. He discounted it much more than the clearance price."

"Probably got the extra friends-and-family discount." Walt fiddled with a fabric piece until he got it just right. "But you never know, if the situation is explained right, Caroline might sell the quilt."

"I don't know about that. The pictures on her website show the quilt draped over the altar at their wedding, so that means it's pretty special to them."

"Still"—Walt shrugged—"wouldn't hurt to ask."

"I suppose not, but—"

The jangle of a door buzzer, similar to the one in Mark's store, broke into their conversation. Lil had helped Walt reactivate it this morning.

"Walt?" Sandy called through the office entry in the living room.

"In the kitchen." Walt put the iron in the caddy just as Sandy popped through the doorway.

"Here's tomorrow's breakfast casserole." She lifted a cake pan.

Lil rose from her sentry at the sewing machine to unburden Sandy. "We just made some coffee. Would you like a cup?"

Sandy rubbed her palms together. "That would be wonderful, thank you. Winter's definitely on its way and I dread it. You'd think after all these years I'd be used to it. I have one more trip to the car; then I can sit and warm up a minute."

After rearranging the items in the refrigerator, Lil slid the nine-by-thirteen cake pan onto a shelf. Sandy had attached a sticky note with cooking directions on the lid. The woman thought of everything.

Lil removed another mug from the cupboard, poured the coffee, and was replacing the pot when Sandy came back through the door, carrying two large disposable pans of cinnamon rolls.

"Some folks don't eat a big breakfast, so we thought we'd provide options." Sandy placed the pans on the counter.

"I might need to sample one of those before we put them out, just to make sure they're customer quality." Walt winked at Lil.

"Oh Walt." Sandy waved her hand. "Help yourself now—we made plenty. Plus our group didn't get any meals over here last week when you came home. Moving up that surgery surprised us, so you two eat some of the food we're bringing over, too. Don't send it all to Jeanie's."

Walt waited for Sandy to sit. He held the back of Lil's chair until she sat down; then he took a seat. A thrill rippled through Lil at Walt's small but caring gesture.

"Have you heard when the funeral's scheduled?" Walt lifted his cup to his lips.

"Tuesday. They're waiting for his sister from Oregon."

Walt nodded his understanding while Lil sipped her coffee and tallied the time the hotel would have guests—at the very least, a week and a half.

"Don't worry." Sandy rapped the table with her knuckles. "We've got you covered for food through next Friday with quiches, biscuits and gravy, Danish, and coffee cake."

"Lil makes a mean frittata. She could cover a morning." Walt's voice held pride in her cooking abilities. "That is, if you don't mind, Lil. I know we'll be busy doing the laundry. It's hard to keep up with the need for towels."

"I don't mind. Let's see how the week goes though. We might find they just don't feel like eating much."

"Good idea." Sandy held her cup in midair. "Never know, we might wind up with too much food."

"The ladies coming to clean can take a break and eat some, too." Walt played with the handle of his empty coffee cup.

"That reminds me. Jan wants to know if you need your uniform pressed for the funeral."

"Shouldn't. I had it dry cleaned and haven't put it on since."

Lil's jaw dropped. Uniform. "Why wouldn't you just wear a suit?" Would she be able to handle seeing Walt in his uniform? Especially after his dream this afternoon? Most people only imagined the horror of the nightmares, but she had a firsthand account. She shivered despite the warmth of the room and her jogging suit.

Walt lifted his brows in surprise. "Sam was a veteran, so the Legion will present a flag and do a twenty-one gun salute at the grave site."

"But you said the other day that you don't help with the VFW." Lil drew her brows together in confusion.

"I don't. The Legion Post I belong to performs the ceremony."

"They're two different organizations, dear." Sandy smiled as she rose from her chair, but her tone indicated that this was something that was common knowledge.

A trickle of anger rolled through her at Sandy's implication but died down quickly. Maybe it was common knowledge. After protesting the war, having a change of heart, and being jilted, Lil tried to block anything to do with veterans, other than health issues, out of her mind.

"Walt, are you going to feel up to attending services this Sunday? If so, I hope you'll join him, Lil."

"If I feel up to it, she'll have to attend or I don't have a ride. The doctor hasn't released me to drive yet." Walt stood, adjusted his walker, and walked toward the living room with Sandy.

Lil trailed a few feet behind then sat on the arm of the sofa while Sandy and Walt continued through the door to the office.

"You know anyone from church would come and get you. Same for the funeral. Just give us a call." Sandy stood with her hand on the doorknob.

The thought that Walt would attend Sam's funeral hadn't even crossed Lil's mind. He'd want to go even if he wasn't performing his Legion duties. His business might be a few miles from town, but seeing Walt's interaction with Bill and Sandy, she knew he was an active community member. She sent up a silent prayer that his church family was willing to come and get him. As much as she enjoyed Walt's company, some time apart might clear their heads enough to get their emotions under control.

"Nice seeing you again." Sandy leaned and waved around Walt. "Lil Hayes. I just can't figure out why your name and eyes are so familiar to me. I'll figure it out though."

Walt closed the door behind Sandy.

"I wonder if she knows Lily and is mistaking you for her since you're twins." Walt walked through the living room, the walker lifted a few inches off of the ground.

"Put the walker down."

Walt grunted but followed her instructions.

"Lily and I are fraternal twins, so we resemble each other but no one would confuse us. Lily's petite like our mother's side of the family, with deep blue eyes and blond, straight hair." She pulled at a cottony ringlet, letting it boing back into place.

"Maybe she's run into you at a doctor's office or something." Walt eased down into his easy chair then picked up the remote control from the end table.

"I always worked in the emergency room, never a doctor's office." Lil shrugged. "Maybe I have a look-alike that knows someone from this area."

"Maybe." Walt shrugged. "Sandy's not originally from this area though. She grew up in Southern California."

Stifling the gasp in her throat, Lil felt her eyes widen. She coughed, trying to clear her past from her throat. Luckily, Walt was engrossed in the news so he didn't notice. Did she know a Sandy? She racked her brain. None that she remembered from her protest days, so that couldn't be the connection. Could it?

Chapter 7

I think I'll go do that bookwork." Walt turned to go into the office. "Think you can spare me from working on the quilt for a while?"

"Actually, I need to run to my camper." It was time to return Tiffany's call. Lil's feelings for Walt were growing stronger, and if his reaction to her war protesting came close to Larry's, it might set Walt back in his recovery.

"Okay. I'll call you on the walkie-talkie if I need you." The clack of the walker hitting the hardwood floor punctuated his words.

Walt's stance was getting straighter, which meant he wasn't having much pain around his incision. She'd promised to help him with the hotel this next week and she would. That would give Tiffany time to line up another nurse.

Lil went to the bedroom to retrieve Walt's idea of modern communication. If he fell in the office, a lot of good a walkie-talkie in the bedroom would do him. Lil walked to the office.

"Here." Lil handed the device to Walt. "Just in case you need it."

Walt peered over his bifocals. "Are you sure you're not a doctor? I can't read your chicken scratch. What does this say?" He held the note up to her.

"It says, 'Need extra pillows in room 2.'"

Frowning, Walt studied the paper. "I don't see that, but since you wrote it, I'll take your word for it."

He pushed down on the arms of the office chair to stand, but the pressure rolled the wheels back, throwing him off balance. "Whoa." He gripped the edge of the desktop.

At his first wobble, Lil's sense of time turned into slow motion. Walt's sharp intake of breath sounded deep and strung out as his body tilted backward.

Her arms flailed as she rounded the counter, grabbing the back of the chair and shoving it out of the way. The whir of wheels, then a thump against something assured her that danger had passed.

Walt rocked forward like a children's inflatable clown punching bag. She needed to steady him before backward momentum came into play. She wrapped her arms around his middle, planted her feet, and braced her legs.

All motion stopped.

Lil's exertion puffed out in heavy exhalations, ruffling the short gray hair around Walt's ears.

After a few seconds, his breathing returned to normal. "Lil, I think I've regained my balance."

Loosening her tight grip, Lil sighed. "Are you sure?" She was reluctant to move away from Walt's calming warmth.

"Yes. Are you all right?"

"Why wouldn't I be?" Lil released Walt's middle, stepping back slowly to make sure he had his footing.

"I heard the whir of the chair wheels and a loud crack. Did I push it so hard it knocked into you?"

Just like Walt to think of someone else before himself. "I pushed the chair out of the way. It ricocheted and hit the wall or the counter. I don't know for sure. I was trying to get to you before you hit the ground."

Lil moved around to Walt's side, pulling on the band of her fleece top to adjust it.

"I will say that scared me a little. Wasn't expecting it." Walt kept both hands clamped to the desk's edge.

"I told you it might take awhile for your balance to even out."

Walt nodded.

"I'm sorry, Walt. The first day I was here, I tried to safe-proof your house while you rested. Guess I missed a chair with wheels that could roll out from under you."

"It's not your fault, Speedy. We didn't plan on using this room for a while." Walt motioned for his walker.

Placing both hands firmly on the grips, Walt angled around. "Maybe we'd better move one of the dinette chairs from the breakfast area over here for the time being."

"Good idea."

"Where's that walkie-talkie?"

"Right here." Lil stretched to reach the communication device then handed it to Walt.

He slid it into his overalls pocket. "There"—he patted the pocket—"a little peace of mind."

He put the ring of master keys in another pocket. "You go on to your camper. I'll just get the pillows and finish up here."

As much as she needed to return Tiffany's call, Lil wasn't leaving Walt alone.

"Just how do you plan to carry the pillows? I'll stay." Lil pushed the rolling chair out into an open space. She grabbed the closest dinette chair and waited for Walt to round the counter before she placed the chair in front of the computer.

"I don't know. It might be a little low."

Walt leaned over the counter. "Well, I won't really be using it much anyway."

Lil studied the chair from various angles. "I'm concerned for your safety."

The door jingled open and several people pulling suitcases came in. For the next hour, Lil helped Walt get everyone settled into their rooms, giving them all extra towels and pillows since the front desk wasn't open all night.

Lil listened while Walt instructed his guests on how the back door worked after hours then told them that a hot breakfast would be served in the morning.

He knew Sam's children but not their children. The family members seemed to know that he had opened the hotel just for them, and they promised not to be any trouble.

Walt watched his guests pull out of the hotel's driveway before he turned tired eyes to Lil. Weariness was etched in the lines of his face.

"My stomach says it's getting close to suppertime."

"Mine, too, but with your doctor's appointment and this"—Lil waved around the room—"I forgot to take something out."

Heading toward the kitchen, Lil noted Walt hitching his step. He'd been on his feet too long.

"Walt, you're limping. Is your hip bothering you?"

The walker scooted along as Walt purposely stepped heel to toe. "I have some pressure, not really pain. Just reverted to that bad habit because it helped for so many years."

"You can take some pain reliever, you know."

"I know." Walt guided the walker to the kitchen table and lowered himself onto a padded dinette chair.

Lil put her hands on her hips and looked around the kitchen as if that would make dinner magically appear.

"I know you like to eat healthy."

Lil braced. Walt had plenty of processed food that she could heat up.

"But I'd like to treat you to supper. The drive-in a few miles from here makes a pretty good pizza, and they deliver."

"Clear out here?"

Walt nodded. "Farther. Won't take a tip either. What do you say? You have to be tired, too. We deserve a treat, don't we?"

"Actually, that sounds really good."

"The number's by the phone. Order any kind you like. I'm not fussy about pizza—just make it a large."

After the pizza was ordered, Lil started to pick up the quilt pieces from the tabletop.

"I can help with that." Walt started to rise.

"You set there and rest." She pointed a finger at him before arranging the various-shaped pieces in a stack and placing them on the counter. She moved the sewing machine to the far end of the table.

Just as she reached into the cupboard for paper plates, the hotel door-opening indicator sounded.

Lil looked at Walt before placing the plates on the counter. "That can't be the pizza man."

"No, he's not that fast. It's probably some of Sam's family." Walt started to get up.

"I'll take care of this. You were on your feet too long this afternoon. You're going to take some pain reliever with your dinner."

"Well, print then, so I don't need a decipher ring to decode your writing."

Lil stopped, placed her hand on her hip, and pulled a face at Walt before she hurried from the kitchen.

❧

"Thank You, God, for the great timing," Walt whispered as he rose from the chair. It should take Lil at least fifteen minutes to get the guests checked in. That'd give him enough time to turn the kitchen into a cozy atmosphere and their dinner into a date.

To get close to the counter, Walt used his walker, then left it behind and steadied his steps and balance by hanging on to the edge of the counter for support. He put the paper plates away.

Making it to the cupboard where his mother's china was stored, Walt carefully lifted out two plates, sliding them along the countertop. He made his way back to the end of the cupboards by the table where he'd left his walker.

Leaving the plates on the edge of the counter, he maneuvered himself between the counter and the table. Once the plates were on the table, he retraced his steps to gather other keepsakes of his mother's—wineglasses. They'd add to the ambience even though he planned to fill them with ginger ale.

Keeping his ears alert for Lil's returning footsteps, he finished setting the table. He lifted the liter bottle of ginger ale from the refrigerator, trying to carry it and push the walker. The walker had a mind of its own, veering off to the side. Tucking the bottle under his arm so both hands could steer the walker, Walt took a step, but the slick plastic bottle slid down the arm of his flannel shirt.

Letting go of the walker, he caught the bottle before it could hit the floor and make a mess. That certainly wouldn't be a romantic evening, scrubbing sticky soda from the floor. Realizing he'd have to leave the soda carrying to Lil, he returned the bottle to the refrigerator.

Glancing at the clock, he found he'd used a full fifteen minutes just getting the table set. Walt stood back. The table looked fancy, but the brightly lit kitchen distracted from the cozy feeling he was going for.

He needed a candle for romantic lighting, but being an old bachelor, he never kept candles around. He had flashlights for power outages. Walt rested his weight through his arms on the walker. His hip did ache; he had overdone today.

He didn't have time to bring a table lamp in for dim lighting. Walt scanned the room, then smiled. Would Lil give him points for creativity? He pushed her machine closer to the place settings and turned it on.

Then he walked to the kitchen light switch and flicked it off. The machine's light gave a soft glow to the table, and the crystal wineglasses sparkled. Just the setting he'd wanted to create because Lil deserved to be pampered. *A Rose of Sharon.*

Walt stood at attention when the door buzzer sounded. Was it a guest or the pizza delivery person?

"Hello." Lil's voice rumbled through his home. "Just a minute and I'll get my purse."

The pizza had arrived. Walt had expected them to deliver to the back door, not the office. He pushed his walker and stepped as fast as his sore hip allowed. He wasn't sure where Lil's purse was, but he was paying for this *date.*

Nerves shot small jolts of electric current through his body, weakening his limbs at the thought. He hadn't dated since the mid-1970s. He gave up because the women he went out with couldn't hold a candle to Nancy.

Walt tried to herd up his rampaging emotions as he hurried through the living room, almost mowing Lil down with his walker.

"Where you going in such a rush?" Lil sidestepped just before the front bar of the walker bumped into her. "I told you to stay put."

With a clear path, Walt kept pushing the walker forward. "I'm going to pay for the pizza."

"I was getting my purse to do just that. Now you go back into the kitchen and rest. Come on."

Walt stopped at the sound of Lil's retreating footsteps. She'd ruin the surprise if she went in now. He wanted to see her face soften and her pretty green eyes sparkle with appreciation, just like they had when she'd seen the table setting the day he'd made the tea party.

"No, Lil. You come with me."

Lil spun around, eyes wide at the commanding tone Walt used.

At least he got her attention. Although, by her stern look, it appeared he might be getting a lecture.

"Please?"

She frowned, opened her mouth, then snapped her jaw closed but held it tight as she walked toward him and followed him into the office.

Once he'd paid and chitchatted with the deliveryman, Lil started for the kitchen with the pizza box.

"Just a minute, Speedy. I need to go first."

Lil stopped and turned. "Why?"

"My legs feel a little weak, so it'd be best if you follow me." His legs *were* weak—not from today's exertions but from tonight's anticipation of a first date with Lil.

"I knew you had overdone today when you started limping. Just because you started feeling better doesn't mean you can resume normal activities. It takes time for your body to heal." Lil brought up the rear of their short parade to the kitchen. "Besides, how am I supposed to help you, carrying a pizza box?"

"Guess you'd have to drop it on the floor." Walt fought back the snicker in his voice.

"Why's it so dark in here. . ."

Lil's voice trailed off as Walt moved to the side, allowing her a clear view of the kitchen table.

"Surprise."

Lil's mouth gaped, her face void of expression.

This might have been a mistake. Walt sucked his pursed lips in and out. Lil was a hard woman to read.

She looked from Walt to the table and back again. "What is all of this?"

Walt's heart pattered as Lil's eyes softened. The corners of her lips quivered.

"Our first date—that is, if you'll do me the honor of having dinner with me." Like a maître d' ushering her to a reserved table, Walt bowed a little and held a hand toward the dinette set.

The pizza box twitched from the tremble in Lil's hand as she nodded acceptance to Walt's invitation.

Speechless. Lil was speechless. This was a first and another unreadable sign. Was that good or bad?

She set the pizza box on the table.

"Before you sit down, would you mind getting the ginger ale out of the fridge?"

Lil gave her head a shake and headed in the direction of the refrigerator.

"I tried bringing it to the table, but it's too bulky for me to carry with this contraption." He lifted the walker.

Lil's head popped up from retrieving the soda. "You need that contraption. Look what happened this afternoon. Walt, you haven't found your new center of balance yet."

Speechless didn't last long.

"I know. I was just saying." Walt stood beside Lil's chair. "Set that on the table. I'll pour it later." He really did need to sit down for a while.

To his surprise, Lil didn't argue or fuss. She placed the bottle on the table, smiled at him, then sat down. He guided the back of her chair as she helped by scooting it under the table.

"Thank you." Every etching in her face shone with happiness.

"So I take it you've accepted my invitation to a dinner date." Walt gave her a wide smile as he poured the soda into the glasses before sitting down.

"I figured that any man who could create a mood using the light on a sewing machine didn't deserve to be turned down." Lil placed her napkin in her lap and reached toward the pizza box.

"Allow me." Walt lifted the lid then pulled out a slice of pizza.

Lil held her plate up to accept her portion.

After Walt plated the pizza, he reached for Lil's hand.

"Let's give thanks."

Grasping Walt's hand, Lil bowed her head. The softness of her hand melted into Walt's palm. The fit of their hands was in perfect partnership, hers not small and lost in the expanse of his, but holding its own against his strength.

"Dear Father, thank You for providing Lil with quick response times, protecting me from near disaster, again. Be with us during the coming week and help us bring comfort to Sam's family. Thank You for this nourishment, the teamwork of the Joy group at church, and for a new friend I've found in Lil. Amen."

Without thinking, Walt brought Lil's hand to his mouth. His lips brushed against the silkiness of her hand.

His gesture surprised Lil. Her sharp intake of breath ended in a squeak that echoed through the silent kitchen. Walt smiled before he turned her hand over and planted a longer, deeper kiss in her palm, hoping it would take root and linger there before he released it.

"Walt." Lil's voice was soft, almost shy. "We can't do this. I'm your nurse."

"This world is too politically correct for me, Lil. I think you're special and I want you to know it. People meet in all kinds of ways. My needing care after surgery was our way." Walt wagged his index finger in the air between the two of them.

"The first day I walked through that door"—Lil looked past him to the back entry—"I'd have never pegged you for a romantic." Lil revealed a shy smile.

Walt shrugged. "If doing something nice for you, Lil, is being a romantic, then I guess I am."

When Lil's eyes locked on his, Walt's heart hitch-stepped. A trace of sorrow filtered through the shine coming from her eyes.

"What is it, Lil?"

She cleared her throat. "Nothing, Walt. Our pizza's getting cold. Let's eat our dinner."

They chewed for a few silent moments.

"Walt, you did use your walker to set the table, didn't you?" Lil lifted her glass.

"Yes." Was that what was worrying her? "I learned my lesson this afternoon." He went to take a drink.

"Don't drink that yet." Lil pursed her lips like Walt could read her mind. "I'd like to make a toast."

She sure can go from shy to bossy fast. Walt grinned at his thought.

"What?" Lil's gaze bored into him.

"Nothing. I'm just having a good time."

Lil grinned. "Me, too. To health and happiness." She moved her glass toward his, the tinkling sound dancing through the kitchen.

"This is real crystal. I'd know that sound anywhere." Lil sipped her ginger ale.

"My mother had expensive taste and she entertained a lot. My father was a doctor. Mom's occupation was community service organizations. What did your parents do?"

"Dad drove a gravel truck. Mom ran the household and took care of Lily and me."

Walt served them each another slice of pizza. "Lil, what's your real name?"

She pursed her lips and stared down at her plate.

"It can't be that bad."

"Well, suffice it to say, I never liked my name the way Lily liked hers. Although there was a short time in the sixties when I liked it because it fit in with the peace move—"

Lil stopped short then filled her mouth with pizza like she was trying to hold her words in.

Walt's glasses slipped down his nose a little as he scrunched his face. "The make-love-not-war peace movement?" He snorted. "Surely Lil can't be short for Sunshine or Rainbow."

Sheepishness crossed over Lil's features as she took a sip of soda. After swallowing, she cleared her throat. "Close."

Walt leveled a look at her.

"Okay, I'll tell you. My grandma, the one that made the quilts, was named Daisy. My mother's name was Iris. My sister's name is Lily. Do you see where I'm going with this?" Lil raised her eyebrows.

"You're named after a flower? But lily is the only flower that starts out with l-i-l."

"No, lily is the only flower that uses the short vowel sound. I'm named after the flower that uses the long vowel sound."

Walt scowled as he racked his brain, searching for flower names that began with l-i-l.

Lil lifted her empty plate. "You were mistaken the other day, Walt. I don't have a lilac quilt because I *like* lilacs. I have a lilac quilt because my grandmother made us quilts that represented our names."

"Your name is Lilac?" Walt was immediately sorry for the disbelief he heard in his voice.

❧

Hands in pockets, Lil pulled her jacket close in an attempt to seal out the chilly night air. She should have buttoned it, but it'd been a long day and she just wanted out of Walt's house. She wanted out of the close proximity that stirred up both of their feelings. She wanted out of this assignment. No, *needed* out of this assignment.

Why hadn't she called Tiffany back? She sighed as she unlocked the camper door. She liked spending time with Walt. In two short weeks they'd begun stitching together the snippets of their lives, time and events overlapping and being appliquéd into their hearts, just like the small fabric pieces that created the pattern of her Rose of Sharon quilt.

She knew now it was time for love to awaken. She didn't believe in coincidence. That replica flour sack material and Mark's knowing about the Lily of the Field quilt—they were God-given incidences.

But surely God didn't want Lil and Walt together. A war protestor and a soldier? A traveler and a homebody? A loner and a socialite?

Well, maybe Walt couldn't be classified as a socialite, but he was active in his community, something that she'd shied away from all these years.

Entering the camper, she secured the door and lifted the walkie-talkie from the counter. A flick of the knob gave a static hello. She pressed the button.

"Walt."

"Lilac."

She shivered at the husky way her name rolled from Walt's lips through the air waves. It sounded pretty when he said it. Made her feel special.

"I'm in the camper, safe and sound. Good night."

"The pain reliever's working. My hip stopped throbbing."

Lil collapsed on her sofa. "I'm glad. Now get some rest."

"I really enjoyed our evening together."

Could the man not take a hint? She needed time alone. Time to think things through.

The *beep-pop* of her walkie-talkie cut through the silence of her camper. "Lil, are you there?"

"Yes." She released the button and lowered the device. The man needed a cell phone.

"You have very soft hands."

She closed her eyes as a soft tingle started where Walt's able lips touched her palm, the tickle of his coarse mustache adding to the pleasure.

Lifting the walkie-talkie to her mouth, she pressed the button. "Thank you, Walt. For everything. I can't imagine a better first date."

Lil dropped the walkie-talkie in her lap then rested her elbow on the sofa arm and rubbed her temples, knowing the conversation wasn't close to being over. Her heart skittered at the thought; her head, not so much.

"When I get rid of this walker, I'm taking you out on the town, a real dinner date and maybe a movie. Or we could take in a museum. Sioux Falls has some interesting ones, and end the day with a nice intimate dinner. Would you like that, Lil?"

Yes! Her heart screamed its response. Luckily it didn't have control of her vocal cords.

When Walt got rid of his walker, a yellow pickup with a fifth wheel would be tearing down the interstate to Texas.

"Lil?"

She couldn't dash the hope in his voice. She lifted the walkie-talkie and pushed in the button to talk. "Both of those sound very nice."

"Good. . ." Static blared, cutting off some of Walt's words.

"Walt, something's interfering."

"I said we can talk about it tomorrow or the day after that. Make some concrete plans."

"Okay. Walt, you'd better get some rest tonight if you want to get rid of the walker."

"Sorry, Lil. Guess I'm kind of wound up."

Car lights flashed past the camper. Lil lifted her blinds and watched a caravan of vehicles parade by.

"Walt, your guests are here. Just warning you in case you hear noises. Don't get up to investigate."

"Okay. They promised not to bother me unless it was an emergency."

The noise after Walt's statement sounded suspiciously like a yawn, his nighttime pain reliever finally kicking in.

"You'd better get some rest. I'll be over early to put the breakfast casserole in the oven." Lil hoped this would end the conversation.

"I miss you, Lil."

Walt's voice, so full of sincerity, melted Lil's heart. "I miss you, too. Now get some rest." Lil flicked the button on her walkie-talkie, expecting that to end the conversation.

"Good night, Lil." Walt's voice was thick and groggy as he started dropping off to sleep. "Your name might be Lilac, but you're my Rose of Sharon."

Chapter 8

Running a hotel was harder work than treating life-threatening injuries in the emergency room. Of course, Lil was used to the latter type of work.

The last few days ran together in a blur. Heat up breakfast, put the food out, make coffee, visit, greet the church ladies, make more coffee, start the laundry, fold the laundry and put it away, prepare lunch and dinner. All the while keeping a sharp eye on Walt to make sure that his balance was steady, that he didn't overdo, and that he used his walker.

Lil flopped down in a chair beside Walt in the laundry room. Today was even more hectic as they tried to get laundry folded before it was time for Walt to get ready for the funeral.

"I really wish you'd come." Walt smoothed out a towel on the table, halved it, tri-folded it, and flopped it on top of the stack.

"Walt, I didn't know Sam."

"I know, but you have met his kids and grandkids. Besides"—Walt sniffed—"I need you there for moral support."

Lil knew this was hard on Walt. It was their age. Friends or loved ones passing on made you consider your own mortality. Wonder how many years you had left. If you'd beat the odds and live past the projected age of insurance life-expectancy tables.

She snapped a towel through the air, grabbed up the corners, and in one fluid motion folded it to match Walt's.

Sam's children were a testament to the kind of man he'd been, a true reflection of kids honoring their father and mother. The only noise they made was when they visited at breakfast. The church ladies couldn't believe how well they kept their rooms, all amid their grieving.

When the buzzing of a finished cycle on the dryer cut through her thoughts, she rose and removed the warm towels, piling them on the table in front of Walt.

He reached for her hand and laced his fingers in hers. "Please?" Eyes filled with sorrow, Walt searched her face.

Compassion turned her heart into a ball of cotton and overruled her mind's reasoning. Lil nodded. "I'll go."

The two of them had the towels folded in record time. Lil gathered the piles up, the residual warmth from the dryer soaking through the thin knit of her turtleneck.

She found Walt locking the front door of the office.

"All of the businesses are closing down during the time of Sam's funeral." He scooted the walker toward the living room. His overalls strap fell off of his shoulder, exposing more of his brown henley shirt. He stopped and pushed the strap back into place with his thumb.

"You've been fighting that strap all morning. Why don't you just tighten it?" Lil worked out the twist in the denim from his last adjustment.

"It's as tight as it can go." Walt turned to show Lil. "I've lost some weight. Must be from all of that healthy eating we've been doing."

Lil harrumphed and looked down at her own frame. "Men. You're so lucky. It's not doing me any good."

"Well, your body is used to eating that stuff. Besides, you look good just the way you are."

Walt's eyes sparked with approval, igniting a brush fire on her cheeks.

"I just hope my uniform fits. We might have to punch a hole in my belt." Walt continued through the house.

They parted ways at the kitchen door.

"It won't take me long to change," Lil called over her shoulder, letting the storm door ease closed on its own.

Twenty minutes later, Lil, donned in the only dress she owned, a dark green sheath, stepped back into the kitchen, her black ballet flats slick against the linoleum flooring.

"I'm back. I hope no one notices this was the same dress I wore to church on Sunday." She hollered the words toward Walt's closed bedroom door.

"Why are you shouting?"

Lil jumped. Mouth open, ready to chide Walt for coming out of the living room and startling her, she turned toward the living room doorway.

No words came out, but her mouth remained gaping. After seeing Walt in nothing but loose sweatpants or overalls, she had no idea what a nice physique he had.

The dark hat he wore tipped slightly on his head was a contrast to his cropped white hair. His tapered uniform shirt accentuated his broad shoulders. The dark pants with a sharply pressed crease down the center of his legs stopped just above smartly shined shoes.

Her heart hammered in her chest and echoed in her ears. She hadn't prepared herself for a man in uniform.

"Lil, is something wrong? Did I mess up my tie?" Walt's fingers fumbled with the collar of his shirt.

"No, Walt. You look handsome." Lil walked over to him and smoothed her hands over his shoulders, resting them on his biceps.

She felt tears sting her eyes. How had she not been able to see the beauty of a man in uniform, the strength and courage belied in the contoured fit?

Walt stood straight in the rigid fashion of a soldier. He tilted his head up when their gazes locked. Lil felt sure he'd see the shamefulness of the way she'd treated heroes returning home from war and order her from his home.

"Would you help me with my jacket? I don't trust my balance."

Lil lifted the jacket from the front bar of the walker. She held it so Walt could slip one arm in, then rounded behind him and helped him insert his other arm. Stopping in front of the walker, she folded down the collar, letting her palms smooth down the stiffly starched fabric.

"Thank you, Lil." Walt put his hands on her cheeks. The slight movement brushed the metal bar of the walker on her dress.

"For what?" The intense look in Walt's eyes lured her face closer to his.

Walt's hard-soled shoes clicked on the vinyl flooring as he took a small step forward.

"For coming with me today and telling me I'm handsome."

His husky whisper tickled her chin as his fingers tipped her head downward, her lips closer to his. Her hands glided back up to his shoulders and rested beside his collar. Her eyes fluttered closed and her grip tightened on his arms as his lips lingered on hers, their closeness weakening her knees.

Walt drew back, running his fingers down her cheeks, resting his hands on her upper arms. The sleeves of her dress rustled from the slight tremble of his hands.

Lil licked her lips, savoring the sweetness of the kiss. Her heart soared when she opened her eyes and saw the warm sparkle of attraction in Walt's hazel irises.

"Let him kiss me with the kisses of his mouth." It definitely was love's desire to awaken in her life, their lives. Walt already thought she was his Rose of Sharon. After that kiss, she knew without a doubt he was hers.

She understood all the descriptive phrases used in the Song of Songs now. *"It burns like blazing fire, like a mighty flame."* Her heart pattered, remembering the electric current of his touch on her cheeks, her arms, her lips.

She sighed, the dreamy response vibrating in her throat. Walt smiled up at her before he pulled her into a hug, the walker rattling its displeasure at being caught in the middle.

This moment was perfect. She'd protect it in her heart forever. Nothing could ever ruin it for her.

Walt broke the embrace, his eyes dancing with teasing. "I bet you're one of those girls who never could resist a man in uniform."

Lil's heart slumped. Nothing but that.

❧

Walt slipped his hat from his head as he entered the church hall. He scanned the room for Lil. She'd insisted on staying to help the church ladies prepare the luncheon rather than accompany him to the cemetery.

Just as well; the twenty-one gun salute never failed to bring strong emotions to the surface. Whenever he heard it, he was transported back to another funeral in a different era, where a hysterical mother and stony-faced father buried their nineteen-year-old son, the son Walt killed by trying to save him.

Yet they'd thanked him, called Walt a hero, and hoped he'd receive a Purple Heart for his efforts. Walt clung to their words, believed them until Nancy clued him in on what she and the rest of the world thought him—a monster.

Walt stepped aside to allow others to pass. He still couldn't see Lil. Earlier, he'd picked the wrong time to kiss her, but he'd needed her comfort. He needed that same comfort now.

As if on cue, Lil, using her backside to open the swinging door, emerged from the kitchen. She carried a large silver serving tray with a vast array of sweets. She set it at the end of a long table. When she looked up, Walt waved a finger to catch her eye.

The simply styled green dress looked good against her ivory skin and brought out the color of her eyes. She'd secured her unruly curls with jeweled hair combs, yet small corkscrews framed her face.

She wore lipstick today. He wasn't certain when she'd put it on because her lips were natural when they'd kissed. Walt rubbed his lips together as his heart became a ball, happily bouncing through his chest.

"Have a seat with your friends, Walt. I'm going to help in the kitchen. After all the ladies have done for us this week, I feel obliged."

A smile curled Walt's lips at her use of the word *us*. "Okay, but come and sit with us to have your lunch when you're finished." Walt reached up and patted her cheek.

"Don't wait for me." Lil wagged her index finger in his face. "You have something to eat. You haven't eaten since breakfast."

Always bossing him. Or was it concern? "I had three helpings of the biscuits and gravy this morning."

"But who's counting?" Lil arched an eyebrow.

"I'm sure *you* were." Walt chuckled. "But I'll eat with the boys."

It was hard to know just how much time passed before Lil joined Walt at the table, accompanied by other church ladies.

"What are you talking about?" Sandy sat in the recently vacated seat across from Walt. Lil slipped onto the empty chair beside him, their chairs strategically arranged so close together that their shoulders touched. He hoped she didn't notice the other side had more elbow room.

Bill piped up. "Just telling war stories. What else do old veterans do?"

Laughter erupted at the table. Walt glanced over at Lil. He'd felt her stiffen, and now a tight smile graced her lips.

Had something gone wrong in the kitchen, or did she feel this wasn't a topic to be discussed at church or a funeral?

Bill launched into a story about Sam in basic training after the two of them had enlisted together. Lil kept her head bowed, eyes riveted to her plate. Yet Walt was pretty sure she was only pushing her food around on her plate as the fingers on her free hand nervously rubbed her paper napkin into shreds. She couldn't be squeamish; she was a nurse. It had to be something else.

"Maybe we should change the subject, guys. The ladies are trying to eat." Walt thought his suggestion might bring a thankful glance from Lil, but her posture remained the same, stilted, her features strained.

"Okay, no battle stories." Bill drew a deep breath. "I'm just glad some of the Vietnam vets are finally getting the medals they deserve. It wasn't right what we came home to."

The already taut muscles in Lil's arm that brushed against his tightened more. She was gazing across the room in the direction of a Sunday school bulletin board. A multicolored rainbow over blue ocean waves, a reminder of God's promise to Noah and humankind.

Her eyes weren't admiring the bulletin board. Her eyes were clouded with the same wistful look they'd had on their very first walk together when this subject came up. She'd never said why, but Walt could tell her feelings on this issue were strong.

"No, it wasn't." Sandy frowned. "I'm ashamed to admit my older sister protested the war. I was in sixth grade when she started. Every night she and my dad would argue at the dinner table. Then when she went to college"—Sandy flopped her hands in the air—"she organized rallies, changed her name from Vivian to Harmony. I never understood it, never."

At first Walt thought Lil snorted, but as the rough coughing started, he realized her sip of coffee must've gone down the wrong pipe.

"Lil, you all right?" He patted her back as the violent coughing continued.

"Fine, just went down wrong," she said, each word a rasp between coughs.

"I'll get you some water." Sandy hurried off to the kitchen.

A tear beaded in the outer corner of Lil's eye and ran down her cheek. As the coughing subsided, she fanned at her flushed face. "Excuse me." Lil cleared her throat hard and accepted the water from Sandy.

After a long drink, her normal peachy glow chased away the cough-reddened hue on her face.

Walt handed her his napkin and she dabbed the moisture from her eyes. "Thank you, Sandy." Lil finished off the water in the Styrofoam cup.

"Feeling better?" Walt wrapped his arm around Lil's shoulders and pulled her into a side hug, expecting to feel her soft warmth melt into his side. Her rigid posture kept her intact in her chair, the stiff arm in his ribs a barrier that separated them. His heart sagged in his chest.

"I'm fine." She flashed him a weak smile, her voice fake and an octave higher than normal.

He'd been around her long enough to know that this was far from fine for Lil.

Walt's arm dropped as Lil scooted her chair a few inches to the side, creating more space between them. Maybe she didn't like public displays of affection. But it was probably more than likely her aloofness had to do with her being his nurse and their growing fondness for each other being unprofessional.

"Walt, will you be able to march in the Veterans Day parade?" Bill tapped his empty cup on the tabletop.

"I don't know. I'm hoping I can. It depends on if I get rid of the walker in a couple of weeks. What do you think, Lil?"

"I'm sure you'll have graduated to a cane by then, but you still might not be up to walking too far. How long is the parade route?"

"Four blocks." Walt faked a stretch and crossed his arms over his chest, hoping no one had noticed his attempt to pull Lil close and her attempt to push him away.

"Maybe we'll have to put you in the convertible with the older guys who can't walk the route anymore."

Walt wrinkled his nose at Bill's suggestion. He'd been marching, the best he could, in the parade since he moved here. This year with a new hip, it should be easier.

"We have a fun Veterans Day celebration." Sandy flattened her forearm across the width of the table and tapped her fingers to draw

Lil's attention away from the bulletin board.

"Obviously, there's a parade. But there is also a trap shoot and a pie social, which we finish off with a ham dinner. It's a blast. You'll have a lot of fun."

"Hmm. . .if Walt's recovery goes according to the doctor's plan, his six weeks of needing a nurse will be up by then."

Lil shifted on her metal folding chair, scooting it even farther away from Walt. She stopped when the legs clamored into the neighboring chair.

Walt winced at a small prick in his heart, like a thumbtack piercing skin. Veterans Day was only three weeks away. He'd been so focused on getting rid of the walker, he'd forgotten that Lil might go with it. Something that, at one time, he'd wanted. Now he didn't want to consider that option.

"Won't you stay and join us?" Sandy smiled brightly at Lil. "You have your camper at Walt's."

Lil gave a small shake of her head. "Sorry, but if the doctor releases Walt, I'll be heading to Texas, hopefully before the first snowfall." Lil crossed her fingers on both hands and held them high.

Lil's words pierced Walt's heart like a razor-sharp bayonet. His pride was the only thing keeping him from letting the pain double him over.

❧

"Are you coming right back?" Walt stood by the back door.

Because she couldn't look at the dejection marring Walt's handsome face, Lil focused on the farmer combining the cornfield across the road.

"No. You need to lie down and rest. This has been a trying day. I'm going to stay in my camper so I don't disturb you." Lil chanced a peripheral glance Walt's way.

The mouth that kissed her a few short hours ago, feeding her soul like manna from heaven, drew into a deep frown. "Lil, tell me what's wrong."

The pleading in his tone weakening her resolve, she drew a fortifying breath.

"I'm sorry."

"Walt, stop apologizing. It's nothing you've done. *Believe me.*"

"Then go change your clothes and come right back."

Lil pursed her lips and shook her head. She allowed herself to look into his hazel eyes. "I have some computer work to do on your case. I'll be back in an hour or so. As your nurse, I'm ordering you to lie down and rest."

"Ordering me?" Anger lifted Walt's last word to a higher level. "Lil, you've been bossing me since you arrived. At first I didn't like it because in my house *I'm* the boss, but then I realized it's just the way you communicate."

Lil fisted her hand and placed it on her hip. "Are you—"

"I'm not finished. This little mood of yours has happened twice. Tell me what's bothering you so it doesn't keep happening."

The angrier Walt became, the faster he spoke.

"No, I'm not going to tell you. It's none of your business," she snapped, raising her voice to cut through his anger.

Walt drew in a sharp breath that seemed to move his upper body back a few inches. "Fine. Go over to your camper and stay there."

In defiance, Walt made a grand gesture of lifting his walker before he turned and marched across the kitchen, slamming his bedroom door behind him.

Lil remained planted on the sidewalk in front of the door. The cold October air permeated her clothes, chilling her to the bone. "I can't tell you, Walt." Her whispered words blew across the camper parking lot, getting lost in the vacant field.

She choked back a sob. Crying would do her no good. It wouldn't change the past, or her feelings, or the fact that Sandy was her college roommate's little sister.

Lil walked to her camper, lifting a hand in limp greeting at a passing vehicle whose horn tooted its hello.

Once inside, she flopped down in her easy chair and slipped off the ballet flats. Sandy was probably thirteen at the time Lil roomed with Harmony.

She rolled her eyes at the name. Vivian was so much prettier than Harmony, but the former name was just too conventional at the time. Lil stayed with Vivian's family over spring break her junior year. Sandy followed them around everywhere. Asking them questions about the war and the rallies and college, just pestering the way little sisters do.

Who'd have guessed that, years later, Lil would run into her again. She'd love to ask Sandy about Vivian, but. . .she couldn't risk it. She couldn't risk running into Sandy anymore either. Sooner or later, she'd remember who Lil was and innocently spill the beans.

"And the truth will set you free."

Lil checked the time. Tiffany should still be in the office. Rummaging through her purse, Lil retrieved her cell phone, pressing the preset number before she changed her mind.

"Tiffany, it's Lil."

"Hello, Lil. After the message you left a week ago, I thought you'd have called back by now."

Tiffany was multitasking, as evidenced by the sounds of the rhythmic click of a keyboard. Holding the phone to her right ear, Lil rubbed her left temple.

"I really need to be reassigned." Lil's heart squeezed tight at the thought.

"Why?"

The *click, click, click* continued, irritating Lil that she didn't have Tiffany's full attention.

The ache in Lil's heart forced out a deep sigh. "You wouldn't understand, but. . .it's because Walt's a Vietnam vet."

"The truth will set you free."

Lil shook her head. Why did that Bible verse keep popping into her head?

"You're right. I don't understand. What does that have to do with his recovery from hip surgery?"

"Everything." *Or nothing.* Lil frowned. Tired and drained from the day, she realized her thoughts didn't make sense.

The clicking stopped. "Lil, is he having flashbacks? Are you afraid he'll hurt you?" Concern filled Tiffany's voice.

"No, no, it's nothing like that." Lil couldn't tell her about her and Walt's feelings for each other. Their relationship had become so unprofessional.

"Then what is it? Does he not respond to your nursing skills? Because you've been a nurse a long time, Lil, and should know every trick in the book to work around that."

"It's not that either." Lil's heart raced and her breaths came quickly. She seldom struggled to find the words to express her thoughts, but something held her back. Her heart pounded harder and her hand shook as if she were watching a horror movie.

Lil's eyes widened as the phone slipped from her fingers, clamoring across the floor with her realization. She was scared. Scared of the recriminations of her past rebellion. Scared of allowing her emotions to influence her mind. Sacred of losing the man she loved.

"Lil!"

Dropping from the chair to her knees, Lil crawled toward the phone. "Tiffany, I'm sorry. The phone slipped from my hand."

"Look, Lil, it's only a couple more weeks, maybe days if Walt's doctor appointment goes well."

Tiffany had obviously logged into the company database and was reading Lil's updates.

"When you hadn't called back, I began hoping that you'd had a change of heart."

I have.

"I hate to tell you this, Lil, but I'm short staffed. I've had two people quit. I have no one to replace you. Can't you stick it out just a little longer?"

"I guess." She made her resignation clear in her voice. No matter how much her heart wanted her to stay, she needed to leave. Fear traced an icy path throughout her body. She shivered. "Good-bye."

Lil tapped the END CALL button. Sitting cross-legged on her living room floor, she bowed her head. She'd been praying for God to provide strength and stamina for Walt. Now it was time to include herself in that prayer.

This relationship just couldn't end like the last one. Lil could never, ever tell Walt the truth.

Chapter 9

After her restless night and nerves jostling her stomach until she felt nauseated, the walk from the camper to the house seemed endless. She missed the buzz and click of the walkie-talkie and having someone to say good night to. Several times she awoke with a start, thinking that she heard Walt calling through the speaker, but it'd only been her dreams.

Her hand trembled as she tried the door. When Walt had started feeling better, he'd get up and unlock the door, welcoming her to his home. Would that be the routine today?

This morning, she'd slipped into her pocket the extra key he'd given her to use, just in case he'd flipped the welcome mat in his home. . .and heart.

The knob turned in her hands. Relief flooded her limbs at the same time the spicy aroma of fresh-brewed coffee invited her in.

Walt sat at the table, fingers looped through a mug handle, reading a magazine. He looked up over his glasses. "Morning, Lil."

"Good morning."

Walt lifted his head and looked at her straight on.

The quietness of her voice must have surprised him.

"Help yourself to coffee."

Lil draped her jacket over a chair back and did as she was instructed. Glad Walt no longer seemed angry with her, she felt moisture form in her eyes. When she blinked back her tears, mist settled on her lashes like frost on the grass.

"What would you like for breakfast?" Lil carried her cup to the table.

"For you to sit down and talk to me." Walt closed the magazine he'd been reading and pushed it to the center of the table.

Lil bit her lower lip before it quivered with fear. She'd hashed it over and over all night. She just couldn't let Walt know about her past. She couldn't stand to see hate flash through his eyes where appreciation had once shone. She couldn't take the chance. . . .

She laid her elbows on the table and folded her arms one over the other.

Walt scooted his chair closer to her, the scrape of the metal legs on the floor slicing through the heaviness in the air. He reached for her hand and covered it with his.

"Lil, I care about you. I know it sounds silly because we've known each other for such a short amount of time, but it's deep. I'm sorry I tried to force you to unburden your problems. It's just. . ." Walt broke eye contact and looked heavenward for a minute before pinning her with his mesmerizing hazel eyes. "I want to be your confidant. Your secret keeper."

If you only knew the secret, Walt, you'd want me out of your house once and for all. Larry had. Now she understood why, but understanding and wanting to live through it again were two different things.

"So I got to thinking it might be easier for you to tell me what's bothering you if I shared something about my past. I don't tell very many people this, Lil. I didn't want the Purple Heart the government awarded me with. I didn't feel I deserved it. Still don't. Other soldiers frame them and hang their honor on the wall. Mine is buried in the far corner of my dresser drawer."

"But Walt, you were wounded in action. You're a hero."

"Of course you'd think that." Walt squeezed her hand, leaning forward, closing the small gap between their heads, trying to close the gap between their hearts. "I can tell that you support our country's troops."

"And the truth will set you free." The pleasant aftertaste of her coffee turned vile on her tongue. She swallowed hard, sending the bitterness burning down her throat. How did he get that idea? She'd sidestepped the subject of war or made no comment at all. She didn't want to tell him her secret, but she now knew it was the right thing to do.

"Walt—"

"No." Walt held up his hand like a crossing guard wielding a stop sign. "Let me share this."

"But Walt, I need to tell you something." She'd found her voice. Blurting it out wouldn't be appropriate, but it might be necessary.

"Lil, don't be so exasperating all of the time." As Walt flopped back in his chair, his hand released Lil's and made a squeaky trail across the tabletop.

The decibel level of Walt's voice caused Lil to draw a sharp intake of breath. Defeat etched the time-kissed creases in his face. Her soft heart took control of her head. Somehow he'd jumped to a conclusion. If he mentioned it again, she'd correct him. Right now, he needed to unburden himself and she needed to make it easier.

"I'm sorry, Walt. I didn't mean to be. I won't interrupt you again."

Pursing his lips until all that was visible was his mustache, Walt's eyes narrowed and his sideways look screamed, *"Doubtful."*

Taking a swig of his coffee, Walt stared into space as if reconsidering his confession.

Lil's hand shook as she lifted her cup. Wrapping her other hand around the warm mug, she managed a sip, hoping it'd settle her nerves.

"Our unit had been on the ground for two days, walking through the jungle looking for the enemy. One of our guys, David Hanson, caught some kind of a bug. Don't know if he drank bad water or what, but that boy was sick, running a fever in that jungle heat; he could barely walk. He was a good soldier and though he tried with all his might, he finally collapsed. We took turns sitting with him while the others went in search of the enemy. Our commander finally decided the area was secure and he radioed for a chopper to pick us up."

Walt sat straight in his chair. His hands ran down the length of his thighs, swooshing the well-worn denim of his overalls legs, silently returning and starting the trip over again.

"Water was in short supply, but we all rationed ours so David didn't get too dehydrated. His sweat-soaked clothes didn't help his chills. At times he was delirious, moaning, crying, and screaming. That made some of the guys uneasy."

Sucking his lips in and out, Walt dropped his gaze until he had his memories in check; then he looked up at Lil.

"It was tense. Some of the guys were certain he'd get us all killed. They wanted to. . ." The bob of Walt's Adams apple was a sign the words were sticking in his throat.

"They wanted to kill him," Lil whispered softly. She knew that happened. On her first nursing assignment, she'd heard a soldier's deathbed confession of how he'd almost turned against his fellow soldier. That's when her shame of being a protestor started.

Slightly nodding, Walt leaned toward her once again, taking her hands in his.

"I told them they'd have to kill me first. Thank God the commander stepped in. After his lecture, he turned to me and told me that Dave was my responsibility until we got back to base camp. It took twenty-four hours for that chopper to come. The thunderous blades, music to any soldier's ears, sounded like the Halleluiah chorus to me."

Walt smiled. "Not only was I getting out of that jungle, but we could get Dave to the medic. I hefted him up over my shoulder, his torso dangling over my back, slung my gun over the other shoulder, and started running with the other guys in the direction of the sound."

A dark veil of sadness curtained Walt's eyes and his smile turned into a grim line. Lil's heart dipped in her chest. Past shame clogged her throat, strangling her. How could she have treated those brave men so badly?

"The clearing wasn't really that far from us, but it was so hot and I'd shared so much of my water with Dave that I was dehydrated, so my muscles didn't want to work. With Dave's extra weight, I struggled with each step. The jungle seemed to come to life with vines snaking around my ankles, limbs dipping downward, catching my helmet or Dave's clothes."

Obviously reliving the moment, Walt's hands tightened around hers, his breath coming in rapid little puffs. "I tripped a couple of times but I made it to that clearing. Nothing had ever looked better to me than that powerful, lifesaving chopper. Knowing the area was secure and that the soldiers inside were covering us, we left the camouflage of the jungle and ran out into the open."

A tremor started in Walt's hands, clacking Lil's ring against the hard tabletop. She wanted to pull her hands free and cover her ears. Instead she closed her eyes. A solitary tear slipping down her cheek, she braced herself for what had to be coming next. "Ambushed."

"Yep." Walt's grip loosened.

Lil opened her eyes. "Is that when you were shot?"

Walt nodded. "I was halfway to the helicopter when the gunfire started. Chunks of ground shot up in the air and rained dirt down on us. The sweat and dirt stung my eyes, but still I ran. I heard the pop of gunfire and felt the velocity of bullets whizzing past me, painful cries of soldiers hit, and through my hazy vision, I saw soldiers drop to the ground."

Guilt gnawed at Lil. No wonder Larry turned her away, couldn't forgive her. Walt wouldn't either. Not after all he'd been through.

Mist forming in Walt's eyes, he swiped at them with his thumbs. "All I could think of was getting Dave to the helicopter, so I just kept running toward the arms pulling soldiers into the gut of the chopper. Just as I got to the chopper, bullets tore up the ground. They pinged against the metal of the helicopter, but I was close enough that someone pulled Dave off my shoulder. I was so much lighter without his weight. I reached up and an arm grabbed me, half in the chopper as I felt it lift up. Then an incredible force pushed me the rest of the way in and my backside burned like fire."

Lil sucked in a breath as her muscles winced, feeling Walt's pain. She searched Walt's face, unable to read the emotion in his eyes. "How can you say you didn't deserve a Purple Heart?"

"Because. . ." Walt hung his head when his voice cracked. "I didn't save Dave. He'd taken a fatal hit."

"But that wasn't your fault." Lil's voice carried like a shout through a canyon.

Walt lifted his head, eyes meeting hers. "I didn't carry him right, Lil. We'd taken off his helmet. I should have protected his head. If I had carried him differently, a mother wouldn't have had to bury her son."

Lil tried to speak but words wouldn't come. The insults she'd hurled at returning soldiers were no different than the grenades they'd thrown during the war. Theirs tore up land; hers tore apart fragile souls. She opened her hands then closed them.

"You don't have to say anything, Lil. I didn't tell you this for sympathy, pity, or to cleanse my conscience. God's healing power did that for me years ago. I finally realized that if He could forgive me, I could forgive myself."

Walt rose from his chair, covering the short span between them. He pulled Lil to him. The fresh scent of the dryer sheets and soft denim tickled her nose as her head rested on his shoulder.

"I told you this, Lil, because whatever it is that you feel you can't tell me, you can tell God. He'll listen and forgive you." Walt's hand ran up and down her arm, the puffy sleeves of her sweatshirt bunching under his hand.

Lil tensed. She knew that God forgave. She'd given Him this burden years ago in the chapel of the small hospital when she was a student nurse. But God wasn't the person she worried wouldn't forgive her. After Walt's experience with Nancy, she knew the truth would cut him to the core. She couldn't do that to him. Wouldn't do that to him.

She lifted her hand to his to stop the comforting movement.

"Hello?" A voice drifted through the living room to the kitchen.

"Breakfast. Your guests are expecting breakfast." Lil pulled free of Walt's embrace. Thanking God for the distraction, she hurried to the refrigerator.

"Lil, I've been awake for a long time. I put the breakfast spread out already."

The walker tapped against the floor. Lil turned to see Walt pass through the living room doorway.

Grabbing on to the counter for support, Lil's legs wobbled all the way to the table. She collapsed in the chair, uncertain if her weak knees were from Walt's embrace or guilt or both.

Walt meant his story to be a comfort to Lil, to give her permission to let go of whatever past mistake she'd made in her life. Instead it just heaped more coals on her head.

There was no way her heart could take the look of betrayal her admission would draw from Walt's eyes, especially after what he experienced during the war—trying to save a fellow solider, losing him, and being wounded by the enemy. She'd owned up to her mistakes once and it cost her the promised happily-ever-after ending to her life story.

Muffled laughter drifted in from the living room, Walt's rich baritone, distinct and infectious, shooting a small current of electricity through Lil. His merriment brought out her smile and lured her from her chair, through the living room, and into the office, like the pied piper's flute.

By the time Lil made it to the office, Walt was sitting behind the computer.

"Sounded like a party in here." Lil rested her forearms on the check-in counter.

"Just recalling old times." Walt waved a dismissive hand through the air. "You know, the you-had-to-be-there kind."

She knew that kind of story too well. Clearing her throat, she turned to the breakfast area. Her stomach rumbled, reminding her she'd skipped breakfast. "Mind if I have something to eat before we get started on the laundry?"

"Help yourself. It wasn't much today—fruit, instant oatmeal, and Danish."

"Walt, that is a hearty breakfast and, for the most part, healthy." Lil glanced out the plate glass window then did a double take. "Snow flurries?"

Walt stood. "Looks like it. Thought that wasn't supposed to happen until later today. Good thing the kids are getting on the road this morning."

"Everyone's checking out? No one's staying with Jeanie?"

Lil tore open a package of instant oatmeal, shook it into a Styrofoam bowl, and held the bowl under the hot water spigot on the coffeemaker.

Walt joined her by the short counter. He cut a square of Danish. "Her sister is staying with her. She's retired and there's enough room for her at Jeanie's apartment."

Lil stopped stirring her oatmeal and laid a hand to her chest. "That's a relief. Sometimes it's hardest afterward when everyone gets back to their routine yet the person in mourning has to struggle to find a new normal."

"True." Walt pulled two cups from the stack and filled them with coffee. He carried them to a table. "Could you bring my Danish? I don't have enough hands."

"No prob—" Lil spun around. Walt shouldn't have any free hands. "Where is your walker?"

A sheepish look crept across Walt's face. "It's over by the computer."

Lil pursed her lips as she carried their breakfast to the table.

"Don't get in a snit, Lil. I've been using it on and off all morning."

In a snit. Lil marched toward the check-in desk area, her Crocs punishing the floor for Walt's bad behavior. She had to stop letting her guard down and watch Walt more diligently.

"Have you forgotten that I'm your nurse?" *And love you and don't want you to fall and get hurt.*

Lil's thought caught her off balance. Her knees weakened and she wavered, wishing she had a walker to steady herself.

&

Since breakfast, Lil and Walt worked in silence. He'd conceded and started using the walker again, even though it prohibited him from being much help clearing the breakfast area.

The church ladies had cleaned and straightened all the rooms for the last time.

Lil, apparently lost in thought, worked at folding a fitted sheet.

Maybe he shouldn't have told her what had happened in Vietnam, but he thought she needed to know. He wanted Lil to be a part of his life, all of his life—his past, present, and future. A grin tugged at the corner of Walt's mouth as he contemplated a future with Lil.

"What do you say we leave this for later and go work on your quilt?" Walt tossed a washcloth down on the table.

Lil growled as the sheet corners refused to cooperate and make a smooth fold. "Who invented these things?" Then she laughed. "But it is easier to make the bed with them. Guess we have to take the good with the bad."

"That's right, Lil, we do." Walt moved closer to her, hoping she heard the double meaning in his words. His arms ached to hold her close, feel her warmth, inhale the flowery fragrance that haloed her.

Still struggling with the sheet, Lil never looked up. "As soon as I wrestle this one into submission, I'll be right there."

Disappointment lassoed Walt's heart, tugging it lower in his chest. Dismissed. That's what she'd done, dismissed him. Had he read everything wrong? The way she responded to his kiss and his embrace?

Walt walked to the kitchen, his only companion the rickety noise from the walker. Without Lil to watch over his every movement, he left the walker by the table and assembled the ironing board.

"What are you doing?"

Walt jumped as Lil's voice boomed through the kitchen.

Heart racing, he turned toward the door. "Look, Lil, in a couple of days, I go back to the doctor. What's the big deal?"

"The big deal is that it's my job to follow the doctor's orders, and his notes said two more weeks of using the walker."

She closed the small gap between them. Using her few inches of height difference, she placed her hands on her hips in an apparent attempt to be intimidating. "And you had the nerve to call *me* exasperating?"

Annoyance flashed through her green eyes and puckered her mouth. She'd never looked more beautiful to Walt. He pushed his arms through the open space her arms created and pulled her to him. Her startled gasp lowered her chin just enough that Walt's lips found hers.

She tasted of coffee and Danish and love.

Lil pushed her hands against his chest but he didn't stop. Instead he drew her closer, deepening his kiss.

A soft moan vibrated from Lil, humming through the kiss, as her hands slid up until she wrapped her arms around his neck. Walt's insides trembled. In Lil's arms he felt eighteen again, young and carefree.

He ended the kiss but held her tight. "Oh Lil," he said, his love-rasped voice barely audible. Never had his feelings been this strong, not even with Nancy. Maybe it was because he and Lil shared the same outlook on life. He knew she'd never turn on him.

She nodded her head, her soft curls silky on his cheek, letting him know her heart agreed with his.

He cleared his throat and loosened his grip. He wanted to look into those vivacious green eyes when he declared his love. It seemed too soon after only four weeks, but life changed quickly and love didn't knock on your door every day.

Cupping Lil's flushed cheeks in his hands, he drank in the emotion pouring from her eyes. It fortified his determination. Her plump lips parted as her eyes roamed his face, like she might be thinking the same thing—*It's love.*

He put a finger to her warm lips. Call it manly pride, but he wanted to say it first.

"Lil."

"Don't say it." Mist formed over her eyes, dimming her love. She'd slightly pulled her head away, giving it small shakes.

"Why not?" This really wasn't going as he'd planned. But why did that surprise him? Lil wasn't like other women, something he'd started thanking God for daily. The thought broadened his grin.

She closed her eyes, drawing her brows together, her years of living emphasized by the lines on her forehead. "Because. . ." She stopped pursing her lips and opened her eyes. "I don't deserve it, Walt. I don't deserve your love."

Walt's smile widened. "Well, I think you do. I love you, Lil."

Her bottom lip trembled.

"You don't have to say it back," he whispered. "Although I'd love to hear it from your lips, your eyes and kiss tell me everything I need to know. You can tell me when you're ready. I can wait."

His words didn't soothe or remove the tortured look from her features. He guessed her heart had been broken once. Her distant looks, the secret she couldn't share, how she found it difficult to voice her feelings—that all added up to a broken heart.

"Walt, I want to tell you something."

A crack of thunder shook the house, rattling the windows. A chorus of pings hit the roof and windows.

"Is that hail?" Lil's voice was back and in full volume.

"Worse." Walt released Lil and walked to the window.

Lil joined him. "I'm glad the folks got on the road when they did."

"Me, too. With these temperatures, this is not good."

Walt moved to the living room window, Lil trailing behind. A thin sheen already glistened on the blacktop in front of the hotel.

Walt stated the obvious. "Ice storm."

"Maybe it won't last long."

꙳

The ice storm lasted thirty-six hours. The governor declared an emergency and closed all the South Dakota interstate exits north and south between the Iowa and North Dakota borders and east and west from Minnesota to central South Dakota.

"What a mess." Lil cracked the door and squeezed through the narrow space, but frigid air seeped into Walt's kitchen anyway.

Walt paced back and forth like a mountain lion on the prowl. "You shouldn't be out in that mess. I should."

"Well, you can't." Lil stomped her boots on the rug, then held the heel of one boot with the toe of the other so she could slide her foot out. She repeated the process with the second boot, soaking the toe of her heavy woolen sock.

A two-inch layer of ice covered the ground. After the first hour of the storm, Lil started the vigil of keeping her camper door free of ice. Thanks to Walt's buying ice melt in bulk, she'd managed to keep his sidewalk and a narrow path to her camper a melted slushy mess by reapplying the solvent about every two hours, but at least it provided some traction.

When Walt paced close to her, he gently pulled an icicle from her curls that escaped the cover of her coat hood. "You shouldn't have to do this."

Lil pushed the hood of her parka back and slipped out of her coat, hanging it over the back of a kitchen chair to dry. She finger combed her curls. "Don't you think I know you'd help me if you could?"

"Yes," Walt conceded before returning to the other end of his pacing track, stopping to look out of windows frosted with ice, obscuring an outside view. He looped his thumbs around the straps of his light blue pin-striped overalls that topped a thermal long-underwear shirt.

"Do you still have electricity out there? I have trouble with that box and thought for sure it'd act up during the storm."

"It's working. My furnace is keeping it nice and toasty, which will help the door not to freeze shut."

"The doctor's office rescheduled for next Tuesday." Walt spoke to the frozen window as he bent, trying to find a sliver of uncovered window to look through.

"Well, hopefully the roads will be clear by then. The sand truck went by. The blacktop's covered in patchy ice. If the sun peeked out it would help, although I'm not so certain that will help the ground cover melt. You might be stuck with that until spring."

"Wouldn't be the first time. By the way, I ran plain water through the coffeepot. I thought you might want a cup of hot chocolate to warm up."

Lil rolled her eyes as Walt kept bending and stretching to try to find some sort of clear spot on the window to see through.

"Did you get any more petal pieces adhered to the fabric?"

"Yeah, they're on the table ready for you"—Walt turned his attention from the window to Lil—"my Rose of Sharon."

Since her back was to him, she allowed herself to grin as a shiver of happiness warmed her soul more than the hot chocolate ever could. He'd been calling her that for the last few days.

She savored the giddy feeling of knowing Walt returned her love. Many times without warning that same giddiness would leap from her heart and holler, *"Surprise!"* exciting a giggle or laugh, but then the truth would tug at her heart, reminding her not to get used to the feeling.

"Thanks to you"—Lil carried two steaming mugs of cocoa to the table—"I'm getting my winter project finished in record time."

Slipping into the chair across from the sewing machine, Walt put his elbow on the table and rested his head in his palm. "I'd like to see what it looks like all sewn together." He started arranging blocks side by side.

"I've got to appliqué all the blocks before I can sew the top together. And if you get a good report on Tuesday, you'll no longer need a full-time nurse."

"What?" Walt's palm slapped against the table, the cups and Lil's sewing scissors rattling their protest against the Formica top.

Lil had internally repeated that mantra so many times over the last few days whenever guilt tightened its grip on her heart that she didn't realize she'd actually said it out loud.

She lifted her eyes from her quilt block. "You knew that day was coming. That you'd be healed and no longer need someone here while you recovered."

By the set of Walt's jaw and sour frown, Lil knew he didn't like or agree with her reasoning.

"You know once the doctor releases you to a cane and six-week follow-up, he'll report it and then your insurance won't cover the cost of the nursing service."

Walt's glare stung more than the pellets of ice the wind had been whipping in her face for the past three days.

"I can pay out of pocket." Walt raised his brows and shrugged, as if the matter was settled.

"Doesn't work that way. There is a shortage of nurses, and my contract with the nursing service says I can't work as an independent contractor." Lil meant the firm nod of her head as the period to end this conversation.

Walt had other ideas. "I thought you were going to Texas as soon as you were done with this nursing assignment. That means you're contract has expired or is on hold or something." He sputtered the last few words and waved a hand in the air.

Lil sighed. So much for pulling the wool over Walt's eyes. "I have a reservation at an RV park in Texas."

"Cancel it. I love you, Lil. I know you love me even if you are too stubborn or scared to say it back. I want you to stay here with me."

She closed her eyes. He wanted her to stay now, but when he found out the truth. . . She shook her head. Then it'd be a different story. It had crushed her when Larry rejected her years ago, and her feelings for him weren't nearly as strong as her love for Walt. She was being sensible not stubborn, but he was right about one thing. She was scared.

Lil opened her eyes. "I told you before I can't stay."

Walt crossed his arms over his chest and glared at her. "Can't stay or won't stay?"

Chapter 10

Lil never answered Walt's question, but he surmised that "won't stay" won out. After their short standoff, Lil spent more time in her camper, using excuses like having to clean it or check for leaks or ice damage.

Loneliness screamed through his house when she wasn't there. It was hard to imagine that he'd been counting the days for her to leave just five short weeks ago.

What could he do to cut through her fears? He couldn't imagine any mistake worse than the one he'd made in Nam. He saw her inner turmoil expressed outward—one minute happy love radiating from her face, the next sorrow curtaining her pretty green eyes.

He stood at the window, staring across the gravel driveway at Lil's camper. Thankfully, between the sunshine and his furnace, the ice melted from his windows. Watching her shadow cross by the camper windows gave Walt comfort, yet he knew that landscape may change with today's doctor's report.

Maybe the X-ray would find a glitch in his healing, something that'd keep Walt using the walker.

A beep, then a static buzz cut through his thoughts.

"You ready to go?"

Walt walked over and picked up the walkie-talkie.

"Yes." He started back to the window and noticed he'd left the walker sitting where he'd stood moments earlier. He hadn't had pain in a couple of weeks and no longer needed to remind himself to walk normally.

Face it, old boy, you don't need a nurse. But he *did* need a nurse—just not for her professional abilities.

"I think we should take my pickup today, just in case we encounter some ice on the roads."

"Probably a good idea, Speedy, because you'll hit it going too fast and put us in the ditch." Walt's voice was light, teasing, and he'd have winked if Lil had been standing by him instead of avoiding him.

Lil looked out her camper window and wagged a finger his way. Why didn't she just come over to the house?

"Get your coat on and I'll pull my truck as close as I can to the door. The sidewalk is clear, but I'm not taking any chances."

The roar of the pickup's motor and the crunch of its tires seeped into the quiet kitchen. Walt opened the door to bright sunshine, deceiving in its promise of warmth as frigid air cooled his face and tickled his nose.

Lil drove the pickup through the yard and parked two feet from his door. With the passenger door centered over the dry sidewalk, all he had to do was take two steps and climb into the cab.

She waited by the open passenger door. "Didn't figure this would hurt your lawn."

The ice cover over the still-green grass was broken and jagged where the pickup tires cut through the smooth glaze. "The ground might not be as frozen as you think." Walt pointed to the tires. "But this won't hurt the lawn at all."

Grasping the built-in handle above the passenger door, Walt, using his good leg, stepped up on a surprisingly ice-free running board. Lil's sturdy hands warmed him through the thick layer of his coat as she held his waist to help him into the vehicle.

Once he found the seat, it was easy to pull himself into a sitting position and get straightened in the seat with both legs together.

"That wasn't as hard as I thought it would be." Walt pulled the seat belt across his chest as Lil snapped the walker to its folded position.

After closing his door, she rounded the front of the pickup, stashed the walker in the backseat, and readied herself for takeoff.

"I have a good feeling about your appointment today." She smiled at Walt as she pulled the pickup into gear.

His heart plummeted to his stomach and it had nothing to do with Lil's driving ability. It was because his gut knew that he was healing, Lil would soon be gone, and his life would return to his normal routines. But that wasn't good enough anymore.

❧

"Shall we go tell Mark and Sarah the good news?"

Walt didn't miss the forced happiness in Lil's voice.

"I suppose so. It's Tuesday and Caroline should be there, too. I want to talk to her about making a Rose of Sharon quilt for a wedding gift for Mark and Sarah. Unless"—Walt stole a glance Lil's way—"you've reconsidered leaving and will help me make them one."

The long sigh and pursed lips created a thick tension in the pickup cab that lingered the rest of the way to Granny Bea's.

Lil pulled into the handicapped parking space right in front of Mark's store. She slipped the placard over her rearview mirror as the click of the passenger door announced its opening.

"Hold it a minute. The asphalt looks dry but there could be a thin layer of ice over it. You don't want to fall and ruin the good news."

"I don't want to use the walker anymore." Although he'd use it forever if that meant Lil would stay.

As if she didn't hear him, Lil slipped from the vehicle, opened the cab's back door, and shut it. He'd opened his door and turned in the seat before he saw what she had in her hand.

"Where'd you get that?"

Lil frowned. "It's yours. Don't you recognize it?"

Of course he did. The quad cane had been his partner for many years. He'd like to change that partner to the hand of his beloved Rose of Sharon.

"I meant when did you get it?" Walt used the passenger door and Lil's shoulder to steady himself as he slid out of the pickup.

"Yesterday while you were napping, I took it out of the closet and put in my pickup. I just knew you'd get a good report." Lil smiled at Walt.

His hand wrapped around the worn handle of the cane and he stopped Lil with his free hand. "I can close my own car door now." With little effort the door snapped shut.

"After you." Lil raised her hand toward the sloped area of the sidewalk.

"Not anymore. We're walking together." Walt snatched Lil's gloved hand in his. He expected, after the tense ride to the quilt store, that she'd try to pull her hand free. Instead her smile widened and her fingers linked with his to create a tight bond, just like their hearts had done over the last few weeks.

Sarah met them at the door. "Look at you." Her eyes dropped to Walt's and Lil's hands. Walt grinned, knowing she wasn't talking about his walking with a cane.

"I got a good report at the doctor."

"I can see that." Sarah eyes now rested on Walt's cane as she opened her arms to embrace him.

Walt took his hand off of his cane to wrap her in a one-armed hug, even as Lil tried to wiggle her hand free of his grasp.

"Mark's in the back room with Caroline. Let's go tell him." Sarah kissed Walt's cheek before releasing him and leading the way to the classroom area of the store.

"Look who's here!" Sarah announced their arrival in the workroom like Walt had just come home from a trip overseas.

Mark and Caroline looked up from a worktable where quilts were strewn.

"Uncle Walt." Mark walked toward him, holding his hand out.

Shaking Mark's hand would've required Walt to break his grasp on Lil's fingers, so he lifted his hand from his cane and squeezed Mark's extended hand. A sly grin crossed Mark's face as he patted Walt on the shoulder.

"How long before you get rid of that?" Mark jerked his head toward the cane.

"A couple of weeks. The doc said I only need it when I'm outside or in a crowded place. I can walk around the house without it."

"As he's been doing quite frequently without the doctor's or nurse's permission." Lil chuckled.

"Caroline. . ." Walt nodded his greeting just before the tall redhead wrapped him in a hug, her corkscrew curls not quite as soft as Lil's as they grazed his cheek.

"You look great. I'm so glad you finally had that surgery." She held him at arm's length. As with Lil, he had to look up to meet her eyes.

"I'd like you to meet Lil Hayes. She's my nurse and—"

"Provided the history behind my Lily of the Field quilt." Caroline shook Lil's hand. "It's so nice to know the original story behind the quilt. I never considered making a quilt that was themed around a name. What a clever idea your grandmother had!"

"It's nice to meet you, too. The love of your work shows in your eyes."

Caroline laughed. "I've been told that before. But quilts are so special and made with so much love that I believe the love rubs off on anyone who touches them."

"You did a splendid job of restoring that old quilt. By the pictures it looks practically new. My sister, Lily, cried over the phone when she saw the pictures on your website."

"I'm glad she approves of the slight alteration." Caroline looked from Lil to Walt.

Walt stepped back out of Lil's sight and gave his head a small shake.

"Well, she is glad that it's in a safe place where people love it as much as she does. Did."

Caroline picked up on Walt's nonverbal cue and focused on Lil. "I'm glad to hear that. It is special to Rodney and me because it brought us together. But it holds an even more special place in my heart because it reminded me of God's promise to care for His children."

"Amen to that." Sarah wrapped her arms around Mark's waist and laid her head against his chest.

Walt longed to have Lil comfortable enough with their love to make a small loving gesture like Sarah did with Mark. Lil only returned an embrace if he initiated it.

Caroline turned back to Walt. "I understand you've started a new hobby during your recovery." She lifted an eyebrow.

"I know I told you all that Mark shouldn't learn to sew because it wasn't manly. But I was wrong. Although I didn't really sew—I just adhered the pieces of the quilt puzzle to make a picture. Lil here did all the sewing." Walt pulled a folded piece of fabric from his pocket and held it out to Caroline. "Thought you might want to see it."

"It's lovely. Good job, you two. At first the appliqué stitch wasn't my favorite, but after a couple of quilts, I think I've perfected it." Caroline handed the block back to Lil.

The jangle of the door alarm sounded, alerting Mark. "I'd better go see if those are customers or some of Caroline's students."

"I'd better get back to work, too, before the boss fires me." Sarah fluffed her short dark bangs with her fingers and giggled.

"Walt"—Lil tugged her fingers free—"I need to pick up some thread while I'm here."

"Okay. I feel a little tired."

Lil's eyes widened. "I don't have to get it today."

Walt held up a hand to shush her. "I just need to sit awhile. I'll stay back here and visit with Caroline until her class arrives."

He watched Lil walk out of the door. *Thank You, God.* Walt had been racking his brain over how to get rid of Lil so he could be alone with Caroline. God's hand was definitely on Walt today.

"She's very special, isn't she?"

Walt continued to watch Lil through the wall window, making sure she didn't change her mind and return to the workroom. "I think so."

"I can tell. In all the years I've known you, I've never seen you radiate happiness the way you have today."

As Lil turned toward the thread section, Walt turned to Caroline. "We need to talk."

&.

"You know, homemade soup does taste better than canned." Walt pushed his bowl toward the center of the table.

Lil arched her eyebrow at him. "That's because the ingredients are fresh. Are you ready for dessert?"

"I'll get it. You've been waiting on me for weeks."

On his way back to the table, a cake pan and knife in hand, Walt bent to see out of the kitchen window. "Looks like we have company."

You have company. "Who is it?" Lil sipped her coffee.

"Sandy. I wonder what she wants." Walt set the pan and knife on the table and walked to the door.

"I'm guessing her Crock-Pot." Lil stifled a little growl of frustration. After the funeral luncheon, she'd hoped to avoid any further interaction with Sandy.

Walt opened the door before Sandy could knock. His visitor shuffled her feet on the rug to clear the moisture from her boots.

"Hi. I dropped by to pick up my Crock-Pot. I'd have been here sooner, but the weather kept me a shut-in." She stepped out of the way so Walt could close the door.

"Would you like some cake and coffee? Lil and I had a late lunch."

Please be in a hurry to get somewhere and say no. Lil knew her thought was unkind, but it was due to self-preservation. If she could get out of town before Sandy figured out how she knew her, then Lil would never have to fall under Walt's scrutiny.

"That would be great. I developed a bad case of cabin fever." Sandy slipped into a chair. "Good thing I have unlimited minutes on my cell phone plan. During that storm, I called every friend and relative I have. Which reminds me. . ." Sandy looked at Lil.

Lil tried to keep her face expressionless as fear cut through her body. "I'll get another dessert plate." Her legs wobbled when she stood.

"I'll get it." Walt started for the cupboard.

"I'll get it." Fear boomed Lil's words out louder and snottier than she'd meant them.

Walt's head snapped around and he frowned.

"Sorry." Lil apologized out of the corner of her mouth as she speed-walked past Walt. Placing her hands on the countertop in front of the cupboards, Lil tried to regain her composure.

Sandy didn't seem to notice Lil's small fear-driven ruckus because their visitor continued on. "I finally figured out how I know you. I was talking to my sister."

Lil's stomach twisted.

"I was telling her about Walt's surgery, and of course your name came up."

Lil's shoulders sagged.

"She couldn't believe it."

Lil's pulse pounded through her ears, muffling Sandy's words. Sweat began to bead on her forehead and she bit her upper lip.

"She asked me to give you her phone number so you two can catch up."

"You know Sandy's sister?" Walt's question came from the center of the room, about where she'd passed him.

"Small world, isn't it?" Sandy kept rambling, unaware that Lil was frozen to the floor like Walt's plaster deer in the yard. However, the tone of Walt's question and his approaching footsteps alerted Lil that he knew something was wrong.

"How do you know Sandy's sister?" Walt stood beside Lil now, his arms crossed over his chest.

"I couldn't believe it when my brain finally made the connection." Sandy laughed. "Of course, I knew why you didn't recognize me. I was just a kid back then, and of course, I had married, so you'd never put the last name with it."

Lil had to stop this conversation. Her hand shaking, she grabbed the dessert plate, turned away from Walt, and walked over to the table.

She sliced through the cake so hard the pan slid across the slick tabletop. If she could just get Sandy's mouth full of cake, she might have a chance to salvage this conversation. Turn it around. By the time Sandy left, Walt might forget about this thread of the conversation.

She scooped a generous piece of cake onto a plate and shoved it at Sandy.

"So do you want her number?" Sandy lifted her fork.

"Um. . .sure." Lil tried to sound happy to reconnect with Sandy's sister.

Walt's hand engulfed her shaky one that was wrapped around the knife.

"I don't believe I want cake right now. So you know Sandy's sister." Walt lifted her chin, but she kept her gaze lowered.

"Know her? They were inseparable back then." The tines of Sandy's fork scrapped across the china plate, granting Lil a small reprieve as their visitor lifted a bit of cake to her lips. Then Sandy lowered it. "They even got arrested together."

"Arrested?" Walt's voice boomed with surprise and sounded much like Lil's normal tone.

Lil finally lifted her eyes at Walt's astonishment.

"For what?" Walt may have asked the question, but the stern set of his jaw and narrowed eyes told Lil that he already knew the answer.

Lil prayed Sandy would choose this moment to take a bite of cake.

"For throwing rocks at soldiers during a war protest," Sandy said before inserting the bite of cake into her mouth.

A sob caught in Lil's throat as Sandy's words registered and settled into Walt's thoughts. Hurt flared in his eyes just before they turned into narrow slits catching her in the sights of his anger.

Her rigid legs muscles began to shake and she lowered herself to a chair before she fell down.

"They were quite a pair," Sandy continued between bites.

"Sandy." Walt's hoarse voice cut through her one-sided conversation.

"Oh, sorry. I guess I'm rambling on. What's new with you two?"

Walt leaned against the counter, extending his legs to trap Lil in the corner.

"Went to the doctor today. Almost have a clean bill of health."

Sandy clapped her hands together. "Oh, that's wonderful!"

Senses returning, Lil scooted the pan toward Sandy. "Would you like more cake?"

Walt's anger was apparent in his stance and the set of his jaw. She needed to buy time. Think of an excuse. *"And the truth will set you free."*

If only it were that easy. The last time she'd told the truth about her past, it didn't set her free but chained her tighter to the mistakes she'd made.

She looked at the Rose of Sharon quilt blocks lying on the end of the table. She'd felt so special when Walt referred to her as his Rose of Sharon.

Her heart ached. She'd never hear those words uttered from his lips again. Never taste his kisses or know the warmth and safety of his arms now that he knew the truth. She was far from being a Rose of Sharon.

"That's good cake, Lil." Sandy placed her empty cup on the table and settled in her chair.

"Sandy, I hate to be rude, but I'm a little tired today and would like to lay down for a nap."

Lil cringed at losing her barrier from Walt's anger.

"Of course, I'm sorry. It's just. . ." Sandy stood, putting one arm through the sleeve of her coat.

"I know. Cabin fever." Walt stepped closer to Lil as he turned slightly to lift the Crock-Pot from the counter's edge. "I really appreciate all the help you and the church ladies gave me."

"It was our pleasure. See you in church on Sunday?" Sandy turned toward Lil.

"Probably not. I don't require a full-time nurse anymore." Walt walked Sandy to the door.

Lil's fears weren't irrational. Walt's reaction was the same as Larry's had been—unforgiving. She placed her head in her hands, covering her face with her palms.

She knew this assignment was going to be a nightmare from the start. But she hadn't planned on a broken heart to boot. Walt's and Sandy's chattering niceties droned through Lil like a cartoon grown-up's *wa, wa, wa.*

No longer trapped between a wall and a wall of Walt, she moved, ready to make her escape.

Keep talking, Sandy. The irony of her change of mind due to her change of perspective brought out a sarcastic chuckle.

Walt stood on his doorstep, Sandy half in and half out of her car. Lil might have a chance to crack the door open, slip through, and race around Walt. She peered out the window, sizing up the situation.

Sandy slid behind her wheel.

Walt's hand was on the storm door handle.

She'd never make it. *The front door.*

As Lil turned on her heel and headed through the living room, the only sound she heard was the thundering of her cowardly heart.

"Lil?"

The firmness of Walt's call sped up her footsteps. She was almost through the door to the office, her heart shattering into pieces like thin ice under a boot heel. She couldn't face Walt or see the disappointment in his eyes where love once shone.

"Is Lilac Hayes, brave war protestor, running away?"

His mocking tone stopped her in her tracks.

"I'm not surprised though. I've found most of the people who protested the war were cowards." A harsh laugh emphasized his point.

Lil's blood boiled. She might have had a change of heart, but protestors never lacked courage. She spun around, eyes narrowed.

"The war protestors I knew weren't cowards. They, *we*, endured criticism, beatings, and arrests." That was the first time in years she'd owned up to being a war protestor.

With his arms crossed over his chest, Walt walked toward her. His angry presence filled the room, making him seem taller, fiercer than before. A force to be reckoned with.

"You led me to believe that you supported America's troops." He stopped a foot short of the doorway.

"I do support our troops."

"But you didn't always, and that's where you misled me after I told you about Nancy and her homecoming surprise."

The angry fire that blazed from Walt's eyes penetrated her to her very soul.

"I didn't mislead you." She snapped each word.

"Not telling the truth is the same as misleading."

Even with a foot between them, Lil felt the angry embers of Walt's hot breath rain down. But even through his anger, his eyes didn't reflect the disappointment and betrayal that Larry's had.

"And the truth will set you free."

At God's nudging, Lil squared her shoulders and took a deep breath. "All four years of college I protested the Vietnam war. I'm not sorry for that."

Though her voice crackled and tears threatened her eyes, she stepped closer to Walt and continued. "I am sorry for all the horrendous names I called the soldiers, all the props I threw at them. I learned too late that names can hurt people, especially when those cruel names forever echo in their minds."

Lil gasped and put her hand to her chest, surprised by the sudden relief in her heart. Her shoulders now felt light and free as she unburdened herself of decades-old guilt and shame.

Apologizing to Walt replaced what Larry never gave her a chance to say. She closed her eyes, the red horror as intense as it had been the day she walked back into the hospital room to beg his forgiveness. His empty razor lay on his bed tray.

"Lil." Walt grasped her shoulders. You're white as a sheet. And you have that faraway look again."

Lil looked intently at Walt, the hot blaze of his anger now a smolder in his eyes.

"Tell me what it is that scares you so much. Is it something you did during a protest?"

"Not directly." As far as Lil knew, Larry was never one of the soldiers she'd called names.

"What do you mean?" Walt's voice was terse, and confusion etched every line on his handsome face.

Lil reached to caress his soft cheek but then pulled her hand back. It really didn't matter that she hadn't called Larry the names. She had called other soldiers names. Had they taken their lives because of her cruel words?

Guilt crept back in to take root in her heart.

"Lil, tell me what's wrong."

She looked into his eyes one last time, memorizing the color, the spark of life, the love.

"I can't."

Chapter 11

She didn't tell Walt either. He'd tried to coax it out of her while she packed up her sewing machine and quilt blocks. But that just escalated their anger, resulting in another argument.

He'd watched her scurry across the driveway, wondering when he'd see her again.

That was three days ago. Other than to catch a glimpse of her shadow passing a window, he hadn't seen or spoken to Lil. She'd even turned the walkie-talkie off.

Walt pressed a button on the remote, blackening the television screen. He had no idea what the weatherman had said. It had been on for background noise. Something to fill in the silence, distract his mind.

It hadn't worked. His anger had long since dissipated, replaced with missing Lil. What could have happened that was so bad she couldn't put a voice to it? There was no way it could be worse than the mistake he'd made in Nam.

A delivery driver walked past the picture window in the living room. Walt pushed down on the heavily padded arms of his easy chair and stood.

He walked into the hotel lobby and opened the door, greeted by frosty air, dry and void of moisture.

"Good morning. Got a package for you."

Walt took the electronic device and scribbled his name across the flat screen.

"Weatherman says it's going to be a nice day."

"Is that right? I missed the weather report this morning." Walt traded the tracking device for the package.

"High of fifty-five. Not bad for early November."

Walt smiled. "Not bad at all. What do you think the temp is now?" An idea brewed in his mind.

"Thirty-nine, maybe. Above freezing for sure. Have a great day."

"Thanks." Walt closed the door. He read the return address label before setting the box on the check-in counter. He'd deal with the package later. Right now, though, if the mountain wouldn't come to him, he'd go after the mountain.

Walt pictured himself marching across the driveway, banging on Lil's door, and taking her in his arms. Instead he grabbed his walker for extra stability and took careful steps to ensure his safety.

He did bang on her door though.

The corner of the curtain moved before Lil threw open the door. "Is something wrong?"

"I'll say it is."

"What is it?"

"The woman I love is trying to close me out and I won't stand for it."

Lil's eyes grew wide. She adjusted the slick jacket of her navy jogging suit and stepped back into her camper.

"Are you going to invite me in, or do I have to stand out here in the cold? Because I'm not leaving until you talk to me." Walt reached a hand up and grabbed the doorframe.

"Just a minute." Lil stepped closer. "Put your good leg on the step first." Lil shouldered herself under his other arm as soon as his foot hit the step. With little effort on his part, he stood in Lil's camper.

Once inside he could see all of Lil's living space. The light paneling and open floor plan made the living space appear bigger, roomier.

Just past the kitchenette there was a short hall with two doors, one on each side. The closed one, he assumed, was the bathroom, the sliding door a closet.

Straight in his line of vision was the bedroom. Lil had left the door open, the lilac quilt from her grandmother covering the bed.

A wayward corn husk whisked past the window. Walt spotted the walkie-talkie and nodded toward it. "The battery die?"

A sheepish look settled on Lil's face. "No, I turned it off."

"Why?"

She shrugged. "I figured you didn't want to talk to me."

Walt stepped farther into the room toward Lil. His overalls leg brushed against an overstuffed chair.

"I think you have that turned around. You don't seem to want to talk to me."

Lil pushed past her counter and stepped into her kitchenette, busying herself at the sink. But from what Walt could tell, she was doing nothing—no water ran, no dishes sat, the sink looked clean.

"Aren't you mad at me?"

"I was. Never could tolerate a liar." Walt shrugged, though Lil stood with her back to him.

"But I didn't. . ." Lil's head snapped up. Spinning around, she glared at Walt.

"Yes, you did, Lil. I'd have rather heard about your protest days and disrespect to soldiers from your lips than Sandy's."

"Right, knowing how Nancy treated you. . ." Lil's voice trailed off and a vacancy clouded her green eyes.

"That was years ago, and although her rejection and disgusting accusations hurt, at least she was being honest with her feelings. Something you aren't even doing now."

Walt's anger returned, pushing the ache of missing Lil aside.

"I had you pegged all wrong. You're no different than Nancy." Walt pointed a finger at Lil. Had she been closer, he might have poked her with it or knocked the chip off of her shoulder.

"Somehow you came to the conclusion I was a different person than I was, *am*." Lil flexed her fingers rapidly before fisting her hands.

The heat of Walt's anger dropped from a boil to a simmer. She was right. He did assume they shared the same political viewpoints.

She lifted her fists to her hips. "I never said that I was different than Nancy."

"That's the problem, Lil; you never said anything." What could he do or say to get this stubborn woman to talk about what was standing between them, their love, their future? Being a protestor might be part of it, but it wasn't all of it.

Lil turned and stared out a sliver of a window. Silence encompassed the room.

A frustrated growl rumbled low in Walt's throat. He turned to leave; then he saw it.

"You finished the quilt?" He walked over to the couch and lifted a corner of the Rose of Sharon quilt.

"Just the top."

Lil pulled the fabric from the back of the sofa. Holding two corners, she lifted her arms high and held the completed work of art like a stage curtain.

"It's beautiful." Just like Lil was. *"How beautiful you are, my darling! Oh, how beautiful!"* He'd always liked the Song of Songs but never fully understood the meaning of the verses until now.

"Thank you. And thank you for helping me make it." Lil folded the quilt top with the patterned blocks out. "I know it's not your definition of manly, but it sure helped me move along with my project. I figured the least I could do is finish it so you could see it before I left."

A pang of loneliness shot through Walt, the force so strong it threatened his balance. He grasped hold of the corner of the wall. The small ache of missing Lil for a few days magnified with the knowledge that she'd be leaving for good.

"Lil, don't go. Stay here. You know how I feel."

Her eyes swam with regret when she met his gaze. "I can't. I'm not the person you think I am. I'll just disappoint you. I've already disappointed you."

Steady now, Walt stepped toward Lil, removing the folded quilt from her hands, resting it on the couch. "Lil, we're not getting any younger. The last five weeks have been the happiest of my life. Even when I found you exasperating, you still made me feel alive and vital."

The corners of Lil's mouth trembled, threatening a grin. "I could say the same about you."

"I know." Walt nodded and squeezed her hands. "Lil, I love you. I want you to stay. To be my wife. To make a life with me."

Walt tugged Lil close, and for a few moments her warmth seeped into him, easing his pain.

Then she pushed away. "I do love you, Walt. And I've daydreamed like a silly schoolgirl of what it'd be like to be your wife. But my past mistakes won't let me go. I've filed your case report. I've received my dismissal paperwork. I'm leaving tomorrow morning."

Walt sucked in his upper lip. He'd experienced pain, but none as extreme as Lil's piercing words. He turned and went to the door.

"Do you need my help?"

He snorted and turned around. "No, I need *you*, Lil. Why do you have to leave? Is someone waiting for you in Texas?"

Her eyes widened, obviously shocked by the firmness in his accusation. "No."

"Then tell me what you're running from. You keep saying your past. You were a war protestor. Big deal. Lots of people were. It was a turbulent time. I'm pretty sure that they moved forward in their lives though." His broken heart was controlling his mouth and setting his course as he turned and closed the distance he'd just put between them.

"Tell me, Lil, what on earth did you do that was so bad you can't say it out loud to the man who loves you?"

Walt placed his hands on her shoulders and bent his head so that, with her tipped-head stance, he could look her in the eye. "I told you the horrible thing I did to get a man killed. Your story can't be that bad."

Her lashes fluttered but she didn't close her eyes. Deep creases furrowed her forehead and she frowned. "It is that bad, Walt, because it's the same. I killed a man."

&

Lil grabbed Walt's upper arms to steady him when he wobbled at her admission. His face paled at the same time his expression went blank.

"Let's sit down."

With a small shake of his head, Walt recovered, straightening to his full height. He ran his hand down her arm. Delightful warmth trailed behind it. His fingers found then clasped hers and he led her two steps to the couch.

"It's not at all what you thought, is it?" With her free hand Lil rubbed the slick fabric that covered her thigh, but didn't attempt to stop the nervous bouncing of her legs.

This was hard. But Walt deserved to know why she couldn't stay and be his wife. She could love him. Would love him for the rest of her life even though she couldn't stay and be his wife.

Of course, once he learned the truth, he wouldn't want her to be his wife.

Walt rubbed his forehead. Confusion danced through his eyes. "Did you kill someone at a protest?"

"Heavens, no! I didn't really kill him, but my past did."

His face contorted as he tried to understand what she was telling him.

How could Walt make sense of it all when she didn't understand her own words?

"Let me start from the beginning. In college, my roommate and I became very political and participated in or organized many protests."

"I understand that part."

"After I graduated, I was sent to a veterans hospital, of all places, for my student nursing. So here I was, a protestor in a veterans hospital and one of my patients was an injured. . ."

"Vietnam vet?" Walt pulled his lips to the side and gave his head a shake.

"Yes. He'd been hurt when someone stepped on a land mine. They amputated his leg overseas but put him in the hospital for other injuries. He was young and handsome."

Lil allowed her heart to remember and revel in that shiny, happy first-love joy. She sighed and smiled.

"You fell in love." Walt touched his palm to her cheek and she leaned into his warmth.

"We did. The seasoned nurses warned me that a lot of soldiers coming home fell in love with their nurses, but. . ." Lil shrugged. "I knew our love was different. What did *old* people know about love anyway?"

Walt chuckled at the face she pulled.

She moved his hand from her cheek, laid it on his thigh, and patted it before she laced her fingers in her lap. What came next was hard, and she didn't need the distraction of Walt's touch.

"He had nightmares." Her knowing eyes looked at Walt.

"It's a sad fact, but most of us do."

Lil pressed her fingers together hard, reddening her knuckles.

"His weren't about the enemy or the gunfire or the battles. They were about what he'd seen soldiers do when they cracked under pressure or fear."

Sympathy moisture filled her eyes when she saw Walt's watery eyes.

"That's when I realized how wrong I was to protest the soldiers. I had no idea what they'd been through, seen, heard. I had no idea how haunting and disturbing it was. I had no idea how the names I called them piled additional guilt on their heads like burning coals."

Silence overtook the room, the only communication between Lil and Walt their gaze, which neither of them broke. Though moisture brimmed in Walt's eyes, his love for her still shone through.

Larry's hate was easier to deal with. Walt's unconditional love unnerved her because she didn't deserve it. Lil shifted a little on the sofa cushion.

Walt reached for her but she leaned away like a wary kitten from a helping hand.

"As days turned to months, we found that we had so much in common that we couldn't help but fall in love. After several surgeries, Larry was healing. His prognosis looked promising and he proposed."

A single tear trickled down Lil's cheek as Larry's hospital-bed proposal played through her memory. "I accepted." She swiped the tear away. "But then I felt we needed to be honest with each other."

She raised her eyebrows and lifted her shoulders in a long, sad shrug. "That's where it all went wrong."

"Lil. . ."

Walt shifted and reached his arms out to her. She wanted nothing more than to fall into them, feel their comfort, draw strength from them, but she'd given in to that impulse one too many times with Walt.

Lil scooted closer to the love seat arm, hoping Walt read the pleading in her eyes. "Don't. I need to finish." Her ragged breath vibrated through her chest, shaking her shoulders.

"So he didn't react well when you told him that you were a protestor." Dropping his arms, Walt rested his hands against the dark denim of his overalls.

Though the expression on his face changed subtly, the love in his eyes never wavered, making her confession even harder. If only they'd flash with hate now, the rest of the story would be so much easier to tell.

"He ranted on and on about how people like me were ungrateful to the men keeping them safe, while the men were losing their lives or limbs in a foreign land. He beat his fists on the mattress, he was so frustrated he couldn't move. He asked for his ring back."

Lil paused and contemplated the toes of her worn sneakers as she gathered her emotions to finish. Surprisingly, it was getting easier.

"I didn't give it back right away. I thought he'd cool off and realize how much he loved me. I mean, love can conquer all, right?" The sardonic laugh gurgled out, echoing through the trailer.

"Lil, it can."

Leveling Walt with the most skeptical look she could muster, Lil cleared her throat.

"After a week, I finally took the ring off and laid it on the bed tray. I asked to be reassigned to a different ward or at least a different section of that ward but student nurses don't hold much weight with a seasoned head nurse. So day after day, I had to bedside nurse Larry while he called me all the names protestors shouted at him."

Nerves bounced her right leg to the beat of her pounding heart. "One morning I couldn't take it anymore. I'd had enough. I'd apologized to him, told him I'd changed my mind and ways but I also couldn't erase what I'd done. He spat out that he'd never forgive me and neither would God."

"That's just not true, Lil. God forgives. . ."

Lil managed a weak smile at Walt's jumping to her and God's defense. "I asked him to stop calling me names. I laid his safety razor and mirror on his bed tray, filled a small washpan with water, and said I'd be right back to clean up the mess. Of course, I said it in quite a different tone and volume."

The pounding in her chest and ears grew louder and her head began to ache. "I didn't go right back. Instead I went outside to cool off. I still loved him, you know," she said, her voice lower in volume until it trailed off into a whisper.

"After fifteen minutes, I went back inside, intending to apologize. He was sick in body and I found out as soon as I entered his room, in spirit, too." Emotion shook her voice as the memory of that day made her hands tremble.

She turned water-filled eyes to Walt. "I messed up. I shouldn't have left him alone. I should have stayed and made sure he used that razor blade for what it was intended."

All the shame and blame of that day lifted from her shoulders as soon as the words left her lips.

When Walt's strong arms wrapped around her, pulling her to his side, he held her tight. Lil didn't pull away, but leaned into him, letting his warmth and love seep into her, making her feel safe. She lifted her arms, hands closing on Walt's forearm like she'd hold a bar for a chin-up, and squeezed.

"Lil, none of that was your fault." Walt's voice was tender yet stern. "You need to forgive yourself."

She nodded against his arm, the rough divots of his thermal shirt scratching across her face.

"I think we should pray." Walt kissed the top of her head.

Chapter 12

L il, I don't understand why you can't stay." Walt stood beside her pickup while she checked the fifth wheel connection to make sure it was secure.

"For the last time, we need some space to make sure this is the real thing, not false feelings that grew just because we were stuck together." She stepped over the connection and sidled up to Walt.

The rolling gray clouds threatened to start dumping snow on them at any minute.

"My feelings aren't phony. They are real." Walt's words huffed out in puffs of vapor hanging in the air a minute before disappearing. He entwined his hand with hers.

"It's only six months. I'll be back by Easter." Lil flipped up the collar of her coat to keep the wind from breezing down her back. "You don't have very good weather for your Veterans Day parade."

"We've marched down the street in snow before. Can't you at least stay through today?"

Shaking her head, Lil pursed her lips. "That'd only make it harder."

"Good." Walt pulled her into a side hug and kissed the top of her stocking cap.

"I'm making one more check inside the camper to be sure everything is secured; then it's good-bye." Her last words whispered from her lips. Walt thought this was easy for her, but it wasn't. She just wanted to be sure this time. Walt needed time to consider all that she'd told him. He may have a change of heart without all the happiness of love fuzzing his thoughts.

"All right. I have some snacks in the house for you. I'll go get them."

Walt slammed the passenger door closed as Lil exited the camper door. Minutes later, package stored in the passenger seat, he met her beside the driver's side door.

"I hope you miss me."

His hand tremored and Lil suspected it didn't have much to do with the below-freezing temperatures.

She wrapped her gloved hand around his bare one. "I'm already missing you."

"Then stay." Walt pulled her into a tight embrace. "My feelings aren't going to change." He held her at arm's length and looked into her eyes.

The intense emotion that shone from them touched her deep within her soul. Her heart cried, "*Stay,*" but she planned to follow her head this time.

"Six months isn't that long. We can talk on the phone, e-mail—"

"Miss three holidays together," Walt protested. "If you stay, then we won't have to feel like the fifth wheel anymore."

It was getting too hard. Lil took a step forward and cupped Walt's face in her hands. "I'll miss you and I love you. I know you don't agree, but this short separation is for the best. It'll give us some time and space to figure out our feelings."

"I don't have to—"

Lil touched her lips to Walt's, stopping him mid-sentence. Her heart swelled with love as Walt returned her kiss.

"I love you, too." Walt's voice was thick and husky as he held her tight, running his fingers through the hair sticking out of the back of her stocking cap.

Lil pushed away. She pointed to the sky. "I'd better get started."

She walked to the pickup, ignoring her heart's urging to look back. The pickup roared to life and she pulled around the small circle of the driveway where Walt stood, his one hand held up in a wave.

She avoided looking out her side mirrors until she was on the interstate heading south. She hoped she was doing the right thing. A few weeks wasn't a long enough time to fall in love. She was doing the right thing, wasn't she?

Lil rubbed her chest where her heart ached. After a few miles she hoped that pain would subside. Usually she was giddy with excitement for her trip to Texas, but today not so much. *Maybe it's just the damp, dismal weather making me feel this way.*

"*And the truth will set you free.*"

The irony in her thoughts brought out a smile. "It's not the weather. It's leaving Walt."

She put her hand down on the bench seat and brushed the corner of cardboard. She glanced over at the three-by-two-foot box. How many snacks did Walt think she needed? Had he packed food in case she was caught in a blizzard?

Lil flipped open a long and short flap of the lid and put her hand to feel around for what Walt had packed. Tissue paper rustled and her hand sank into something soft. A pillow?

She tried to peer into the box while she drove, but all she could see was tissue paper. She patted across the paper, the package's contents still soft. She tried lifting it with one hand, but it was too heavy and awkward.

Curiosity getting the best of her, Lil signaled to take the approaching exit. She slowed on the off ramp then checked her mirrors. No one was behind her, so at the stop sign she pushed the gear into PARK.

Pulling the box closer, she tore the tissue paper away and gasped. "Walt, my dear, sweet Walt." Blurry eyed, Lil ran her hands across the yellow fabric with white flowers, the worn pastel flour sack as familiar to her as her own embroidered lilac quilt.

She lifted the Lily of the Field quilt and buried her face in it. How in the world did Walt get Caroline to part with it?

There was only one way to find out. She pulled the pickup into gear. Checking both ways, she turned to go over the overpass and get back onto the interstate going north.

That man! That wonderful, wonderful man. Why on earth was she running from him? Thankful the posted speed limit was seventy-five miles an hour, she realized that the fifteen minutes she'd been away from his side was fifteen minutes too long.

Tapping her fingers against the steering wheel, time seemed to stand still. Just when her patience was running out, she saw the hotel and RV campsite sign standing high on iron poles.

Lil braked at the stop sign, sending a silent prayer for a clear path as she pulled onto the blacktop and made the half-mile trip to Walt's driveway.

She saw him slowly walking around the outer drive of the RV park. His back was to her. She thought about honking the horn but didn't want to startle him or cause him to stumble.

Forgetting about the bumpy ruts, Lil bounced through the driveway at the same speed she'd entered on Walt's first day home. The fifth wheel lurched and jerked. Lil took her foot from the gas and checked her side mirrors. The camper straightened. When Lil looked out the windshield, Walt cut catty-corner across the camper site, hurrying toward her.

Stopping the pickup in the middle of the driveway, Lil slid from the driver's seat and ran to Walt's wide-open arms.

"How on earth did you get Caroline to part with that quilt?" She threw her arms around Walt's neck.

"I can be very persuasive." He hugged her back. "I guess this means you're pleased with your gift."

Lil tilted her head back so she could see Walt's handsome face. "Very pleased. But you know I'll return it to Lily."

"That was the plan. Caroline and Rodney felt it should go back to its rightful owner." Walt dipped his head and kissed her cheek.

"I need to thank them."

"I hope not in the same way you're thanking me." Mischief danced in Walt's hazel eyes.

Lil raised her brow at him.

"Well, they'll be at the parade this morning. If you think you can stay. . ."

"I'm not going to Texas. I don't need any time to figure this out. I love you, Walt."

Walt's deep kiss took her breath away.

"Let's get your camper set up and then get into town for the parade."

Arms wrapped around each other, they headed for Lil's pickup.

"I think I'm going to have to get some bigger speed limit signs, now you're sticking around, Speedy."

Lil laughed out loud.

Once her camper was set up in the best camp spot in Walt's lot, he changed into his uniform.

Sitting beside Mark, Sarah, Rodney, and Caroline, waiting for the parade to begin, Lil didn't feel like a fifth wheel at all. As the color guard led the parade, Lil stood and placed her hand over her heart.

Her solider carried the American flag with a step as spry as that of the young man who'd proudly served his country.